LOVEBIRDS

Amanda Hampson grew up in rural New Zealand. She spent her early twenties travelling, finally settling in Australia in 1979 where she now lives in Sydney's Northern Beaches. Writing professionally for more than 20 years, she is the author of two non-fiction books, numerous articles, and novels *The Olive Sisters*, *Two for the Road*, *The French Perfumer*, *The Yellow Villa* and *Sixty Summers*.

Other books by the author

The Olive Sisters
Two for the Road
The French Perfumer
The Yellow Villa
Sixty Summers

LOVEBIRDS

AMANDA HAMPSON

VIKING
an imprint of
PENGUIN BOOKS

VIKING

UK | USA | Canada | Ireland | Australia
India | New Zealand | South Africa | China

Viking is part of the Penguin Random House group of companies
whose addresses can be found at global.penguinrandomhouse.com.

Penguin
Random House
Australia

First published by Viking, 2021

Cover images by Shutterstock and Alamy
Author photo by Christian Trinder
Cover design by Adam Laszczuk © Penguin Random House Australia Pty Ltd
Typeset in 12.5/18 pt Adobe Garamond by Midland Typesetters, Australia

Printed and bound in Australia by Griffin Press, part of Ovato, an accredited
ISO AS/NZS 14001 Environmental Management Systems printer

A catalogue record for this
book is available from the
National Library of Australia

ISBN 978 0 14379 213 0

penguin.com.au

MIX
Paper from
responsible sources
FSC® C009448

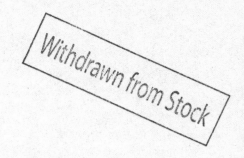

For Tracey & Christian Trinder

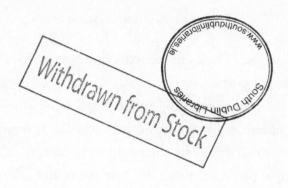

1

pretty boy

Her bag was packed but still she resisted leaving. She glanced around the kitchen for anything left undone. No dishes in the sink. Benches wiped clean. Plants watered. Not a single item out of place. It calmed her to see everything in order.

She dreaded this journey, knowing that, when she arrived in Nullaburra, there would be no Ginny coming out onto the verandah, her arms wide for a welcoming hug. No sitting together in the sunroom, talking and laughing over a bottle of shiraz as the sun dipped behind the hills and the shadows crept across the vineyard. No Ginny at all. Elizabeth pulled herself back to the task of departure. 'I'm on top of this now,' she informed Eric. 'Nearly ready to go.'

Eric made no comment. He'd been subdued for the last couple of days, which was most unlike his usual chatty self. He'd been the only witness to Elizabeth's gusts of furious tears as she railed against the world and all the dreadful people who survived while beautiful souls like Ginny were taken early. But in his silence, Elizabeth sensed a quiet empathy. He was giving her space to grieve.

She hung the grey linen dress, bought some weeks ago in preparation, on the front door handle. It wouldn't do to forget that. Everything else she could work around. She added an extra couple of shirts, a pair of loose pants and a jumper to her overnight bag: comfortable clothes to wear around the house. Paul would want to talk, of course, and she would be there to listen and commiserate. Paul and Ginny had been her closest friends for more years than she wanted to calculate, and Ginny had been her best friend for half a century.

Eric perched on the windowsill where he could watch the birds in the garden and admire his own reflection at the same time. He had other favourite spots: the back of the sofa, the picture rail and sometimes on Elizabeth's shoulder or head while she cooked dinner. He liked to walk over the crossword as she puzzled over it and, even though he was no help with clues, she counted that as participation. It wouldn't do to forget him either.

She offered him an upturned finger. He looked up and tipped his head to one side, bright-eyed. She thought he looked particularly handsome in the morning light, almost regal with his turquoise breast, stripy head and tiny necklace of black spots circling his white throat. She rubbed his chest gently with her finger and he gave a little shiver of pleasure.

'Hello, pretty boy,' she said in her most loving voice. 'Hello, sweet thing.'

'Hello sweet thing,' Eric chirped. 'Swe-et thing sweet thi-ng.'

Elizabeth found herself smiling for the first time since she'd heard that Ginny had gone. Clever little bird. If it wasn't for Eric, there would be whole days when she didn't hear the sound of her own voice. She sometimes joked around with him in different accents. She did a passable Stallone – 'Hey, wise guy' – and Bogart – 'Here's looking at you, kid.' It was hard to tell how amusing he found her but she enjoyed hearing him repeat these phrases.

Most people assumed that budgies were barely one up from goldfish in the thinking department, and while Eric was no towering intellect, not given to reciting poetry or expounding his political opinions (both points in his favour), he was intuitive and a quick learner. He wasn't just a feathered echo chamber; he had excellent recall for phrases as well as tone and nuance, and often added consoling little tuts. Sometimes he would rub his head against Elizabeth's knuckle in a show of spontaneous affection and she knew that, in his own budgie-ish way, Eric loved her. In the past, she had considered getting a female to keep him company, but was unsure how she would feel about Eric lavishing his attentions on a lady friend.

Now that she had a firm grip on her emotions, she could be strong for Ginny's family. She would find words of comfort for them, and offer a shoulder to cry on for Ginny's children, Adam and Polly. She would deliver the eulogy, which she had worked on late into the night, with emotion but without tears. She didn't want to impose the rawness of her grief on anyone. Privately, she wondered if she would ever get over this loss. After a lifetime of friendship, it was difficult to imagine a world without Ginny.

Eric normally lived in a large palatial cage on a stand and she transferred him to a smaller cage for the trip, fixing the latch carefully. 'Come on, young man,' she said. 'We're going on a road trip.' His tiny eyes brightened; there was nothing he loved more than a car trip. It was the closest he came to flying.

3

'I can't bear it I can't bear it,' he chirped.

'That's all behind us now, sweet thing,' explained Elizabeth, making a note to teach him a fresh phrase on the road. He had a Siri-like ability to pick up phrases and could be tricky to reprogram. It wouldn't do for him to repeat this one in Paul's hearing.

She walked around the house one more time, glancing briefly into each room. She'd lived in this house for more than forty years. Every room held memories of different stages of her life: as a young married woman, as a mother to babies and then two growing boys. With Ray and without Ray. She had once been the central figure here, but her sons had been gone for years. They had families of their own, and she had drifted into the periphery of their lives.

The house was 1950s solid cream brick, unprepossessing from the outside but the rooms were large and the ceilings high. In the living room, glass doors opened onto a paved patio and sunny garden. In the garden was an elm tree that she and Ray had planted as a sapling. Now it had wide generous branches and she often sat on the bench in its dappled shade on summer afternoons. The house had once brimmed with music and life and slamming doors, but these days it was quiet. The only disturbance was Geoffrey next door with his industrial leaf blower that roared like a jet taking off. Around and around his house, up the ladder and on to the roof, then out to the pavement, up and down the grass verge and finally the street and gutter. No leaf left behind.

Until recently, her neighbour on the other side had been Maud McBride, who was very elderly and too frail to go out. By prior arrangement Maud would hang a gaudy souvenir tea towel from Fiji in her front window when she needed Elizabeth to shop for her, change a lightbulb, take out her rubbish or track down a strange smell in the kitchen – of which there were many. She'd recently gone into care and Elizabeth was surprised how much she missed her, or perhaps missed being needed. That house had been empty for a while, but now there was a new resident, a young man with dreadlocks who kept putting his bins out in front of Elizabeth's house. She hadn't spoken to him yet but had left a couple of terse notes, spending as much time writing them as debating whether to sign off 'Elizabeth' or 'Mrs O'Reilly' – settling on the latter to emphasise the seriousness of the matter.

Now it was time to go. She gathered her things and locked the front door carefully. She secured Eric's cage on a booster in the passenger seat of her car. He babbled companionably as they set off into the thick of the Sydney traffic towards the freeway and, beyond, her old hometown of Nullaburra.

In her late teens, Elizabeth had famously run away from Nullaburra with no plans to ever return. But life was longer than she could have imagined at seventeen and she'd returned countless times over the years to see her parents, while they were alive, and Ginny and Paul. These days, there was a pleasant familiarity as she entered the outskirts. She rarely went into the centre of town, taking the first turn-off and crossing the river as she headed directly to Ginny's place. She always looked forward to her first glimpse of the white double-storey house on the hill with its generous verandahs and gingerbread trim. She had first visited as a child and it had never lost its sense of wonder.

As she drove up the long curving driveway, she was disappointed to see a couple of cars parked in front of the house.

It would have been nice to have Paul to herself for a little while so they could have a proper talk. Paul evidently felt the same because, before she had even switched off the ignition, he appeared on the verandah and came down the front steps to meet her. She got out of the car and almost collapsed weepily into his embrace before remembering she was to be the strong one.

'Liz, so good to see you.' Paul held her at arm's length and looked at her closely. 'Are you all right?'

'Of course,' she said thickly. 'It's not like we haven't been expecting it.'

He nodded. 'Come on in. We have a full house – the kids are here.'

Elizabeth sensed a discomfort in Paul but it wasn't the time to question him. She lifted Eric's cage out of the car and handed it to him. 'Just let me get my bag out of the back.'

'Leave it there for the moment, Liz. As I said, we've got a full house, so we've had to billet a few people out.'

Elizabeth's face set in the stony expression she knew, from past experience, people often took exception to and she attempted to loosen it, forcing a tight smile. It was appalling to hear herself bundled up with 'a few people'. Who on earth were these people? Ginny wouldn't have allowed her to be 'billeted'. Or perhaps she would, actually. On reflection, Ginny would have told her to pull her head in and not make a fuss.

'Of course, no problem,' said Elizabeth. 'I'll fit in with you, Paul.'

Paul wrapped an approving arm around her shoulders. He made squeaky kissing sounds at Eric, who lifted his beak in the air disdainfully. After a moment, he gave Paul a cheeky sideways glance and said, 'Hey wise guy wise guy sweet thing.'

Paul laughed out loud and Elizabeth was pleased that Eric had worked his charms on cue. She took the cage back from Paul and they made their way up the wide steps to the front door. At the top of the stairs, Elizabeth paused to turn and gaze out over the property; the marching rows of vines wreathed in bright green were a sight that always brought her pleasure. It felt like a homecoming just to be here with Ginny's family.

As they crossed the verandah Paul said, 'I'm sorry, Liz. I know you'd prefer to stay here, but with the kids and their families, that's literally every bed in the place taken.'

'No, no. It's my fault. I didn't think. I should have booked into the motel.'

'No need for that expense. Judith's more than happy to have you at hers.'

This stopped Elizabeth in her tracks. Ginny's sister was the *last* person she wanted to stay with. Surely Paul knew that? Surely Judith knew that?!

'What's up?' asked Paul, pausing to wait for her.

'Nothing. My knee just locked up,' she improvised, giving her knee a cursory rub. Her only thought was how to extricate herself from this awkward situation. She didn't enjoy staying with other people; Ginny and Paul were her only exception. This house was her second home and they always referred to the bedroom off the verandah as 'Lizzy's room' – and why Judith would offer to have her there was anyone's guess.

As she entered the hallway, with its polished timber floor and familiar smell of beeswax and lavender, Elizabeth felt a crushing pain in her chest at the absence of Ginny. It knocked the breath out of her and put the trivial matter of her own temporary displacement in perspective. It was only for a few days.

Paul led the way to the dining room, a high-ceilinged room dominated by a conservatory table, where Elizabeth had enjoyed countless meals with the family over the years and, before that, with Ginny's parents and siblings when she was young.

Adam and Polly and their partners sat around the dining table, which was covered in dishes of food in containers of various shapes and sizes, presumably dropped in by well-wishers. By rights, thought Elizabeth, these should have gone into the freezer for Paul to have in coming weeks, instead of being consumed in one decadent feast, and in the middle of the afternoon! There were half-a-dozen bottles of wine open, and everyone looked wrung out. Polly's two daughters and Adam's young son lay on the Persian rug beneath the bay window, playing a board game – just as Ginny and Elizabeth had done as children. That, at least, was a wholesome scene.

Adam got up from the table, gave Elizabeth a hug and sat down again, but his wife, Abigail, and Polly and her husband barely acknowledged her. Elizabeth had pictured herself in warm embraces with Adam and Polly, reminding them how much their mother loved them and how special Ginny had been. She'd imagined it like a scene in a sentimental American film where the character of Elizabeth was played by an actress who exuded warmth and empathy, who murmured words of wisdom that were received with tearful gratitude. The real Elizabeth stood marooned halfway across the room holding a birdcage, her arm lifted in an awkward salute that she quickly withdrew as the two couples resumed their conversation.

Elizabeth had known Ginny's children all their lives. She'd been present at their births and marriages. Over the years, she'd had intimate knowledge of their personal lives: Polly's struggles with fibroids, Adam's low sperm count, Abigail's drink-driving charge. She heard it all, although never from them. But Elizabeth could see that she had already been demoted to someone who had once known their mother.

When the grandchildren noticed Elizabeth, they jumped up and galloped towards her, squeaking with excitement, stretching their hands towards Eric's cage. Eric fluttered his wings as he retreated backwards into a corner. Elizabeth felt a flush of panic and briefly considered dashing for the safety of her car. Why didn't someone stop them? The parents thought it was funny, for God's sake!

'That's enough, kids,' said Paul gently. 'Budgies are highly strung, so you mustn't touch him.'

'Aww.' His granddaughter pouted. 'Can't we just pat him?'

'No, you can't,' said Elizabeth, instantly regretting how abrupt she sounded. The parents stopped laughing. The children stopped jumping. The room went still and silent. Elizabeth softened her tone. 'Budgies are very sensitive. Stress can kill them.'

Through clenched teeth, the child released a piercing shriek that rang in Elizabeth's ears for a full minute like a distant train whistle. The girl began to weep and retreated to her mother's lap. The two boys threw themselves resentfully back on the rug as though their board game had been reduced to second best. Polly stroked her daughter's hair, perhaps imagining the child had been traumatised by being refused something she wanted.

Elizabeth put Eric's cage up on the mantelpiece safely out of reach. She took the cover out of her bag and placed it over the cage. As she turned back to the room, she caught sight of Paul shaking his head slightly at Polly, as if to dissuade her from some course of action. He turned to Elizabeth. 'Come into the kitchen, Liz. I'll make you a cup of tea.'

'Tea time,' confirmed Eric. It was one of his favourite expressions. 'Tea time.'

Elizabeth followed Paul down the hall to the kitchen at the rear of the house. As she passed the large gilt-framed mirror that hung in the hallway, she caught sight of herself and, as often happened, took a moment to recognise the woman she saw there. The body shapeless in comfortable pants and cotton shirt. The faded hair, short and sensible. The stubborn set of the jaw. As always, she had the urge to dispute this image. Insist that this was not really her, but some trick of the light. Or perhaps it was a trick of life, one that everyone experienced sooner or later. The only part of herself that she recognised was that flicker of uncertainty in her hazel eyes. She often saw it in photographs, even those taken of her as a child, and was never sure if it was visible to other people. Ginny recognised it, of course. And Ray — he could read her eyes.

She gave this imposter in the mirror a kind smile and noted the immediate improvement. But from the dining room, she heard Abigail say, 'Aye, aye, m'hearties!'

Polly said, 'Watch out or you'll find yourself walking the plank.'

Adam suggested they keep their voices down but Abigail just laughed her dirty laugh. She was often rude to Adam, and Ginny too, when she could get away with it, and flirty with Paul. Elizabeth had never liked her and she probably knew it.

Paul put the kettle on while Elizabeth assembled the teapot, with its colourful knitted cosy, and the tiny milk jug that had once belonged to Ginny's grandmother, along with a couple of Milk Arrowroot from the biscuit tin. She put them on a tray and followed Paul out to the sunroom. She regretted leaving Eric on the mantle; she'd expected they would join the family at the table. She was hesitant to go back for him and draw further attention to herself.

Paul must have noticed her anxious glance. 'You be mother,' he said. He got up and went back down the hall, returning a moment later with Eric's cage. Elizabeth flushed at the muffled burst of laughter from the dining room.

Paul sat down and wrapped his hands around the hot mug, breathing in steam from the tea. 'Don't judge them too harshly, Liz. They're as broken-hearted as we are. It hasn't fully hit them yet. They're relieved too – the waiting is over. That's been the worst part. And, to be honest . . .' He gave an embarrassed shrug. 'They've been drinking all afternoon.'

'They're afraid of the pain,' said Elizabeth. 'I understand that. It's only natural.'

Paul nodded but said nothing.

Elizabeth dipped her biscuit in her tea. 'How will we manage without her, Paul?'

'I don't know. I'm trying not to think about that.' He was silent for a moment. 'You've managed without Ray all these years. Not something you expected to do.'

Elizabeth wondered if he had only now realised how difficult it had been for her, and it occurred to her that their friendship might struggle to survive the loss of Ginny. Perhaps Ginny was the only thing that held them together. 'That's a little different,' she said. 'But I suppose at some point you have no choice but to accept the situation.'

'I'm sure you're right,' he said, but changed the subject. 'Now, let's talk about tomorrow.'

Elizabeth nodded, although she would have preferred to continue chatting in a more philosophic way. She didn't want to think about tomorrow.

'It's very simple, as Ginny wanted. A service at the funeral home chapel at eleven. Then they'll take her away. She probably told you she didn't want people to go to the crematorium . . .'

'Yes, she always hated going there for funerals. But it's hard to think of her —'

'I know, but that's what she wanted; not a funeral but a celebration. We'll come back here for a light lunch, just family and close friends.'

'Can I do something, Paul? Make tea or scones. I'd like to do something.'

Paul smiled. 'You don't want to make scones for a hundred people, Liz.'

'A hundred?' echoed Elizabeth in dismay. 'That's family and close friends?'

'I expect there will be twice that many at the chapel. Teachers and students from school. She touched so many people's lives over the years. Anyway, she planned it all and thought of everything. The lunch will be catered with fancy "horses derves" and seafood and champagne.'

'Moët, no doubt,' said Elizabeth fondly. 'Extravagant to the end.'

'As she said, you only die once. She wanted her friends and family to see her off with a decent bubbly. Now, Liz, don't let me forget – Ginny left an envelope for you. I just have to dig it out but she was very insistent that you get it. Remind me tomorrow before you leave.'

It was news to Elizabeth that she'd be leaving tomorrow, but she managed to say nothing. She certainly didn't want to stay at Judith's a minute longer than necessary. She felt suddenly teary. 'I wish I'd seen her one more time before she went, Paul.'

'Better that you didn't, love. She didn't look too bad when you saw her last, but as I said, she went downhill very quickly at the end.'

They sat in companionable silence for a few minutes, nursing their tea, then Paul drained his mug and shifted to the edge of his chair. Clearly their time together was coming to an end and Elizabeth cast around for a way to prolong it. In that moment, she had the strongest sense that tomorrow would be her last time in this house. It was a realisation that was as unfathomable as it was definitive. How could that be? Surely Paul wouldn't sell the place? Or would Adam move his family in and take over the winery? Seemed unlikely. It wasn't lucrative enough to support a family; Paul and Ginny couldn't have managed without her teaching income. Anyway, now wasn't the time to ask about Paul's plans for the future. She would have to wait to hear in due course.

Elizabeth knew she would not feel at home here tomorrow when this house was filled with strangers. She would be the outsider. She looked around the room, greedily taking it all in, remembering the many hours spent here over the years in all seasons, listening to Ginny's funny stories about her students and fellow teachers, Elizabeth matching them with often almost unbelievable tales during her years working in the justice system. Occasionally, they would remember Paul and call out for him to join them. He was always amused by the girlish hilarity that erupted after the first glass of wine, but he rarely did. It had occurred to Elizabeth, from time to time, that he may have been a little envious of the closeness of their relationship, but he certainly never voiced it.

She and Ginny had been best friends since they were ten years old. Over the years, Ginny had become a pillar of the local community and Elizabeth had increasing responsibilities in her own career. It was only when they were together that they could really let loose. They brought out the best and the worst in each other, but in the end, there was nothing Elizabeth could do to save her oldest, most loved and cherished friend.

'If you need any help with sorting her clothes . . . you know . . .' Elizabeth gave a shrug, already regretting her offer since she couldn't bear to do that job.

'Polly will fix all that. I'm sorry. I haven't even asked after your family, Liz. How are your boys?'

Elizabeth's gaze drifted to the window and the bright day outside. 'No change. I don't see Danny's little girls very often. It's not him – Melissa's very close to her own family. When Tom gets out next year, I'm hoping Danny might be able to help get him back on track.' She paused. 'Things are still a bit of a mess.'

'And Zach, how old is he now?'

'He's fifteen.' She gave a heavy sigh. 'Claire and I haven't spoken since Tom's trial, so I haven't seen Zach for nearly a year.'

Paul smiled sympathetically, and she had to dig her fingernails into her palms to keep a grip on herself.

'Anything from Ray?' he asked.

'I'm a bit worried actually. Normally when I write, I hear back a couple of weeks later. This time it's been at least a month – or more.'

'You could go and find out for yourself, Liz.'

'If Ray wanted to see me, he would say so. If he needed me, he would ask.'

'Would he?' asked Paul. 'Would he feel he could ask, especially after all this time? It's got to be more than twenty years, Liz.'

'Thirty, actually.' She avoided his gaze while she finished her tea.

Paul got up. He seemed impatient or exasperated, but she couldn't be sure. 'Actually, let me get that envelope now, then that's one thing I can cross off my list.'

A moment later he was back, handing her an envelope with her name written in Ginny's hand, then he was guiding her towards the front door and, before she knew it, Elizabeth was back in her car with Eric by her side and Paul waving her off. Was she imagining the expression of relief on his face, or seeing it all too clearly?

As she drove away, she was seized by a desperate sense of loneliness. Ginny and Paul were her only close friends these days. The only ones who really knew her and in whom she could confide. Unexpectedly, it seemed those days were over.

2

the letter

As she entered the outskirts of town and passed the Nullaburra Travel Inn, Elizabeth was tempted to stop and get a room. It was only out of consideration to Paul that she kept driving until she arrived at Judith and Bruce's house near the centre of town.

Judith answered the door with a welcoming smile. For a moment, Elizabeth stood there, overnight bag in one hand and Eric's cage in the other, and stared in silence. Judith's usual grumpy expression had vanished; her frown and entire forehead had been ironed flat, giving her face an elongated look, like a weary old greyhound. Elizabeth wondered what Bruce, a man violently opposed to anything that didn't exist in the previous century, thought of this malarky. But Elizabeth made no reference to the modifications, not even a raised eyebrow. 'Hello, Judith,' she said. 'You look well.'

'Hi, Liz, come in. Put your stuff in the first room on the right. Do you want a cuppa?'

'I've just had one with Paul . . . thanks,' she added slightly too late, unnerved by a sense of stepping into enemy territory.

'It's after five – we can have a glass of something!'

'Sure,' Elizabeth agreed, although she hadn't anticipated that billeting would involve being treated like a bona fide guest. Judith rushed off to the kitchen with an odd sense of urgency, pointing in the direction of the spare bedroom on the way.

The small guestroom was crowded with furniture, a dozen cushions in autumnal colours meticulously arranged on the double bed along with two towels rolled into tubes and decorated with an artificial frangipani. A glass and jug of water sat on the bedside table. It was like the set of a play, awaiting the arrival of an important guest – a role that Elizabeth had not accepted. She put her bag on the floor and Eric's cage on the bedside table. She gave him some seed and topped up his water. 'Here we are. All is well,' she said, reminding him of the new phrases she'd taught him in the car.

'I can't bear it!' he said, staring out of his cage with a dismal expression.

'*All* is well,' she repeated several times but he remained tight-beaked, unconvinced.

Elizabeth had been to this house for various events over the years and always disliked the place. It was cluttered and fusty, as though it belonged to much older people. The depressing colours, maroon and olive green with brown furniture, were reminiscent of her grandparents' nursing home. She wandered into the living room and sat down, gauging when she could reasonably excuse herself and go into town for something to eat.

Judith brought out a bottle of shiraz and arranged the glasses and coasters on the coffee table along with little bowls of nuts and crackers, evidently attempting to replicate Ginny and Elizabeth's traditional get-togethers, which was touching but disturbing at the same time.

Once Judith had laid everything out, chatting nervously all the while, she made herself comfortable in an armchair, fussing around with the cushions as though settling in for the foreseeable future. She poured the wine and lifted her glass in a toast. 'To Ginny.'

Elizabeth obliged with a response and took a sip of wine. It was hard to relax knowing that Judith had something on her mind and, based on past experience, most likely a grievance or three.

'Liz, I'm so glad we've got this time together. Look . . .' She stopped and a flush mottled her neck. 'Here's the thing. I'd . . . I'd like us to be friends.'

Elizabeth wondered if she'd heard correctly. She considered all possible responses and finally settled on: 'O-kay. Um . . . what brought this on?'

Judith gave a tinkling laugh. 'Ginny always said I never got your humour.'

Elizabeth was not trying to be funny; she was genuinely bewildered. 'We've been enemies for half a century, why stop now?'

'Frenemies,' Judith corrected.

'What?'

'Friendly enemies. Look, we've both lost someone we loved. We both have a gap in our lives. Why not fill it with each other? As a tribute to Ginny's memory.'

Seeing that Elizabeth was not convinced by this reasoning, Judith continued, 'I'm going to come clean with you, Liz. Full disclosure. I was always a bit jealous of you. Right from when we were little.' She held up her hands in mock surrender. 'I'm being really honest with you here.'

'Why?' asked Elizabeth.

'Why be honest? Or why was I jealous?' Judith laughed nervously.

'Both would be helpful.'

'From the start, you and Ginny were thick as thieves. That was one thing. I idolised my big sister and you stole her from me.'

'We were just children. It's quite natural to feel that.' Elizabeth noticed her voice had taken on a soothing tone, one she might use with someone threatening violence.

'And then I got to high school, and you and Ray were like celebrities.'

'Oh, come on, Judith. We're talking Nullaburra High, for crying out loud! Celebrities? That was all in your mind.'

'I was just a kid and Nullaburra High was my whole world. You were like grown-ups. Everyone knew that you and Ray were having sex.'

'Do we have to go into all this? Seriously? Especially right now. I can't see the point. If you've wasted half your life festering on this . . .'

Judith took a reckless gulp of wine. 'Okay, sorry. I got a bit off track. I didn't plan to say that.'

'What did you plan to say? Just say it so I can go and get some dinner.'

'Oh, Liz, please eat here with us. I've done a lamb roast. I thought we'd get our business out of the way before Bruce got home, and then we could all enjoy a meal together.'

Elizabeth closed her eyes so she could roll them undetected. It was bad enough being billeted; the last thing she needed was to be 'business' to be got out of the way, let alone while the roast was cooking. Bruce was the most tedious man on the planet, obsessed with outlandish conspiracy theories. He was probably at a meeting of the Flat Earth Society right now. And Judith was a Petri dish of imagined slights that had mutated and multiplied over the years. The idea of spending an hour with them was barely tolerable.

Judith pushed on. 'Okay, where was I? Yes . . . so I was jealous at school and then you and Ray ran off and —'

'Let's not go into every detail because it was all a very long time ago.' Throwing diplomacy to the wind, Elizabeth added, 'And, anyway, how do you explain being so awful just in this last year? All the nasty, *nasty* texts you sent me. Shouting at me over the phone. I never told Ginny about those incidents, by the way.'

Judith blinked hard. 'Sorry about that. When Ginny got ill, I resented the influence you had with her. And her travelling to Sydney for chemo, not even listening to what I had to say about a more natural approach —'

'Judith. The treatment Ginny elected was *her* choice. That's what she wanted to do. If she'd wanted to treat herself with garlic infusions and dream catchers, then I would have respected her decision. I was supporting what she wanted.'

'Judging by that comment, I don't think you would have, quite frankly.'

Elizabeth got up. She was about to erupt or burst into tears. 'It's irrelevant. Ginny's gone and no amount of hashing this out will bring her back. And how you think you can repair the damage of decades while dinner's cooking is completely beyond me.' She went to the bedroom, picked up her overnight bag and Eric's cage and, before she had time to reconsider, was in the car driving away and muttering furiously under her breath.

She drove through town, now hungry and wrung out with grief. She briefly considered going home to Sydney but that wasn't an option. She wanted to stop and get some food but felt so wobbly that if she opened her mouth to order a sandwich she might just start bawling. She pulled into the carpark beside the river and watched the water flowing past. There was a moment when the sun dipped low and the surface was burnished with green and copper, and she thought of Ray. They had often come to the river that first summer, not to this part near town, but further down where the willows grew right to the edge. Sometimes they'd stay all night and she would cycle home in the soft morning light, her heart full of love and dreams. It was a time when the world and everything in it was brilliant and glorious.

It occurred to her now that every single part of Nullaburra was overprinted with memories of the past and people she had lost. She simply couldn't bear it any more. Now that Ginny had gone, there was no reason to return. All of a sudden the tight knot of grief in her chest unravelled and she was sobbing, gasping sobs that came hard, as if being torn out of her.

'Sweet thing!' cried Eric, hopping about his cage anxiously. 'Sweet thing tea time!'

She wanted to stop but on and on it went until her head ached. When it was over, she dried her face, dug out her toiletries bag and rubbed some cream into her skin. She chatted in a cheerful voice to Eric, reassuring him again that all was well. This stress wasn't good for either of them.

She walked across the road, bought a hamburger and ate it sitting in the car. She thought about sleeping in the car but she'd be a wreck tomorrow. She remembered the envelope and got it out of her handbag. It was a single folded sheet of paper, the writing in Ginny's familiar hand but shaky like an old woman's.

My dear Lizzy,

I have thought so much about you in these last days. I feel there are things that I need to tell you, that you will only hear from me, your oldest friend.

Having been in your life for so long, I know you in all your dimensions, from the sweet girl to a woman who has dealt with the harsh blows of life with incredible strength and fortitude. But with all the dramas of these last couple of years, I have seen you change from my kind, generous, loving friend to someone else.

I understand that you have come to the end of your tether, but there have been times when I didn't agree with your approach. I loved you too much to tell you and should have been more honest. You have withdrawn from people you love to protect your heart, but now you need to deep dig once more and find the courage to reunite your family. Only you can do that.

You need to start by finding Ray. You have to close that chapter of your life so you can start a new one. My deepest fear for you is that if you don't act now and make things right, you are at risk of alienating everyone you love. I don't want you to be alone and lonely. You don't deserve that — you have done so much for your family at your own expense and you have so much love to give, my darling Lizzy.

Be brave, do it now before it's too late. I have every faith in you.

Love always, Gin.

P.S. We both know Judith can be difficult but she has a good heart. Think about putting your grievances with each other behind you. It would be nice to have an 'old' new friend. It was my suggestion that you stay with her while you're here to give you two a chance to bond.

3

skipping

1962 Lizzy sits in the shade of the classroom eating her sandwich. She takes tiny bites to make it last as long as possible. She feels invisible here in the shadows; it's a welcome break from the uncomfortable notoriety of being the new girl. When the sandwich is finished, she has nothing to do with her hands. She experiments with folding them in her lap, then tucks them behind her knees while she watches the other children play on the quadrangle.

The boys play handball, heckling and shoving each other roughly. The girls play four square or hopscotch in spaces marked out on the concrete. Two older girls hold the ends of a long heavy rope while children run in from both sides, chanting as they jump, 'Salt, vinegar, peppers! One, two, three, four . . .' Occasionally someone trips, knees are scraped, bony elbows skinned. Lizzy wants to join in these games but is too shy to draw attention to herself. She might trip on the rope and have her dress fly up. She blushes thinking about the possibilities.

The teacher reads her book in the sun while she eats her

lunch. She looks up occasionally with a dreamy gaze, as though arriving back from another world. If a fight breaks out, she picks up her whistle and blows it so hard and long that the children cover their ears in distress. She only gets up for gushing wounds and, even then, reluctantly.

Lizzy can't imagine how she will ever find a place for herself here. She's ten years old, this is her third school and making friends gets harder each time. She's never wanted the pressure of popularity, just one good friend. She feels such longing as she watches other girls sharing confidences and sandwiches, giggling and conspiring together. When the teacher asks them to partner up in class, they never have to look around, fearful of being the one left out. For Lizzy, school life is a game of musical chairs with no place for her. Now she sees a girl walking towards her and expects the worst. The teacher calls the girl Virginia, but the other kids call her Ginny. She stands out with her pale skin, honey-coloured hair and blue eyes. She's one of the popular girls. Her friends squabble to sit next to her at lunch. The friends hang back, scowling, but Ginny has a generous smile, the look of someone holding in laughter. 'Hello, I'm Ginny. You're Elizabeth.'

Lizzy nods. 'I know.' She doesn't blame the friends for sniggering.

'Do you like being called Elizabeth?'

'Mum and Dad call me Liz or Lizzy.'

'Snap!' Ginny smiles. 'I thought so. I hate being called Virginia.' She offers her crooked little finger. Lizzy hesitantly hooks her own finger around it, still wondering if there's a trick in store. It wouldn't be the first time friendship has been offered and snatched away for entertainment. But Ginny gives it a squeeze. 'Ginny and Lizzy. It fits.' She pulls a handful of crumpled elastic out of her pocket. 'Want to play?'

Lizzy smiles. She's spent hours playing Elastics between two chairs at home. Now her moment has come.

Lizzy's parents have recently bought a grocery shop in Nullaburra. They worked hard for years to save for their own business and now they work harder than ever. She and her parents, and her older brother, Doug, live in a house behind the shop. The yard between the two buildings has become an obstacle course with pallets stacked against each other, piles of flattened cardboard boxes ruined by rain and a line of washing held up by a wooden prop. The house itself is gloomy with draughts that come up through the floorboards and make an eerie whistling sound that Lizzy finds terrifying. When it's windy, sheets of wallpaper flop from the walls and her mother uses a stapler to stick them back up. Her father sets traps for the rats that scuttle through the roof space in the night and talks about getting a snake to put up there.

All day her parents dash across the yard from the shop to the house and back again. The business is like a baby that needs constant attention or it will die and take their life savings with it. Home is an extension of the shop: the living room is part storeroom, the kitchen doubles as an office. Half the kitchen table is given over to the shop's accounts, ledgers and stacks of bills, and her mother's prized possession, an adding machine with neat rows of buttons and a handle on the side. She works the machine with dexterity and speed, using her left hand to trace the figures in the ledger, while the right dances across the keys and turns the handle with a flick of her wrist. Sometimes, when Lizzy is home alone, she gently presses the buttons and mimes winding the handle. She must not be caught touching the sacred machine.

Everything is secondary to the business. Meals are haphazard, the cupboards stocked with dented tins and two-day-old bread. Conversations are about bills, suppliers, stock and customers. Doug does the deliveries and collects gossip about their customers, reporting back on who has a new fridge, television or car. Her parents like to speculate on where people 'got their money'. Lizzy has no idea what this means and imagines the ways in which people might get money, perhaps buried treasure or robbing a bank or even by murdering someone. But she never asks questions. She just tries not to get in the way.

When she's invited to afternoon tea at Ginny's house, her mother seems pleased but is too busy to drive her out there. 'I don't have time to be chauffeuring you around. It's only a couple of miles – you can easily ride your bike. Just take a torch in case it's dark on the way back.' She gives Lizzy a tin of biscuits and a jar of piccalilli relish to take with her. 'Just a courtesy. They don't need anything from the likes of us – silvertails, from what I hear,' she adds with a sniff. 'Doesn't make them any better than us. Just remember that.'

Lizzy has no idea what this means and thinks about it as she rides past paddocks of grazing cattle. The Moncurs have ploughed up their paddocks and put in neat rows of posts and wire fencing, leaving the white house at the top of the rise surrounded by barren chocolate-coloured earth. Her knees tremble with nerves as she rides up the long driveway to the house. She leans her bike against the verandah and stands chewing at her thumbnail as she gathers the courage to walk up the steps and knock on the door. The longer she delays, the more convinced she becomes that she has the day or time wrong – or has misunderstood the invitation altogether. She imagines herself pedalling madly down the hill, escaping before her error is discovered, and is about to fly when Mrs Moncur opens the door, pretty in a floral dress and bright lipstick. She smiles and welcomes Lizzy in.

'Come through . . . Lizzy, isn't it? The children are out in the garden.' Mrs Moncur seems delighted with the biscuits and pickles. They walk down the wide hallway; on the walls are framed portraits of the family – the sort taken in a studio by a professional photographer. With only a year between them, the children are arranged in order with Marty the eldest, then Ginny and Judith.

Mrs Moncur and Lizzy arrive in a large kitchen with an adjoining sunroom at the back of the house. 'We'll have afternoon tea soon so you're not all starving when we start the games,' says Mrs Moncur.

In contrast to the bare fields surrounding the house, the garden is a green semi-circle edged with flower beds, shrubs and shading trees. Ginny, Judith and Marty are already in the garden with a couple of Ginny's friends from school, girls who Lizzy knows resent her friendship with Ginny but wave hello politely.

While the children play tag, Mrs Moncur puts out plates of food on a table on the verandah and calls them up to eat. There are devon sandwiches with tomato sauce, cut into triangles, sausage rolls and fairy bread. She pours them each a drink from a large jug of orange cordial with ice cubes tinkling against the glass. She slices up a whole block of neapolitan ice-cream and puts each slice between two wafers. It's all so extravagant that Lizzy has a sinking feeling she has misunderstood and this is a birthday party. She doesn't know when Ginny's birthday is and she was the last to arrive – did the others bring presents? She glances into the kitchen looking for a birthday cake. She feels a stomach-ache starting that soon disappears when Mrs Moncur tells them to run off and play. No cake with candles, but there are hula hoops and old stockings for three-legged races.

Mrs Moncur sits on the verandah steps with a drink in one hand and a cigarette in the other. She laughs loudly and applauds their efforts, never telling them to quieten down or go away.

Late in the afternoon, the children are allowed to roam the house and play hide-and-seek. Marty suggests sardines and Lizzy is picked as the first to hide. Panicked by the responsibility, she runs upstairs and rushes blindly into a bedroom. She shuts herself in a wardrobe that smells of hairspray and cigarettes, and sits quietly in the dark. After a few minutes, Marty opens the door. He crawls in among his mother's clothes and shoes and pulls the door shut behind him. In the blackness, Lizzy feels his lips press hard on hers, slobbery and tasting of Juicy Fruit chewing gum. Then there is only the sound of his breathing. Lizzy pushes herself into the corner of the wardrobe, holds her breath and wonders how she will ever face him in the light of day. She doesn't have to wait long. The door swings open and light pours in. Judith stands over them, squinting at Lizzy. 'You're not allowed in our parents' room. It's out of bounds. You will be in so . . . so . . . so . . . much trouble. Mum won't let you come here ever again.'

'Shut up, you idiot!' shouts Marty. 'Go away!'

'I'm telling Mum!' Judith launches a kick in his direction. 'Telling!' He reaches out and grabs her ankle, toppling her backwards onto the floor. 'Telling!' He leaps out of the wardrobe and sits on her, hand over her mouth as he threatens to lock her in there.

Lizzy crawls out of her hiding place, her face burning. Ignoring the two of them, she walks slowly downstairs. She doesn't know what to do, how to make things right. She doesn't know where to find Ginny. In the kitchen, Mrs Moncur listens to the radio while she peels potatoes. 'Hello, Lizzy, everything all right? Would you like to have dinner with us and stay over? I can telephone your mother if you like.'

'Thank you, Mrs Moncur, but I need to go home. Thank you for having me.'

'It's been a pleasure! Come again – anytime!' she says. 'Don't be a stranger.'

Lizzy nods dumbly. The spectre of Mrs Moncur's disappointment weighs heavily as she switches on the torch and rides off into the twilight.

4

fairy floss

1965 The one Saturday a month when Lizzy doesn't have to work in the shop, she and Ginny ride their bikes to the Moncur house on Friday afternoon and back to school together on Monday morning. They share every moment, every thought and dream, as well as clothes, hairbrushes and homework. On hot afternoons they lie on the twin beds in Ginny's room and read comics while they sing along to the radio, content in their own little world.

Lizzy's mother always grumbles about that weekend off; she thinks Lizzy should work as hard as they do. Lizzy doesn't mind the work but is bored by the constant dramas in the shop: the freezer that keeps breaking down, the endless discussion about the two new cash registers needed for decimal currency next year, and the rats infesting the yard. There was a time when she was alarmed by these problems but she has begun to suspect that her parents enjoy any break in the monotony of their routine.

In the Moncur household they set the table every night, with cloth napkins, and sit together for dinner. Mr Moncur introduces a topic for discussion and everyone is encouraged to put forward a point of view. Recent topics: Why were Aborigines still not counted in the census? Was it right for Australia to get involved with the American war in Vietnam? Could Australia ever have a woman prime minister?

At thirteen, Lizzy knows nothing about current affairs but she soon begins to notice newspaper headlines and takes more interest, imagining herself offering some startling insight in a future discussion. In her house, meals are usually eaten on fold-out tray-tables in front of the television. One evening, she attempts a discussion about the Freedom Ride of Aboriginal student activists, as they watch it on the evening news.

'That's their business. Nothing to do with us,' says her father. 'We let them into university, and this is all the thanks we get; a bunch of so-called educated long hairs driving around the country stirring things up.'

'They're trying to bring the issues to the public's attention,' says Lizzy. 'The way they're not allowed into places and segregated —'

'Issues? Segregated?' scoffs her brother, Doug. 'Where are you getting these words, Miss Snotty Nose? You don't know what you're talking about.'

'Don't speak to her like that,' says her mother. 'Anyway, we don't talk politics in this house. Lizzy, get up and change the channel. I'm sick of all this news.'

'It's not politics . . . it's stuff we should know about.'

'Who made you the expert on world affairs?' asks Doug through a mouthful of food.

'It's not world affairs, it's our —'

'Stop arguing, you two,' says her mother. 'We've got more important issues around here. Doug, can you bring that delivery inside, put it all in the back room? It's going to rain tonight. You can help him, Miss – burn off some of your teenage anger. And bring the washing in while you're out there.'

'I'm not angry —'

'That's enough,' says her father. 'They might have time to sit around talking about "ideas" up at the Moncurs, but we've got more important things to worry about. Come on, take your dishes out and get to it.'

Out in the yard, Lizzy uses a flattened box as a shield against the pegs that Doug hurls at her to entertain himself. Eventually he gets bored, takes one box inside and thankfully doesn't come back. Lizzy moves the rest of the delivery and brings the washing in. She tries to avoid being alone with Doug. He seems to get a strange pleasure from twisting her arm or bending back a finger until he sees tears in her eyes.

Once the chores are done, Lizzy spends the evenings in her bedroom, doing her homework while she listens to the transistor radio she bought with her earnings from the shop. It's the size of two bricks with a big fat battery inside and she loves it more than anything else she owns. She lies in the dark for hours listening and feels connected to the world beyond this house. She sings along to her favourite songs until Doug bangs on the wall and shouts, 'Shut up! It's like hearing a bloody dog being kicked to death.'

She wonders what made him think of that particular example.

For Ginny's thirteenth birthday, Lizzy is invited to join the family on their annual visit to the Royal Easter Show in Sydney. She and Ginny talk about it for weeks beforehand, debating what to wear and which rides to go on in the fairground.

When Mrs Moncur discovers that Lizzy has never been to Sydney, she suggests they extend the trip. 'We could visit the Show in the morning and in the afternoon go into the city. We can take Lizzy to David Jones and go for a walk in the botanical gardens.'

'Would you like to come with me to see the Opera House building, Liz? Much more interesting than David Jones,' says Mr Moncur with a wink. 'The shells are in place now. History in the making.'

'I don't want to go to David Jones,' says Judith. 'Or the boring Opera House. I want to go to the sideshows and ride on the Ferris wheel.'

'Shopping's boring,' says Marty. He gives Lizzy a sidelong glance. 'But if Lizzy wants to go, I guess it's okay.'

'I say it's Ginny's birthday, she should decide,' says Mrs Moncur.

'We do the same thing every year,' says Ginny. 'It would be nice to do something different this time.'

They set off from the Moncurs' in their butter-yellow Rover, a car that seems very luxurious to Lizzy with its polished timber dashboard and leather upholstery. The four children are squeezed together in the back seat where they squabble on and off all the way to Sydney.

The excitement of the Easter Show is almost unbearable. Lizzy and Ginny are allowed to go off on their own with instructions to meet the family at midday. Lizzy has never experienced crowds like this, the noise and smells: a heady combination of hot oil, sugar, petrol and animal dung. So much happening at the same time. She feels like a visitor in a foreign land as Ginny takes her on a whirlwind tour through the animal yards and to see the preserves and fruit and vegetable competitions. They watch the rodeo rides and career around in dodgem cars. In side-show alley, Lizzy manages to win a large pink soft toy that looks like a cross between a cow and a cat and makes them laugh hysterically every time they look at it.

Mrs Moncur and Marty are waiting for them at the meeting point but Mr Moncur has gone off to look for Judith, who has gone missing in the crowd.

'I hope he doesn't find her,' Marty whispers to Lizzy, his sugary breath warm on her cheek. She knows he's saying this to be funny but is surprised at his meanness. How would he feel if something happened to Judith?

An announcement comes over the loudspeaker about a lost child who fits Judith's description. They follow Mrs Moncur to the office to find Judith eating fairy floss and enjoying the attention. As soon as they get outside, Mrs Moncur asks her, 'How much fairy floss have you had, Judith?'

Before she can reply, Judith promptly vomits down her own dress. Pink foam splatters over Mrs Moncur's cream shoes, as if Judith has coughed up an organ. Marty laughs shrilly but Ginny and Lizzy know that the day is turning sour. Sure enough, the afternoon activities are cancelled and the sickly smell of fairy floss fills the car on the way home.

'Next year . . .' says Ginny, when she and Lizzy are alone in her room. 'Next year, we'll be fourteen. We can take the bus down to Sydney on our own and do what we want.'

For Lizzy, life moves so slowly that next year seems unimaginably distant and her disappointment at missing out on the fabled David Jones store and the Opera House and botanical gardens is so profound, she's not sure she will ever get over it.

5

fringe dweller

Nullaburra's two motels were both full and Elizabeth suffered a fresh pang of regret at her impulsive exit from Judith's. She drove out to the caravan park north of the town, which was unlikely to be booked out at this time of year. As she pulled in, she saw with dismay how neglected and grubby it had become. It had once been a place where families came for their summer holidays and parents sat in cheerful groups outside the cabins drinking beer on hot summer nights while their kids ran wild. Now there was a sense of desolation, with shabby caravans on blocks and relocatable cabins. It had become home to fringe dwellers and those on the brink of destitution. She noticed a green shipping container half-hidden in the bush and immediately suspected a meth lab, but perhaps that was just her gloomy frame of mind.

'Sorry, buddy,' she told Eric. 'I didn't think this through.'

'Sorry bud-dy all is well all is well,' Eric responded cheerfully.

One of the cabins had a stick-on sign saying 'Office' over the door, so she knocked and waited. Through net curtains she could see the bare, bony legs of an elderly man stretched out on the bed watching a shopping channel on TV. The man eased himself off the bed and opened the door. His face was creased and baked brown, his few remaining teeth varnished with nicotine. He was almost bald with an unfortunate crust of hair growing along the edge of his ears. With barely a word, he pocketed her cash and handed over a folded set of linen, a threadbare towel and a key.

Elizabeth carried her bag and the cage into the cabin, closed the door and let Eric out. He sat on her knuckle, tilted his head to one side, and asked, 'How's yer day how's yer day?'

'Not so good, little buddy, but thanks for asking. You're cute,' she told him. With nothing else to do, she spent a few minutes coaching him to respond with, 'You're cute too.' The two of them batting compliments back and forth cheered her up slightly.

The cabin was cleanish but the air was heavy with mildew, underpinned by the greasy odour of fish fingers. She thought wistfully of her lovely room at Ginny's with its ornate pressed-tin ceilings and the big sash windows that looked out over the rolling hills of the vineyard. She had stood at that window so many times, mesmerised by the sight of birds swarming over the bare vines in winter, the froth of buds in spring and ruby leaves of autumn. Elizabeth and Ginny had played among the vines as children and later helped with the harvest. In these last years they had often walked the property in the evenings. Those times already felt like the distant past, a place she had once inhabited with people she had once known.

She made up the bed, averting her gaze from the stained mattress so as not to imagine the activities of previous occupants, and chatted with Eric while she organised herself. 'It's not that bad,' she reassured him. 'Just an odd smell. It's only one night.'

Eric wasn't that interested; he was busy pecking at the grapes she'd lined up on the table for his dinner. She turned on the television for company. It was tiny and fixed so high on the wall that her neck cracked loudly every time she looked up at it. There was nothing for it but to go to bed. The sheets seemed clean but the pillow had a revolting meaty smell that was hard to ignore. Exhausted, she drifted off to sleep only to be woken by nearby shouting and sometime later a siren and a blue light spinning wildly around the walls. Then all was quiet and she slept.

She woke at first light feeling sweaty and disoriented. To avoid whatever bacterial infections lurked in the communal shower, she made do with a flannel wash. She now realised that once she left the cabin there would be nowhere to change, so she slipped on her black low-heeled shoes and the grey linen dress, which now looked unpleasantly rumpled. There was no mirror, let alone an iron to fix it, so it would have to do. She had a jacket she could wear over the top.

Back in the cafe near the river, she ordered coffee and breakfast, wondering how she would fill the hours until the funeral. Her shoes felt tight and the dress cut into her neck. There was a little button at the throat that was more comfortable when she unfastened it.

The next problem was Eric. After her quick exit from Paul's yesterday, she didn't have the nerve to drive out and leave her boy there. She couldn't possibly take him to the service but nor could she leave him in the car for an hour. In the end, she spent so long deliberating that there was only one option left.

Elizabeth was the first to arrive at the chapel and the attendants were still getting themselves organised. She asked one of them if she could leave Eric's cage in the office. The young woman looked dubiously at Eric, as if she'd been asked to care for something much larger and more dangerous. 'He's really no trouble,' Elizabeth assured her.

The woman went over to the office. She returned a few minutes later and murmured something about insurance, eliminating that final possibility.

The chapel was attached to a funeral home and had a modern exterior with a more traditional church-like interior, designed to add a touch of gravitas to proceedings. The Order of Service pamphlets were stacked on the table inside the door. Taking one, Elizabeth settled herself on the end of a pew towards the back and tucked Eric's cage in beside her. She gave him a nice big piece of cuttlefish to keep him occupied and put the cover over his cage. People began to arrive and she noticed several looking down curiously at the cage. She overheard a man behind her say, 'There's a lady with a birdcage there. They must be releasing doves.'

'Oh, bless!' said the woman with him. 'What a beautiful idea.'

Elizabeth was about to turn around and set them straight when she caught sight of Paul and his family walking down the centre aisle. She opened the Order of Service and ran her finger down the list and up again but her name still didn't appear. It suddenly dawned on her that there had been no discussion about her eulogy yesterday. An oversight? Or was that the reason Paul had hurried her along?

Paul sat down in the front row with Polly and Adam and their families all side by side. Elizabeth parked her handbag on her seat and hurried to the front to speak to him. He looked up with a smile. 'Hello, Liz. Good to see you here. I thought you might have left town.'

Elizabeth had no idea what he was talking about. 'Paul, my eulogy . . . I'm not on the Order of Service.'

Paul got up and ushered her over to one side where they could speak in private. 'I'm sorry, Liz. We should have discussed this yesterday. Polly has organised it all and there wasn't time for everyone to speak.'

'Paul, I'm not "everyone". Ginny and I have been friends since we were ten years old. I knew her longer than you did, not that I'm saying . . . I just don't understand . . .' She struggled to keep her voice low and not draw attention to herself.

Paul put a restraining hand on her shoulder and said firmly, 'Perhaps you could read it at the lunch, Liz?'

Elizabeth wanted to insist that she had things to say about Ginny that no one else could. She wanted to show how hurt she felt at being dismissed and overlooked, but it clearly wasn't the time or place. She shook her head, more in bewilderment than refusal, went back to her seat, and sat down with a heavy sigh.

'Odd smell odd smell odd smell,' noted Eric under his cover. 'You're cute too.'

All around, heads turned, looking for the source of these words. People nearby began to titter. Elizabeth kept her eyes fixed on the altar. A single thought occurred to her: this was Polly's revenge. And Elizabeth knew exactly what it related to. She felt heartsick at the realisation. Ginny had always said her daughter had a spiteful streak. Neither Paul nor Adam would have wanted to leave Elizabeth out of the service but they wouldn't argue with Polly. And, although it went against her nature, this time Elizabeth would have to let it go, admit defeat and accept her punishment. At least she now understood what was going on.

The Nullaburra Primary choir, all dressed in neatly pressed uniforms, gathered in front of the altar and sang 'You Raise Me Up' in pure, beautiful voices, accompanied by three young violinists. It was a perfect choice for Ginny, who had nurtured hundreds of children over her years as a teacher. That was the dramatic difference in their careers; Ginny had inspired and educated young people whereas Elizabeth's world had been in damage control, finding ways to catch those tumbling through the system towards prison. Ginny had nurtured dozens of students who had gone on to gather accolades in the wider world. Elizabeth's efforts had some success but just as many failures. She pondered what piece of music would be appropriate at her own funeral, but couldn't think of a single inspiring song that would encompass her life.

As the choir finished, a baby began to wail, which was fortunate since Eric now began to chirp, 'Tea time tea time.' Elizabeth found some emergency slices of apple in her bag and slipped one into his cage to keep him quiet.

Paul didn't get up to speak, which didn't surprise Elizabeth; he was a naturally reserved man. Both Adam and Polly read eulogies they had written, neither looking up from the sheet of paper in front of them. They were followed by the school principal, who had only been with the school a couple of years and referred to Ginny as Virginia. Elizabeth shook her head in despair. No one talked about Ginny growing up, her girlhood, her teenage years. It was all about her service as a mother, grandmother and teacher. Her personality had been buried under the weight of her good works. Elizabeth found it dispiriting to think that, in the end, Ginny's value was measured entirely by her worthy service to others, like a donkey or a guide dog.

Eventually it was over. The children sang a couple of hymns and everyone rose and began to move out to the forecourt of the funeral home. Elizabeth was glad to be out in the sunshine of a warm spring day. Paul, Adam and Polly stood near the door, thanking people as they filed out. Elizabeth embraced Paul and Adam but made do with rubbing the back of Polly's hand in a comforting way as she forced a smile. Polly gave Eric's cage a pointed look and turned away to the next person in the line.

Mourners stood around chatting, greeting and embracing people they knew. Elizabeth put Eric back in the car and lowered a couple of windows an inch. She hovered politely on the edge of the crowd, waiting for this part to be over. She saw familiar faces but didn't feel up to talking to them, and she kept her distance from Judith and Bruce. She wasn't in the right frame of mind for the inevitable apology she would have to make. She sent a friendly little wave Judith's way and was blanked in return. It was times like these that she wished Ray was here, to comfort her and talk everything through on the way home. He knew some of these people and, regardless of whether he wanted to see them or not, he'd know exactly what to say to everyone.

The funeral car slowly crossed the forecourt and Elizabeth said her silent goodbyes as she watched it creep down the drive and turn onto the road. It still didn't seem quite real that this was her beloved Ginny disappearing into the distance.

As the crowd began to disperse, one of the attendants, a young man in a dark suit with his hair slicked back in a ponytail, came out of the chapel and slid the glass doors closed. As they locked together, Elizabeth caught sight of a woman wearing a potato costume reflected in the glass. It took a moment to realise it was her. She looked down at her dress. She hadn't noticed it was such an unflattering bulbous shape. Her hand crept to the button at her throat as she realised the dress was on backwards. She followed the attendant into the office and asked to use the bathroom. He pointed the way down a hall.

When Elizabeth came out of the bathroom a few minutes later, the office was in darkness and the main door was dead-locked. She tapped on the glass with her fingers like a trapped bird and watched helplessly as people got into their cars and drove away. Last to leave, without a backward glance, was Ponytail speeding off in his blue Barina.

Elizabeth didn't have the energy to be angry; there was almost an inevitability to the situation. On the reception desk she found a tiered plastic holder with a selection of business cards and called the funeral director. Once the initial confusion was cleared up and apologies delivered, she sat and waited until the Barina came to a skidding halt outside.

Because of that kerfuffle, she was one of the last to arrive at Paul's place – would she ever get used to calling it that? She went straight to the dining room and tucked Eric's cage in the corner beside the credenza, out of sight and earshot. The poor little chap, what a disruptive couple of days for him.

A waiter with a tray of drinks stood at the living room door. She took a glass of champagne and was so thirsty she drained the glass and returned it to the tray. Not recognising anyone here, she stood gazing out of the living room window, as if admiring the view, while actively counting the minutes until this part of the ordeal was over.

'Lizzy?'

Elizabeth gave a start and turned to see Ginny's brother, Marty, bearing down on her, his teeth set in a wide grin. Bald with a faded red beard, his complexion told a florid tale of sun and alcohol, probably in tandem. For a horrible moment she thought he was going to kiss her but, catching her expression, he stopped short. 'I thought it was you. How the hell are you, Liz?' he asked.

'I'm okay, Marty. And you?'

'Aww, we've lost a good 'un,' he said, shaking his head. It sounded like an all-purpose phrase he'd settled on to keep things simple. 'A good 'un,' he repeated, experimenting with a more wistful tone.

'Yes, she was the best. We were lucky to know her,' agreed Elizabeth, hoping this would signal an end to the inanities. 'And how have you been, Marty? Still up in the Far North?'

'Yep. Hot and happy up there. And yourself? You still working?'

'I'm not sure how I feel about being asked if I'm "still" doing things – as if I've got one foot in the grave. I'm only sixty-seven, Marty.'

He shrugged. 'Yeah, well, I'm sixty-eight. I just assumed you'd be retired by now.'

'Not at all. Far from it.' As the words left her mouth she realised what a short-sighted fabrication this was. Why had she even said it? Marty only had to bring it up with Paul and she'd be revealed as a liar since she was no longer employed. It was the concept she objected to, the whole 'put out to pasture' business.

'That's great, Liz. Good on you,' he said with misplaced admiration. 'I'm glad to see you here. You were Gin's closest friend. Hanging out here with us when we were little kids. My God, how long ago was that?!' He gave a harsh bark of laughter at this cruel joke called time.

'Yes, I was her closest friend. Thank you, Marty. I was supposed to speak at the service, but I was bumped,' she said quietly. 'I managed to get on the wrong side of Polly.'

Marty grimaced. 'Big mistake. Been there, done that. What was your crime?'

Elizabeth hesitated, glancing around quickly. 'I was just standing up for Ginny. Someone had to do it. They treated her like a servant. Inviting her on that holiday to Bali and then leaving her in the hotel every night with the kids while they went out drinking with their friends. Even after she was diagnosed, they . . .' She pulled herself up before she hit warp speed on this topic. 'Anyway, doesn't matter now.'

'Families,' said Marty. 'They don't take well to outside interference, but I know what you're saying. Ginny loved the kids and she was big-hearted. Couldn't say no.'

'Yes, that's it,' agreed Elizabeth, letting the subject drop.

'And your boys . . .?'

'Tom and Danny,' Elizabeth reminded him.

'Oh yeah, I heard Tom was doing a spell inside for assault. That surprised me. He was such a great kid. I remember he came up and helped with the harvest here one year.'

The usual hot, prickling sense of shame washed over Elizabeth. Someone like Tom ending up in prison was so unlikely that even people with good manners let their curiosity get the better of them. 'He's not a kid any more,' said Elizabeth. 'He's forty-four. Not something I ever thought would happen in our family, Marty. It still surprises me. The whole thing was a stuff-up from start to finish.'

'And Ray? Has he been found?'

'What is it with everyone asking me about Ray all of a sudden?' said Elizabeth. 'He's not a missing person, you know. He's not lost.'

Marty seemed unfazed by her terse response, but a couple of people standing nearby turned to look at her. 'Well, he disappeared, didn't he?' said Marty.

'But he announced his own disappearance. It's a different thing.'

'So, where do you reckon he is?'

'I know where he is. He's up north.' Elizabeth gestured vaguely in a northerly direction and Marty's eyes followed obediently, as if he might see Ray there in the distance. For years no one had asked after Ray but now, all of a sudden, he was not just on her mind but on everyone else's as well.

Elizabeth was about to excuse herself when they were joined by a heavy-set woman in a purple cheesecloth dress, her long grey hair woven into a thick plait. To Elizabeth's critical eye, she had the look of someone who had embraced hippiedom in later life. Marty introduced the woman as his partner, Jenny. 'And this . . .' he said with a grand gesture towards Elizabeth, '. . . is Lizzy O'Reilly.'

Jenny looked Elizabeth up and down. 'Oh, wow. I've heard a lot about you,' she said. 'You're nothing like what I imagined.'

'Sorry,' said Elizabeth, more bemused than annoyed. 'This is the best I could do on short notice. I'm not sure why you'd even hear about me. I've barely seen Marty in the last thirty years.'

Jenny laughed. 'First love and all that . . .'

'Never forgotten,' Marty chortled, giving Elizabeth a wink.

Elizabeth blinked. It was difficult to imagine that a wet kiss in a wardrobe half a century ago could be interpreted as love – she wasn't even a willing participant. She didn't know where to begin unravelling this, so she made her excuses. They exchanged empty promises about keeping in touch and she moved on. She now planned to square things off with Paul and make her escape.

The waiter reappeared with a tray of blinis topped with avocado and fat prawns. She took one and popped it in her mouth whole, to save possible mess. She took another, in case he didn't come her way again, and, since she was about to get on the road, a third.

Now Paul was making his way towards her. Not wanting to appear greedy, she quickly slipped the second blini in her mouth and hid the third one behind her back. Her mouth was so full, it felt like she'd stuffed a wet flannel in it.

'I'm sorry about the business at the chapel, Liz,' said Paul, joining her. 'As you can probably gather, it was all taken out of my hands.'

Elizabeth nodded, her mouth locked in a bulging smile.

'I'm sure you understand. I need to let the kids have more control. We all have to grieve in our own way.'

Elizabeth continued nodding, and added some agreeable sounds.

'I'll do the rounds and see you later.' He drifted away to greet people and she took the opportunity to stuff the third blini in her mouth. She retrieved Eric and made a discreet exit through the kitchen door, running to her car, head down like someone caught in crossfire.

6

to the sea

As soon as she got home, Elizabeth tore her dress off, went into the kitchen and stuffed it in the bin. Then, much as she had enjoyed the dramatic gesture, she retrieved it and took it to the laundry. She would wash the thing and take it to the Salvos store tomorrow, wishing it a happier life being worn the right way around and hopefully to a more pleasant occasion.

Eric was delighted to be home and freed from his cage. Babbling happily, he went straight to the window to preen and admire himself. 'You're cute too!' he assured his reflection. 'Odd smell odd smell.'

'Tea time,' she told him as she put the kettle on.

'Tea time tea time!' he agreed, strutting along the windowsill.

Revived by a cup of tea, Elizabeth took a long hot shower and washed her hair twice to erase the smell of that pillow and cleanse herself of the whole dreadful experience. She put on a cotton robe and lay down on her bed. She'd barely closed her eyes when her phone began to ring in the other room. It almost never rang these days, so she rolled off the bed and hurried to answer it.

When she saw the caller was her daughter-in-law, Claire, she hesitated and, by the time she considered the pros and cons, the phone stopped ringing. She listened to the message. 'That was Claire,' she reported to Eric. 'She said it's urgent.'

He twitched his head from side to side. 'S'urgent s'urgent.'

'I suppose I have to call her back.'

Elizabeth loved her daughter-in-law and adored her grandson, Zach, but couldn't seem to forgive Claire for her role in Tom's downfall. While it wasn't her fault that Tom had committed a crime, it was partly her betrayal that triggered the whole catastrophe. But Elizabeth was aware that it was this sort of stubborn attitude that Ginny had been referring to and so she returned the call before she could talk herself out of it.

'Hi, Liz, thanks for calling me back.' Claire either had a cold or had been crying.

'No problem. What can I do for you?' asked Elizabeth.

'I need your help. It's Zach.'

Elizabeth's heart gave a lurch. 'What's happened?'

'He's in a bit of trouble, actually. Can we meet? I'd really like to talk it all through with you in person.'

'Can't you tell me now?' asked Elizabeth. A dizzying wave of anxiety caught her unawares and she sat down heavily on the sofa.

Claire sighed. 'Please, Liz? It's a bit complicated.'

They agreed to meet the next morning, at a cafe near the hospital where Claire worked, and Elizabeth lay down on her bed feeling more churned up than ever. Zach in trouble. The whole family was falling apart and she couldn't help but feel at least partially responsible.

When Zach was younger, Elizabeth had pictured herself as

a cool nana, the sort who spontaneously high-fived and said things like 'Wassup, dude?', perhaps accompanied by a secret handshake. At one time she'd even watched these handshakes on YouTube. But it wasn't the sort of thing she could practise with Eric, and she had a creeping suspicion that Zach would not think it was cool any more. Almost to the day that he turned fourteen, he changed from a sunny little boy to a scowling stranger who never used two words if one would do. She had imagined that she could be Zach's shelter from the storms of adolescence, but his overnight transformation had taken her by surprise. She soon heard herself speaking in the brisk, no-nonsense tone she'd once used with young offenders when she was a probation officer. 'Come on, Zach. Your mother asked you to do something. Let's just get it done.' Despite her best efforts, she had been guilty of scolding him for mumbling, poor posture and a negative attitude and had unwittingly etched the demarcation lines between them. But then her attentions had turned to Tom's unfurling disaster and her relationship with Zach suffered the blow of neglect.

When they were teens, her sons had played football, wagged school, fought with each other, chased girls and played video games together on an Atari hooked up to the television in the living room. But Zach lived in a different world. He was either out in the ocean surfing with a tribe of wild-haired boys, or shut in his room with his Xbox. His life was private, beyond the gaze of adults. She hadn't seen him for almost a year and, to her deep regret and guilt, felt as though she barely knew him now.

When Elizabeth arrived at the cafe, Claire was already there dressed in her nurse's uniform. She got straight up and gave

Elizabeth a firm peck on the cheek, as if expecting resistance. 'I've ordered you a flat white,' she said. 'I hope that's still your coffee.'

'Yes. Thank you. So, what's happened?' asked Elizabeth, sitting down.

'How are you, Liz? I miss you. We both do, me and Zach. I was so sorry to hear Ginny passed away. She was so lovely, and such a dear friend to you.'

Elizabeth hesitated, not trusting herself to speak. 'Yes, she was.'

'Are you all right?' Claire leaned forward, gazing at Elizabeth. 'You must be —'

'I'm fine. You've got me worried, Claire.'

Claire gave her a long sorrowful look and then capitulated. 'You might have read in the papers that there was a fire in our local surf club a few months ago?'

Elizabeth shook her head. 'I don't remember it, but go on.'

'Unfortunately Zach was involved. He and his mate found a can of petrol in a skip in the carpark of the surf club. There were a lot of kids down there and they started a bonfire. Some building materials caught fire and then the surf club itself. They obviously didn't mean for that to happen. I was on night shift and, next thing, I got a call to come down to the police station.'

'Who was the mate?' asked Elizabeth.

'Jackson was the other boy. He's not a bad boy either. They just don't think things through.' Claire paused as if reading Elizabeth's thoughts. 'Zach's fifteen now, Liz. I don't have that much control over him these days.'

'Have they been charged? Do you have a lawyer?'

'We have a lawyer and he's in court next week,' said Claire.

'Oh, Claire, why on earth didn't you call me earlier? Why didn't your lawyer refer the case to go to conference? Has Zach had previous warnings?'

Claire nodded as tears welled up in her eyes and Elizabeth had to look away. Claire often let things roll along, thinking everything would be all right until it absolutely wasn't. Now it would be more difficult to sort this out.

The coffee arrived and Elizabeth was glad to have a moment to gather her thoughts and choose her words. She wanted to handle this properly. 'Claire, I'm not meaning to sound harsh. I just wish you'd called me when he was first arrested. I'm thinking of Zach.'

'I'm sorry. I was embarrassed, to be honest. Please help us, Liz. You know the system, how things work. I'm lost with it all. We have to keep him out of . . . you know. I can't believe this is happening to our family. We're not the sort of people who even know criminals . . .'

'No one is immune. As we have discovered.'

'Could you take him?' blurted Claire. 'Take out a guardianship, or whatever. The court would look on that favourably, wouldn't they?'

Elizabeth was speechless for a moment. 'You can't just give him away, Claire.'

'I'm worried sick about my boy. I just want what's best for him. I can't think what else to do. I'd do anything!'

'There's something else going on. What aren't you telling me?'

Claire stared at her for a long moment and Elizabeth saw how much she had aged in this last year. She was almost unrecognisable from that young woman radiant on her wedding day with a circlet of flowers in her long hair. More heartbreaking were memories of Tom on that day, handsome in a cream double-breasted suit. These days he lived in prison greens.

'I've got an ovarian cyst. I had to put off the op because of all this. I need to take sick leave and get some rest. I'm just completely exhausted,' Claire said tearfully.

Elizabeth didn't know what to say. She knew that she had to put what happened with Tom behind them. She couldn't bear anything to happen to Claire. 'You'll bounce back. Women always do. We don't have a choice.'

Claire gave a faint smile. 'I knew you'd know the right thing to say, Liz.' Elizabeth had no idea if she was joking; Claire wasn't the sarcastic type. 'Will you at least think about it? Look, I need to get to work but . . .'

Elizabeth nodded and stood up to go. 'We can request that the Liaison Officer refer it to a Youth Justice conference instead of Children's Court. Text me the contacts of the people you're dealing with and let them know I'm involved now.'

'Thank you, Liz, I'll do that straight away,' said Claire. 'I appreciate it.'

Elizabeth gave her daughter-in-law what she hoped was an understanding smile. 'I'll get the coffees. You head off to work.' Claire got up and gripped her in a fierce hug. Taken by surprise, Elizabeth managed to lift one partially trapped arm and give her a pat on the back.

Elizabeth paid the bill and crossed the road to the beach. She found a hat in her bag and squashed it on her head. She sat on a bench and watched the surf roll in, wave after wave, and tried to take comfort in the majesty of nature while she ordered her thoughts.

She knew Ginny was right. She had to be the one to bring her family back together. Right now her biggest problem was her own stubbornness, and her inability to back down. She worked hard to keep her thoughts to herself, but opening her heart was a more complex and difficult task.

If only Ginny were here to help guide her through this metamorphosis. She watched the gulls flying low and free over the surf, half hoping for a sign that Ginny was with her still in spirit. If only Ray was here and she could lean on him. But there was no one, she was completely alone.

7

the Irish boy

1968 Lizzy wakes before the alarm. She gets out of bed and looks out the window to see two sets of headlights crawling up the driveway, bright spots in a grey dawn. Mr Moncur comes out onto the front verandah to greet the pickers as they pile out from the cars, the sound of laughter and the sweetness of ripe grapes in the cool morning air. The grapes will be harvested today and the whole family has been drafted for work.

Lizzy lifts Ginny's blanket and tickles her feet. 'Wake up, they're here.'

Her friend groans and rolls over to the wall. 'In a minute . . .'

Lizzy pulls on shorts and a t-shirt. In the bathroom she splashes her face and runs her fingers through her hair. Recently cut in a short, boyish 'Twiggy' style, she imagines it makes her look more worldly and sophisticated than her sixteen years.

On the front verandah, the pickers help themselves to bread rolls and eggs and bacon from a metal tray set out on the table. But as soon as Lizzy steps outside, all heads turn in her direction and a prickling blush spreads up her neck. Her t-shirt suddenly feels too thin, her shorts too short, her feet too bare.

'Here's our little lark!' cries Mrs Moncur, hurrying out with a tray of coffee mugs. 'Bring out the coffee pots, please, Lizzy.'

In the kitchen, two coffee percolators bubble on the stovetop. Lizzy switches off the elements and carries both pots back outside. The pickers stand together in the driveway, talking in hushed, early morning voices as they eat. As she fills each of the mugs, hands reach in and grab them with mumbled thanks. 'Thanks, Lizzy,' says one with a teasing note in his voice.

She glances up in surprise. Ray O'Reilly. He's a couple of years ahead of her at school, a recent arrival and the topic of much discussion among the girls. She can't believe he knows her name, then realises Mrs Moncur just said it. She glances around at the other pickers, all much older than him. 'How come you're doing this?'

'Money? Why else?' He laughs quietly into his coffee.

She searches for something intelligent and witty to say. 'So, d'you like the school?'

'It's okay. Preferred my old school in Sydney.' He pauses, then adds, 'End of the year when I finish, I'll be going back there . . . to the city.'

'Do you want more coffee?' asks Lizzy. She tips the pot to refill his mug but it's empty. She blushes so hard the roots of her hair tingle.

'I better go anyway,' he says with a lopsided smile. 'See you later, Lizzy.'

She takes the mug from him and watches as he follows the other pickers into the vines. He glances back over his shoulder and gives her a wave. She wants to wave back but hesitates, then it's too late.

'Oh, I missed out on everything,' says Ginny as she surveys the food trays with nothing left but glistening fat and yellow flecks of fried egg.

Lizzy picks up the trays. 'I didn't get anything either. Come on, we'll make our own.' She wants to tell Ginny what just happened, but not yet. For the moment, she needs to hold it close, examine it frame by frame. The way his dark brown eyes held hers. The lock of hair that flopped over one eyebrow. The sinew of muscle in his forearm as he held the coffee mug. As she glances back towards the vines, she notices the spill of sunlight on the grass, the call of birds and the softness of the air on her skin. Everything seems sharp and bright.

Lizzy and Ginny work together all morning, cutting fat bunches of grapes and putting them in buckets. Marty's job is to collect the full buckets and replace them with empty ones. Lizzy's bucket never gets past half full before he's back to get it, making an annoying comment or asking her for the umpteenth time how she's going. She gazes off into the distance hoping to catch sight of Ray but he's one of many figures, bending and straightening, as they work the lower part of the vineyard.

When she and Ginny walk back to the house, the pickers are gathering in the shade of the utility shed to eat their lunch. Chatter and laughter rise and fall in the midday heat. She doesn't dare glance over to see if Ray is among them.

'Did you see that new boy from school's here?' asks Ginny, who stares quite openly at the men.

'Ray O'Reilly,' says Lizzy, the words sweet on her lips.

*

Nullaburra High has grown fast through the sixties from a couple of hundred students to over five hundred. The school has a brand-new assembly hall and library. Lizzy has often seen Ray there at lunchtime, studying or reading. He's an oddity in a school where indifference is admired and effort is condemned as 'try hard'. It seems he's not aware of these unspoken rules. He's friendly to everyone but friends with no one in particular, passing through with no need to be accepted or part of a group. He has the faintest Irish lilt that marks him as an outsider and is often mimicked by the boys but admired by the girls.

Before the harvest, Lizzy had never spoken to him. It wouldn't have crossed her mind, even given the opportunity. But when she next goes to the library, Ray smiles and gives her a wave. He pulls out a chair beside him at the table and beckons for her to sit down.

'How are your hands?' he asks in a hushed voice, spreading his palms to show the cuts and grazes.

Lizzy displays her own. 'Not too bad. Gloves are probably a good idea.'

'I felt like an old man from all that bending.' He mimes holding his aching back, his face a grimace of pain. 'I had to get up at four-thirty the next morning and help my uncle with the milking. More bending.'

'Do you do that every day?' asks Lizzy. 'Is your uncle making you do that?'

'Not really . . .' He pauses as if considering how much to tell her. 'My dad wanted me to leave school and get an apprenticeship as an electrician like him. We were arguing about it all the time. My stepmother suggested I could help her brother on the farm and finish school here.'

'Stepmother? Is she wicked?' Lizzy smothers a giggle. She's never known anyone with a stepmother.

Ray looks thoughtful. 'She has a long, crooked nose with a wart on the end . . . No, actually, she's a good sort. She's trying to help and I was glad to get out of there, to be truthful.'

Lizzy tells him she has to work in her parents' shop on the weekends. 'It's not that bad. I can tell you the price of fairly much any tinned vegetable – always handy to know. A great conversation starter. Peas are on special this week, by the way.'

Ray grins. 'Fantastic. I'll be in to stock up.'

When she sees him in the library a few days later he asks, with mock seriousness, if peas are still on special. She confirms they are, adding that creamed corn is also discounted, and laughs at his pursed lips. The librarian asks them to be quiet or leave. They go outside and walk around the edge of the playing field, talking until the bell rings. After that they meet in front of the library every lunchtime but never bother going in. They walk slowly around the playing field talking until it's time to go back to class.

Lizzy has never encountered someone who is so interested in the world. Ray has ambitions to be a journalist and hopes to get a cadetship with a newspaper. He talks about travelling: he wants to work as a foreign correspondent and learn other languages. In the library, he's been studying Latin for the new Higher School Certificate exam – a subject taught at his previous school but not at Nullaburra High. He explains the Romance languages to her, something she's never heard of before. 'If you speak Spanish and English, you can travel to half the world, not just Spain but Mexico and South America.' The idea of going overseas, let alone to South America, has never crossed Lizzy's mind. She'd be happy just to leave Nullaburra.

Talking to boys has never come easily to her and being shouted down by her older brother all these years hasn't helped. She's either tongue-tied or unnecessarily loud with nothing in between and occasionally shows off in a way that makes her cringe afterwards. But with Ray, there's an easy naturalness, something she's only ever known with Ginny.

Ray tells her that when he was nine, his mother left and went home to Ireland. He has a younger half-brother called Andy and his stepmother is called Cynthia. He seems very fond of them both. His father rarely gets a mention.

'Would you forgive your mum if she came back now?'

'Course I would. I can't see her coming back now, though. I'll go to Ireland one day and find her. When I'm a famous journalist,' he says.

Lizzy thinks about Ray's mother and how he must have felt losing her like that. She often wishes her own mother would go far away – but not forever.

One Saturday Ray comes into the shop, parking his motorbike out the front. He buys three cans of peas, which makes them both laugh. He courteously introduces himself to Lizzy's mother but as soon as he leaves, her mother wants to know who he is, why he's hanging around and where he's from.

'He goes to my school and he's from Sydney. You don't ask that about other customers.'

'He doesn't sound like he's from Sydney,' says her mother. 'And he's sort of dark looking.'

'He's Irish, Mum. He came here when he was a little kid.'

'I see . . . A Catholic then, I suppose. Well, I don't want to see you on the back of that motorbike. And he's too old for you any-way – you're only sixteen.'

'He's only eighteen . . .'

'Cut the backchat, Miss. You know what I'm saying. Stay away from him. That's an order.'

Lizzy has no intention of staying away from Ray. She couldn't if she tried. Over the next weeks they spend every lunchtime together. On Friday or Saturday nights they often make up a foursome with Ginny and her boyfriend, Chris, and go to the pictures or a local dance. Sometimes they just drive around Nullaburra in Chris's Falcon looking for something to do, or park down by the river. Lizzy feels intoxicated in Ray's pres-ence, as if nothing else is quite as real. The touch of his hands on her skin, his kisses, gentle and passionate, and the murmured conversations between them are beyond anything she has ever experienced.

Over that summer she often climbs out her bedroom win-dow in the night and rides her bike down to the river to meet him there. They kiss and hold each other, and talk until the early hours. When summer fades and it's too cold to go to the river, Ray meets her on the corner of her street with his motorbike and they ride out into the dark countryside to his uncle's farm. They wheel the bike quietly into the hay barn where it's warm and the hay smells sweet and grassy. In the privacy of the barn they make love for the first time. It's a little uncomfortable at first, but over that winter, sex becomes a natural part of their relationship. Lizzy sometimes wonders if anyone has ever felt as deliriously and dizzily happy as she does. One night in the barn, with the packed hay prickling her skin and their clothes in disarray, Ray murmurs in her ear, 'Te amo.'

'What does that mean?' she asks, giggling at the strangeness of it.

'It's Spanish. It means I love you.'

Lizzy wants to say she loves him too. She has loved him from that first moment at the harvest. She thinks of nothing but him. But that simple declaration is beyond her. She doesn't know how to start. She has never uttered those words to anyone, let alone in a foreign language. And never heard them from anyone – ever. She's overwhelmed by the responsibility and the trust he's placed in her. She knows he's disappointed but still she can't say the words.

On the ride back to town there's frost in the night air and skeins of mist float above the paddocks, eerie in moonlight. Her eyes sting as she shelters in the lee of his warm back. He drops her at the corner of her street. They press their cold lips together. And still the words won't come.

As she walks away, she knows she can't let him ride off into the freezing night, down those lonely country roads without knowing the truth. In the moment before he kickstarts the bike, she calls out, '¡Te amo!' Feeling like an idiot, wondering if she even said it right. At first she thinks he hasn't heard. She calls out again, louder and stronger. He climbs off the bike, kicks the stand down and opens his arms out wide to her.

8

the window

1969 Lizzy and her parents stand out on the street and watch two men on ladders affix a new sign to the shopfront that reads 'Clayton's Self-serve Mini-mart' in red block lettering on a mustard-coloured background.

'People already know they can serve themselves,' Lizzy points out. 'And everyone knows we're the Claytons.'

'It sounds more American,' explains her mother; she often borrows *McCall's*, and *Good Housekeeping* magazines from the library and considers herself an expert on all things American. 'People want to feel shopping is glamorous. You can pick things up and read the labels.'

'How is it glamorous picking up your own tin of baked beans?' asks Lizzy.

'At Clayton's Self-serve Mini-mart, you get the best of both worlds with personal choice and personalised service,' her father says in the radio announcer voice he sometimes adopts to amuse her mother.

'You missed your calling, Ted,' says her mother, not for the first time, a compliment he always enjoys.

School is over for the year and the summer holidays stretch ahead with shelves to be stacked and sales to be rung up on the till. It's bad enough being with her parents all day but made worse at the moment because the only topic of conversation is Nullaburra's first supermarket under construction nearby. A dozen shops and some houses have been demolished to make way for an enormous building with a dedicated carpark. One minute her parents are fretting about competition and potential discounting, the next they're scoffing at the grandiose aspirations of the enterprise in Nullaburra, where people are notoriously cheap. They discuss it endlessly with customers, many of whom share their scepticism. Her parents think these customers are showing loyalty but Lizzy thinks it's more likely the fear of change. Still, she has to agree that the new sign on the shopfront does make the business look more modern and up-to-date.

'That's a shot across the bows for the Coles family,' says her father. 'Let them know that Clayton's mean business and we don't take kindly to "out of towners" muscling in where they're not needed.'

'They won't last a year,' says her mother. 'In the meantime, we need to batten down the hatches. I don't want any more fuss about you going back to school, Liz. You've got your School Certificate. That's all you need. You have to think about the family, not just yourself all the time.'

Lizzy gathers herself, determined to continue this battle but her father takes her by the arm, holding it a little too firmly for her liking, and draws her attention back to the sign. 'Claytons – that's us. This is our family business. Not just Mum and me – the whole family, including you.'

Lizzy pulls her arm away. 'You didn't care about Doug going off and getting an apprenticeship. I'm not spending the rest of my life working in this shop.'

'Don't speak to your father like that, Miss. You're not too good for it. Doug's worked full-time in the business – you haven't. Too busy out chasing that boy with the motorbike that I told you to stay away from. You can't get away with any nonsense in this town, you know. We're not stupid. Besides, we make these decisions. Not you.'

'And you can take that scowl off your face too,' adds her father. His own expression transforms to a beaming smile as he sees a customer approaching. 'Hello, Mrs Griffith! What do you think of our new sign?'

Mrs Griffith shades her eyes from the afternoon sun, squinting up at the sign. 'Very smart. Now, do you have those stock cubes I asked for?'

'Yes, of course. I ordered all three flavours,' he says, ushering her into the shop.

As soon as they're alone, Lizzy's mother turns to her. 'And don't go getting yourself pregnant. That boy's too old for you and that sort will be long gone back to where he came from. We're not having you here with a big belly.'

Lizzy follows her father inside, forcing herself to pretend nothing's happened. She doesn't need any extra attention right now. She waits at the till, counting the minutes. On the dot of five, she hands over to her mother to cash up for the day. As she races across the yard, she can hear the phone ringing in the house and snatches it up before it rings out. 'Hello? Ray?' she asks, breathlessly.

'Yep. It's me. I didn't get the cadetship. There's a lot of competition. They'll take me on as a copy boy but I have to get my shorthand and typing up to speed,' he says. 'Anyway, at least I'm in the door, and they want me to start on Monday.'

Lizzy tries hard to be thrilled for him. In the last few months he's written to every daily paper searching for work. 'This next Monday?' she asks in a wobbly voice.

'Don't worry, Lizzy. I'll come back and see you soon. Promise. Don't cry.'

'I'm not crying, I'm just . . . um . . . so are you going to stay down there now?'

'Yeah, I found a place this afternoon. It's a room, quite big with a bit of a kitchen and shared bathroom. My uncle's coming down on the weekend anyway, so he can bring my stuff. Come and see me when you get some time off. Next weekend?'

'Yeah. I'll try.' She doesn't want to tarnish his joy. They talk until he runs out of coins and are cut off without saying goodbye. Lizzy goes to her room. She lies on her bed and sobs into her pillow until her throat is raw and her face swollen. Life without Ray is unimaginable. She thinks about the girls he will meet at the newspaper. It makes her chest hurt. And she cries some more.

On Saturday afternoon she and her mother wash the lino floors and disinfect all the surfaces. Her mother scolds her for sulking, imagining it's still about having to leave school, but Lizzy hasn't even begun to grieve about that. She has to behave herself and come up with a good excuse to get away next weekend. Ginny will cover for her, she always does.

After dinner Lizzy goes to her room and lies on her bed, staring at the ceiling and listening to the tinny sound of television laughter from the living room. She drifts into sleep and wakes to a tapping on the window. She kneels on her bed and looks out to see Ray's face appear out of the blackness. She lifts the window open wide. He pulls himself in and tumbles onto her bed, the leather of his jacket cold on her skin, his cheek warm against hers. 'I thought you were staying down there?' she says.

'Yeah, but you sounded upset. I thought I'd better come back and cheer you up.'

She holds his face between her hands. 'You rode all the way back here for that?'

He kisses her softly as he peels off his jacket. 'Course.' He tells her everything that has happened in the few days they've been apart, full of enthusiasm for his new life.

Lizzy only has one piece of news.

'Oh Je-sus,' says Ray. 'They're as bad as my father. It's that generation trying to stand in the way of us getting ahead. They can't make you work in the shop.'

'Keep your voice down. You don't know what they're like — all guilt and threats.'

'You're joking. Try coming from a Catholic family. If you're not going back to school, why stay here? Come down and get a job in Sydney.'

'Mum and Dad would never let me go. Ever. Even when I turn eighteen it'll be a battle. I probably will have given up hope by then anyway.'

He's silent for a moment, then reaches for her hand. 'Come with me now, Lizzy. Tonight.' His serious tone makes her tremble all over. The thought of leaving with him is terrifying, but him going without her is so much worse.

'You don't have to decide right now . . .' he says. 'If you don't want to . . .'

Lizzy pulls away from him and gets off the bed. She stands looking around the room, scanning her life up until this moment, then she drops to her knees beside the bed.

'What are you doing down there?' asks Ray, sitting up. 'Praying?'

Smothering her giggles, she reaches under the bed and pulls out a duffle bag. 'Packing, you dope.'

In years to come, she will always remember the sense of freedom, the wind tearing at her hair, her arms wrapped around Ray's body as they fly through the night. She will always remember the sight of the city's sparkling clusters of light as they cross the Harbour Bridge to begin a new life.

9

distant gunfire

In the week after Ginny's funeral, Elizabeth dreamed of Ray almost every night. In some dreams he was the central figure, in others a shadowy presence. Each morning she woke thinking about him. Why hadn't she heard from him? That's what was bothering her. Even after all this time, she still had conversations with him in her head. She wrote to him every few months. Her letters weren't long but always reassuring. She kept bad news to herself. He always replied promptly to let her know all was well at his end. But now, it was almost seven weeks since she'd written to him – and still nothing back.

She was due at Claire's at six that evening to discuss Zach's case. She was nervous about seeing her grandson. She had no explanation for her absence over this last year that would be acceptable to a fifteen-year-old, and any excuses she had would imply that her suffering had been more important than his.

The day ahead seemed endless. She kept busy, cleaned the house, nattered with Eric and hung out a load of washing, and it was still barely lunchtime. She sat down at the kitchen table with the weekend crossword, but the questions seemed garbled and she soon became frustrated. Restless, she had the urge to put everything around her in order but her dominion was as tidy as it was ever going to be.

'All in order. Neat as a pin,' she told Eric, who sat on her head while she cleaned out his cage. 'Good girl. Good girl.'

'Good girl,' he repeated encouragingly. He learned new phrases quickly and forgot most of them, but occasionally he surprised her with one she had quite forgotten. He inspected his freshly cleaned home, chattering happily to himself, then tucked his head under his wing and dozed off. He wasn't exactly a sparkling conversationalist but at least he never argued with her, unlike her sons, who seemed to be waiting to pounce to con-tradict or correct her. She didn't ruffle Eric's feathers the way she did theirs.

In the end she set off for Claire's far too early and, just to torture herself, drove down the street where Tom and Claire had once lived. She parked opposite their old house and indulged herself with memories of that golden day when they took possession of their first property. Elizabeth had brought along a bottle of French champagne and they all stood together in the garden and raised a toast to this milestone. Danny was there with his daughters, Lily and Grace, who were tiny. Zach was only ten and excited about the good-sized lawn to play on. She recalled it as a perfect day; her two sons discussing the structural aspects of the house, her three grandchildren running excitedly through the empty rooms while she and Claire discussed colours and furniture arrangement. It was more than they could afford at the time but Elizabeth had no doubt that they could handle it: both were making good money.

They couldn't have imagined that four years later this house would be sold to pay Tom's legal fees.

As she got out of the car at Claire's place, the front door opened and Nathan came out – the last person she expected to run into here. Seeing her, Nathan recoiled for a second, then walked off unhurriedly down the street. As if he owed her nothing. As if he hadn't betrayed Tom in the worst possible way. She watched him go. He was tall, well-built and loose-limbed, always so sure of himself. He'd been Tom's best friend since university and later his business partner, almost part of the family – but not any more.

Elizabeth knocked at the front door, then, seeing it had been left unlatched, walked straight in, catching Claire by surprise. 'Why is Nathan hanging around?'

'Hi, Liz. He just dropped in to see how we're getting on. Can I get you a drink?'

Elizabeth followed her into the kitchen. 'Where's Zach while all this is going on?'

'Nothing is going on.' Claire sounded exasperated. 'He'll be home shortly. He just went for a quick surf.'

'A surf?' asked Elizabeth. Was she the only one taking this situation seriously?

'He'll be easier to deal with after a surf. He'll be back soon, don't worry. And you're a little early anyway. Any news?' Claire opened the cupboard and got down a bottle of gin. She wiggled it at Elizabeth, who gave a nod of approval.

'I'll wait until Zach gets here. I don't want to go over everything twice.' Elizabeth sat down on the sofa and looked around the room. It was quite pleasant for a rental property. Although it was a shabby old beach house, Claire had a talent for nesting; she was good with cushions and throws.

Claire brought over two gin and tonics with lemon and ice, and sat down on the opposite sofa.

'He's not half the man Tom —' Elizabeth stopped herself, not knowing whether to refer to Tom's superiority in the past or the present tense and let the subject drop.

The front door banged shut and Claire called out, 'Is that you, Zachy? Nana's here to talk to us. We're in the living room.'

Zach appeared in the doorway. In barely a year, he had transformed from a gawky adolescent to a young Adonis. His wetsuit had been pulled down to his waist revealing a lean muscular torso. He had Tom's dark eyes and hair, long, tangled and sun-scorched. For a moment she was quite dazzled by his beauty but he returned her admiring gaze with one of cold suspicion. 'Haven't seen you for a while,' he said, his mouth full of metal and bands.

As a little boy, Zach would have run to her for a hug, dragging her off to see something he'd found or a skateboard trick he'd mastered. She wished he would cross the room now and give her a spontaneous hug, but she didn't deserve that and wasn't about to initiate it.

'Just have a quick shower and we can talk,' said Claire.

Zach ignored her and instead sat down beside her on the sofa in his wetsuit.

Elizabeth took this as her cue. 'Okay, we're intervening now before your case goes to court. I can't understand why your lawyer didn't do this from the outset.'

'He's a friend of a friend and not that experienced in this area,' admitted Claire.

'I've spoken to your Liaison Officer about taking it to a conference with a convenor instead. You'll admit responsibility, Zach, and then —'

'Nah,' interrupted Zach. He arched his back and stretched his arms overhead like a cat limbering up. He glanced longingly in the direction of the kitchen.

'Are you hungry?' asked Claire.

Elizabeth's head did a wobble of confusion. 'Nah to what?'

He shrugged. 'Wanna go to court.'

'Why would you want to go to court?' asked Elizabeth. 'You've already had a caution for a similar offence, albeit a lesser one. You don't want to risk a sentence and a criminal record.'

'Wait.' He looked perplexed. 'Al be it. What?'

'Although,' translated Claire. 'Albeit.'

'Whatever. Anyway, I don't want that lawyer. He's a kook. I'll defend myself. Your honour, I plead not guilty.' He turned to Claire to enquire about more important matters. 'Did you get Weet-Bix?'

Elizabeth had to work hard to keep her irritation in check. 'This isn't a TV show, Zach. Pleading not guilty, when it's clear that you *are*, will not help your case. On the contrary. They want to see you're repentant.'

Zach frowned. 'Meaning?'

'Meaning it will make matters worse if they see that you're not sorry for what you did and deny responsibility. In the Children's Court —'

'*Children's* Court?!' said Zach, clamping his arms across his chest. 'No way.'

'Just listen to Nana, darling,' said Claire. 'She knows what she's talking about.'

'I want to go to the same court Dad was in. Will it be in the papers?'

'Now, listen to me, Zach.' Elizabeth reverted to her steely tone. 'You were arrested and charged. The justice system is now in control. Not you. You wouldn't be in an adult court. You are legally a child.'

He gave her a long withering stare. 'Debatable.'

'It is not *debatable*,' said Elizabeth. 'It's a fact. And they want to see you taking responsibility for your actions.'

Anger flashed in his eyes and threaded through his body like a charge. 'It. Was. An. Accident.'

Elizabeth leaned towards him. 'Would there have been a fire if you and Jackson hadn't started it? Yes or no?'

He stared at her for a moment and, without another word, got up and left the room. She waited for the inevitable slam of his bedroom door. At that age, Tom had been a champion door-slammer, throwing them open and shut until there was a handle-shaped hole behind every door. But now there was only silence and Elizabeth wondered if a winner had been declared. After a moment, they heard the muffled sounds of explosions and automatic gunfire.

'*Call of Duty* . . . Xbox,' said Claire apologetically. 'He is just a child. We need to help him.'

Elizabeth held her tongue. There were many things she'd like to say to Claire and in the past probably could have. But she had lost Claire's trust too. So she remained silent.

'Don't take any notice of Zach's comments,' said Claire. 'You do what you think is best. I'll make sure he cooperates . . . well, I'll try anyway. So, if he admits responsibility then we can go to this conference thing rather than court?'

Elizabeth agreed. 'They prefer to keep kids out of the courts.'

'What do you think about the other thing? You know, the guardianship?'

'I don't think that's necessary. Let's see how we go in the conference and take it from there. My closer involvement may be enough.'

'I went to see Tom last week,' said Claire, watching the ice swill around in her glass.

Elizabeth nodded. 'Good. How was he?'

'He's okay. I wanted to tell him what was happening, with me and Zach.'

'How did he take it?'

Claire's lip quivered but she held on. 'Not very well. He feels trapped.'

'It's not just a feeling. It's a reality. Did he really need to know?'

'He's still Zach's father. We're still a family, Liz. He needed to be told and I wanted to do it in person.'

The fusillade of gunfire stopped abruptly. Elizabeth turned towards the bedroom. 'He just put his headset on,' said Claire.

Elizabeth got up and walked over to Zach's door. She opened it just wide enough to have a peek inside. The bed was in a knot, the floor a mass of tangled cables and clothes with his wet-suit lying on top. Zach sat facing a large monitor, with oversize earphones clamped on his head. On the screen soldiers ran half-crouched through a burnt-out building amid rapid explosions. After a moment she realised Zach was controlling an automatic weapon, killing everyone in his path at such a frenetic pace that her eyes struggled to keep up. She flinched as blood exploded across the screen and Zach commented to some unseen comrade,

'Ohhh, sniped! I was on a fat kill streak. Oh man, I was one off my chopper gunner.'

Elizabeth quietly closed the door. It was as though she had intruded on something private and intimate: Zach's secret life where he spoke another language.

Sitting down, she asked Claire, 'I'm wondering how you see things going with Tom, as in getting back together?'

'Liz . . . I don't know. And I don't think it's fair to ask me. There are things we need to work out.'

'So that's a maybe?'

Claire bit her lip and said nothing, and Elizabeth was forced to make do with that.

10

little creatures

For Zach's conference meeting, Elizabeth dressed in what, only a few months earlier, had been her work suit. Now the jacket pinched under the arms and the skirt pulled taut across her hips. Looking at her image in the full-length mirror, she wondered if it had always fitted so poorly and she'd just been too busy or careless to notice. She ran her fingers through her hair. Short and practical, making the point that she didn't care about her appearance. She couldn't remember exactly when she'd adopted this look – probably after Ray went away, a time when she wanted to be invisible. She wondered how he would see her now. She doubted that even Ray could see past this plain exterior to the sweet Lizzy he fell in love with. He probably looked a little ragged himself these days. He was forever fixed in her mind in his early forties; now he was in his late sixties. Earlier in the week, to her relief, there had been a letter from him. He admitted to having been 'under the weather' and assured her there was no cause for concern. He joked about getting old and forgetful but there was something about the tone of the letter that left her unconvinced.

*

The Youth Justice conference convenor, Mrs Giles, who had already been in touch with Zach to discuss his case, led the proceedings. The Police Liaison Officer and the deputy president of the surf club (who, Elizabeth was relieved to note, was a motherly looking woman), Claire, Elizabeth and Zach all sat in a circle facing each other. It was meant to be an informal setting but Elizabeth imagined it was still intimidating for Zach to be the centre of so many adults' attention.

Zach was dressed in a crisply ironed white shirt with a black tie, hair slicked into a knot at the nape of his neck. He showed none of his earlier combative attitude and answered the convenor's questions briefly and respectfully. When asked, he explained exactly what had happened and admitted fault. Elizabeth wasn't convinced it was genuine. There was a glibness in his delivery that made her suspect bribery might have played a part.

Claire forced a smile now and then. One of those smiles was for Elizabeth when Mrs Giles mentioned that his grandmother's increased involvement in Zach's life was a very positive factor. Between the six participants, they agreed on an Outcome Plan in which Zach would write the surf club an apology letter and commit to twenty hours of community service for the club. A curfew of 9 pm and he could not associate with his co-conspirator, Jackson. He would be monitored by his caseworker, Angela, over the next six months.

'I'd like you to come back and meet with me again for the final determination, please, Zach,' said Mrs Giles. 'It's very important that you don't break this agreement, or get into any more trouble. Do you understand?'

Judging by Zach's annoyed expression, he had thought this was the only meeting he would have to endure, and that was usually the case. But perhaps Mrs Giles was also not entirely convinced by Zach's performance.

When it was over, Elizabeth, Claire and Zach stood out on the street together wondering what to do next. Elizabeth felt an urge to point out that the conference was the beginning of the process, not the end of it. But if she started going on about it, he'd probably walk away. So, instead, she suggested they go to the Italian restaurant across the street for lunch.

'What do you think, Zachy?' asked Claire.

'They have good pizza,' Elizabeth assured him. Zach turned his princely gaze towards the restaurant, which she took as acquiescence. She set off across the road to avoid any debate.

Once their orders had been placed, a silence fell on the group. Elizabeth reminded herself how important it was to choose her words carefully, not just the content but the tone. 'Well done, Zach. You spoke very well.'

'Thank you, Nana,' said Claire meaningfully. 'So did you.'

Zach shook his head slowly, lips in a tight line of annoyance. Elizabeth sympathised to some extent. Claire did tend to infantilise him, but eventually he said, 'Fine. Thank you.'

'Very important that you follow the conditions, Zach, especially the curfew,' said Elizabeth. 'Angela *will* check up on you, that's her job. Don't risk getting caught out.'

Claire nodded obediently but Zach's attention was on the pizza oven. These constraints were going to be difficult for him, and Elizabeth knew that he couldn't be trusted because he had no understanding of how damaging a criminal record would be for his future.

His pizza arrived and he worked it over with the efficiency of a waste disposal unit, doubling each slice and folding them sideways for maximum input speed. Still chewing, he pushed his chair back from the table. 'Use your card, Mum?'

'You're not leaving now? We haven't even been served yet,' said Claire in dismay. 'Nana needs to talk us through everything . . .'

Zach stood over them, waiting for the answer to his question.

'Yes, all right. Use the Visa in my desk drawer.' Claire sighed. 'Make sure it's a legitimate site, not a dodgy one.'

His eyes narrowed. 'Can you not? Of course it's legit.' He tilted his chin in Elizabeth's direction. 'See yah.' He walked out of the restaurant, yanking at his tie, pulling the hairband off and loosening his shirt. By the time he stepped onto the street, he was a wild boy again.

The pasta and salad arrived and they began to eat. Elizabeth was actually relieved that Zach had gone and the atmosphere was a little less fraught. Tension at the table always gave her wind. 'So you bribed him to behave himself, Claire?'

'The latest Black Ops,' she admitted and, seeing Elizabeth's expression, added, 'It's an Xbox game.' She sighed. 'Yes, I know what you think, Liz, but the end justified the means. He behaved himself. We got through this part and that's all that matters right now.'

'I agree, but he has to stay out of trouble.'

'He doesn't mean to get into trouble.'

'Of course not. Young men have a particularly poor sense of outcomes. He needs our help to understand the long term —'

'Liz, he's *fifteen!* You've forgotten what they're like. He has no idea why he does things. I have tried to be tougher and it's led to the most horrendous rows. Then he walks out the door.

What can I do? I've got my hands full with work and health problems.'

'You could be a bit more fierce with him. He thinks he's leader of the pack and that's dangerous.'

Claire's mouth turned down resentfully, just as Zach's had when he was asked to come back for another meeting.

'Stop taking crap from him,' said Elizabeth. 'And anyone for that matter.'

Claire raised an eyebrow. 'Does that include you, Liz?'

'That's the spirit,' said Elizabeth with a smile as she stabbed at the penne with her fork. 'That's more like the old Claire. Give it back.'

'I remember you once told me that you disliked timid women.'

'Disliked is a bit strong. I get irritated by them, perhaps . . . I was one once, you know,' said Elizabeth. 'Perhaps that's the reason.'

'I never dreamed I'd become timid, but you're right,' admitted Claire. 'I am a bit afraid of Zach. And I was of Tom too. They both have hot tempers and I've made myself small, like a little creature that rolls into a ball so it can't be seen. Was Ray like that? Was he angry? Is that where it comes from?'

Elizabeth thought about this. She had a general policy of not discussing Ray but, in the spirit of having an honest and open discussion with Claire, she would bend that rule. 'There were two Rays. Before and After. The "before" was the most kind, gentle, thoughtful man. The "after" . . . well, that man was still there but there was anger and, to be honest, there were times when I had to tiptoe around him.'

Claire nodded. 'It's exhausting having to second-guess yourself.'

Elizabeth agreed. She knew what she had to do now. It wasn't something she wanted to do, but it was the right thing. 'Claire, I considered the idea of having Zach come to stay with me for a while so I can keep him on track, but my place is too far from school and the beach – which would just create more problems. So I thought . . . why don't you stay at my place for a few weeks? It's quiet and peaceful and you can relax there. I'll move into your place and manage Zach so you can have a break.'

Tears welled up and spilled down Claire's cheeks, and Elizabeth glanced around to see if anyone noticed she was making someone cry. She handed Claire a napkin and said, 'It's really no big deal.'

'It is a big deal, Liz. I know it is. The only thing is, I don't know how Zach will feel about it.'

'I know. I'm not his favourite nana right now but I'll make it work. Somehow.'

'Thank you. So much. Speaking of nanas, Mum's planning to come over soon, just for a few days. Would you mind if she stayed at your place as well?'

Elizabeth had always felt a little competitive with Claire's mother, Adele. She lived in Perth and visited several times a year, her visits heralded for weeks in advance. She was one of those older women who fought the fading with an arsenal of colour. No menopause mauve or panicky pink for her; she was all cobalt blue and fire-engine red with contrasting headscarfs, lime-green spectacle frames and snazzy boots in animal prints. Elizabeth had often wondered where she got the energy to dress up like a peacock every time she went out. It wasn't as if you could look like that one day and dash out for milk in a grubby tracksuit the next. She wondered if Adele ever felt trapped by the expectation she'd created. And what did she get out of all that effort? Anyway, Elizabeth wasn't competitive on the glamour side of things, it was more about Claire's and Zach's affections. She knew Adele would be aware that Elizabeth hadn't been exactly supportive until recently, so some extra effort was needed. 'Of course not. Treat my home as your own, Claire.'

'Thank you, Liz. I do appreciate it.' She got up and gave Elizabeth an awkward hug and sat down again, as if a weight had been lifted off her. 'You probably don't need my advice but I will say this. When it comes to getting what he wants, Zach can and will argue for days – weeks if need be. He's got incredible stamina and focus, and things can escalate quickly. So, choose your battles.'

Elizabeth wondered what those battles might entail. It was a long time since she'd wrangled teenagers; she hoped she was still up to it.

11

reconnaissance

Elizabeth spent her first afternoon at Claire's cooking, all part of her plan to win Zach over. She had brought Eric's large cage with her and set it up in the adjoining dining room, so she could chat with him as she worked. Zach arrived home at five o'clock, wearing a filthy school sports uniform. He planted himself in front of the cage and Elizabeth introduced him to Eric.

'Weird name for a budgie. He doesn't look like an Eric.' Zach peered into the cage as if trying to find the bird's Eric-ness.

'What does an Eric look like?' asked Elizabeth, going back into the kitchen to toss a salad together.

He shrugged. 'Old?'

'Hey wise guy,' said Eric. 'Wise guy.'

Zach looked around as though he was hearing things. He peered into the cage with more interest. 'Fresh. He talks. He sounds kind of digital. Hello, Eric.'

'Hello Eric,' repeated Eric. 'Sweet thing.'

'So you can teach him like . . . anything?'

'Pretty much,' said Elizabeth.

'Pretty much,' confirmed Eric, which made Zach splutter with laughter.

'I let him out sometimes but we must make sure the outside door is shut, or he'll fly away. Budgies can't survive in the wild.'

'How long have you had him?'

'About six months. I got him when I retired and was home all day. He's quite good company.'

Zach turned to look at her with his steady gaze but said nothing.

'I thought we'd have an early dinner. You must be hungry.' Elizabeth put plates on the table and served out the lasagne she'd made. Zach sat down and began to eat but when she tried to add salad to his plate, he pulled it away so violently that a lighter dish would have been airborne. No salad then.

'I don't really get why you're here,' he said between mouthfuls. 'When's Mum coming back? Why did she go?' He paused. 'Is it because of me?'

'Do you think it could be?' asked Elizabeth.

'Dunno. Maybe. So, you're at ours, she's at yours.' He frowned. 'I don't get it. First you don't come around for months, like a year? Then you're, like, living here?'

'Yep, it's all or nothing with me,' said Elizabeth. She was pleased to see the lasagne was going down well. He cleaned up his plate, licked his knife and looked around for more.

'There's plenty there if you want it,' she offered.

'Nah. I'll have some later.' He got up from the table, slung his plate in the sink and went to his bedroom. As Elizabeth pondered how to tackle the issue of his poor manners, he emerged from his room, pulling up his wetsuit.

'Don't forget you need to be back by —' she began. But he was gone.

The way he wolfed his food and left the table, as though he lived in a backpackers, was unacceptable. She put it on her mental list of small battles to fight when bigger battles were won, the most important of all being his curfew. The worst thing that could happen was him getting into trouble after curfew. But right now, she realised, there was an opportunity to do some reconnaissance. She needed to know his hangouts and where to find him if necessary. She put her unfinished meal in the fridge, grabbed her sunhat and left the house.

She followed him at a distance, the way she'd seen it done in movies. He didn't look around. Obviously being stalked by his nana was not something he was particularly concerned about. He crossed the road and took a shortcut down a hidden path between the houses. This exercise was already proving useful. The path led through to a road that ran parallel to the beach, beyond which was a set of timber steps that traversed the sandhills.

Once he'd disappeared over the other side, she climbed the stairs and found a sheltered spot on the beach. There were a dozen or more surfers clustered out on a gleaming platinum swell. Someone raised an arm and Zach responded with a salute. He walked out on a small promontory of rocks, the sort of place fishermen were swept off in high seas. He stood at the end, staring into the water, making some calculation, and then launched himself on his board into the crashing waves and paddled languidly out. Once he joined the other surfers, he became as indistinguishable as a seal in a colony.

Daylight saving had kicked in earlier in the week and the late afternoon sun was warm for October. Now she was sitting down,

Elizabeth had no real desire to get up and go back to the empty house and reheated lasagne. There was also a risk that he might see her leave. There was a pleasant onshore breeze and she enjoyed watching the sea from a safe distance. Her legs, stretched out in front of her, looked pale and doughy. Since there was no one around, she pulled her dress up to her thighs, lay down and put her hat over her face.

She woke disoriented with a gritty taste in her mouth, shivering with cold. The sun was setting and she was alone on the beach, apart from a man walking his dog along the shoreline. Dogs weren't allowed on the beach and she considered doing her civic duty by informing him, but he was walking briskly and her duty didn't extend to running after him.

She got home to find Zach standing at the kitchen bench eating a large piece of lasagne out of his hand, like a slice of pizza.

He looked her up and down. 'What happened to you?'

'Nothing. Why? Did you heat that up?' asked Elizabeth.

''s fine. Did you go for a walk?'

'No. Yes. Why?'

'Was that you lying down on the beach?' He had a look of distaste on his face that had nothing to do with the lasagne. 'Can you not?'

'So, you knew it was me,' said Elizabeth.

He frowned. 'What do you want me to do?'

'I don't know. Check I was alive? If I'd been there all night, would you have come back to get me?'

He considered this for a moment but was unable to reach a conclusion.

Elizabeth sighed. 'Just rinse that plate in the sink and put it in the dishwasher. Not near it. In it.'

He did as he was told and went to his room. She retrieved the plate and rinsed it properly. The plan for taming Zach had been clear in her mind. Tough love. But Claire was right, he seemed to have a knack for sensing when she was going to take a stand on something, and then his easy compliance tipped her off balance.

12

dancing queen

The first week went relatively smoothly from Elizabeth's point of view. Surprisingly, Zach was no trouble to get off to school. He rose from his bed at the last possible moment and slid into his clothes as he walked to the kitchen. Holding a bowl under his chin, he shovelled soggy Weet-Bix into his mouth while he looped his backpack over one shoulder. He finished breakfast with a frenzied clanging of the spoon while in transit to the front door and, with a final triumphant crash of his bowl on the glass hall table, he was gone. The whole operation took around seven minutes; an impressive display of time and motion efficiency and all conducted without a single word being spoken.

He was home every evening playing Xbox in his room and explained that he didn't have homework because he did whatever was set during the next class and, by the end of the day, it was all complete. Elizabeth wasn't quite sure what she thought about this, but his logic was impressive. They had some brief exchanges but no arguments. As long as she didn't cause him any bother he didn't care about her being there and she was free to hover in the misty periphery of his consciousness, like a faithful servant.

While Zach was at school, Elizabeth could let Eric out of his cage to explore his new environment and sit on her shoulder while she did the chores. At the end of the week, she congratulated herself that a smooth transition had been completed.

She waded through the mess on Zach's floor, stripped his bed and changed the sheets. The bedding smelled of salt and sweat and pizza, odours that took her back to a time when her boys were young. Tom had gone off to his first week-long holiday camp when he was ten years old. She'd missed him so much that before she went to bed each night she would bury her face in his pillow to comfort herself. Younger and less adventurous, Danny preferred to be at home with her. He was more of a gentle dreamer. It made her sad that the men she loved were all distant from her now. Picking up Zach's pillow, she inhaled his boyish odour and felt the sting of nostalgic tears.

Friday afternoon brought heavy grey clouds and sticky humidity. Elizabeth lay down on her bed to rest before Zach got home. The heat felt oppressive, worrisome so early in the year. She got up and turned on the overhead fan, slipped off her dress and bra and put on an old cotton t-shirt. She lay down again and closed her eyes. The first blowfly of the season buzzed around the room. It landed on her bare leg and, when she flicked at it, landed on the other leg, then back to the first. She reached out and grabbed her bra and gave the fly a good whack. Moments later it was back and she realised that there would be no rest until this pest was dead. She got up and followed it around, whacking at it ineffectually with her bra. It buzzed out of the room and, just as she got her hopes up, buzzed back in.

With bitter determination, she pursued the fly into the dining room, opened the outside door and tried to steer it out. Discarding the bra, she picked up the newspaper and tracked the fly back and forth across the room, vaguely aware of what a sight she was in her undies, breasts flopping about loosely under the t-shirt. In his cage, Eric perched on his swing and watched intently as she scolded the insect. 'Oh for God's sake, there's an open door! Save your own life, you stupid fly. Get out! Out!'

Executing a clumsy leap, she managed to whack the thing with a perfect backhand in a successful mid-air strike. She landed heavily on one foot, stumbled and almost lost her balance but managed to right herself and complete the manoeuvre, feet together, arms above her head like a proud gymnast.

'Out,' Eric squeaked. 'Get out get out!'

She heard a sound behind her and spun around to find Zach and two of his mates in school uniform standing in the living room. Clutching the newspaper to her chest, she ducked into the kitchen and stood pressed against the fridge, grimacing as she imagined the last few minutes from their point of view. The worst part was that the boys weren't even laughing, just silent.

'Who's that?' asked one in a quiet, fearful voice.

'Neighbour,' improvised Zach. 'Um . . . you know, that thing . . . Alzheimer's.' Elizabeth heard the boys go into Zach's room and close the door softly, as if to avoid disturbing the beast. A moment later, the sound of gunfire exploded in his room.

Her face still burning, Elizabeth retreated to her bedroom where she stayed all evening, wondering how she could ever come back from that showstopper. She was getting ready for bed when Claire rang.

'Hi, Liz. How's it going? Everything all right?'

'Yes. Of course,' Elizabeth assured her. 'Why?'

There was an awkward pause. 'I had a message from Zach. Something about you dancing in the living room . . . naked?'

'Oh *pffft*,' replied Elizabeth. 'Is that exactly what he said?'

'Hang on, I'll put it on speaker and read the message. Okay . . . here we go. He said: "she is dancing in living room no clothes why?"'

'No clothes is not the same as naked,' Elizabeth pointed out. 'I did have some clothes on.' She didn't like the way Zach referred to her as 'she', as if this was one of a series of complaints against her. Claire was silent, forcing Elizabeth to elaborate. 'I had undies and a t-shirt on, if you must know. And I was actually . . . oh, it doesn't matter.'

'Look, I'm very grateful to you, Liz, and I don't want to interfere, but I think it would probably be better if you did that sort of thing in your room. He also said you'd been following him.'

'Not continually – just the once. I wanted to see where he went.'

'And where did he go?' asked Claire.

'To the beach.' It sounded perfectly obvious and a bit childish – not exactly the shrewd reconnaissance mission she had imagined.

'To keep Zach on side, I do think we need to respect his privacy.' Claire sounded so uncomfortable that, even though Elizabeth did not believe for one millisecond that fifteen-year-olds deserved privacy, she agreed to curtail her more indiscreet activities.

They chatted for a while about other things. Claire said she was enjoying the peace of Elizabeth's house, and her operation was scheduled for early the next week. As they came to the end of their conversation, Elizabeth asked her, 'Claire, what would your song be? You know, a song that sums up your personality and your life. Like your theme song.'

'"Dancing Queen",' said Claire without hesitation.

'Right . . . I meant to play at your funeral, for example.'

'My funeral? Why do you ask? Do you know something I don't know?'

'No, just that they played "You Raise Me Up" at Ginny's funeral. It was so perfect and I've been thinking about it ever since,' said Elizabeth.

'Probably still "Dancing Queen" to cheer people up and get them on their feet dancing.'

Elizabeth thought this sounded like a scene from a rom-com, not a real-life funeral, but she agreed that it was a nice idea.

'What were you dancing to this evening?' Claire asked in a friendly tone.

'The sound of a fly buzzing. I was trying to kill it.'

There was a splutter on the other end of the phone followed by gales of laughter. Claire had such a pretty laugh; it was a pleasure to hear it, even from a distance.

As they said their goodbyes, Elizabeth caught a note of fondness in Claire's voice and tried to remember when she'd last heard that from anyone, apart from Eric.

13

a world away

1969 The first morning of her new life, Lizzy wakes to a room awash with sunshine. It takes a moment to realise she's not dreaming – it's wondrous and terrifying at the same time. She rolls onto her side to watch Ray while he sleeps, noticing his thick dark lashes and heavy brows that knit together when he's concentrating, and the shadow of the night on his jaw. He's so beautiful that she feels a rush of joy and fear. He wakes slowly and pulls her to him with a sleepy smile: 'Come here, you.'

The one-room flat is up a narrow flight of stairs above a car showroom. It's shabby, with patchy wallpaper and scarred timber floors, simply furnished with a table and two chairs, a saggy double bed and a sofa. The makeshift kitchen has a small bench-top hotplate that doubles as a grill, a cold water sink and a large rattling fridge. The bathroom is down the hall and shared with the flat next door, which is currently empty. Large sliding windows along the back wall of the flat open wide and look over the yard where the cars are cleaned, and a high chain-mail fence covered with scarlet bougainvillea.

For breakfast they eat grilled cheese on toast with a glass of milk. They tumble back into bed to make love and sleep and wake in the afternoon heat. With no coins for the hot water meter, they share a cold bath. In the evening they ride over to Bondi Beach and sit on the warm sand, where they eat fish and chips and talk about their future children's names. Ray would like Kathleen, after his mother and, although Lizzy prefers something more modern like Lisa or Cilla, she finds the sentiment touching. They toss boys' names back and forth and finally settle on Thomas and Daniel.

On Monday, Ray goes to work and Lizzy calls her mother from a phone box that stinks of urine and cigarette smoke. She hardly gets a word in as her mother's fury whips down the line. 'Are you out of your mind? How do you think me and Dad felt yesterday finding you'd sneaked out? Just a scrap of paper saying you'd gone to Sydney! We've been worried sick.'

'I'm sorry, I just thought —' begins Lizzy.

'Oh, I'm dying to hear this. You just thought you'd run off on the back of a motorbike with a boy I *told* you to stay away from. Now we're stuck without someone to help in the shop. And the whole town is talking about what a little slut you are.'

'Mum, that's not true. You know it's not true. I just wanted to say . . .' Lizzy pushed the cigarette butts around the floor with the tip of her shoe. She didn't know what she wanted to say. She just wanted to get this conversation over with.

'We could have the cops on you, you know,' says her mother. 'You're not eighteen yet. You've got no business running off like that. You broke our hearts.'

'You don't have to worry about me, Mum. I'm going to get a job.'

'Can I remind you that you've got a job? Either come home today, or not at all.'

The line goes dead. Lizzy stands holding the receiver, relieved the conversation is over but reluctant to break her connection to home. After a moment, she hangs up, pulls open the door and walks out into the blue day.

She wanders past small boutiques, coffee lounges and bookshops, never daring to go inside. Paddington is a world away from Nullaburra – it's interesting and glamorous. Young women are dressed in bright mini-dresses in florals and stripes, and trouser suits and go-go boots, the sort of clothes she's only ever seen on television. She walks as far as Paddington Town Hall and along the backstreets, past rows of white terrace houses with lacework balconies and flowers blossoming through wrought-iron fences. On her way home, she buys lamb chops from the butcher, and potatoes and carrots at the greengrocer.

She wanders slowly past the car dealer's glossy white showroom where the cars – Jaguars, Rovers and Triumphs – are all squeezed in at odd angles. Inside, a man sits at his desk talking on the phone. Middle-aged and jowly with thick sideburns, he wears a brown three-piece suit, despite the hot day. This must be their landlord, Mr Geddes.

As she walks away, he suddenly appears at the showroom door. 'Hello there. In the market for a new car, are we?'

'Um . . . no, thanks. I don't even know how to drive.'

'I could teach you, if you like. I can just see you behind the wheel of one of these Jags.' He grins. 'Would you like a cold Coke?'

Lizzy regrets stopping and has no idea how to excuse herself from this conversation. 'No, thanks. I'm just staying upstairs . . . with Ray.'

'Uh huh, I see. Well, anytime. I'm always here.' He clicks his heels and gives a mock salute, as though putting himself at her service.

She smiles and shrugs, giving him a little wave as she opens the door to the upstairs flats. At the top of the stairs, she turns to see him holding the door open with his foot. He gives her a wink and that salute again. If only she knew what it meant.

When Ray gets home, he says the landlord has just asked for an extra five dollars a week now there are two of them. 'He said he'll make it three dollars if you wear shorter skirts.'

'What did you say?' asks Lizzy crossly.

'That we'd find another place?' Ray tears off his shirt and tie, and splashes his face at the sink.

'Didn't you want to punch him?'

Ray laughs. 'You 'burra girls! Fists first, questions later,' he teases. He dries his face off and wraps his arms around her. 'He said he was joking and backed down on the increase. What do you think?'

'He's okay. I don't mind him. And the place is good.'

'I'm too tired to go around punching people anyway. I reckon I did a good ten miles at work today. Next week I'm on night shifts, four in the afternoon 'til midnight.'

Lizzy makes him a cold cordial. He sits down on the sofa and pats his thigh invitingly. She drops onto his lap, puts her arm around his shoulders and kisses him. 'Were the people nice to you? Are there lots of pretty girls?'

'No girls as pretty as you. Yeah, the people are good. They shout a lot. There's four of us copy boys. We hang around and wait for things to deliver. It never stops there, Lizzy. All day and night. I went everywhere, all over the building from the news room, to the presses, the delivery dock. It's like a huge factory making this newspaper. It's just . . . crazy, but exciting too.'

'Compared to milking cows, you mean?' suggested Lizzy.

'Yeah, good to get out of those damn gumboots. Did you call your mum?'

Lizzy nods. 'She was really cross. I'll try again when she's calmed down.'

'No regrets?' he asks, earnest and concerned.

She kisses his frown away. 'Never. But I do wish I'd brought more clothes and my savings passbook. I'll look for a job tomorrow.'

Ray pulls his wallet out of his back pocket. 'Take whatever you need. Get something nice to wear for job interviews and money for bus fares and lunch.'

'Thanks,' she says. She pulls a few notes out of his wallet and hands it back. 'Do you want me to wash your shirt out?'

'S'okay, I'll do it. What's for tea?'

'Meat and two veg,' says Lizzy. 'Um . . . how do you cook, you know, real carrots?'

Ray laughs out loud. 'You'll make someone a wonderful wife one day, when you're properly trained.'

Lizzy grabs his wrists and pins them against the back of the chair. 'An old rich bloke with sideburns and a three-piece suit! Not some newspaper boy.'

'You wait, Lizzy Clayton. My day will come. Our day. From now on, all the days are our days.'

A week before Christmas, Lizzy starts work as a junior in a large jewellery shop in Pitt Street. She buys the tea and biscuit supplies for the staffroom and washes up the cups and saucers after morning and afternoon tea. She cleans the glass shelves with methylated spirits that makes her eyes sting, and sometimes she has to crawl into the display window and remove dead insects.

Every afternoon she takes the bus up to Oxford Street with a bag of jewellery for repair to Mr Berkovics, the jeweller and watch-maker. He works alone in a meticulously organised office above a record shop and always invites her to have coffee with him while he does quick repairs on the spot. He has a magnifying loupe that he clips onto his glasses and a thick foreign accent that takes her some time to get used to. He has opinions about each item of jewellery, respect for valuable pieces and disdain for trinkets. 'Ah, but people are sentimental,' he says. 'They spend more money to repair a cheap little chain than it cost because it means something to them. Me, I have no sentiment for things, only people.'

Mr Berkovics is from Hungary, a place that Lizzy only knows from the postage stamps she used to collect. He's what her parents call a 'reffo'. She had always pictured them as wild-eyed outlaws who grabbed what they could from decent hard-working people, taking jobs and opportunities that didn't belong to them. But Mr Berkovics is kind and sad. He listens to classical music on his transistor radio and brings her small sweet cakes from home. He teaches her to do simple repairs, fixing chain links and clasps. He explains the difference between rose, white and yellow gold, and how to breathe on a diamond to see if it's genuine. He soon becomes her first new friend.

She calls home on Christmas morning from the same stinking phone booth as two weeks earlier. This time it really hurts when her mother hangs up on her. It's the first Christmas she has ever been away from her family.

Today she's nervous about meeting Ray's family when they go there for Christmas lunch. They've bought a cookery book for Ray's stepmother, Cynthia, some socks for his father and a red Volkswagen Beetle Matchbox car for his little brother, Andy, who is eight. 'What do I write on the card to your dad?' she asks Ray as she wraps up the presents. 'I can't write Dad when it's from both of us.'

'Let's not do cards,' says Ray. He looks handsome in a white shirt and narrow red tie, his hair slicked back, tendrils curling around his neck. He smooths down the front of his shirt and straightens his tie nervously. After a moment he adds, 'The other thing is, that my dad doesn't like me calling Cynthia by her name . . . but, you know, she's not my mother, so it's sort of difficult. She doesn't mind.'

On the train to his father's place in Marrickville, Ray's normal exuberance seeps away as he stares out the window, lost in thought. When Lizzy slips her hand into his, he gives a start. 'We won't stay long,' he says. 'Promise.'

Andy answers the door, his little face alight with excitement. With his fair skin and short-back-and-sides haircut, he looks nothing like his older brother. But they obviously love each other and embrace in a wrestle-hug. Cynthia is welcoming and pleased to see them. Lizzy likes her straight away. But Ray's father, a heavy-set man with watchful eyes, barely acknowledges Lizzy and doesn't leave his armchair to greet them. When Ray hands out the gifts, his father gives the package a squeeze and puts it aside. 'I can guess what that is,' he says. He has a strong Irish accent that Lizzy didn't quite expect. Ray has only the faintest hint of an accent but it's more pronounced when he speaks to his father.

Cynthia is delighted with her cookery book and Andy with his toy. 'It's the racing one,' he says, taking it for a spin along the edge of the dining table. Lizzy notices that despite his sourness, Ray's father watches the boy with an indulgent smile.

There's roast chicken with gravy and vegetables for lunch, and Cynthia has set the table with Christmas crackers and festive paper napkins. Ray's father sits down at the head of the table and mutters grace. He carves up the chicken and helps himself first, glancing at Ray as if he has something to say but is under instructions to keep quiet. Lizzy's grateful for Cynthia's small talk and Andy's chatter that keeps the conversation going.

Almost as soon as they finish the homemade Christmas pudding with custard, Ray pushes back his chair and says they need to go as there aren't many trains today.

'And did you go to Mass last night?' asks his father.

'Dad, let's not talk about that today. We can have that discussion some other time. When Lizzy's not here. And it's not Christmas.'

'Do stay a bit longer. We're going to watch the Queen's address,' says Cynthia, appealing to Lizzy.

Ray's father shoots Cynthia a look of irritation. 'She's not my queen.'

'She's Australia's queen, though, dear. We have this discussion every year,' she tells Lizzy with a laugh. 'It's part of our Christmas tradition.'

'There is no address this year,' says Ray. 'She's written something instead.'

'Always the smart alec,' says his father.

'Dad, I'm not being a smart alec – it's in the papers.'

'Oh yeah, I forgot you're a newspaper man now. You need a haircut. You look like a wog . . . like a pikey. I don't know how you got any sort of job looking like that.'

Cynthia murmurs, 'Patrick, no . . . please . . .'

Ray stands up. 'Not today, Dad. I'll come back some other day so you can insult me, if it makes you feel better. But let's leave today be. We'll just go now.'

Cynthia quickly gathers up the dishes and Lizzy helps her take them out to the kitchen. 'I don't know why he does this but it usually gets worse before it gets better. We haven't even given you your gift,' says Cynthia.

Back in the dining room, Ray's father is practically shouting. 'And what do you think you're doing running off with a teenager? I'm surprised they haven't locked you up. And what's she? Not one of us. Never said grace before in her life.'

Ray holds up his hands as if fending off a blow. 'Stop, Dad, please. We're going now. We can talk about this some other time.' At the door he calls out, 'Thanks, Cynthia.'

His father turns scarlet. 'Have some respect!'

'We'll see you next year, Ray. Or anytime. Thank you for coming,' says Cynthia, leaning in the kitchen doorway. 'Lovely to meet you, Lizzy. Come again, dear.'

Andy runs out to the gate. 'When will you come back? Can I come to your place?'

Ray wraps his brother in a hug and lifts him off his feet. 'Yeah, maybe. I'll try and organise it. We'll see you soon, Andy Pandy.'

As they walk to the station, Ray apologises, on the brink of tears. Lizzy tells him it's fine. It doesn't matter. In the train, she rests her head on his shoulder and, when they arrive at Central Station, he leans down and gives her a kiss. 'Let's just walk around. Better to be with strangers.' They walk the city streets all the way back to Paddington and have cheese on toast for tea.

Later, as they lie in bed, Ray says, 'There's stuff I haven't told you about my family. Things we don't talk about. But probably you should know.' He's silent for a moment, then says, 'Back in Ireland, I had a little sister. Her name was Caitlin. She died when she was two from diphtheria.'

Lizzy finds his hand under the sheet and intertwines her fingers with his. 'How old were you?'

'I was about five. I don't really remember her dying or anything like that, but I do recall we used to go to the cemetery every Sunday after Mass. We'd take some flowers – you know, just bits we'd pick on the way. What I remember most is that there was a little angel carved on the gravestone and it was my job to clean it with a toothbrush. I remember going to Caitlin's grave with Mum to say goodbye. I knew we were going to Australia but didn't really understand what it meant. I didn't know we were leaving my grandparents and all. Well, when you're a kid, you don't have a clue what's going on. But I know Mum would have found it hard to leave Caitlin behind, that's for certain.'

'But why did they want to come out here?' asks Lizzy.

'Dad was offered a job. I told you he's an electrician, well, he's what they call a journeyman electrician who works on industrial projects. He was offered a job with a construction company, Addersals and Sons. He still works for them.'

Ray rolls over and props himself up on one elbow. He strokes her cheek tenderly. 'There's one more thing I have to tell you. I said to you ages ago that after my mum went back to Ireland,

Dad put me in a boarding school. That's not really true. It was actually a boys' home. There were other boys like me, who only had one parent, but also boys who were orphans. Dad used to come and see me sometimes but, truly, it was the worst year of my life. Nothing good happened there until Cynthia came along. She visited with Dad this one time, and I thought she was nice. They said there'd be a special surprise for my tenth birthday. I thought it might be a train set or something but they came and took me home.'

'So does that mean your parents got divorced?'

'I suppose. I don't know if Dad and Cynthia are properly married in the Church. I wasn't there and, to be honest, I don't care. I'm just glad she came along.'

Lizzy presses her cheek against his. 'I wish all those things hadn't happened to you. But I think it's made you strong and more mature. You turned out perfectly in the end.'

He laughs quietly and holds her close. 'It's not the end yet, Lizzy. It's just the beginning.'

She lies awake thinking about his mother who left him as if she didn't care at all, as if her love for little Caitlin was stronger than for the boy who lived. But Lizzy has seen a photograph of Ray and his mother. He's six or seven and sitting on her lap, his hair flattened neatly against his head and a sulky expression on his face. His mother is pretty with dark hair to her shoulders and a shy smile. The way she has her arms wrapped around him, anyone could see that she adores her son.

14

golden summer

1970 The first summer of the new decade passes in a haze of golden days and hot sleepless nights. When the windows of their flat are wide open, there's cool night air but also the insistent buzz of mosquitoes and the dawn call of kookaburras. When the windows are closed, the room is airless and suffocatingly hot. Lizzy often dreams she's back at the mini-mart, unpacking endless boxes of product onto the shelves, as if this new life is a dream and they are playing at being grown-ups. But she wakes each morning to find that Ray is real and she can't believe her own happiness.

As they lie in bed one morning, watching the sun creep into the room, he tells her that when she stepped out onto the Moncurs' verandah in her white shorts, with her tanned legs and short blond hair, 'all sleepy like a little chick just hatched', he just knew she was the girl for him. 'I mean, who picks grapes in white shorts?' He laughs.

'Oh, so I looked helpless with no common sense, did I?'

'No, you didn't look helpless at all. You looked a bit shy

and . . . a little lonely. Like me. You were so beautiful, I stopped breathing for a minute. I could have actually fainted.'

Lizzy laughs. 'I don't believe you.'

Hand on heart, he says, 'It's the absolute truth. You took my breath away.'

'And you mine,' she says, kissing him.

Lizzy writes to her parents every week, just a short letter to let them know what she's doing. They never reply. She sometimes rings Ginny from the telephone box. If anyone needs to call Lizzy or Ray, they have to ring the car dealership and Mr Geddes comes puffing up the stairs and knocks on the door. When Lizzy takes a call on his phone, he pauses what he's doing and blatantly eavesdrops, as though this is the cost of the service. Once, when Ginny rang, Lizzy had to resort to pig Latin, 'ehay isyay isten-inglay inyay osay Iyay an'tcay aysay uchmay' – *he is listening in, so I can't say much.*

Ginny was initially shocked that Lizzy had run away with-out consulting her, but she approves of romantic gestures and has promised to come and visit as soon as she can. On the other hand, Mrs Moncur has been very cool when Lizzy rings, and Judith just hangs up.

Ray attends night school one evening a week, learning short-hand and typing. Sometimes when he and Lizzy finish work at the same time they meet up and walk around the city for an hour or so. It's one of Ray's favourite pastimes. He's curious about all sorts of things; a trait that Lizzy finds strangely endearing. He has a large map of the world stuck up on the wall of their flat and often stands staring at it while he gets ready for work.

She wonders what he sees in those different coloured shapes that mean so little to her. He sticks drawing pins in the places he's planning to go, Ireland being the first one. But he likes to work out itineraries for trips through Europe or South America, connecting up the drawing pins with red string to form jagged paths across continents. He's been teaching himself Spanish with a cassette recorder and repeats the sentences over and over under his breath so as not to disturb her.

One evening after work, walking in the city, they happen upon the Spanish Club down a side street. Despite her shy resistance, Ray convinces her to have a look inside the club. A man in a dark suit greets them in Spanish. After an embarrassingly long pause, Ray comes up with a response. He threads the foreign words together, speaking in an odd faltering way, and beads of sweat gather at his temples with the effort of it. Lizzy finds it painful to witness, but the man wears a patient smile and nods encouragingly, and she can't help but be proud of Ray, who has conjured up this ability out of nowhere.

The man invites them into a large room where people sit at tables, talking and drinking wine or beer. Ray buys them both Cokes and they sit down, not knowing what to expect. Soon, a guitarist sets himself up on a high stool and a middle-aged woman with black hair tied at the base of her neck pulls up a stool beside him. He strums the guitar with dramatic strokes and the woman sings in a throbbing, discordant voice. After a moment, another woman walks into the room wearing a long floral dress, tight over her body with heavy frills cascading from the knees. There's a sprinkle of applause as she fixes the room with a furious gaze and stamps her feet on the timber floor, raising her hands slowly above her head, castanets clicking. To Lizzy's ears the noise is deafening, but Ray is ecstatic. He talks excitedly all the way home and wonders if there might be an Irish club, maybe Italian, French – Greek! 'Lizzy, we could travel all over the world right here. Think of the interesting people we could meet hidden away in this city.'

'It's a bit of a problem if they don't speak English, isn't it?' she asks.

Ray just laughs and puts his arm around her shoulders. When they get home, he entertains her with his own version of the flamenco. He struts up and down, stamps his feet and clicks his fingers, glaring at her furiously until she's almost crying with laughter. Afterwards, he stands before his map and adds a marching line of drawing pins across Spain, from Barcelona to Madrid and into Portugal, like a general planning to conquer Europe. Lizzy doesn't know what to make of this enthusiasm. The only places she's ever thought of going are Disneyland, or London to see Buckingham Palace and Big Ben. The idea of going to places where people don't speak English seems crazy to her, but not to Ray.

15

bouncing fairies

On Saturday morning, Elizabeth was keen to avoid Zach in the hope that last night's image of her cavorting about in her underwear would fade from his mind. She bought a barbecued chicken and left it in the fridge with a note saying that she'd be back after lunch.

She set off to the children's bookshop, where she spent an hour pondering a gift for Grace's seventh birthday. In the end she bought two books for the birthday girl and one for Lily as well, and lashed out on gift-wrap and ribbons to make the gifts look pretty.

With the Saturday sport traffic, it took well over an hour to reach Danny and Melissa's house in Dulwich Hill. They lived in a squat brick bungalow with a wrought-iron gate that, today, was decorated with colourful streamers. Elizabeth stood staring at it for a full minute. Grace was having a birthday party? Wasn't it normal practice to invite grandparents to these events? She knocked at the front door and, through the frosted glass panel, saw Melissa's profile with her distinctive top-knot appear and disappear again. After a moment, Danny came down the hallway and opened the front door.

Elizabeth forced a bright smile. 'Hi, Danny!'

'Hi, Mum.' Danny looked at her carefully. 'You okay?'

'Of course, why?' He was standing slightly above her on the threshold. She could see past him into the backyard where giggling children were chasing each other.

'You looked a bit odd, that's all,' he said. 'What's happening?'

'I just dropped by to give Grace her gift. And Lily too, of course.'

'Cool. Thanks, Mum.' He reached out to take them but she instinctively clasped them to her chest.

'Can't I see the girls?' she asked. 'Is it a party?'

He glanced over his shoulder uneasily. 'No, no . . . just her little cousins.'

'Danny, I'm their nana. I have my Working with Children clearance, you know.'

'Maybe some other time, Mum. It's just . . .'

Elizabeth took in the row of shoes lined up neatly on the little rug inside the front door. Danny's gaze followed hers. 'It's Melissa's mum and sisters. They're cooking lunch. I promise I'll bring the girls to your place next week. Okay?'

'Okay,' she agreed reluctantly. 'I'm living at Claire's for the moment, so bring them over there.'

He frowned. 'Why?'

If she told him about Zach running amok he would tell Melissa, which would be another black mark against the O'Reilly family, and she didn't want that. Melissa's family were close and cosy, and very well behaved. 'I'm going to have the kitchen done,' she said, already aware this was a ridiculous excuse because, sooner or later, it would be evident that she hadn't had her kitchen done. 'Well, thinking about it, anyway.'

'You're living with Claire because you're thinking about having your kitchen done?'

'Not exactly. She's living at my place.'

'Because . . . she's thinking of having her kitchen done?' he asked, half-smiling. 'What's really going on, Mum?'

Elizabeth shoved the two gifts at him. 'That's where I'll be next week anyway. Bring the girls, I'd love to see them. Melissa too.'

She was saved from having to explain any further by the appearance of Melissa's mother, Doris, looking curiously down the hall. When she recognised Elizabeth, Doris came to the front door and gestured for her to come in. 'Elizabeth! Very nice to see you. Come in! We making lunch. Plenty for all.'

Doris had beautiful manners. She was small and round, and always immaculately dressed in black pants with a contrasting top; today's was jade green and blue. She was a similar age to Elizabeth but, with her black hair in a short bob, she looked ten years younger.

The lure of seeing the girls was too much to resist. Elizabeth glanced at Danny, who lifted his eyebrows in acquiescence. 'Well, just for a moment then,' agreed Elizabeth.

Danny stood aside and she was halfway up the hall when he said, 'Mum. Shoes.'

'I'm only here for a minute,' she protested but, at his stern look, went back and put her bag and the gifts on the floor while she bent down and took her shoes off, lining them up neatly with the others.

The kitchen-dining area was full of people. Melissa and her three sisters were at work in the kitchen, where the air rang with the fragrance of hot sesame oil, ginger and garlic. Their husbands sat around the table drinking designer beers while they discussed something that involved constant reference to their phones to support their argument. While the men's conversation was in English, when Melissa and her sisters were together they always spoke in Cantonese, despite all having been born in Australia. In the early days, Danny had mentioned that they used to tease him about being the token *gwailou,* but over the years he had managed to blend in and these days no one seemed to notice.

But every time Elizabeth was plunged into this family, she felt uncomfortable, clumsy and foreign. As if she had found herself in a strange land with no understanding of the language or culture. She was increasingly envious of people who travelled and were comfortable anywhere in the world. In all this time, other than once attending a conference in New Zealand, she'd never left the country. It was one of her great regrets. For many years she didn't have the time or money, and later she had no one to go with and wasn't confident to travel alone. It seemed she had left it too late. Ginny had once invited her to join them on a wine trip to France but Elizabeth didn't think Paul would appreciate her tagging along. And she wasn't at all interested in wine.

'You like tea, Elizabeth?' asked Doris.

'Thank you, I won't . . . I'll just . . .' Elizabeth glanced towards the backyard and the tiny objects of her affection.

'Have some tea, Mum,' said Danny. 'You're not in a hurry, are you?'

Elizabeth scanned the kitchen for possibilities. The tea was likely to be green, which she loathed. It tasted like steeped grass clippings. 'Do you have . . . normal tea?' Realising how that sounded, she added, 'Black tea with milk?'

'That would be white tea?' suggested Danny. And, while that was accurate, she sensed he was having a go at her. He seemed to find her discomfort annoying, which only exacerbated the problem.

While Melissa made the tea, Doris brought in a pair of towelling scuffs for Elizabeth's bare feet, as though she were a hotel guest.

'Thank you. I don't . . . all right, thank you.' Elizabeth put the slippers on. She stood at the kitchen bench and sipped her tea so quickly it seared her throat. 'Lovely. I'll just go out . . . see the girls . . .' She was now incapable of finishing a sentence.

She went out and stood on the back steps. Neither Melissa nor Danny were gardeners and the yard, mainly rough grass and straggly shrubs, was dominated by a large circular trampoline enclosed in netting that, today, was a basket of bouncing fairies.

Lily, Grace and three other little girls were dressed in bright lycra and taffeta tutus and the two boys wore wizard's capes. They chased each other in a game of tag and bounced off the nets, shrieking with excitement.

Elizabeth wanted to go out to them and soak up their joy and be seen by them. She longed to feel their spindly little arms around her neck and smell their warm sugary breath. She looked down at the terry-towelling scuffs curtailing her freedom like shackles. She wondered if it was okay to go out in bare feet and then put the slippers back on? Or should she go back to the front door and collect her shoes and bring them out? The whole business was fraught. She called out to the girls but they were too busy chasing and screaming. She stood and watched them for a few minutes, then realised it was futile, so she went back inside and made her excuses.

'I guess you have to rush back to work on those kitchen plans,' said Danny, as he walked her to the front door. 'Mum, I don't get why you come around, keen to see the girls, and five minutes later you're itching to leave.'

'I don't know what they must think of us, Dan. With Dad gone, and Tom away . . .'

He opened the front door for her. 'They don't look down on us, if that's what you're getting at, Mum. It's all in your head.'

Elizabeth wanted to take him into her confidence, tell him about Zach's troubles and Ginny's letter and her concerns about Ray. She wanted to ask for his advice. He was the most level-headed of the family, and she valued his opinion. But pride stood in her way. She didn't trust him to keep these private family matters from Melissa – when there was no reason why he should.

'Have you heard anything from Dad yet?' he asked.

'Yes, there was a note, but . . .' Elizabeth bent down to put her shoes on.

'There you go. He's just getting absent-minded.'

As she stood up, he leaned over and planted a kiss on the top of her head. She said goodbye, then stopped halfway down the path and turned back to him. 'Danny, do you have a song that's yours – you know, like your anthem?'

'You're kidding, right?'

Elizabeth laughed. 'Oh, of course. "Danny Boy". Silly me.'

Danny waited dutifully in the doorway until she was in her car. He gave her a wave and closed the door. She imagined him strolling back down the hall to the warmth and fun of the family, Melissa glancing over at him with raised eyebrows. *All okay?* And him nodding with a slight smile to reassure her. They were that kind of couple.

Elizabeth was alone in the world once more. As she set off for home, she wished she'd brought Eric along, so she could have unburdened herself to him. She felt a pang of missing Ginny. They had always shared the trifles of their lives, re-enacted word for word trivial disputes and commiserated over that rude person in the post office queue, defending each other before the story was even out. Later, when Ginny was ill, they spoke every day, often more than once. Conversations that were occasionally serious but more often hilarious as they remembered and retold stories from the past. Now, in place of those conversations, there was empty silence, and it was hard for Elizabeth to imagine how she would ever fill it.

16

out in the night

Elizabeth arrived back at Claire's to find that Zach and the barbecued chicken had gone somewhere together. It was early afternoon but she already felt uneasy. She tried Zach's phone but it rang out. When he wasn't back by dinnertime, a creeping anxiety overtook her. The responsibility weighed heavier by the minute. It wasn't just the importance of the curfew, but the added fear that something might happen to him on her watch. She had no contacts in Zach's world. She didn't know his friends or any of their parents. She didn't want to trouble Claire; it was pointless bothering her over every little thing, although at this stage it was hard to know whether this was a little thing – or not.

By the time the curfew ticked over without a word from him, she was consumed with dread and decided she would drive around the area to look for him. It wasn't a very practical plan but it was all she had right now.

The suburb was quiet at night and the streets empty apart from the occasional person with a dog to walk. She drove along the beach road and pulled into the carpark at the surf club.

A few teens who looked like members of Zach's tribe, foundlings washed up by the ocean, stood around chatting together. On closer inspection none were him. She wound down the window and called out, 'Do you know Zach O'Reilly?' Several glanced in her direction, then went back to their conversation. 'It's an emergency!' she added. One of the girls called back, 'Try the skate park.'

The skate park was all swirling concrete with steep curved ramps. Floodlit in the centre, the periphery was dark and populated by shadowy figures – not exactly nana-friendly at night. Now and then, one of these figures would detach from the group to cross the centre, swoop up the lip of the bowl, teeter for a moment on the ridge and fly back down. Just when she thought it would be impossible to identify Zach, she recognised him airborne over a central jump. She waited until he landed safely and called his name. He either didn't hear or was ignoring her, because he skated off towards the far end of the park.

'Zach! I need you to get in the car. Now!' she shouted. Breaking into a jog, she headed in his direction, puffing with exertion and indignation.

As she got closer she heard one of his mates say, 'Isn't that your mental neighbour?'

She didn't catch Zach's response but the next minute, he skated off past her and into the night.

By the time she arrived home, hopping mad and determined to have it out with him, he was in his room, the door closed. She calmed herself by debating various consequences: turn off the internet, lock up his skateboard, ground him – she couldn't see that one working. She was barely in the door when she got a call from Claire and answered crossly, 'Yes?'

'Hi, Liz, how's it going?'

'How do you think it's going? He's a slippery customer. I'm going to have to attach a tracking monitor to him.'

There was shocked silence on the other end.

'Joking,' said Elizabeth. 'He told you he was out after curfew?'

Claire sighed. 'He didn't see it as being "out out". He was just at the skate park with his mates. To him it's as normal as being in his own backyard.'

'Except that his *actual* backyard isn't a magnet for drug dealers and police. He was out after curfew.'

'Do you want me to come home, Liz? It's obviously harder than you realised and Zach is my responsibility.'

'It would take a lot more than this to defeat me, Claire. But I suggest that, when he comes bleating, you take a firmer stance. He's been treated like a little prince for too long. Now he needs a reality check. He must be home before the curfew.'

'I know. You're right. I can see that. I've been trying to make things up to him for so long. We wanted so much for his childhood to be different from Tom's and . . .' Claire stopped but it was too late.

Much as she resented the comment, Elizabeth dug deep for a conciliatory phrase to smooth out this conversation, 'Yes, well . . . these things happen. We can't make life perfect for our children, unfortunately.'

'That's true,' Claire agreed. 'What do you want to do?'

Elizabeth knew by now that she could not summon back the sunny little boy she once knew. The adolescent Zach was a different person altogether and she had to adapt. 'I want you to stay there and rest after your op next week. Just relax until you're well,' she said. 'I am equal to this task.'

'I know you are. More than equal.'

'Take care of yourself, Claire.'

'Mum arrives tomorrow – she'll take care of me,' said Claire. 'Thanks, Liz.'

They said their goodnights. Elizabeth decided against discussing the matter with Zach and instead chopped up an apple to hand-feed to Eric. She'd had so little time to devote to him lately. He pecked away, happy at the attention, gave her a sidelong gaze and said, 'Go home loser.'

For a moment she thought she was hearing things, but he cheerily repeated the phrase several times and there was no mistaking it. She couldn't help feeling betrayed, as if he had switched allegiances. She threw the rest of the apple outside for the possums and went to bed in a huff.

As she lay in the dark, puzzling over how to make a shift in her relationship with Zach, her thoughts turned to Tom and what she might have done differently there. It was still in the back of her mind that she could have done something. Had she known about his financial problems, she would have sold the house to help. But she didn't know and wasn't asked for her advice or assistance. Still, it was hard to accept that she had been powerless to avert that catastrophe.

Tom and Nathan had studied law together and later formed O'Reilly & Donaldson, Solicitors. Elizabeth had thought Tom was settled for life in that business but he had a restless nature and wanted something more 'lively' as a sideline. He bought a couple of rundown cafes. Neither seemed like a good investment but he applied himself and learned everything he could about the business. He had Ray's ability to immerse himself in a subject and soon understood the mechanics of it all: staff management, inventory and marketing. He had both cafes refurbished, doubled the turnover and sold them at a profit. Elizabeth was proud and pleased for him, but it turned out that was just the beginning.

With his new-found confidence, he bought a bigger operation, a bistro in Rushcutters Bay. But the restaurant business was more complicated. Customers had higher expectations, the inventory and staff were more complex to manage, and Tom's lack of experience began to show. There were dramas with staff. Managers were hired and fired, and bad reviews began to overtake good ones online.

'There's something fundamental not working in the place,' Tom told her. 'I just can't put my finger on it.' Elizabeth knew he would figure it out: getting to the bottom of things was one of his strengths. He installed cameras, which revealed nothing. One evening, during the dinner service, he wandered about the restaurant to observe the staff and the processes. When he inspected the coolroom, he noticed a box tucked away at the back of the racking. Inside were half-a-dozen plastic shopping bags stocked with fillet steaks, foie gras, seafood, cheeses and expensive bottles of wine. He had suspected someone was stealing; now he realised that everyone was. The kitchen staff were a band of thieves. He'd thought he had their respect and that they were all on the same team, but he'd been conned. He confronted the staff that night, dismissed them all and closed the restaurant. It was a decision made in anger and everything began to unravel from that moment.

As she waited for sleep to come, Elizabeth tried to visualise a different future for Tom. She imagined him back home with Claire and Zach. Beyond that, she couldn't see what his future might hold. He would never practise law again and he had lost his enthusiasm for the restaurant business. She knew he would find his way somehow, but it didn't stop her fretting. She wondered what Ray would say about it all. She would value his wise counsel now, but he knew nothing about it because she had kept it from him.

That night she dreamed Zach was riding a horse, galloping along a beach like someone in a travel ad. He was shirtless, his hair flying behind him like a mane, and he laughed with the same innocent joy she'd seen in Lily and Grace. She woke wondering what it all meant. When Zach came out for breakfast, neither of them mentioned the incident at the skate park. She had decided that telling him off was pointless and now had a different strategy in mind.

She watched him build a tower of Weet-Bix. 'Can you ride a horse, Zach?'

'Dunno . . . Gonna buy me a pony?' His mouth twitched to suppress a smirk.

She ignored the sarcasm. 'I remember you wrote a wonderful story once, about Fred the barking horse.'

'Oh, yeah, and that one about the man with a hat that was a rabbit.'

'Kept his head warm but sometimes left raisins —'

'Sultanas,' he corrected. 'Because he was a sultan. I didn't know what a sultan was, thought it was to do with sultanas.'

'Do you still write stories?'

'Not unless I have to.' He hunched over his bowl to shorten the distance the spoon had to travel to his mouth.

'What are you really good at now?' asked Elizabeth. 'What are your strengths, do you think?'

He considered the question briefly. 'No-scope head shots. Three sixty no-scopes.'

It wasn't quite what Elizabeth had hoped for but she got on board. 'I gather you're referring to a long-range sniper shot to the victim's head without telescopic sighting.'

He looked slightly offended, as if she had intruded into his secret life. He shrugged and began to scrape up every last fibre of cereal and drop of milk in the bowl. The repetitive clink of the spoon grated on Elizabeth's nerves. To keep him talking, she flipped two slices of bread into the toaster. 'I'm going to see your dad in a couple of weeks. Would you like to come?'

'Not allowed,' he said, letting the spoon drop noisily.

'Says who?'

'Says Dad. He doesn't want me to come.'

'What does Mum say?'

'Dunno.' He shrugged.

Elizabeth plastered peanut butter on the toast and slid it in front of him. 'What do *you* think about it?'

He shrugged again and met her gaze. She had a sudden vision of him peering out from a suit of armour and wondered if the horse in her dream and the armour went together.

'He calls me Thursdays. Six minutes. Sucks.' He pushed his chair back and moved away from her and this conversation, taking his toast with him.

17

over the cliff

In the days that followed, it seemed to Elizabeth that there was a fragile truce in place. She told Zach that he *had* to let her know where he was going and when he'd be back. It fell short of her objective that he ask permission but she reasoned that taming any wild creature needed patience. She reminded him of the Outcome Plan conditions but was instructed to cool her jets. She explained again that if he broke his agreement with the court, Youth Justice would escalate his case and he said, 'Cool.' But he did reveal that he'd arranged to start his community work at the surf club over the weekend.

On Friday she ran her errands and stocked up at the supermarket. She got home to find the house reeking of burned food. In the kitchen, every cupboard was open and there were dirty dishes all over the bench. Two frying pans had bacon rinds stuck to them like scorched tapeworms. There were half-a-dozen plates encrusted with congealed egg, an empty packet of bread, an empty egg carton, and butter melting on the bench. Four spatulas, all covered in egg. Her gaze travelled the benches, to the floor and up to the ceiling – to see the remains of an egg adhered there, which solved the mystery of the multiple spatulas. She sighed at the realisation that school wasn't even out for another hour.

Eric's cage was empty. She heard herself make tiny mewling sounds as she ran around frantically searching for him. Had they set him free outside? Or on fire? Had the little barbarians actually murdered him? She walked around the back garden and called his name, feeling increasingly hopeless. The realisation slowly dawning that she would never see Eric again. She went back inside, sat down on the sofa and burst into tears.

'He-ad sh-ot head shot!' Elizabeth looked up and there was the dear little chap perched on a picture frame in the living room. Clever boy! She made kissing sounds and he fluttered down and landed on her outstretched finger.

'Hello, my beautiful boy. I'm so sorry.' He sat on her shoulder while she laid out budgie-sized treats in his cage: chopped-up strawberry and pepitas. She put him in the cage and closed the door with relief. She would have to leave him locked in her room or get a padlock for his door.

'Shuddup!' he said happily as he waddled around his cage. 'Shuddup loser,' he told his reflection in the mirror. 'Shuddup.'

'Okay, wise guy,' she replied. 'That's enough of that talk.'

It took an hour to restore order in the kitchen, scrape the mess off the bench and clean the ceiling. She made dinner and called and texted Zach but got no response. She put on her pyjamas and made herself comfortable on the sofa, confident that he fully understood he had to be back by nine. She would play it cool. Cool Nana. She channel-surfed but found it impossible to concentrate.

The curfew passed. She turned the television off and stared at the blank screen as if Zach's whereabouts might be revealed there. Hopefully not on the late night news. She had the same knot in her gut that she used to have when Tom and Danny were teens. If there was going to be trouble, it was always on a Friday or Saturday night. She remembered the feeling of relief that they were asleep in their beds on Sunday morning. Now here she was again, watching Friday night pass in slow, sinister increments.

She picked up her phone and saw that, impossibly, she had missed two calls from Zach while she was in the bathroom. She tried to call him back but there was no answer. Her gut was roiling as she paced up and down the living room trying to imagine what trouble he was in now.

The phone rang again and Zach said in a hushed voice, 'Can you come and get me?'

'Of course. Where are you?'

'I'm on the headland. Near the golf course. The police are here,' he said. 'Park near the beach . . . we'll get down the cliff.'

'Cliff? Zach, no! That's dangerous —'

But he was gone. She grabbed her keys and ran out of the house.

It was only a ten-minute drive. As she pulled into the car-park she could see a fire engine and police car parked up on the headland where the golf course met surrounding bushland. There were people standing around but they were too distant to recognise. She got out of the car, gritting her teeth as she stumbled down the gravel path to the beach in her slippers.

The full moon lit a shimmering path from the horizon as she hurried towards the cliffs of the headland. Now her eyes had adjusted, she could see a dark figure making its way slowly down the cliff face. It wasn't a sheer cliff – there were furrows and the occasional narrow track – but it was high enough for serious injury and probably unstable. She hardly dared breathe, as if her breath might blow him off course. If only she believed in prayer, now was the time to request divine intervention. She wanted to scream out to him, but that would be pointless and distracting. As she slogged through the soft sand towards the cliff face, she realised there were other figures edging their way down. She looked around helplessly but there was no one else. The parents of these kids were home in bed, out to dinner or watching television, and completely oblivious to the drama playing out in the moonlight.

Before she could get close to the cliff, the climbers began to jump down, one after the other, onto the sand and run off along the beach. She tried to run after them. She called Zach's name but her voice was drowned out by the crash of the waves.

In a moment, they had gone and she was alone on the beach again.

Swearing under her breath, she made her way back to the carpark. As she came over the sandhills, she saw a police car parked beside her car, and dropped to her knees to give herself a moment to think. How would she possibly explain why she was down on the beach at this time of night in her pyjamas and slippers? She lay flat on her belly and lifted her head occasionally to see if they were still there. They must have done a licence plate check because after a few minutes they drove away.

She got up, brushed herself off and shouted Zach's name a few times, knowing he was long gone.

He was not at the house when she arrived back. She had a shower, washed off all the sand and sat in the living room in the dark, trying to calculate her next move with a cool head. No more Nana Nice Guy.

She heard the click of the front door opening. When she flicked on the light, he was halfway across the living room, reeking of alcohol and bumping into furniture. His hands were bloody, his clothes torn and filthy.

Her pent-up anxiety and frustration exploded. 'What the *hell* is going on, Zach?'

He blinked hard and opened his eyes wide as though rudely awakened.

'You could have been arrested tonight! Worse, you could have been killed falling down that cliff. What is wrong with you?'

He rallied and raised his fists in a fighting stance. 'Oh yeah. Come at me, bro!'

'What? Don't take me on, Zach.'

'Come on then . . . square up,' he said and attempted some fancy footwork that sent him staggering into the coffee table. 'Let's see what you're made of, champ.'

'Oh, for goodness sake. Don't be ridiculous. What do you think you're playing at? Climbing down a cliff in the dark. Not just in the dark, but pissed. Where did you get that alcohol?'

'What do you care?' he shouted, dropping the playful drunk act. 'Why are you even here? You don't care about us!'

Elizabeth knew this conversation had to happen, but not right now and not like this. 'I do care, Zach – more than you can imagine. I'm sorry . . . I'm sorry . . .'

'Don't bother. I couldn't care less. I don't fucking care —' Zach stopped himself as a burp erupted from deep inside his chest.

'Oh, bloody hell!' said Elizabeth. 'Quick, get in the —'

Too late. Vomit erupted from his mouth and flowed slowly like lava down his chest. He pulled up his t-shirt in an effort to catch it. Elizabeth grabbed a throw from the sofa and caught the overflow before it reached the carpet. Furious as she was, when their eyes met, she realised that this was the most honest moment they had shared. She saw shame and confusion, and a sort of lost hopelessness in him. She recognised the fearful look in his eyes and wondered how she had ever missed it.

18

these last days

1970 Lizzy and Ray buy an engagement ring and plan a small party to make it official as well as celebrate Ray's twentieth birthday. Lizzy sends her parents an invitation and a few days later an envelope addressed in her mother's handwriting arrives. Inside is a glossy greeting card with 'Congratulations on your Engagement' written in silver script, surrounded by fluttering doves trailing ribbons. Lizzy recognises it from the Hallmark stand beside the counter in the mini-mart. The message inside says, 'From Mum and Dad and Doug'. To Lizzy, it represents a declaration of peace and she's quietly confident that, when the time comes, her father will walk her down the aisle.

Ginny arrives on the afternoon train to help with the party arrangements. She and Lizzy assemble plates of Sao crackers topped with cheddar cheese and slices of tomato, and make a dip of mushroom soup and cream cheese to have with potato chips. Ray buys a crate of beer and a couple of bottles of sparkling wine.

Lizzy's gift to him was a portable record player she'd

128

had on lay-by for weeks, and a jazz album, recommended by Mr Berkovics' friend in the record shop, called *Kind of Blue* by Miles Davis. Ray's already played it four times today, so she considers that a success.

The first guest to arrive is Aunty Gwen, who lives on the other side of the harbour in Lavender Bay, where she runs a guesthouse. Gwen is quite the opposite of Lizzy's mother; she's as glamorous as a film star with a taste for floaty clothes, dangly earrings and Camel cigarettes. 'Don't worry,' she says, thrusting a bouquet of flowers into Lizzy's arms. 'I'm not here to spy for your mother.' She scans the room curiously. 'So this is the love nest. Oh my goodness, is that the handsome lover?' She gives a low whistle. 'No wonder you went out the window.'

'Ray, this is my Aunty Gwen,' says Lizzy, beckoning Ray over.

'Just Gwen. Let's drop the aunty business.' Gwen offers Ray a limp hand as if expecting him to kiss it, which leads to an awkward handshake and makes her laugh.

While Ray fetches Gwen a drink, she tells Lizzy, 'You'll find Sydney is an easier place to live. People are more open minded, especially if you move in the right circles. Or the wrong circles — so much more interesting.'

'We don't really have any circle yet,' says Lizzy, putting the flowers in the sink.

Gwen's eyes are drawn back to Ray. 'Your mother said he's in newspapers. She made it sound like he owned one.'

'Not exactly.' Lizzy laughs. 'Maybe one day.'

'I suppose I should ask to see the ring.' But instead Gwen lights a cigarette and gives Lizzy an assessing look. 'I can see you're happy, Liz. Don't take it for granted. He seems like a sweet boy but men need a close eye kept on them.' She shrugs. 'They can be . . . troublesome in my experience.'

Mr Berkovics and his wife arrive with a bottle of wine and the gift of a small brass clock. Lizzy had imagined Mrs Berkovics would be large and world-weary like her husband, but she's bright-eyed with a darting gaze, and petite in a fitted black dress. Her English is perfect with only the slightest accent and, by the time Lizzy brings their drinks, she and Gwen are engaged in an animated conversation about London, where Gwen once lived with her first husband.

'My wife loves people. She speaks six languages,' Mr Berkovics tells Lizzy as he sips his wine. 'She can always find someone to talk to.' He gazes at his wife with an expression of helpless love.

Lizzy laughs. 'Six! You must tell Ray – that's one of his goals.'

'It's a good goal. It will last all his life. What other ambitions does he have?'

Lizzy glances over at Ray. 'Being a foreign correspondent somewhere . . . anywhere.'

'And you, Lizzy. What are your dreams?'

Lizzy shrugs, embarrassed by the ordinariness of her aspirations. 'Nice house. Children. Same as most people.'

Mr Berkovics nods. 'But Ray is not most people. Maybe these two ideas can work together, but not at the same time.'

Lizzy barely registers this comment before Ginny comes over and introduces herself. She tells Mr Berkovics that she's heard a lot about him and he looks pleased. 'We are good friends, aren't we, Lizzy?' he says.

Lizzy agrees, so glad to have Ginny there who has the ability to talk to anyone and always makes people feel welcome.

It's something she's grown up with – the Moncurs often entertain guests from the city, or even overseas.

Lizzy's parents' social life takes place behind the counter; they don't invite people home. She can't imagine guests in their living room with large boxes of toilet paper stacked around them. Or sharing the kitchen table with the ledgers and the adding machine.

Ray has invited Cynthia and his father, not expecting them to come. But now here they are at the door, with Andy as well.

'What a sweet nest you have,' says Cynthia, accepting a glass of sparkling wine. 'We're so happy for you both, aren't we, Patrick? Congratulations. And happy birthday, Ray dear.' She gives him a warm hug and kiss on the cheek.

Ray's father nods and extends his hand. 'Congratulations, son. You're an adult now. I suppose you know what you're doing.' He gives Lizzy a nod of acknowledgement.

'Thanks, Dad,' says Ray, and Lizzy can see in his smile that he needs his father's good opinion more than he would like to admit.

'Aren't they the gorgeous couple?' says Gwen, coming over to introduce herself.

'They are,' agrees Cynthia. 'We're very happy for them.'

'Mum said we're going to the wedding even if it's in the . . . something . . . office,' says Andy in a loud voice.

Cynthia laughs, blushing. 'We have to wait for an invitation.'

'We haven't set a date,' says Ray. 'Probably end of the year or early next year.'

'Registered for your National Service, lad?' asks Ray's father.

'If you want to avoid the dreaded ballot, it's better not to register,' says Gwen tartly. 'Keep your head down until it's over.'

'You don't have a choice,' says Ray's father. 'It's the law. Don't put daft ideas in his head. There's enough in there already.'

Gwen bristles. 'So you think it's reasonable to send boys, barely old enough to shave, off to be killed in Vietnam in an American war?'

'Oh, all right . . . one of those are you – pinko?' He gives Lizzy an annoyed look, as if she's responsible for Gwen's radical opinions.

'Patrick, please,' begins Cynthia. 'Anyway, I read in the paper that if you get caught not registering you are automatically conscripted. So better to do the right thing, I suppose.'

Ray holds up his hands in surrender. 'It's fine. I'll register this week.'

'Pat's not really *for* the war . . .' Cynthia tells Gwen. 'Or against.'

'Very Swiss of him.' Gwen raises a sceptical eyebrow. 'Well, you can always skip the country if your number comes up in the ballot, Ray. Plenty have.' She moves away to talk to Ginny before Ray's father can muster a comment.

Just as the evening seems to be getting complicated, Lizzy looks around to see Mr Berkovics and Ray's father enjoying a discussion. Gwen, Cynthia and Mrs Berkovics are chatting together like old friends. Ginny sits on the bed talking with a late arrival, one of Ray's work friends called Paul. Andy stands on a chair while Ray gives him a tour of the wall map. Everyone is occupied and, for the first time this evening, Lizzy can relax.

A month after Ray registers, a letter arrives from the Department of Labour and National Service requiring him to attend a medical examination. A few weeks after his appointment, his call-up papers arrive and he's conscripted into the army. It all happens so quickly. Ray is a little shocked but cautiously optimistic. The chances of being sent to Vietnam are slim, and over the last year there have been protest marches all around Australia, and overseas as well. He's certain that the government, under increasing pressure, will soon withdraw Australian troops.

Lizzy and Ray often walk down to Oxford Street in the evenings now and watch the television news in a shop window: fuzzy black-and-white images of helicopters, tanks and men in army clothes and floppy hats. It all seems so remote, another world, and it's hard to imagine this could have anything to do with them. But it lurks on the edges of Lizzy's consciousness and she sometimes wakes in the night, gripped by a fear she has never experienced before – that Ray will be taken from her, and there is nothing she can do to stop it.

It has rained overnight but the dawn sky is clear as Lizzy and Ray wait in the street for a taxi. In a couple of hours he will be on an army bus headed to Kapooka, a place neither of them had heard of until recently, where he will begin his National Service training.

Lizzy's face is swollen from crying all night. She wants to have every last minute with him but also to get the pain of parting over quickly. It will be three months before she sees him again and the weeks ahead seem bleak. She will be counting the days as she waits for him to come home on leave, even knowing that he will have to go away again.

With his duffle bag on one shoulder, Ray puts his arm around her and looks into her face. 'It's just training, Lizzy. It's not like

I'm going off to war. You don't have to worry about me. It's going to be fine.'

Lizzy knows he has been dreading the rigorous training and the uncertainty about where he will be posted when it's complete. His whole life has been disrupted and his valued freedom snatched away from him.

'I'll write to you every day,' promises Lizzy.

'I'd love that. Tell me everything that happens so I don't miss a thing.'

'I love you,' she says.

He pulls her into a hug and squeezes her against him. 'And I love you, my sweet Lizzy.'

As a taxi approaches, he holds her close and she sobs on his chest. When it pulls up beside them, he opens the door, greets the driver and throws his bag in the back seat. He leans down and kisses her. 'Home soon, baby.'

She stands alone in the street and watches the taxi disappear into the distance. Then there is nothing left to do but climb the stairs to the empty flat and watch the sun come up on her first day without him.

A few days after Ray leaves, Lizzy's mother rings her at work one morning to say she will be coming down on the train to meet Lizzy at lunchtime that day. If that's not surprising enough, when she arrives, her mother insists on having lunch at Coles Cafeteria.

'Don't tell your father,' she says, as they walk down George Street together. 'I want to see what's on offer.' She stands at the entrance of the cafeteria, mesmerised by the long line of customers snaking past the counters and the tables packed with lunchtime diners.

'Mum, you're in everyone's way. I've only got an hour,' says Lizzy.

They join the queue, edging forward as the assistants fill people's plates with pies and chips or roast meat and vegetables, all with a slop of brown gravy on top. Lizzy expects her mother to complain about the noise, a hundred conversations punctuated by crashing crockery and cutlery, but she gazes around curiously.

As they sit down, Lizzy notices that, under her cardigan, her mother is wearing her blue nylon work smock with Clayton's Mini-mart embroidered on the breast pocket.

'I just hope you haven't got into something that's going to ruin your life, Liz,' her mother says between mouthfuls and, without waiting for a response, continues. 'Oh well, it's probably too late to worry about that now. Honestly, running away . . . how stupid can you get? I bet his family aren't too pleased, either. Anyway, you're almost eighteen, responsible for yourself and that's that.' She looks up from her meal and frowns at Lizzy. 'So now he's gone off, just be thankful you're not pregnant. You're not pregnant, are you? I suppose you're on the pill – doctors are handing them out like sweets now.'

'His name is Ray, and he hasn't just "gone off" . . .'

'We don't expect you to come home. We've hired a girl and she's an improvement on you, I must say. Doesn't daydream as much, and the customers like her.'

'That's good,' says Lizzy and she means it.

'When *Ray* comes home,' her mother says, as if to humour her, 'you can get married. If he'll have you still.'

Lizzy's eyes burn at the implication. Her mother pats her hand. 'He'll be fine. Most of these conscripts aren't being sent overseas, anyway. But good on him, fighting for this country. Very patriotic. Anyway, me and Dad don't think you should be in the city on your own, so I've asked Aunty Gwen if you can board with her in the meantime. You can help around the place. She could do with an extra hand.'

Lizzy realises that, with Ray gone, she has somehow fallen back into her parents' care by default. While it's not ideal, in the week since Ray left she has felt lost. When she comes home from work, Mr Geddes wanders out of the showroom and waylays her with small talk, but he's kinder now, more sympathetic and fatherly. Still, she doesn't sleep well and dreads coming home to the empty flat.

'Aunty Gwen lives close to the ferry and you'll get some fresh air on the way to work.' Her mother mops up the gravy with her bread and pushes her plate away. 'That was good. We could do with a place like this in Nullaburra. Don't tell your father I said that.'

Her mother refuses to spend money on a cup of tea and has brought a thermos with her. They walk across to Hyde Park and sit on a bench near the fountain. Lizzy watches the cascading water sparkle in the sun, only half listening as her mother describes the shelving arrangements of the new Coles supermarket, compares the prices of various products and discusses the 'discounting war' they've been forced into.

Lizzy turns her attention to the people walking past. Young people like herself on their lunchbreak. Lively and fashionably dressed, they chat and laugh with friends. There's an odd moment when she sees herself detach from the conversation and join these other young people, naturally falling into step with them. Not just walking away from her mother and this tedious conversation, but her family and the world of Nullaburra. The feeling lasts a split second and is followed by a pang of disappointment that she's still sitting on the bench, listening to her mother while they drink cold tea from plastic mugs.

Gwen's guesthouse in Lavender Bay is a spacious three-storey building with five rooms set aside for guests, who are mainly commercial travellers and business people who stay regularly. The rooms are comfortable, lavishly decorated with floral bedspreads, crushed velvet cushions and tasselled curtains.

Gwen herself lives in a cosy flat on the top floor. There's a covered-in balcony off the living room that will be Lizzy's bedroom. It's sunny and bright, with rows of louvre windows that look out towards the harbour and the bridge, and the city beyond. There's a single bed in one corner, a chest of drawers and a small desk.

Soon after Lizzy moves in, her parents drive down and bring her precious radio and a suitcase of clothes she'd forgotten about, and she begins to feel more settled and at home.

In the evenings she has to collect the breakfast orders. In the mornings, before she goes to work, she helps Gwen prepare the breakfasts and delivers them to the guestrooms on trays. She leaves home every day smelling of fried food and stands outside on the ferry deck in the hope that the sea air will eradicate it before she gets to work. As promised, she writes to Ray every evening and posts the letter on her way to work, as she counts down the days until he comes home on leave.

19

salt and pepper

Elizabeth prodded the pile of red seeds on her plate with her fork. They were tasteless, with an odd texture; gritty and soggy at the same time. It occurred to her that Claire may have accidentally served her some of Eric's selection of seeds. Boiled birdseed.

Claire herself ate absolutely anything healthy. Add the word 'super' to the word 'food' and she was in. Like kale, for example, another unpalatable food and the poor relation of silverbeet, which Claire lovingly massaged with cold-pressed coconut oil just to make it edible.

'All right, Liz?' asked Claire, who was barely eating anyway.

'Just wondering what this is,' said Elizabeth.

'It's quinoa. You know that, Liz. It's very good for you. Not to your taste?'

'It doesn't quite meet my minimum expectation for flavour, consistency and palatability. I'm not sure even Eric would rate it very highly. The vegetables are delicious though.' Elizabeth glanced over at Eric, who was enjoying his visit home. He patrolled the

138

windowsill to cast his eye over any changes in the garden or new birds in his territory.

Claire smiled. 'We can test that theory. Looks like there'll be plenty left over.'

It was an odd experience for Elizabeth to be a dinner guest in her own house. She couldn't complain: Claire was keeping the place very clean and tidy, and the plants all looked in good health. Unlike Claire, who looked a little washed out after her surgery. Adele had been here earlier in the week to take care of her but then rushed off back to Perth to keep up with her volunteer commitments.

'Do you ever get lonely here?' asked Claire.

Elizabeth thought about this for a moment. The years after Ray left were the loneliest of her life but she had been frantically busy and had little time to dwell on it. Wherever she was, she had a nagging feeling she should be somewhere else: finishing a probation report, picking up a child from sport, shopping for the week, packing lunches. By the time the boys left home, she was inured to loneliness in all its forms and had hardly noticed it, until recently.

'It's a big house for one person,' continued Claire. 'You could easily downsize.'

Elizabeth looked around, trying to see the place through Claire's eyes. When she and Ray bought the house in the seventies, Roseville seemed like an outer suburb of Sydney, but over the years the city had extended far beyond them. The furniture was a little shabby and dated, the rugs on the polished floor were tatty around the edges. This house had been her protective shell, a place to retreat from the world. It wasn't only her home, it was Ray's for whenever he might need it. 'I suppose

I could,' said Elizabeth and, changing the subject, 'Has Zach been in touch?'

'I saw him last week when Mum was here. We met after school and we message every couple of days. It comes down to me contacting him, unless he needs money, of course. I think everything outside his group is a bit of a blur.'

Elizabeth smiled. 'Nothing a good haircut wouldn't fix. He looks like a sheepdog.'

'Oh, I wouldn't go there, Liz. You haven't seen him really angry yet.'

Elizabeth shrugged. The cliff incident would remain between her and Zach.

'He said the caseworker has been checking up on him,' said Claire.

'Angela, yes, she came on Monday. She seems very pleasant. Zach is polite with her.' Elizabeth paused. 'Look, I owe you an apology, Claire.'

'Oh?' Claire looked up from her dinner.

'I may have possibly implied you weren't . . . I don't know, keeping a proper eye on Zach? But I have to admit, he has thoroughly got the better of me in the last few weeks. I've been backfooted the entire time.'

Claire nodded. 'I know. It's like you're constantly in damage control with no idea how to prepare for the next surprise. Tom and I were so distracted in the last couple of years, Zach started living his own life and it's been impossible to rein him back in.'

'How do you feel about him seeing Tom in . . . the centre?'

'Does he want to?' asked Claire.

'Hard to tell. We had a brief conversation and I got the impression it was Tom's objection that stood in his way.'

'Well, I don't have a problem with it. It might be good for him, given what else is going on. For both of them.'

They ate in silence for a moment, then Claire asked, 'Why did you leave work? You said you'd never retire. Was it because of Tom?'

'It was my decision. I didn't have to leave.'

'Well, why did you?' Claire refilled their wine glasses and there was something in that gesture, and Claire's frank gaze, that made Elizabeth want to be more honest.

'I didn't like being the subject of gossip, and the butt of jokes – only some of which were behind my back,' admitted Elizabeth. 'I was embarrassed professionally because of what happened with Tom. And, because I worked in Corrections, I had to declare a conflict of interest. I had access to confidential files and that sort of thing.'

She paused and took a sip of wine. 'It definitely put me under a lot more pressure. Then there was a complaint made by one of my team. I think the word "crabby" was used. I'd been known as a trailblazer in the department over the years and I didn't want it all to end badly.'

'I wouldn't say crabby,' said Claire. 'Perhaps . . . salty. Occasionally a little peppery. But never dull.'

Elizabeth smiled. 'Ray used to call me his Sweet Lizzy, and I sometimes think the sweet part of me went with him when he left.' She paused, feeling like she'd said too much. 'It wasn't Tom's fault,' she said. 'I wouldn't want him to think that.'

'I understand. I know it came as a shock to you, but things had been difficult at home for some time. When Tom got caught up with the unfair dismissal case, Nathan came to see me because he was worried about Tom – not just as his business partner, but as his friend. Of course, what happened was wrong, I'm not trying to justify it, but that's how it started.'

Elizabeth nodded. 'You don't have to explain it to me. It's . . .' She wanted to say it was none of her business but couldn't go quite that far and they both fell silent. Elizabeth finished her quinoa as a sort of penance. It wasn't as bad as she'd first thought. 'Ginny wrote me a letter just before she died . . .'

Claire nodded sympathetically. 'Ginny dying must have been so hard for you.'

Elizabeth still had the tight feeling in her throat every time Ginny's name came up. 'Yes. It was. She told me I needed to sort out things in the family.'

'I see,' said Claire, her tone guarded.

'Starting with Ray. I feel something has changed, something's not right, and I've been thinking of going up north to find him.'

Claire's eyes widened with surprise. 'Really? I thought you were permanently . . . estranged.'

'I wouldn't say estranged – that's an angry separation. It's not like that at all.'

'What is it like?' asked Claire. 'I've never really understood.'

Elizabeth wasn't sure herself. There wasn't a definitive term for it. 'It was something he needed to do. I understood that.'

'But Tom said he left without warning, or even saying goodbye.'

'It was a difficult time for him,' said Elizabeth.

'But . . .' said Claire. 'It's not over for you.'

'No,' Elizabeth admitted. 'It's not.'

'When were you planning to go? I'm not sure I could handle Zach right now.'

'Perhaps a week or two? Whenever you're ready to come home. No pressure.'

'I really admire your loyalty to Ray,' said Claire. 'Considering how everything turned out in the end.'

'As I said, we haven't come to the end yet,' said Elizabeth. Claire didn't know Ray. No one knew him like Elizabeth did. It wasn't loyalty, it was simply understanding the truth of the man.

Claire gathered their plates and put them in the sink. She leaned against the bench and looked at Elizabeth. 'I know what you're thinking, Liz.'

'No one knows what I'm thinking,' Elizabeth deadpanned.

'You're thinking about my lack of loyalty to Tom.'

'Not at all,' said Elizabeth. 'I'm wondering if you have a toothpick.'

20

corrections

Elizabeth made several attempts to discuss the plan to visit Tom with Zach but he doubled down on his refusal. She suspected this was mainly because he didn't want to think about it. A week later, the school secretary called Elizabeth in the middle of the day and asked her to come in and meet with the principal – immediately, if possible.

When Elizabeth arrived, Zach was sitting outside the principal's office looking typically unconcerned. The principal, Mrs Marshall, came out and invited them both in. Elizabeth introduced herself and asked if they could have a word in private first. Mrs Marshall agreed and Elizabeth followed her into the office. Closing the door behind them, she sat down.

'So, you're the nana,' said Mrs Marshall. She didn't look at Elizabeth but scanned something on her computer monitor that made her frown. Elizabeth remained silent until she had the woman's full attention. While she waited, she noticed Mrs Marshall's shapeless black dress and limp hair and unhappy expression: a woman who had no time for herself.

'His mother isn't well at the moment, so I've stepped in,' said Elizabeth.

Without any enquiry about Claire's health, the principal went on to explain that Zach had vandalised a fellow student's phone. He'd already been given three warnings for other misdemeanours and was now going to be suspended for two weeks.

Elizabeth nodded, listening without interruption. 'Firstly, I would like to apologise for Zach's behaviour, and he will replace the phone, of course.'

'That goes without saying,' said Mrs Marshall. Her eyes strayed back to the computer screen and she gave a huff of annoyance at whatever she saw there.

'You are likely aware that Zach is under a corrections order and still has his final determination ahead,' said Elizabeth. 'Suspension is the last thing the court wants to see on his report —'

'Well, he should have thought of that earlier. I suggest we bring him in and explain the consequences to him in person. Zach needs a wake-up call.' Mrs Marshall turned to her computer. 'Excuse me, I just need to attend to this,' she said, tapping at the keys.

Elizabeth waited and planned her next move. Mrs Marshall finished her business, and seemed surprised to find Elizabeth still there.

'You wouldn't put a child into the justice system as a wake-up call, Mrs Marshall,' said Elizabeth, her tone even and reasonable. 'I agree he's done some stupid things. I'm not excusing that behaviour, but there are extenuating circumstances. Zach has just been through the worst year of his life. Everything he knows has been turned upside down.'

'I'm not sure what you expect from me, Mrs O'Reilly.'

'Respectful negotiation?' suggested Elizabeth.

Mrs Marshall raised her eyebrows. 'I have obligations to other students, and we have procedures. I don't just have one Zach, you know. I have a dozen.'

'I understand. It must be difficult,' said Elizabeth. 'But right now, Zach's future rests with you.'

'That's a little dramatic, don't you think?' Mrs Marshall sat back in her chair and folded her arms over her chest.

'Not at all. Once kids enter the corrections system, they go down a rabbit hole many don't come out of. It changes their perception of themselves at a time when they're trying to work out who they are. I'm sure you'll agree that fifteen is a vulnerable age.'

Mrs Marshall frowned. 'What's your background, Mrs O'Reilly?'

'I worked in the justice system for more than thirty years – the first ten as a probation officer, the last ten designing rehabilitation programs.' Elizabeth had the woman's full attention now and pushed on. 'We know that the vast majority of kids who get support, instead of punishment, never reoffend. I think those of us in a position of authority have a moral obligation to protect young people – and keep them out of a system that could destroy their future.'

Mrs Marshall gave her a long look. 'What did you have in mind?'

'I'll apply to take him out of school for two weeks, for family reasons. So, essentially, he's off your hands and my responsibility. Let me see what I can do with him.'

Mrs Marshall opened a file on her desk and flicked through

his reports. 'His marks have dropped quite badly in the last year.' She closed the folder. 'I suppose we could de-escalate it to a final warning and replacement of the damaged property.'

'Thank you,' said Elizabeth. 'Is it possible to make that a verbal warning?'

Mrs Marshall's lips set in a firm line and Elizabeth took that to mean probably not.

Elizabeth had hoped to continue with her calm, reasonable approach on the drive home with Zach and help him use this set-back to analyse his own behaviour. But she'd expected him to be at least the tiniest bit contrite. He was not only unrepentant but quite uninterested. Now she was just ranting and, if he suggested she cool her jets again, would quite likely blow a gasket. 'I literally do not know how to tell your mother. I can't tell her . . . I'm so embarrassed this happened on my watch. What is going on with you? Are you going to apologise?'

'To who?' he asked, not bothering to look up from his phone.

'To me? To your mother? To the boy with the damaged phone?'

'That kook gets a new phone. It's got nothing to do with you,' he replied. 'And you just said you weren't gonna tell Mum. Sooo . . .?'

'Of course I have to tell your mother!' His coolness made Elizabeth furious. She pulled over and stopped the car. 'Okay, hop out. You can walk home.'

Zach got out and ambled off down the street. They were only five minutes from the house, so he arrived before her and she ended up lugging his heavy backpack inside, where she dumped it on the floor. She went straight into the kitchen and switched the modem off. Within seconds, he rushed out of his room pale with shock. She positioned herself between him and the modem. 'Here's the deal, Zach. I want you to come and visit your dad. Something needs to change. You won't listen to me or Mum. Maybe you'll listen to him.'

Zach shook his head. 'No deal.'

She stood her ground in silence.

'No deal!' repeated Zach, angrier now.

Eric fluttered around his cage, picking up on the tension in the room. 'No deal!' he cried. 'No deal no deal!'

'He doesn't want me there.' Tight-lipped, Zach launched a kick at the coffee table, knocking it over and scattering books on the floor. 'Why don't you stay out of it?'

'I can try to book us in for Saturday.'

His face darkened and he took a step towards her. 'Just turn the internet back on.'

Elizabeth kept her voice low and calm. 'The internet stays off until we reach an agreement. *And* you pick that table up.'

For a moment he stared around the room as if looking for something to break, then he shouted, 'Okay! Okay! I'll come. Jesus! Turn. It. On.'

'Now the table, please.'

He picked up the table by one leg and slammed it on its feet. 'Turn it on!' he said, heading for his room. 'Turn it on!'

'Turn it on!' echoed Eric. 'Jesus turn it on!'

'Yes, thank you, Eric. I will indeed turn it on. Just remember who's in charge here, buster,' she told him. It was a victory, but she was shaken by the interaction. She was too old for all this teenage argy-bargy.

She requested a call from Tom. She had six minutes to make her case, but surprisingly he agreed straight away. 'I can hardly get two words out of him on the phone, let alone a conversation,' he said.

'Two words is a conversation with Zach. You're doing well. I'll make the booking now.'

'Thanks, Mum. Yeah. Thanks.' Tom sounded resigned and it seemed to Elizabeth that the time was right for him and Zach to meet.

For years, terms like defendant, remand, conviction and imprisonment had been the language of her work. She had seen people flinch at the mention of them and now she knew what that felt like. When it came to discussing Tom, those same words stuck in her throat. She had been guilty of shutting down discussion about his situation and had never spoken about it with Zach. Now he needed a reality check, that would have to change.

On the drive up to the correctional centre, Zach listened to music through earphones, his face concealed inside his grey hoodie. It was like having the grim reaper as a travel companion. Elizabeth wondered what he was thinking and how he felt about seeing Tom. Most likely he was thinking about something else entirely.

At the centre they queued with other visitors, went through the various checks, showed their IDs and put their phones in a locker. Zach had to leave his hoodie in the locker, which he didn't like at all. He had a baggy long-sleeved t-shirt underneath but looked vulnerable stripped of his outer layer. His nervousness was palpable and, when she touched his arm briefly, he jumped. She gave him some change to buy snacks from the vending machines for Tom and that kept him busy while they waited.

They went through the security check into the visitation room and took their seats. Zach put a tube of Pringles and a packet of M&M's on the table. He rearranged them several times nervously, as if he had brought them for a show-and-tell presentation.

There was always a variety of people visiting prisoners, and a couple of women there today were familiar to Elizabeth. She exchanged a smile with an older woman whom she had chatted with several times in the waiting area who was also visiting her son. There was another woman Elizabeth was familiar with; she always looked on the brink of a breakdown. She had six kids that all had to be farmed out to relatives so she could get here and see her husband who, in all honesty, did not look worth the effort. Every story was a tragic one, Elizabeth knew that first hand. Every man in here had once been someone's little boy.

Restless with nerves, Zach tried to move his chair closer to the table and discovered it was bolted to the floor. He slumped in his seat unhappily and frowned. As prisoners began to be escorted into the room, he observed each reunion, taking everything in.

Then Tom was walking towards them. He wore white overalls and the forlorn smile that broke Elizabeth's heart every time she saw him here. He'd always been confidently well-dressed and spent money on sharp haircuts. With his prison trim he looked older and a little defeated, and she wondered what it would take for him to get his confidence back when he got out of here.

Zach stood up, glanced at Elizabeth, remembered his instructions and sat down again. Tom joined them at the table and took Zach's hands in his. 'Hey, Zach. How are you, buddy?'

''K.' As soon as Zach's hands were released, he withdrew them inside his sleeves and folded his arms tightly across his chest as though he was in a straightjacket.

'How are you, Tom?' asked Elizabeth.

'I'm fine. Just worried about this young fella,' he said without taking his eyes off Zach. 'How are you going living with Nana?'

Zach gave Elizabeth a sidelong glance as if she had a gun in his ribs. 'Okay, I guess. Eric's cool.'

'And I'm not?' asked Elizabeth, only half joking.

A flash of metal as Zach grinned despite himself. 'No.'

Tom smiled. 'What's this Nana tells me about school?'

'Nothing . . . just threw something.' He paused to see if that was enough detail. 'Into a fan,' he added.

'And did some damage, by the sound of it,' suggested Tom.

Zach shrugged. 'Yep.'

'You know, Zach, it takes just one dumb move to backfire and . . . *boom*. You already know that from the surf club. And you need to remember you're not off the hook yet – far from it. If you keep up this behaviour, you're going to end up here.'

'Like you,' said Zach in a sullen voice. He unfolded his arms and rubbed some invisible dirt off the table with his sleeve.

Tom shook his head. 'I can't begin to express how much I regret what I did. Learn from my mistake, son. Don't be an idiot like me.'

Tom met Elizabeth's gaze. She shook her head slightly. That was enough lecturing. Enough prostrating himself. She could see by Zach's expression that he wasn't really taking this on. No one was going to talk him out of anything.

'How's the surf been anyway?' asked Tom. 'Pumpin'?'

Zach curled his lip and shrugged. 'S'okay.'

'Zach's off school for a while,' said Elizabeth. 'So I'm thinking of taking him up north with me to find out what's happening with Dad.'

'Riiight . . . Why's that?' asked Tom.

'Few reasons. One is that Ginny wrote me a letter . . .'

Tom frowned. 'Before she died?'

'No, after she died. Of course, before she died!'

Zach ducked his head to hide a smile.

'Funny,' said Tom. 'You know what I mean – like a deathbed letter?'

Elizabeth nodded. 'She said she didn't agree with the way I'd handled some things.'

Tom laughed. 'She'd want to be safely on the other side before she made that statement. Was that it? Nothing else. Just a short letter with big writing?' He mimed writing in the air with his finger.

'I should have brought it with me. There were a few things, but one of them was that she thought I should go and see Ray . . .'

Tom shook his head sympathetically. 'Mum, I don't know what good it's going to do. If Dad wanted to see us, he would have come back by now. He's had long enough.'

'I think it could be good for Zach,' said Elizabeth.

'What does Claire think?' asked Tom.

'She doesn't have a problem.'

'Wait. What are you even talking about?' asked Zach.

'It's a long story, Zachy. One day we'll have a good talk about it,' said Tom. 'I'll be out in a few months. It's not that long. We'll go for a surf together, eh?'

There was a shout somewhere behind them and, before they could work out what was happening, alarms sounded. The two guards in the room moved towards the table where an argument had broken out and Elizabeth saw it was the woman with all those children and the hard-faced husband, who was now on his feet. More guards materialised, prisoners were removed and visitors escorted back into the reception. It was chaotic but perfectly executed at the same time. It all happened so suddenly that she and Zach found themselves standing in the reception area in a daze for a few minutes. It was over. They collected their things and wandered out of the building into the warm afternoon.

On the drive home, Elizabeth felt miserable as she always did after seeing Tom. Zach didn't speak once. Shrinking into his hoodie, he seemed to be trying to disappear altogether but gave the occasional sniffle and wiped his face with his sleeve.

21

the road north

Zach was less than cooperative about the idea of a trip up north. Elizabeth didn't give his resistance too much attention. She continued to produce meals that couldn't be eaten on the move and held him captive for a few minutes at least. She bought a fold-out map of New South Wales and spread it out on the dining table when he was trapped by a large bowl of spaghetti bolognese.

'So this is, like . . . the whole state?' he asked, as if he'd never seen a paper map before.

Elizabeth pointed out Sydney and traced the road north. 'We're here, and we'll be going all the way up this highway.'

He scowled. 'Trek. How long's that going to take?'

'Couple of days. It'll be cool, Zach. Road trip.' She twitched her shoulders in a cool rapper move.

He looked pained. 'Do I have to go?'

That he was asking this question was heartening, and the first indication that she had any authority over him at all. 'There's good surf spots all up the coast. We have to stop overnight somewhere. You can bring your board.'

He continued to look over the map. 'What are the purple and red lines?'

'The purple are the main roads, like the freeway, and the red are more secondary roads.'

He traced the lines with his fingertip, murmuring place names under his breath. 'Currabubula, Bingara, Narrabri . . .' He paused, his lips still shaping the words. After a moment he said, 'Okay, fine.'

'Okay fine okay fine,' repeated Eric. 'Jesus turn it on!'

'If Eric comes too,' Zach added.

Elizabeth had planned to leave Eric with Claire but if that's what it took, so be it.

She knew she had to move swiftly and leave within the next few days, and now it was her turn to get nervous about the trip. She began to wonder if she'd unwittingly been waiting thirty years for a decent excuse to go and find Ray. She went out shopping and bought two flattering casual dresses. In the change room, she had a long critical look in the mirror and noticed her eyebrows had become patchy and faded, giving her face a blank look. On impulse, she went into a brow bar to have them renovated.

The young woman's touch on her face and the hovering and fussing, as if the state of Elizabeth's eyebrows was of national importance, made her yearn for more attention. She remembered those years when her body wasn't her own, with a baby on the breast and a toddler clinging to her leg. The years when her body was the centre of comfort for others. Now she was like a pariah or a queen. In the last six months, apart from a peck on the head from Danny and a hug from Claire, no one had touched her. Increasingly, no one even saw her. In the street, people looked right through her. In cafes, staff attended to visible customers and she had become resigned to it.

When completed, her eyebrows looked quite startling, shapely and defined, slick and arched, framing her eyes. She allowed the young woman to sell her a lipstick called 'Sugar Plum' and some mascara as well. In fact, she would have bought almost anything just to prolong the self-indulgent pleasure of this transaction. None of this was for Ray, she was just brightening herself up. She thought about buying him some wine but hoped he'd stopped drinking and didn't want to encourage that anyway. He would have to feast on her eyebrows alone.

On the day of their departure, she woke Zach at 5 am. The sports bag she'd told him to pack lay discarded and empty on the floor of his room. He was sprawled facedown across the bed and difficult to wake. There were several false starts when he lapsed back into unconsciousness. 'Whhhy do we have to leave so early?' he asked groggily.

'Traffic. Come on, get some clothes in that bag. I'll make you something to eat for the road.'

While he dragged himself out of bed, she hurried to the kitchen and threw a ham and cheese roll together. He came out of his room a few minutes later carrying the sports bag and grabbed his surfboard from the laundry. Elizabeth followed him out to the car with Eric in his small cage. Zach threw his bag into the back seat, carefully slid the board into the back hatch and got in.

'Don't you need to pee?' Elizabeth asked as she strapped Eric's cage into the back seat.

'Nah. I'm fine.' He reached for the roll.

'Zach. Don't be so lazy. Go and pee. You'll be busting in a couple of hours.'

He turned to argue the point and paused, evidently trans-fixed by her eyebrows as he looked from left to right and back again silently. With an exasperated sigh, he went back inside. His sports bag still looked empty. Elizabeth leaned over and unzipped it. It contained his wetsuit and two pairs of undies, neither of which looked clean. She gave her own exasperated sigh, took the bag back inside and packed it with clean clothes.

They finally set off into the dawning day and Elizabeth felt a jitter of excitement: the sense of a beginning with no idea where this journey might lead.

She had imagined that, in the confined space of the car over several days, they might have a conversation more than a few minutes long – a proper discussion. In reality, Zach was more like a kidnapping victim, sulky and withdrawn, ears plugged with his buds. Clearly he'd rather be anywhere but trapped in this car with her.

Elizabeth felt as though she was chauffeuring someone of high office who couldn't be spoken to, like royalty or a rock star. After an hour on the freeway, the silence had thickened to a point of discomfort. She became self-conscious about clearing her throat and then couldn't stop. She pulled out a tissue and blew her nose with one hand, disturbing the silence with all the subtlety of a brass band.

She turned on the radio. There was an interesting discus-sion on the ABC about gender politics. That was something she and Zach could definitely discuss; he must have some opinions on that topic. 'What are your thoughts on this gender-neutral pronoun?' she suggested as an opener. But the topic was clearly not to his taste. He pulled his hoodie further over his head, slid down in the seat and went to sleep.

When she stopped for coffee, Zach was still asleep. He woke when she got back into the car and handed him a takeaway coffee and a muffin.

'What's this?' he asked suspiciously.

'Coffee?'

He looked as if she'd just offered him a line of coke. 'I don't drink coffee. I'm fifteen.'

Elizabeth burst out laughing. 'Sorry, Zach. I just thought . . . I don't know what I thought. Don't fifteen-year-olds drink coffee? Try it. Better for you than vodka.'

He had a sip, shook his head and handed it back. He opened the muffin. As they set off again, he assiduously removed every blueberry before eating what was left.

After a while he asked, 'Does he know we're coming?'

'Grandad? No. He's difficult to contact. He doesn't have a phone or a computer or anything like that.'

'Why?'

'He doesn't need them, or want them, I suppose.'

'Will he be angry about us coming?'

'No. He always asks after you when he writes. I've sent him photos,' said Elizabeth. 'He's sad that he hasn't met you.'

'I don't get it. Why be sad? Why not just come and see us?'

Elizabeth had been anticipating this conversation and how to phrase it in a way that Zach could process. 'Grandad had a sort of breakdown, many years ago. He made the decision to go and live away from other people, completely on his own. He thought it was the only way he could manage. So, that's what he did.

I think he'd be afraid to come to see us. It would be overwhelming for him . . . like he was coming out of a quiet forest into something like a war zone.'

'He lives in the forest? Like a feral?' He had a scornful way of asking questions, as if he thought everything was stupid and was only asking to confirm his opinion.

'Yes. He's right in the rainforest with no one around.'

He shook his head dismissively. 'That sucks.'

'You probably get used to it after a while.'

Up until this moment, he had barely taken any interest in their destination but now he seemed unsettled by the idea of a remote rainforest. Not surprising when Elizabeth considered how narrow the scope of his world was. He lived in a triangular universe consisting almost entirely of home, school, the beach – and online. Not that her world was much larger these days.

They stopped overnight at Coffs Harbour. Elizabeth had booked a motor inn close to the beach and, as soon as they'd checked in, Zach went straight out into the surf.

When she was settled, Elizabeth walked down and sat on the beach to watch him. When it came to surfing, he had enormous patience and tenacity. The way he paddled for a wave, half caught or missed it, sliding off the back, then sat and waited for the next one. Then he would catch a wave, flying between sea and sky in a mist of spray. It was beautiful to watch, like a graceful dance. But, just as quickly, the ride was over and he was paddling back out again.

When he'd had enough, they walked back to the motel together and she suggested he have a shower, and then they could go somewhere nearby for dinner. But that was not to be.

Elizabeth went for the pizza and they ate it sitting on their beds watching *Bondi Rescue*.

She cut up a small tomato and some cucumber for Eric and tried to program him with new phrases like, 'Hello, Zach. Waass up?' in an attempt to amuse Zach.

But Eric had his own ideas. 'That sucks that sucks!'

Bored with television, Zach looked around the motel room discontentedly. 'Can I sleep in the car?' he asked.

'What? Why on earth do that when there's a perfectly good bed here?'

He scowled. 'Can I?'

'Can I?' asked Eric. 'Can I?'

'No, you can't, stickybeak,' said Elizabeth. 'Not you, Zach – Eric.'

The car was parked right outside the door and she supposed it was safe enough. He could lock himself inside and wouldn't need the car keys. 'I guess so. Brush your teeth and take the room key in case you change your mind. Take a pillow and a blanket.'

While he was in the bathroom, she brought his surfboard inside so he had space to stretch out in the hatchback. It would be fine to sleep in with a mattress but very hard without one. She glanced over her shoulder and wondered what other guests would think seeing a child sleeping in the car. But there was no one around.

Zach came outside carrying a blanket and pillow. She handed him the motel key. 'Night, Zach.'

He mumbled something and she was saddened by the defeated droop of his shoulders. It was as though he wanted to behave better, or at least differently, but was controlled by some malevolent force. Did he want her to be firmer or softer? It was impossible to tell. Anyway, she wasn't up for an argument right now: she needed her beauty sleep.

Sometime in the night, she heard the car door close. She waited for the sound of the key in the lock, but it didn't come. She got up and looked out the window but couldn't see if Zach was still in the car. She slipped outside and peered into the back. Apart from the bedding, it was empty. She looked around helplessly. Where could he have possibly gone? She went inside and checked her phone. It was 11 pm – where the hell was he?

She scouted around the building, checked the pool area and stood out on the street trying to work out what to do next. Did he not know what the time was? Or think his curfew didn't apply here? She debated the idea of driving around but didn't know where to start. She went back inside to wait and lay in the dark, her ears attuned for the sound of his return.

It was after midnight when she heard the key turn in the lock. The smell of rotting food preceded him. There was a rustling of sheets as he climbed into the other bed, accompanied by the putrid smell.

Elizabeth sat up and flicked the bedside lamp on. 'Where have you been?' He cowered under the covers. She got out of bed, marched over and ripped the sheet off him. His jeans and hoodie were stained and filthy. 'Second question. Why do you stink?'

He pulled his hoodie up over his head and curled up in a fetal position.

'Zach! No one is going to sleep until this is sorted out. I've had enough. More than enough. Just explain yourself and we can get some sleep.'

'Nothing to explain,' he said. 'Couldn't sleep. Went for a walk.'

'Okay, and then . . . it started raining rotten food?'

There was a long silence. 'These eshays came out of a take-away. They start, like, following me. And saying stuff. I started running. There were three of them chasing me.' His voice cracked. 'I hid in a dump bin behind a supermarket.'

Elizabeth sat down on the bed beside him and patted his shoulder on a clean spot. 'You really are a dope sometimes. I wish you'd just think about it for five minutes and realise when you're putting yourself in danger.'

'I was really, really scared.' He sounded on the brink of tears.

'I don't know what goes on in your head sometimes.'

'Neither,' he admitted.

'Okay, go and have a shower and get some clean clothes on.'

'I didn't bring any other clothes,' he said.

'You obviously haven't looked in your bag yet. Did you even brush your teeth – or just run the water? An old trick your dad used to pull.' She gave a little *hehe* laugh that sounded more like Homer Simpson than her but it got a weak smile. 'Off you go. Quick sticks. Then we can get some sleep.'

Elizabeth sealed his filthy clothes in a carrier bag and got him a glass of water. He came back from the shower smelling much better and got into bed, and she turned off the lamp. 'Goodnight, Zach. Sleep well.'

There was a long silence and then, 'You too.' Followed by something muffled that sounded like 'Nana'. And Elizabeth found herself grinning like a fool in the darkness.

22

heartbreaker

1971 'Troops home for Christmas,' says Gwen, glancing up from her newspaper. 'You'll have your boy back in no time.'

Lately, Lizzy's felt a little envious of Gwen and the certainty of her life. Every morning Gwen reads the paper over tea and toast, then she'll go down and collect the breakfast trays, potter around doing the dishes and gossiping with Rosa, who comes in to clean the rooms. In the afternoons, when the work is done, she'll lie on the sofa to read and smoke or have a friend over to play cards. This is Gwen's world, comfortable and predictable. Not in limbo like Lizzy's, as she waits on an uncertain future.

Lizzy picks up her handbag and heads out into the cool morning. She stands at the ferry wharf, watching the colour of the water change from grey to silver as the light clouds dissolve into a clear blue sky. She wonders what Ray will see when he wakes in a few hours' time: green paddy fields or dense jungle, or long dry grass littered with landmines. Every evening she watches the television news and tries to make sense of the images of soldiers trekking through dense jungles, and distressed Vietnamese people clutching armfuls of tattered belongings, their villages destroyed.

During his months of training, she and Ray lived from hope to hope: that he would serve his time on home ground, that he would be put into Signals rather than Infantry. But then he was allocated Infantry and sent to Canungra for jungle training – which everyone knew only meant one thing. He was shipped out to Vietnam on short notice without the chance to even come home and say goodbye. Now her only hope is that he comes home alive.

Ray's letters tell of unbearable humidity and mould that spreads like a virus through everything: clothes, books, food. They have to deal with mosquitoes, scorpions, leeches and ring-worm. Boredom and fear, and days of waiting, followed by the terror and chaos of contact with the enemy. He says the troops are burned out and drink to stay sane, and that neither the North or South Vietnamese want them there. No one seems to know what the point is any more. The war itself was lost long ago; all that remains is for America to admit defeat so they can all go home and get on with their lives. His early letters were full of his homesickness and the culture shock of adjusting to life in the camp at Nui Dat. But, as time passes, he writes less about his experiences and more about plans for their future when he comes home.

In years to come, her most vivid memory of that first summer will be lying on her narrow bed to watch the play of light on the white net curtains and listen to her radio, every song background music to her despair. She waits for a letter. She waits for Ray. Waits because she doesn't know what else to do.

In the end, Gwen shakes her out of her miasma. 'Listen, lovey,' she says one evening as they sit down to dinner. 'You can't spend your life waiting around for blokes. It's not healthy. While your fellow's away, do something useful to better yourself.'

'Like what?' asks Lizzy.

'Night school. Go and finish your schooling. Get your Higher School Certificate. Every woman needs an education.'

'Not according to Mum and Dad.'

'Don't take this the wrong way, Liz, but do you want to be a shopgirl forever? You're smart. You could go to university and get a degree.'

'A degree? In what?'

'Work that out when you get there,' says Gwen. 'First things first.'

With nothing to lose, Lizzy takes her advice and signs up for night school three evenings a week. There's no time to mope – weekends are taken up with study and assignments. Gwen offers to teach her to drive in her old Mercedes and they set out on Sunday mornings with Lizzy nervously behind the wheel.

During the holidays, Ginny comes up to Sydney for the weekend. They top and tail in Lizzy's bed and talk until the early hours. Bleary-eyed, they make the guest breakfasts together and spend Saturday roaming the botanical gardens and the city. As they walk through Hyde Park, Lizzy describes the odd but liberating experience she had there with her mother. As always, Ginny listens carefully and tries to understand the significance of the moment. 'I think that was an "out of body" experience,' she says. 'Sometimes when people nearly die, they see themselves from above. You saw yourself being free.'

'It takes a while to get used to being free,' admits Lizzy. 'Am I still in your parents' bad books?'

Ginny weighs the question up. 'Maybe a tiny bit but they were okay about me coming to stay. Mainly because you live with Aunty Gwen and they think she's a "stable influence".'

Lizzy laughs. 'They don't know Gwen, that's for sure.'

'What do you mean?' asks Ginny, her eyes bright with curiosity.

'Oh, she's not that bad but she drinks a lot. One night she had a few too many whiskeys and slid right off the sofa onto the floor, and the really funny part was she didn't even spill her drink, just continued talking.' Lizzy mimes Gwen slipping onto the floor with a moment of wide-eyed surprise and they laugh so much people turn to look, which makes them laugh more.

Lizzy is about to elaborate on Gwen's other nocturnal habits when she suddenly feels a little disloyal. She knows Gwen pops downstairs on the nights Mr McIntyre, a commercial traveller for a haberdashery firm, is staying. And Lizzy once came home early from night school and walked in on Gwen, flustered and pulling her clothes together, as Mr Cowell, the refrigeration salesman, rushed off down to his room. But Gwen has compromised her own privacy to accommodate Lizzy, and she doesn't want to repay that kindness with gossip.

On the Saturday evening, she and Ginny take the bus to a party at Paul's house in Newtown. He's been in touch since he and Ginny met the previous year, and she seems to think he shows promise. They weave their way through the crowded hallway of the house into a dark living room where people dance and sing along to Deep Purple's 'Black Night'. And then into the kitchen, which is packed with long-haired student types drinking bottles of beer and arguing about politics. Paul is nowhere to be seen. Lizzy wonders if they are even at the right party and already regrets coming.

A man with long dark hair and a white t-shirt leans in the doorway. He catches her eye and beckons her over. She ignores him and turns to Ginny. 'Let's just go.'

Ginny points out to the backyard where Paul can be seen talking to a young woman. It's obvious, even from a distance, that the two of them are in the midst of a heated argument. 'Let's get a drink,' Ginny says. 'See what happens. We'll give it an hour.'

Bottles of spirits sit on the kitchen bench. Lizzy finds some mugs in the cupboard and fills them from a bottle of Pimm's. They scull the first drink and take another one into the living room, where they dance together. Lizzy rarely drinks and the second one goes straight to her head. When Ginny takes their mugs for a refill, the man in the white t-shirt reappears and Lizzy finds herself dancing with him. He tries to catch her eye but she looks away and hopes he will lose interest.

Led Zeppelin's 'Heartbreaker' fills the room and it feels good to lose herself to the music. She closes her eyes. Her body moves without thought. The man's arms encircle her and his lips press on hers. She's not sure if this is real or her imagination. Did she secretly want to feel the intoxication of being desired? His tongue forces its way into her mouth. She tries to pull away. Then she's stumbling backwards as he pushes her against the wall and kisses her hard. The music that only moments ago made her feel wild and free sounds discordant and drowns out her cries.

Her arms pinned against the wall, she turns her head from side to side to avoid his hungry mouth. He changes position to hold her more firmly. She manages to free one leg and brings her knee up hard into his crotch. He lets go and she runs down the hall, pushes through the crowd and out onto the street.

People standing on the pavement turn to look. Someone asks if she's okay. She shakes her head, sits down in the gutter and tries to throw up but nothing comes. She desperately wants to go home. In a moment, Ginny appears and sits down in the gutter beside her. Lizzy bursts into tears and they sit together until it passes.

As they walk back to the bus stop, Ginny says, 'That was Paul's girlfriend.'

'Not for long, by the look of it,' says Lizzy with a sniff.

They grin at each other, and Ginny's face, gilded by the street light, is so comforting that Lizzy takes her arm. 'It's still early. Let's walk home.' Ginny agrees and they walk for hours through the city, and across the Harbour Bridge. They arrive home at midnight and squash into the narrow bed, falling straight into sleep.

Later in the year, Lizzie goes home for the long weekend. It's her first trip since she left eighteen months earlier and she's surprised at how ordinary it feels. She notices how shabby and uncared for the house is, and wonders if it was always like this.

The shop has seen some improvements with new shelving and display stands, and bunting looped across the ceiling that already looks limp, as though the party is long over. The best part about being home is that Doug has gone; he now lives in a share house with a couple of mates on the other side of town. But it's business as usual with her parents and she helps her mother with the shop cleaning on Saturday afternoon.

Her father seems pleased that she's continuing her education; her mother is more sceptical. 'You would have been better to go to secretarial school and learn a trade. Something useful,' she grumbles.

Her father agrees to lend her the delivery van to visit the Moncurs on Sunday afternoon. Lizzy puts in a big effort with her appearance for the visit. She wears a short brown corduroy pinafore with a black poloneck underneath and knee-high boots. She styles her hair now in a fashionable shaggy cut, carefully adds mascara to her lashes and pale pink to her lips. She would have preferred to arrive in style at the Moncurs' in Gwen's Mercedes. The delivery van with 'Clayton's Mini-mart' on the side doesn't have quite the same effect.

Ginny's waiting on the verandah when she arrives. 'I bet your folks will have you doing deliveries before you go.' She laughs as Lizzy walks up the front steps.

'Probably. Mum wants me to help her rearrange the fridge–freezer on Monday morning before I leave.' Lizzy stands at the front door and looks out over the green vines, birds flocking overhead, and feels a rush of affection that she will never feel for the house behind the shop.

As always, Mrs Moncur greets her charmingly and welcomes her back. If there is a little coolness beneath the surface, it soon begins to dissipate. There are scones with fresh cream and jam for afternoon tea, and they sit in the sunroom and chat like adults. Marty and Judith hang around, staring openly at Lizzy, but eventually they get bored and wander off.

'I was so pleased to hear you'd gone back to school, Lizzy. Very sensible,' says Mrs Moncur. 'Now, tell us all about the joys of living in the big city. It must be exciting being in the thick of things. And look at you, Lizzy, so mod and groovy!'

Lizzy talks about her studies and her new job as a filing clerk in the Department of Social Services. Mrs Moncur asks interested questions about the opportunities for advancement in the department. 'Lizzy, I know you're engaged and I see you have a pretty ring, but please don't be in a great rush to get married. When Ray comes back, let the dust settle. You will have been apart for some time and . . . you both will have changed. Life is longer than you think. You don't need to keep jumping out of windows. When the time is right, a door will open and you can simply walk through.' She laughs and lights a cigarette. 'Listen to me, quite the philosopher. It's just we're very fond of you, as is Ginny, of course. We don't want to see you get into anything . . .' She stops herself. 'Marriage is easier to get into than out of, that's all I'm trying to say.'

Lizzy nods. 'Thank you, Mrs Moncur. I will keep that in mind.'

Mrs Moncur laughs. 'You probably won't, but just remember there is a fine line between impulsive and reckless. Good to know where that line is. Ditto for you, Ginny. Oh, I can see you've both had enough of me now. Go on. You girls go off and share your secrets, I'll tidy up here.'

Upstairs, they lie on Ginny's bed and talk about the next year when she'll move to Sydney to start university, and when Ray will come home and life will start for real.

It's late afternoon by the time Lizzy leaves and, as she drives back towards town, she remembers the first time she rode her bike out to the Moncurs' and how afraid she was. She thinks carefully about Mrs Moncur's advice and, for the first time, feels a sense of trepidation about the future.

23

the man in overalls

As far as Elizabeth was aware, there was only one person who knew Ray's exact location, and that was Baz Ackland. It wasn't that Ray was hiding, he simply had no address. She knew he lived somewhere in the foothills of the Nightcap mountains and that the closest village, Wissam, was about forty minutes away.

Wissam was a tiny hamlet with a combined general store and post office. There was a sprinkling of shops on one side of the road and a public park and playground on the other. She had never actually been there but, in the last few years, had been able to explore the area with digital mapping. Online, she had traced the road through the village, flanked by lush farmland, and beyond into the dense rainforest of the foothills. But, after winding deeper into the countryside, the map petered out and left her stuck, scrolling back and forth, around and around.

Baz knew the location of the property because he owned it and had once lived there. He and Ray had served in Vietnam together but Baz had been sent home early after losing his right foot to a landmine. He'd bought a few acres of virgin rainforest and built a cabin. He lived there for a while and sold honey from his beehives and marijuana from his bush crop. But the isolated life didn't suit him, and he'd moved down to Lennox Head to take over his grandmother's farm, which he later inherited.

When the boys were young, Elizabeth and Ray had gone up to Lennox a couple of times a year, staying for long weekends and sometimes for New Year's. There were always children who ran wild while the adults sat around the fire pit eating home-grown lamb and drinking Baz's famous honey-fermented beer. He'd been an early adopter of permaculture and self-sufficiency and, for a while, the place had flourished. Later, when things became difficult for Ray, they stopped going altogether.

Now, as she drove slowly up the driveway of the Lennox farm, Elizabeth could see the place was neglected. Baz's clever improvisations, the waterwheel in the dam and the windmill that generated power, had both fallen apart. The house was shedding paint, the gutter was broken in one corner and the roof had started to collapse. It looked almost abandoned. But Baz's old cream-coloured Land Cruiser was parked outside, its paintwork cracked and streaked with rust, as though it were bleeding. Elizabeth pulled up and parked behind it.

Zach took out his earbuds and looked around uneasily. 'Creepy.'

'Creepy,' agreed Eric. 'Creepy go home loser.'

Zach pressed his lips together to hide his glee. Elizabeth glanced at herself in the mirror and wondered if this was an appropriate occasion to debut her new lipstick. 'Baz is a little . . . eccentric,' she said.

Zach yawned and stretched. 'Meaning?'

'You'll see,' said Elizabeth as she got out of the car.

The front door was wide open. She stepped inside and called out Baz's name a couple of times. The living room was a shambles: books, clothes, magazines, tools, building materials, bags of cement and a wheelbarrow full of bricks – all muddled together. There were animal droppings on the floor and a pungent odour filled the air, like a combination of mothballs and sour milk.

Zach stood in the doorway and examined the mess with interest. 'I can hear a TV,' he said. 'Out the back.'

Elizabeth heard it too. She called out again, louder this time, 'Baz! Hello?'

A sudden explosion rocked the house and dust showered down through cracks in the ceiling. She and Zach instinctively dropped to their knees. Zach crawled in behind the sofa and Elizabeth followed, passing Eric's cage to him. The floor was thick with dust and what looked like rat or mouse droppings, but Elizabeth hardly gave it a thought. They sat in the cramped space with their backs against the wall, knees bent and feet tucked under the sofa. 'What the hell?' asked Zach, clearly shaken. 'What the hell!'

'No idea,' said Elizabeth.

'Someone's coming,' he whispered.

Heavy, uneven footsteps advanced from the back of the house, accompanied by a tapping sound, like castanets. Elizabeth peeked out and saw a man who vaguely resembled Baz, with thin grey hair stretched across his head and tied in a wispy ponytail, and a dense, full beard, like a possum at his throat. He held a rifle in one hand and stood pressed against the doorframe, as if to avoid being someone else's target, while he scanned the terrain outside. He was joined a moment later by a grubby billy goat with large curved horns.

'Is that the guy?' Zach mouthed.

Elizabeth nodded, heart thudding in her chest. It was hard to believe that only minutes earlier her chief concern was whether the occasion warranted breaking out her new lipstick.

'Okay,' whispered Zach, taking command. 'Identify yourself and order him to lay down his weapon.'

Her words came out as a squeak. 'Baz. It's Liz. Ray's wife. Put the gun down, please.'

'Baz! Baz!' squawked Eric, helpfully. 'Liz! Liz!'

Baz looked around wildly, rifle at the ready. Suddenly he shouted, 'Who's there? Where are you? Where the fuck are you?! I know what you're doing. You can't fool me.'

The goat kicked up its hooves in a little dance of excitement, and shook its head from side to side as if looking forward to an opportunity to utilise its vicious horns.

'Put the gun down, Baz, please,' called Elizabeth, her voice calm but still several octaves higher than expected.

Baz held the gun at chest height and turned in a slow circle as his eyes scanned the room. Without another word, he spun around and walked back the way he'd come.

The goat stood on the doorstep and looked outside, then its head swivelled in their direction. It trotted over and stared behind the sofa with its flat yellow eyes. Extending its neck, it curled its lips back and began to nibble at Elizabeth's hair. She tried to push it away but it was not so easily dissuaded. 'Shoo! Shooo!'

'Be quiet,' whispered Zach. 'He'll hear you.'

'Zach, there's a goat eating my head,' she hissed. 'Take Eric and move along. Gimme some room.'

Zach did as he was told and shuffled further along the narrow space as the goat moved forward to get a better grip. Elizabeth leaned backwards, put her foot firmly on the goat's forehead and pushed as hard as she could. The goat pushed back, enjoying the game.

'Is that a good idea?' asked Zach.

'I don't know. It's just what I normally do when I'm stuck behind a sofa fighting off a goat. Got any better ideas?' She leaned right back on her elbows, put both feet on the goat's head and used all her strength. After a short tussle, it lost interest and backed away, its hooves tapping off into the distance.

'Now what?' asked Elizabeth.

'I dunno,' said Zach. 'You're always telling me you're in charge. Let's see what you got.'

'We could make a run for it. If we can get out the front door without being seen, and get to the car . . .' The plan already sounded risky. 'What do you think?'

'Reckon you could do a commando crawl?' asked Zach.

'I think so. I've done a plank before.'

'Cool . . . you won't get far with a plank.' He got on his knees and raised his head slowly to look over the back of the sofa.

'Oh, Zach, be careful,' Elizabeth whispered.

He ducked back down. 'I reckon he's camping.'

Elizabeth turned to him. 'What?'

'Yeah, just sitting there waiting for us. I see it on COD all the time. Loser tactic. He's gonna get a double kill. Head shot. What we need is a grenade launcher —'

'What are you talking about?' she hissed. 'You sound as crazy as him!'

'We could melt him right through that wall,' insisted Zach.

'Zach, I don't want to *melt* him. He's a family friend.'

The sound of Baz shuffling up the hall silenced them.

Elizabeth peered out from behind the sofa. Baz stood in the middle of the room with a steaming mug in each hand. 'Come out, come out, wherever you are!' He sounded more bemused than crazy now. 'Where the fuck are you? Eh?'

'I'm here, Baz.' Elizabeth crawled out and struggled to her feet.

'What are you doing down there, mate? I thought I was hearing voices from the great beyond. The great beyond!' he repeated, slopping tea on the floor.

Elizabeth dusted herself off. 'So you made hot drinks?'

He laughed. 'Tea solves everything! Good to see you, Liz! Welcome!'

'Baz, I heard what sounded like a shot out the back.'

'Oh, that was a mistake. I wake up suddenly and fire one off sometimes. Nothing personal. How long have you been in there?'

Zach emerged, holding Eric's cage. 'Baz, this is Zach, my grandson. Tom's boy,' said Elizabeth.

Baz's face lit up. 'The boy's the image of Ray, isn't he? Is he? My eyes are a bit stuffed. Bloody cataracts. But he looks good to me. Good-looking lad. He's got a touch of the Irish blood in him, I can see that much.' He handed Elizabeth a mug and fist-bumped Zach, who watched him carefully.

'Now, you, ol' girl. Give us a hug. It's been too long. Fucking years!' Baz put down his tea, opened his arms to Elizabeth and locked her in a tight embrace. Up close, he had a musky odour that reminded her of the pet mice the boys once kept. It was one unpleasant smell after another in this house. 'What a surprise!' He held her at arm's length. 'Lizzy, just as beautiful as ever. As ever!'

Elizabeth laughed. 'You better get those cataracts done, Baz.'

'And who is this little chap?' asked Baz, looking into Eric's cage. 'Little chap.'

The goat reappeared and Zach lifted the cage away from its curious lips. 'This is Uncle Eric,' said Zach.

'Head shot!' said Eric as he hopped around and fluffed his feathers anxiously. 'Head shot what the hell.'

'What's he saying?' asked Baz, peering at Eric. 'Did he say something?'

Elizabeth and Zach exchanged looks. 'Hedgehog, I think,' suggested Elizabeth.

'Hello, Eric! This is Vladimir,' said Baz and he gave the goat an affectionate rub. 'He's a Grand Duke, actually, but you can just call him Vladimir. He doesn't mind "Your Imperial Highness" but that's a bit of a mouthful. Come and sit down. What a treat! What a tremendous treat.'

He picked up a pile of newspapers from the sofa and tossed them in a corner, indicating with a flourish that they should sit. He sat down on a stack of magazines, then pulled one out from under him and showed Elizabeth the cover. '*The Economist*. Saving them until my eyes get fixed. Not that I plan to anytime soon, but . . .' He looked up at Zach. 'You're probably hungry, young fella. Have a fossick around the kitchen, see what you can find. Check in the freezer.'

Zach looked at Elizabeth. She gave him a nod. 'Don't touch the gun,' she said.

He looked slightly offended and wandered off towards the kitchen.

Vladimir stood, eyeing Elizabeth's hair with intent. 'Don't worry about Vlad,' Baz reassured her. 'He's a bit highly strung sometimes. Russian aristocracy, you know what they're like.'

'Not from personal experience, no,' said Elizabeth.

Zach reappeared and perched on the arm of the sofa.

'Find something?' asked Baz. 'Something? Anything?'

Zach shook his head. 'Not really hungry.' Elizabeth could only imagine the state of the kitchen if it didn't meet Zach's standards. He was *never* not hungry.

'Baz, I was wondering if you'd heard from Ray recently?' said Elizabeth.

'Depends what you call recently.' Baz couldn't take his eyes off Zach. 'Play football, young fella? You've got the looks for the Premier League. Or you a rugby man? Rugby man? AFL?' Elizabeth had forgotten Baz's irritating habit of asking questions without waiting for an answer or repeating a word or phrase like his own personal echo – a habit he shared with Eric, now she thought about it.

'Play soccer at school,' Zach admitted.

'Do you now? I've got a soccer ball here somewhere. We can have a kick around.' He put his tea down and got to his feet. To Elizabeth's surprise, Zach obediently followed him out the front door in search of a ball.

She was about to take a sip of tea when she noticed a foreign body, a small drowned cockroach, floating in it and quickly put the mug aside. She picked up a couple of magazines, noting both were years out of date, and wondered how long Baz had been putting off having his eyes fixed. Vladimir hadn't moved and his goaty smell wafted over her in nauseating waves. She picked up Eric's cage and went outside.

Zach and Baz came out of the utility shed chatting amiably, although she couldn't catch what they were saying. Baz held a deflated ball and a bike pump. There had been a standing joke about Baz that, regardless of how untidy the house was, he could still lay his hand on almost anything.

When they were both satisfied with the firmness of the ball, Baz kicked it high in the air with his prosthetic foot. Zach waited for it to bounce and land again, then trapped it with his foot. 'Nice work!' shouted Baz, scarlet with the effort. 'Nice work!'

Zach dribbled the ball around the patchy grass in front of the house and kicked it into the paddock. Despite his awkward lope, Baz dashed after it like an excited puppy.

'Don't make him run, Zach!' called Elizabeth. It was some years since she had done first-aid training and she began to go through the CPR steps in her head. But Baz still had some kick left in him, and next thing the ball flew past the house, bounced off the Land Cruiser, ricocheted off the shed with a loud bang and hit something in the high weeds that smashed like glass. Vladimir trotted over to investigate.

Baz limped back and sat panting on the front step. 'Sorry about the gun, Lizzy.'

'Why sleep with a gun? You're a danger to yourself, Baz. And the front door was wide open. If you're worried about intruders . . .'

'Door shut or open, doesn't matter, those bloody cats find a way. They're smarter than you think. Anyways, I don't sleep, just doze off occasionally. It's not getting better. If anything, it's getting worse.'

They watched Zach flick the ball from one foot to another.

'Hey, Lizzy, remember the old days?' said Baz. 'One big happy family. The kids. The parties. The conversations. The wine and weed nights. Lamb on the spit. Jeez, they were good times. I can taste that lamb now. Best times of my life. Happy days. Happy. Days.' He gave a shuddering sigh. 'How *is* Ray doing?'

'That's why we're here. We're going up to see if he's okay.'

'I don't think that's the answer, you know . . . going off on your own. Tried it. Hated it. Bloody miserable. Alone with your thoughts. Lot of old mates did it but, you know, we're social animals. We have to be with other people. Still, I don't see a soul from one month to the next here.'

'Why haven't you had your eyes done, Baz?'

He shrugged. 'Don't want to throw good money after bad. I'm stuck here anyway. Know my way around. I expect I'll wake up dead one day. No one will even know I've shuffled off. And you know what? I won't mind. I could speed up the process, but that can be messy. And I was brought up a Catholic, like Ray. Everlasting damnation is something I'd like to avoid, if at all possible.'

'But fixing your eyes could make all the difference . . .'

'Look at that boy. Takes me back. Good to see a young person. Full of life. Life, eh? What a lottery that turned out to be.'

'Baz, I need to know exactly where to find Ray,' Elizabeth interrupted.

'It's a fair way up in the hills. No signs to speak of. Dirt road. I can draw you a map. Don't rush off, mate. Bunk down here for the night. I'll make us a bite to eat. We can knock over a bottle of something. Bottle or two.' He gave her a wink.

Elizabeth had sensed this was coming. She felt sorry for Baz, but not enough to stay the night and eat from his kitchen. 'I think we need to keep going, thanks all the same. But how do you get around, Baz? Do you need me to get anything for you?'

'I can see, just not that clearly.' He gave a breathless laugh. 'Story of my life, hey? Like looking through a layer of plastic. Don't mind it actually. Bit frustrating sometimes. Getting to the supermarket is easy, reading packaging is not. You wouldn't even think about threading a needle. Anyway, nothing much to look at around here. Nothing I haven't seen a thousand times. You know, this place used to be freedom for me, now it's a prison. The loneliness, Jesus . . . it's like a physical pain.'

Elizabeth looked out over the empty paddocks. Tall straggly weeds had taken over long ago, the fences were falling down. The farm had once overlooked rolling green fields all the way to the ocean. Now the suburbs marched up from the coast and the treeless hillsides were dotted with beige and cream houses. Soon Baz would have neighbours. 'Is there anything we can do for you, Baz? Any needles you want threaded?'

Baz smiled. 'Thanks, mate. I'm right. Just having a whinge. Hang on, let me find some paper. I'll do you a map.'

He got up and went inside. Zach wandered in circles, thumbs working frantically on his phone while he dribbled the ball with his feet. Elizabeth envied his dexterity. 'Baz is going to draw a map, then we'll get going,' she called. Zach slipped the phone into his back pocket and walked over.

Baz came back with an old envelope and a stub of a pencil. He sat down on the step and put a cross on one corner of the paper. 'This is us here then, and then . . . hang on . . .' He turned the envelope around. 'This is north. Hold it. Where'd I put that cross?' He squinted at the ragged piece of paper. 'North?'

'If we head for Mullumbimby and then up to Wissam?' Elizabeth suggested. 'What happens after that?'

'How do you spell Mull . . . um . . .?' asked Zach, phone in his hand.

Elizabeth spelled it out for him. Baz combed his fingers through his beard thoughtfully as if teasing out the information. 'You go through the town. Towards the mountain. There's a few twists and turns. I can picture it . . . there's a big gum right on the turnoff . . . big gum . . . a ghost gum.'

Elizabeth was fast losing hope that they would get anything useful from this exercise. Zach located the village in Google maps and expanded the view but it was futile; there was no way Baz could see the detail. 'Look, don't worry,' said Elizabeth, getting up to leave. 'We'll head up there and ask around. Someone's bound to know him.'

Baz pulled a glum expression. 'I want to help, Liz. I really do.'

Elizabeth reassured him that it was fine. She gave him a brief hug and he grabbed Zach's hand and pumped it enthusiastically. 'Great to meet you, son. Come back anytime. Bring your dad. Tom came here a lot when he was a boy. We'll have another kick around. Kick around, eh? You, me and your dad.'

'Happy days!' added Eric and Baz laughed, wheezing like an old squeeze box.

As they drove away, Zach delivered his verdict: 'He's a kook. But kinda cool.'

'Glad you didn't melt him now?'

Zach weighed up his weaponry ambitions against the sacrifice of Baz. 'Debatable.'

As they left the farm, driving along country roads, golden afternoon light spilled down the paddocks. Clusters of trees cast shadows and there were small creek crossings from time to time. It was pleasant driving but Elizabeth had no plans to continue up to Wissam tonight – it was too late in the day. They would get a motel near the coast or in Mullumbimby and then head inland first thing.

Her mind drifted back to the years when they used to stay at the farm. Those people had been the closest thing that she and Ray had to a tribe. But, in the end, apart from their history, there was nothing to hold them together. They would talk about their comrades, the pranks and personalities, stories that sometimes sounded like memories of some terrible boarding school or prison. But under the surface, something darker was at work. Marriages began to collapse; there was one suicide after another. Ray felt there was too much suffering and he couldn't be around it any more. She tried to remember some of the people they knew back then, people they considered friends, but struggled to connect names to faces.

In the rear-view mirror, she noticed a vehicle coming up fast behind them. When she reached a passing lane, she pulled across to let it overtake. She heard the roar of a Land Cruiser in full throttle and glanced across to see Vladimir, head out the passenger window, giving her the dead eye, and Baz waving frantically from the driver's side.

'Oh, brother,' she said. 'Zach, take a look at this.'

Zach looked over and started laughing. 'What the hell?'

'What the hell what the hell!' came the cry from Eric in the back seat.

Baz shouted something but his words were lost to the noise of the engine. He pointed ahead like a man with a cavalry behind him.

'Are we following them now?' asked Zach.

Elizabeth sighed. 'Seems like we have a goat and a blind man leading the way.'

'Um . . . visually impaired, you mean.'

'Beg your pardon – visually impaired.'

'And what's the thing with the goat?' asked Zach. 'The Grand Duke and all that?'

'I have no idea,' said Elizabeth. 'And I daren't ask.'

Baz pulled into the next rest stop and Elizabeth parked beside him and got out. Vladimir flipped his front hooves out the open window in an attempt to escape but Baz hauled him back inside and wound the window up.

'Glad we caught you two!' Baz shouted, getting out of his vehicle. 'You three!' He came around to Elizabeth's car. He was now wearing a pair of grey and orange mechanic's overalls with 'Aston Martin Racing Team' printed across them.

'I gather it's no coincidence we're going in the same direction, Baz.'

'You'll need help, mate. You won't find him by looking. It's bloody bushy up there. You'll be lost in the ranges for weeks. They'll be sending in helicopters.'

At the mention of helicopters, Zach got out of the car and took an interest.

'Yes, I get the picture,' said Elizabeth. 'That's very kind, Baz, but . . . I'm not sure we need a whole deputation turning up —'

'He'll be happy to see me. Don't worry about that,' said Baz. 'Don't you worry.'

'You couldn't go and see him some other time?' This was not how Elizabeth had pictured the reunion, but she had to weigh that up against not finding Ray at all.

'The place is hidden away. I know because I hid it. I'm your man.'

'Do we really have to bring a goat along with us?'

Baz looked affronted. 'Come on, Liz. Don't be an old dragon. I can't leave Vlad alone at home. You brought a budgie.'

'Ouch, roasted,' commented Zach. 'Good point.'

Elizabeth conceded defeat. 'Okay, well, we're planning to get a motel tonight. We could go into Byron or —'

'Nahhh . . . they're a bunch of wankers down there. Rip-off merchants. Greenies, righties, lefties, hippies, capitalists, nihilists —'

'Nihilists?' asked Elizabeth. He made it sound like the beach resort was in the grip of an existential crisis. She took a deep breath. 'Okay. What do you suggest, Baz?'

'Just head on up to Wissam. It's only an hour to Ray's place from there. Plenty of spots to kip down. Won't be a problem. What do ya say, Zachy? Let's rock and roll, baby!'

Elizabeth looked at Zach. If she'd said something like that, he'd be disappearing into his hoodie with embarrassment but now his hoodie was sealed in a plastic bag, and he gave a cheerful shrug.

24

the horse blanket

By the time the two cars left the highway and turned inland towards the dark hills rising in the distance, the light had almost gone. The forest became dense and the road was empty apart from Baz leading the way. They drove on into the night, the road twisting and turning, and Elizabeth became increasingly nervous about where they would end up, wondering if they were already lost.

'Where's he taking us?' asked Zach. 'I'm starving.'

'What the hell,' agreed Eric. 'What the hell.'

'Do you think Eric actually understands everything we say?' asked Zach.

'To be honest, probably not. He is very clever but I think, to some degree, he picks up on intonation. Are you able to see where we are now?'

Zach glanced at his phone. 'No service. Might be okay higher up.'

Over the years, Elizabeth had occasionally daydreamed about living up here with Ray. She saw herself pottering around, adding feminine touches to a quaint, rustic shack. There she was in a straw hat and cotton frock, collecting fresh eggs from the hens and vegetables from the garden. But that was a fantasy and, now, as she drove through the blackness guided only by the beacon of Baz's rear lights, she was back to worrying whether Ray even wanted to see her – let alone the whole entourage.

Having explored Wissam online, arriving in the village was a little surreal, like being on the set of a familiar film. There were a couple of street lights in the village and she could see a few changes had taken place since the area was last updated online. The cafe looked newly painted and the cottage next door was now an eco shop, so perhaps the place attracted more visitors these days.

Baz pulled onto the gravel verge beside the park opposite the shops, which had public amenities, picnic tables and barbecues. Elizabeth swung her car around to face the opposite direction and lowered her window to speak to him.

'Je-sus,' shouted Baz. 'My night vision's *stuffed*. Couldn't see a thing towards the end. Just following my headlights.'

'Baz, there is nowhere to stay and nowhere to eat here. I knew this would happen.'

'And I'm hungry,' added Zach in a plaintive voice.

'Mate. I've got a swag or two in the back. And an esky. We'll be right. We're not going to make it up there tonight but we're close.' He gestured into the darkness beyond.

'We haven't eaten and we are not sleeping outside,' Elizabeth insisted.

'There's a restaurant open. Ten minutes,' said Zach, looking up from his phone.

'Okay, Baz – hop in with us,' ordered Elizabeth. 'We'll get

something to eat. And there might be accommodation as well. But no goat.'

Baz got out of his car with Vladimir on a chain and secured the goat to the front bumper of the Land Cruiser where he could reach a patch of grass to nibble on, and got in the back seat of Elizabeth's car.

'Baz, can I ask why you are wearing mechanic's overalls?' asked Elizabeth as they drove out of the village.

'Only clean thing I had in a hurry. Straight out of the packet. Very comfy, I have to say. I like 'em. I like 'em a lot. There's an idea. I could start my own clothing range. Everyone's doing it. What do you say, Zach? Want in? Build an empire? We could call it Bazack . . . Bazack Enterprises.'

'Don't Bunnings already sell those?' asked Zach.

'Or Zacbaz . . . Doesn't really roll off the tongue, does it?' Baz chattered on, outlining his plans to build an empire – all of which sounded ridiculous to Elizabeth. Zach was silent but she sensed that he found Baz quite entertaining.

The restaurant was an old pub beside a petrol station in the middle of nowhere, and surprisingly busy. There was the usual menu of fish and chips, steak and chips, and roast beef dinner. They ordered at the counter and were given a buzzer to take to their table.

The bar was crowded with men wearing hi-vis shirts and boots encrusted with clay. They held schooners of beer and had loud voices. In his work attire, Baz fitted in perfectly. He looked around with a grin. 'The joint's hopping. I'll have to come here more often. Hopping.'

'It's not exactly your local, Baz,' said Elizabeth. The place was noisy, but cosy too in a way. She put the cover over Eric's cage and slipped it under the table. Baz went to the bar, brought back a couple of schooners and put one in front of Elizabeth. 'Not for me, thanks, Baz. I'm driving.'

'One or two won't hurt. Lighten up, mate. A bevy will do you the world of good.'

'I'll have it,' offered Zach straight-faced.

Baz pushed it across the table to him. Elizabeth pushed it back. 'He's fifteen.' Baz winked at Zach, as if to make her the un-fun one, and she gave him a warning frown.

As they were finishing their meals, one of the hi-vis men sauntered over and asked Baz for a quick word. He got up and followed the man to the bar. After some discussion, the two of them went outside. Elizabeth began to wonder if Baz was still in the weed distribution business and they were about to get involved with the local drug cartel.

'What's he doing?' asked Zach, after a while.

'No idea,' said Elizabeth with a sigh. 'I better go and find out. Have a look at the desserts. I'll be back in a minute.'

She found Baz in the parking area with his head under the bonnet of an old Mustang, Hi-vis holding a torch for him. With Baz's poor vision, the engine must have been pitch dark but, with some authority, he asked the man to get in and start her up.

'Baz, what are you doing?' Elizabeth called.

'Hang on, Liz . . . Bit more juice, mate. Yeah . . . how does that sound now?'

Hi-vis got out of the car and seemed pleased. Baz dropped the bonnet and the two of them walked back into the pub together, chatting like old mates. Elizabeth followed them inside where Hi-vis gave Baz a few friendly slaps on the back and another schooner of beer.

'How could you fix his car if you can't see properly?' Elizabeth asked, when Baz sat back down at the table. 'Did you tell him you're not actually a mechanic?'

He laughed and held his hands up, pivoting them at the wrists as though they were sculptures on display. 'Hands of a surgeon. Nothing wrong with my hearing neither,' he added. 'I've been fixing cars for yonks.'

'What's a yonk?' asked Zach.

'It's a very long time,' explained Elizabeth. 'So, what's the plan? We'll have to go and find a motel.'

'Lizzy, no need,' said Baz. 'I've got all sorts in my Cruiser. Bits of this and that. We'll make it work. No need to start throwing money at it. Sleep under the stars. Happy days.'

The idea of sleeping under the stars, in something that Baz kept in the back of his car, did not appeal and Elizabeth was about to insist, when Zach said, 'Cool.'

Nevertheless, she asked at the bar if they rented rooms and was told that the upstairs rooms were used for storage these days. Even sleeping in a storage room was preferable to sleeping outside, but she resigned herself to bunking down in her car.

They arrived back at the carpark to find Vladimir standing on the bonnet of the Land Cruiser, bleating pitifully. Baz ignored the goat's imperious complaints and, by the light of a torch, pawed through the bits and pieces that were strewn throughout his vehicle.

To Elizabeth it looked like a drug-runners cache, ready for any eventuality on land or sea, but it was probably just an accumulation of years of stuff that he'd never got around to taking out. He located a couple of old swags, slung one at Zach and offered the other to Elizabeth. Or, as an alternative, a filthy-looking horse blanket, which she reluctantly accepted. The park was fairly well lit and had toilets, so at least she wouldn't have to pee behind a bush.

Zach had spent this time untangling Vladimir and getting him down off the bonnet of the Cruiser. When he tried to lead the goat to the tap in front of the amenities block, Vladimir ungratefully began to butt him. Zach grabbed hold of the two curved horns as though they were handles and ended up walking backwards as the goat rocked its head from side to side to shake him off.

'Baz! For God's sake,' said Elizabeth. 'That goat's dangerous – do something!'

Baz glanced up from his endeavours and called out, 'Don't let him pin you down, mate. He's in a playful mood. Give him something to distract him. A snack. Any little morsel.'

'Like what?' shouted Zach. He let go and grabbed the branch of a tree, swinging his legs up and out of the way of Vladimir's horns.

'Anything will do. He likes cigarettes, cheese . . .'

'I don't have a cigarette,' said Zach. 'Or cheese!' He hooked his leg over a branch and pulled himself to safety. Vladimir's hooves were planted on the trunk of the tree and the goat stared up at Zach longingly. 'I hope he can't climb trees,' said Zach.

'Don't you have a carrot in there somewhere, Baz?' asked Elizabeth.

'I have a lot of shit in here but not a carrot, I'm afraid. Hang on . . .' He rummaged into his belongings and, after a moment, found a crushed straw hat. 'I'll sacrifice this,' he said and hurled it like a frisbee towards Vladimir, who quickly abandoned Zach and skipped over to inspect it.

Elizabeth was exhausted and desperately wanted to lie down. After some discussion, Baz chained Vladimir up to a tree for the night, and he and Zach found a grassy patch in the park and laid their swags down.

Elizabeth moved Zach's surfboard to one side, lowered the back seats of her hatchback and spread the horse blanket out as a mattress. She put on another layer of clothes, added some extra padding around Eric's cage and settled down on top of the prickly blanket. One thing she knew for certain, it was going to take a lot more than a slash of 'Sugar Plum' to make her look decent in the morning.

'Happy days,' said Eric with a wheezy chuckle.

25

the homecoming

1972 'He's on the grog, you know,' says Gwen. 'While you're at work all day, that's what he does. Sits around and drinks. I never see hide nor hair of him.'

Lizzy pulls the tray of toast out from under the grill and flips each piece over, burning her fingers as she does every day. 'So how do you know then?'

'I know a closet drinker when I see one. Coming back from the shop with a bottle under his jacket. He's all day in your room, then doesn't even want to come upstairs for dinner. Pass me those plates, Liz.' With an expert touch, Gwen slides bacon and eggs onto the plates. She adds a spoonful of baked beans from a pot simmering on the stove and a few slices of fried black pudding for Mr McIntyre.

Lizzy adds two slices of toast and pops metal covers on the plates to keep them warm. She silently fills the small teapots with boiling water. She doesn't know what to say. Gwen means well but it doesn't feel right to talk about Ray behind his back. 'We'll find our own place soon,' she says. 'When he gets a job.'

'Lizzy dear, I'm not trying to get rid of you. I feel for the boy but I can't see him getting a job when he hardly leaves the house. That fellow, Paul, has rung a couple of times. I buzzed your room but Ray doesn't pick up. You need to get him to a doctor. They're handing out Valium for a lot less. It's not just for neurotic housewives, you know – his nerves are in shreds. He's like a cat up the curtains and I can't see him coming down without some proper help.'

Lizzy knows she's right, and there are other things as well, things Gwen doesn't know anything about. Ray has gut problems that send him dashing to the bathroom; he has inflamed, itching rashes in his armpits and groin that Lizzy dabs tenderly with calamine lotion every evening. He won't see a doctor, and she knows it's because he's afraid it may be something serious he's not ready to face.

Ray arrived on a midnight flight and she was at the airport to meet him. In those first moments in each other's arms, they wept with joy and relief. His letters had been full of glorious plans for their future and sweet declarations of love, but now he's distant and withdrawn, and irritable in a way he never was before. It's as if there's a current running through him; he snaps and sparks at every little thing, and his eyes are clouded with uncertainty.

Gwen has given them one of the guestrooms until they find a place of their own. It's a spacious room with a double bed, a wardrobe and an armchair. It has large sash windows with a view across the harbour to the city.

Gwen dubbed it the honeymoon suite, but Ray's first week home has been far from a honeymoon. The kisses and caresses and late-night murmurings that Lizzy had dreamed about have been absent. He's been reluctant to even touch her and slept the first few nights in the armchair, afraid he might lash out at her in the night. He barely sleeps, and when he does, sometimes wakes with a shout of terror. He says he's afraid to close his eyes. If she wakes and finds him gone, he's usually in the back garden. Standing quite still, the only movement the glow of his cigarette, he cuts a lonely figure. Some days he spends hours lying in the bath smoking, not seeming to care as the water slowly goes cold.

The dawn brings him rest, and he's asleep when Lizzy leaves for work. When she gets home, he's there in the bedroom, leaning on the sill of the open window as he smokes and gazes out towards the city. Like an old man, she thinks, dreaming about the life he once had when this city was his domain. An old man in the body of a 22-year-old.

In all their time together, they have rarely disagreed, each generously deferring to the other, but now Lizzy feels she can't do anything right. He complains about her clothes flung on the floor, the damp towel on the door handle, the mess of cosmetics on the dresser. Disorder rattles him, and she struggles to keep up with these changes and understand his need for order.

When he shouts at her one evening for accidentally banging the bedroom door, she bursts into tears and he puts his arms around her, apologising over and over. They sit down on the bed together, his arm tight around her shoulders. 'I just need time, Lizzy. It's much harder than I thought. It's like I've been to hell and dropped back on earth but I'm not really here. I'm stuck somewhere in between. I can't explain what it's like . . .'

'I want to help you,' she says. 'Ages ago, you talked about writing something, for the paper. You could show what it's really like there —'

Even as she speaks, he's shaking his head. 'I don't even want to think about it. Even if I did – if I could write the truth – no one would believe it.' He gives a bitter laugh. 'The government probably wouldn't allow it.'

He gets up off the bed and paces the room restlessly. 'They want us to believe there was a point to it all. There wasn't. There was no point. We went into a country and helped the Yanks slaughter people – for what? Our blokes died for absolutely no reason . . . thousands of Americans died for no reason and Vietnamese, old people, women, kids . . . hundreds of thousands of people died.' He sits down in the armchair and reaches for his packet of cigarettes. She notices how his hands shake as he lights one. He exhales in a defeated sigh. 'You're always asking me what it was like, Lizzy, and I'm never going to tell you because you don't need to know.'

'But . . . it might help you, Ray,' she says. 'I want to share it with you. You don't have to be strong and deal with everything on your own. I want to understand.'

He pauses, thinking. 'In films, someone gets shot and falls down dead with a puddle of blood on the ground. It's nothing like that. Mines are full of bits of metal. They blow bodies apart – mates who you've lived side by side with for months. You've seen the photos of their mum and letters from their girl and now they're nothing, if you didn't drag what's left of them out of the jungle . . .' He stops himself to take a few breaths. '. . . and that's not the worst of it.'

'People have different experiences,' he continues. 'Some guys had no contact with the enemy – they have to put up with the heat and boredom, and the deafening sound of artillery. It's just the luck of the draw. But from the first time you have contact, the fear never leaves you. The whole time I was there, I was absolutely terrified. I've seen tough men, experienced regular army, just bawling with terror. I saw a soldier start screaming – just out of the blue – on and on. He couldn't stop himself. They had to take him away. You're trapped in hell and there's no escape. You have to make yourself numb to everything. Or you'll start screaming . . . and you won't stop.'

His face is contorted with pain and Lizzy sees something wild and unpredictable in him, as if he could run from this room and keep on running and never come back. But he doesn't. He drops to his knees in front of her and gazes up into her face. 'You keep asking me if I'm happy to be home, Lizzy. I don't know. I don't feel anything. I've forgotten how.'

He lays his head in her lap and she folds herself over him. As she strokes his back, she feels some of the tension ease from his body. He lifts his head, takes her face gently in his hands and, for the first time since he's been home, kisses her in a long sweet kiss that she will remember forever.

Lizzy thought Ray would be keen to resume normal life as quickly as possible and make up for lost time. He'd been in line for a cadetship, the first step towards his long-held ambition to be a journalist. But he hasn't been into the office or even contacted anyone from the paper. He says the cadetship will be long gone and he's probably too old anyway. She's sure that's not true and suggests they meet Paul and Ginny for a meal. Ray agrees reluctantly but then puts it off and cancels at the last minute. She wants to look for a flat, so they can move out of Gwen's, but he makes excuses and puts that off as well. He doesn't want to go anywhere or do anything. It's now three weeks since he came home and he hasn't been to see his father and Cynthia. He talks about wanting to see Andy, and she knows he means it, but still he doesn't go.

She feels awkward about staying so long with Gwen. The offer of the room was only for a week or so. 'If you want to stay longer, you can pay me some rent,' says Gwen one evening. 'Just what you can afford, love.'

'Thanks. I'll talk to Ray,' says Lizzy. 'See what he thinks.'

'You can't expect him to make these decisions any more, Liz. He doesn't have the wherewithal.' Gwen gives her a long look. 'Just sit down here for a moment. I want to talk to you.' Lizzy does as she's told, worried about what's coming next.

Gwen pours her a glass of sherry and she takes a sip; it's thick and sweet in her mouth and she feels a bit sick.

'I don't want to have to say this, Liz, but there's no one else to do it. Think about what you're getting into if you marry this boy. Ray's handsome and smart, and I'm sure he's decent but . . . war changes men. I was twelve when our dad went off to the war. He was a decent man, but he fought in New Guinea and whatever happened to him there turned him into a monster. When he was on a bender, Mum and us two girls would have to barricade ourselves in the bedroom. I remember to this day the sound of things smashing against the other side of the door. If he got hold of you, he'd take off his belt and lay into you. It only stopped when he got really sick and couldn't drink any more.'

Lizzy remembers her grandfather giving her and Doug each a shilling and a pat on the head when they visited him in the nursing home. Her mother may have hinted that he was 'difficult' but this is the first she's ever heard about him being violent. 'Mum's never mentioned anything about that.'

'No. We don't talk about it, even among ourselves. I suppose we're ashamed.'

'Anyway, Ray would never be like that. He's gentle and kind —'

'I reckon they're the ones who get hit the hardest, the sensitive ones,' says Gwen. 'Don't cope with it. Whatever happens to these chaps, it's unimaginable. Soul destroying. You need to decide if you want to deal with that, because it's not going to magically go away.'

'I do,' says Lizzy. 'I can.'

Two days later, she comes home to find him sitting on the bed, his bag packed. He's waiting to say goodbye. He explains that he's going to a mate's place up the coast at Lennox Head. 'Lizzy, you need a break. I need a break. Just for a week or two. I'll try and get my head together. I'll be back soon.'

She tells him that she understands, because she wants to be understanding. She kisses him goodbye and watches him walk down the street to the station. The lightness in his step brings tears to her eyes. It hurts that his spirits have been lifted by the prospect of going away when he's only just arrived home.

Ginny and Paul come to see her at Gwen's place. Together, they walk down to the park in Lavender Bay and sit on the grass to look out over the harbour. It's a view that Lizzy never tires of seeing. The bridge forms a great arch across the water, Luna Park on one side and the city on the other, with the cranes of the Opera House construction just visible beneath the bridge. There's a sharp autumn breeze off the water and Lizzy pulls her jacket around her miserably. She explains that Ray has gone up north for a break but she can see Ginny and Paul are puzzled by his behaviour. She makes excuses. She doesn't know what else to say.

'Is he still having trouble settling in?' asks Ginny. 'Can't be easy.'

'And people are very anti-war now,' says Paul. 'It's rough for our boys coming home and being called murderers and baby-killers. It's not as if Ray wanted to go in the first place.'

'Ray doesn't say much about it,' says Lizzy. 'He gets annoyed with the stuff on television, I know that. One of the guests at Gwen's asked if he killed anyone over there.'

'That's disgraceful,' says Ginny, shocked. 'How awful for him.'

'Curiosity,' says Paul. 'That's human nature for you.'

'No, that's terrible. How did Ray cope?' asks Ginny.

'Not very well,' says Lizzy. 'He's fed up with everyone having an opinion about Vietnam when they don't know what they're talking about – even the newspapers.'

Paul nods. 'He's right about that. The Americans have controlled most of the information that came out of there. But now, people have started to realise what's really been going on and it's changed their attitudes. That's the only reason we're withdrawing our troops.'

Lizzy wishes that Ray could talk to Paul: he's always so sensible and understands the politics behind it all. He and Ray often had long, sometimes heated, discussions about these topics. It was the basis of their friendship but Paul's understanding is theoretical, and he doesn't know what Ray's been through or how he's suffering.

Ginny gives her a sympathetic smile. 'Have you set a date yet?'

Lizzy shakes her head. In his letters, Ray was keen to get married as soon as he got back but he hasn't mentioned it and nothing is certain at this point.

'He'll come right, Lizzy. It would be too much to expect for him to just fit back into his old life. He must feel quite lost,' says Ginny.

That night, Lizzy goes over and over the conversation. She realises that Ginny is right. Ray is completely lost and he's not going to find his way alone. Someone needs to guide him back into the world, and that person can only be Lizzy.

A week later, Ray calls and asks her to post his heavy jacket to him. It's colder up the coast than he anticipated. She doesn't ask when he's coming back and he doesn't make any promises. A few days later, Paul rings her to say there could be something at the paper for Ray, and when he gets back, he needs to come and talk to the boss.

Lizzy takes the bus to Paddington in her lunch hour. As she walks along the backstreets to their old flat, she experiences the sort of nostalgia that she imagines old people feel revisiting a place where they were happy in their youth. The time that she and Ray had here is already a sweet and distant memory.

Mr Geddes sits at his desk as if he's never left, his brown suit a little tighter than when she last saw him. He looks up when Lizzy walks into the showroom and grins. 'Got your licence, have you, little lady?'

Lizzy nods. 'I can't afford any of these cars though.'

'Just dropped in to see me, did you? That's nice.'

A middle-aged woman wearing a business suit bedecked with gold chains appears from the back room, carrying a stack of brochures.

'This is my wife,' Mr Geddes says. 'Marge, this is the old tenant from the top flat.'

Mrs Geddes gives Lizzy a brief smile and turns away to restock a brochure stand.

'The boyfriend had his number come up, poor beggar,' Mr Geddes continues. 'Did he end up going off to fight the gooks?'

Lizzy nods. 'He's back now and we're looking for a flat. I was just wondering if one of the upstairs flats is available?'

'They both have tenants but we could kick one of them out,' suggests Mr Geddes.

'We are not kicking anyone out,' says Mrs Geddes without turning around.

'This boy's been off to fight for his country. Fly the flag, Marge.'

'Don't worry,' says Lizzy. 'Thanks anyway.'

'Hang on,' says Mr Geddes. 'What about Denison Street? That's coming up next week.'

'It's more expensive,' says Mrs Geddes. She stops fiddling with the brochures and looks at Lizzy with more interest. 'It's a proper one-bedder with a little garden. Forty dollars a week.'

Lizzy hesitates. That's almost her entire wage and she would have to dip into their savings until Ray found a job. Mr Geddes hauls himself out of his seat. 'How about this? We do it at the same price as upstairs for the first couple of months, then the full rent. Get you kids back on your feet.' He turns to his wife. 'Good tenants. Patriots. What do you say?'

Mrs Geddes gives him an exasperated look. 'What am I supposed to say?'

The flat is a pleasant surprise. On the ground floor of a terraced house with two rooms, it has a proper kitchen, basic furniture and a small back garden – everything they need.

Lizzy pays the first week's rent and withdraws two hundred dollars from their joint account to buy a 1965 Ford Falcon she sees parked on the street with a sign in the window. A week later, she moves all their belongings from Gwen's place into their new home.

First light Saturday morning, she sets off to drive to Lennox Head ten hours away. She knows there will be difficult times ahead for her and Ray. Over the past weeks she's become aware that there are many things Ray struggles with now: crowds, noise, planes, enclosed spaces, darkness. No doubt there will be more but she vows to make Ray's world a place he can live in.

In years to come, Ray will often recount the story. He had begun to realise that moving forward was impossible for him. He didn't know how to start and had lost his ability to make all but the smallest decisions for himself. He had lost faith in himself and, at a time when he felt both worthless and useless, Lizzy had driven all that way in the hope of taking him home.

26

into the wild

Elizabeth tried to get comfortable in the back of her car. If she scrunched her knees up, they soon began to ache, but to straighten both legs, her feet had to be on either side of the front seat – inelegant and still not comfortable. After a restless night, she was woken by Eric imitating the pub buzzer and sat up suddenly, clipping her head on the interior light.

She wiped the condensation off the window and peered out. In the dawn light, her travelling companions looked like untidy mounds of earth dumped in the park. The goat had slipped his collar and, noticing movement in the car, came over to press his pink nose and lips moistly against the back window. To escape Vladimir's hooded gaze, Elizabeth curled up on the horse blanket and listed the discomforts of the night for Eric's benefit. 'All in all, one long nightmare,' she concluded. 'As I knew it would be.'

Eric listened and babbled cheerfully, pleased to have her undivided attention. When she had finished complaining, his patience was rewarded with some spinach leaves and a couple of grapes. She cleaned his water container and refilled it from her bottle, pulled on her jacket and crawled out of the car. The sun was a pale wash across the fields and the air fragrant with the smell of eucalyptus.

Zach was tucked up in his swag with his hoodie, retrieved from its plastic bag and still filthy, now pulled up over his head. Nearby, Baz snored creakily. His ponytail lay curled across his cheek like a limp strand of seaweed. He looked old and frail, and Elizabeth resolved to be more patient with him today.

She used the public toilet, washed her face and changed her clothes. There was no mirror so she was spared the finer details. When she came out, Baz was up and already dressed, having slept in his mechanic's overalls. Just another example of the outfit's versatility, he explained. He got his esky from the Land Cruiser and dumped it on one of the picnic tables.

'Chucked all this stuff in from the freezer. Just need to work out what's what and who's who in the hood.' He took out various plastic-wrapped pieces of meat and stared at them before putting them aside.

Elizabeth picked one up and inspected it. 'Looks like a rabbit.' It occurred to her that it could just as easily be one of the feral cats Baz had complained about earlier. 'Let's not have rabbit for breakfast,' she suggested.

'We'll keep that out. We could do that in a stew tonight. See anything that looks like bacon? Sausages?'

'The cafe will be open soon,' said Elizabeth as she surveyed the unappetising frozen lumps of meat.

'We don't want to waste money on triple-baked, fermented . . . activated avocado and goji berry muesli. This is good simple fare we've got here. Protein.'

Resigned to doing things Baz's way, Elizabeth peeled back the plastic on one of the packages and handed it to him. 'This one looks like bacon.'

'Good, just chuck that on the barbecue. I've got a few eggs here somewhere.'

The smell of food roused Zach from his slumber. Drawn towards the hotplate, he stood yawning as he watched the bacon bubble in its own juices. Baz threw some frozen slices of bread and some eggs on to complete the meal.

When everything was done, they clamped it all between slices of fried bread and ate with their hands. To Elizabeth, the food tasted of everything that had ever been cooked on the hotplate, and she hoped her stomach would cope.

Baz reassured them that he knew exactly where to go from here and, when breakfast was done, they packed up the cars and set off towards the mountains. As they drove, Zach stared out the window at the fields dappled with sunlight and dotted with grazing cows and reported gloomily: 'There's nothing here but trees . . .' He scanned the landscape for something else worthy of his disdain. '. . . and grass.'

Elizabeth nodded. She wasn't really in the mood to chat, distracted by the thought that very soon she would see Ray. Now it was absolutely imminent, she was worried about what they might find and questioning the wisdom of the entire operation. Her gut churned with anxiety, or possibly the early symptoms of food poisoning.

The farmland was left behind as the road snaked upwards, deeper into the forest. Soon they were driving along the spine of a ridge with trees either side growing up from steep ravines. The road was narrow with ditches on both sides and a sheer drop beyond them. Elizabeth kept her eyes straight ahead, not daring to look down.

Once they had crossed the ridge, the land widened again and they were surrounded by dense rainforest. The road came to a dead end with three options of dirt tracks leading into the bush. One clearly led to a communal property marked by a ragged collection of home-hewn letterboxes on posts, and the other two tracks were unmarked. Baz paused for a moment and then set off confidently up one of these tracks, Elizabeth following behind.

After a while, they came to a large, cleared area with a good-sized house and various outbuildings. Not at all what Elizabeth had envisioned. A woman with hennaed hair almost to her waist was out working in the garden. She straightened up and stared as the two cars pulled up.

Baz got out of the Cruiser and came over to Elizabeth's window. 'Sorry, I've led us astray. Came up the wrong track,' he said. 'Gimme a minute. I'll just say a quick hello.'

He went over to the woman, who threw up her arms in delighted recognition. They embraced and launched into an animated conversation. Elizabeth began to suspect this wasn't an accidental detour at all but an impulsive decision on Baz's part.

'What is going on?' asked Zach, lolling against the window. 'Who is she?'

'I don't know.' After ten minutes or so, Elizabeth got out and walked over just in time to hear Baz say that he would be happy to take a look and suggest it could be the timing chain, presumably referring to the woman's old ute parked nearby.

'This your wife?' asked the woman with a smile as Elizabeth joined them.

'Nah. Ray's missus,' Baz told her. 'Liz. Susie.'

Elizabeth said hello but didn't offer to shake Susie's hand, which was covered in soil. She was older than she looked from a distance but had a strong, attractive face. Baz obviously thought so too, the way he beamed at her delightedly.

'Ray's missus,' repeated Susie. She glanced past Elizabeth to the car. 'Who's the kid then?'

'Our grandson, Zach,' said Elizabeth. 'We're on our way to see Ray now.'

'I've been away for a couple of months up in the Territory, painting. Only just got back, so I haven't seen him. He okay?' she asked.

'That's what we plan to find out,' said Elizabeth, turning to Baz with a meaningful look.

'I'm just going to take a quick look at Susie's starter motor,' said Baz. 'Then we'll shoot off.'

'Now?' asked Elizabeth. 'Baz, come on, can't it wait?'

'Well, I'm here now,' said Baz. 'May as well.'

'Okay, fine. But we'll go on ahead and see you there.'

'Bazzy, you get on your way, babe. We can catch up while you're here. And say hello to Ray for me. I should've checked on him when I got back. I feel bad now.'

Baz agreed somewhat reluctantly, and they got back in their respective vehicles and set off towards the road, where Baz made a tight turn into the second unmarked track. This one led more directly into the foothills and was thickly forested on either side of the track, apart from the occasional clearing full of sunlight and morning mist.

'Zach, look,' said Elizabeth. 'Wallabies.'

Three large wallabies and several smaller ones paused and stared at them. Zach looked at them for a moment. 'How can people live out here?' He glanced at his phone. 'No service.' His head slumped in a gesture of despair.

The unsealed road was in a poor state, forcing them to slow down to a crawl as they bumped along. They climbed uphill over ruts like judder bars that made the car rattle and shake. In other places the ground was so uneven that it was more like driving on a creek bed than a road. Baz's vehicle was better suited to the terrain but the Cruiser still rocked from side to side with Vladimir bobbing around in the back.

'How much further?' asked Zach.

'I have no idea. I haven't been here before, you know that.'

Hunched over the steering wheel, Elizabeth concentrated on the track and making sure nothing got ripped off the underside of the car. Even so, she became aware that Zach was staring at her. 'What?'

'You're quite small really,' he said.

'That's because I'm sitting down. I'm taller standing up.'

'No, really. How tall are you?'

'I don't know. Five two. Something like that.'

'Meaning?'

'Feet. Five foot two inches,' said Elizabeth as she slowed to navigate around a deep fissure in the track.

'We don't have feet any more, not since . . .' He looked at the useless phone in his hand and sighed.

'1974,' offered Elizabeth.

'Anyway, you're small,' he concluded.

'Okay, I'm glad we settled that . . . Surely it can't be much further.'

After some thought, he said, 'You should be called Nano, not Nana.'

'I'm not actually called Nana. I have my own name, but fine.'

She'd been trying to engage him in conversation for weeks without success, and now, when she was almost sick with nerves, he'd finally found a topic he wanted to explore.

'Do I have to meet him?' he asked.

Elizabeth glanced over at him. 'Are you nervous?'

He shrugged. 'Dunno. You?'

'Yes. Yes, I'm very nervous, Zach. I haven't seen him for thirty years.'

'That's like twice as long as I've been alive. Are you even going to recognise him?'

Elizabeth shrugged. 'And will he recognise me?'

She felt the weight of Zach's hand rest for a moment on the top of her head in a consoling pat. The prince's blessing. It was only a moment but her head retained the warmth of his touch long after it had gone, and it was more comforting than she could have imagined.

Up ahead, Baz stopped and they pulled up behind him. When she got out, Elizabeth could see that the main track ended here. Now it seemed they would continue on foot.

Zach peered through the windscreen. 'Do I have to come? We can stay here.' He nodded towards Eric's cage. 'Eh, li'l buddy?'

'Nightmare,' agreed Eric. 'Nightmare.'

'Zach, you're one of the main reasons we're here,' said Elizabeth.

He turned to stare at her. 'Definitely debatable.' But he opened the door and got out.

'Tuck your jeans into your socks, Zach.' Elizabeth found some insecticide spray in the door pocket and passed it to him.

'Give yourself a good spray with this, especially around your lower half.'

'Why?'

By now she recognised that mutinous expression and decided not to mention there would be not only mosquitoes, but ticks and leeches. 'Just a precaution. Little insects, mozzies and things.' She gave him an encouraging smile and got a mistrustful look in return. As she fetched Eric's cage, she glanced around for Ray's car but couldn't see it.

The air was warm and alive with bird calls. Elizabeth was glad they were here in the spring; the summer humidity would be almost unbearable. Baz got out of his car with Vladimir on a chain. He stood for a moment and stared at Elizabeth as if trying to read her thoughts. 'You ready for this, mate?'

27

the cabin

All these years and all this way, Elizabeth had never felt less pre-pared. Her heart thumped wildly in her chest and she could feel her pulse throb through her hands and feet. She had waited so long for this without truly being aware that she was waiting. It was no longer something she could idly daydream about. She was facing the reality of Ray's life and Ray himself. She had no idea what to expect, what sort of state he might be in. Her great-est fear had always been that he could die here alone. As she set off up the path, the full intent of Ginny's letter came home to her: the need to finalise things with Ray, however that played out, and she drew strength from Ginny's wise counsel.

Carrying Eric's cage, she followed Baz, Vladimir and Zach up the dirt track. They walked for about ten minutes until they came to a clearing with a jumble of buildings, not quite as pic-turesque as she'd imagined. There was a rough, hand-built cabin with a deck out the front and a rusting corrugated iron roof. There was a sizeable vegetable garden enclosed in wire netting and, behind it, a covered area like a workshop with a workbench, tools, pieces of timber and a number of blue plastic barrels, presumably for safe storage. But no signs of life.

Baz shouted Ray's name but nothing came back apart from the chime of bellbirds and the distinctive cry of a whipbird. The door into the cabin had a flyscreen but it wasn't locked and, with some trepidation, Elizabeth stepped inside. It was one room, sparsely furnished with a basic kitchen, the shelves above the sink neatly stacked with plates and cups hanging on hooks. Along one wall, a bookshelf packed full of books, a pot-belly wood stove in the corner and, at the far end, a bed, neatly made with a quilt. Everything in its place.

She picked up a shirt that hung on the back of a kitchen chair and brought it to her face. Every fibre smelled of Ray.

'What are you doing?'

She turned to find Zach standing in the doorway. 'Just . . . seeing if it was Ray's,' she said, guiltily tossing the shirt back onto the chair.

'Oh. I thought you were blowing your nose. That would be weird,' he said.

'I agree. It would. Doesn't look like he's here at the moment.'

Zach stalked around, carefully assessing the place.

'What do you think?' asked Elizabeth.

'What?' he asked.

She gestured, arms open wide. 'The place.'

'Oh, I was looking for a modem.' He glanced around again. 'Kinda cool. So, are we going?'

'We've barely been here five minutes, Zach.'

'But if he's not here . . .'

Elizabeth handed him Eric's cage. 'Take your buddy outside so he can get some fresh air. I'll be out in a minute.'

When he'd gone, she walked around the room. Everything was old and worn, from the bedding to the furnishings. It was neat and spartan, like the home of a monk. There were a couple of framed photos on the wall, one of her and Ray at their school formal and another of a family picnic held for Tom's tenth birthday. They looked like a normal happy family, and she remembered it as a happy day. On the bookshelf were a few books on Shackleton and his expeditions, some novels: Hunter S Thompson, Hemingway, and Joan Didion, a book called *Self-reliance* by Emerson and Thoreau's *Walden* and half-a-dozen books about permaculture, bird species and the history of the area.

She went back out onto the deck, which was almost as big as the cabin itself, and stood for a moment, taking in the view that met Ray every morning. After the dim interior, the green of the rainforest was dazzling. Beyond the clearing the trees became tall and dense, with long loops of vines slung from one to the other like ropes. There were clusters of large rocks and boulders; darkness and shadow with splashes of light.

Vladimir, chained to a post, was knee-deep in edibles but had contorted his neck to nibble on a vine just out of reach. Zach slumped mournfully in a chair on the deck and was a picture of suffering until Baz walked up the steps, holding something that looked like a long thin rag.

'What's that?' asked Zach.

Baz held it up high for him to see. The skin was as fine and crackly as paper but with the patterned imprint of the snake that had discarded it. 'Eastern Brown, if my eyes are serving me. Big bugger too. Watch yourself walking around, stamp your feet. Stamp. Stamp. Stamp.' He demonstrated stamping his feet in case anyone had missed the point.

'I'm not walking anywhere,' said Zach, alarmed.

Baz laughed. 'We could carry you out on a stretcher. Chop down a couple of saplings for poles. Or one of those fancy things they used to carry queens and gentry around in. What were they called, Liz?'

'It was well before my time, but a sedan chair, I believe. I don't think that'll be necessary,' said Elizabeth. 'Zach will be fine.'

'Want this, son?' Baz dangled the snakeskin in front of him.

Zach stared at it for a moment and then gingerly took it. The tail had broken off but the open mouth of the snake was imprinted in the skin. 'Are they dangerous?' he asked.

'Oh my word yes. One of the deadliest snakes in the world. Deadly. Deadly,' said Baz with satisfaction. 'But before we go condemning our slippery serpent friends, let's not forget, the deadliest creature on earth is *man* —'

'Baz, do you think we should go and look for Ray, or wait here?' interrupted Elizabeth. 'There's no car here, so he could have just gone out for the day, I suppose.'

Baz lowered himself into a rickety chair. 'We'll hang here. Let's sit tight and have a cuppa.' He gazed around him. 'It's paradise, isn't it? Zachy? Whaddyah think?'

Zach looked around. ''S'okay. Bit boring.'

'I'm surprised Ray hasn't done more with the place in all these years,' said Elizabeth. 'It's pretty basic.'

'That's the point. That was one of my conditions. No renovating. No building. It's not to do with the council – nothing here is approved anyway. I didn't want the place all fluffed up with vanilla-scented candles and plantation bloody shutters. And low-voltage lighting . . . like some kind of resort.'

Zach and Elizabeth exchanged looks. 'I don't think there's much risk of that, Baz,' she reassured him.

After a moment Zach asked, 'What's a plantation shutter?'

While Baz explained, Elizabeth went inside. On the shelf above the sink, there was tea and coffee and sugar sealed in mason jars. The stove was a two-burner portable that ran off a gas bottle, and the water had to be pumped up from a tank somewhere, spurt by spurt. The kettle took forever to boil on the gas ring – this was a life lived more slowly, and after all, what else was there to do? She could see already how this might have suited Ray, and also how difficult it would be to leave a place where the only sounds were birds and insects and the wind in the trees. To face the cacophony of the city would be overwhelming.

As she stood waiting for the kettle, the morning light filtered through the window over the sink and she noticed there was a fine layer of dust on the timber benchtop. She wondered if Ray had been gone longer, perhaps a few days or even a week.

She took three mugs of tea outside. Baz was still going on about plantation shutters as part of a global conspiracy to distract the human race from what was truly going on.

Zach's head had sunk into his neck like an old man's. He clearly regretted asking. From time to time, he glanced at his phone as if trying to make a connection through sheer willpower. 'How long are we staying?' he asked again.

'Soak up the beauty. Write a poem. Do a painting. Look at that . . . and that . . .' Baz said, pointing at trees randomly.

Zach gave him the scornful look he usually reserved for Elizabeth. 'Why'd you leave here if you love it so much?' he asked.

'Fair question. Couldn't handle the isolation. That's the truth. Was okay at first, had a bunch of mates camp up here and help me build this place. All mucking in together, getting stoned, playing music. Then everyone went home and the party was over. Well and truly over. I did my bees and grew some crop but, before long I was getting wasted every day and started to think twice about the whole business.'

'So, what did you do?' asked Zach.

'Went to live with my nana down at Lennox. That was her farm down there.'

Zach grinned. 'Your nana? How old were you?'

'Just a kid. Probably twenty-three. Around about. She wanted to move up to her unit on the Gold Coast, so I took the place over. I think she felt sorry for me having lost my foot.'

'How'd you lose it?' Zach sounded genuinely interested.

'Stepped on a landmine. Blew the whole foot off, boot and all. Just gone. Didn't know what had happened. Threw me twenty feet in the air and smashed my arm when I hit the ground.'

Zach winced in sympathy. 'That'd hurt.'

'World of pain, matey. You've got no idea. World. Of. Pain. Had shrapnel all through me. Still do. It kind of works its way up to the surface and you can feel it under the skin. Was just lucky I didn't lose both legs. Or my life, for that matter. Just lucky. Probably a bit of bad juju going on. I was so keen to get out, I had thought about shooting myself in the foot.'

'Unlucky to step on a landmine,' Elizabeth pointed out.

'Lotta people don't survive that. Plenty of ugly ways to die or get injured in war. Die slow or quick. Single bullet or a grenade. Or just lose your bloody mind. Take your pick. Take your pick. None of it's pretty. In the end, it's the mind that gets fucked up. When you get rewired to run into danger instead of away from it . . . it messes you up big time.'

Zach was silent. He wasn't looking at his phone. He appeared to be thinking.

Elizabeth finished her tea. She noticed a hook under the roof over the deck, and got up to hang Eric's cage from it. Despite the nice view, she felt guilty that Eric had to suffer two days in his small cage, the cost of her indulging Zach and making her own life easier. She went down into the vegetable garden. There was plenty to choose from: carrots, potatoes, zucchini, several varieties of spinach and strawberries, as well as vegetables she didn't recognise. She picked a few beans and spinach leaves to chop up for Eric, with a whole strawberry for his dessert.

Vladimir was straining on the chain, keen to get inside the fenced area. She bolted the gate carefully and skirted around the goat, only to feel a warm trickle of something drip down her ankle. He had managed to get good coverage of her foot and soak the hem of her pants as well. It could have been her imagination, but Vladimir looked pleased with himself. She walked back up to the deck and left the beans and spinach on the table.

'Ugh. What's that smell?' asked Zach.

'Eau de Vladimir,' said Elizabeth. 'The bloody thing peed on me.'

Zach started laughing and, when Baz explained that Vladimir only peed on people he liked, and she should be honoured, Zach laughed even harder. Elizabeth was less amused. The bathroom was in a shed beside the cabin, and she took off her shoe and pants and gave the offending areas a good wash. The toilet, she discovered, was outside, behind the bathroom. It was a long-drop arrangement, fashioned from a half-buried wheelie bin with a lid and a piece of board that could be laid across it as a seat.

When she got back, Baz had fallen asleep in his chair, mug in hand, mouth wide open to reveal a graveyard of dental neglect. Every once in a while he took a shuddering breath and between times didn't seem to breathe at all. Zach met her gaze and grinned.

'Need anything from the car?' she asked.

'The internet?' His eyes closed slowly to illustrate the depth of his suffering.

Back at the car, she gathered a few snacks she'd put aside for emergencies. Now she had a quiet moment to herself, she had the strongest feeling that Ray had been gone a while. She needed to look more carefully and try to work out when and where he might have gone.

She searched the cabin and found his suitcase stored under the bed, his winter clothes packed neatly in it. So he either hadn't gone far, or hadn't planned to leave for very long.

The place didn't look as if he had prepared to be away for any length of time. She opened the fridge under the bench and checked the date on the carton of milk she'd used earlier but it was the long-life variety and would last another year. There were a few eggs, which he must have bought because there were no chickens, a bunch of celery tied up with string and a bowl of beans that looked relatively fresh, perhaps picked a few days ago.

When Baz woke, she suggested that they widen the search into the surrounding bushland. Zach wasn't keen but decided it was better than being left on his own.

They trooped off, following Baz as he led the way along a narrow track. All around them were tropical palms, and overhead a canopy of tall trees. Baz halted the procession for a moment as a blue-tongue lizard crossed their path. It paused for a moment to stare at them with its prehistoric gaze and moved on, disappearing into the undergrowth. From time to time, they stopped to shout Ray's name and Elizabeth fretted that he might be injured, or worse. If he couldn't reply, it would be impossible to find him.

After a short, steep climb, the rainforest opened out to an area of large flat rocks. Beside it ran a creek that fed down from the mountain, creating rock pools, before tipping off the escarpment in a waterfall that cascaded into the valley below. From here, they could see over the vast green forest to low hills and the distant haze of the ocean.

Baz cupped his hands and shouted, 'Ray! Raaay!' with only a faint echo in reply.

Looking at the sheer drop to the valley below, Elizabeth realised how easy it would be for Ray to simply walk off the edge, and he would never be found. It was difficult to tell if she was being overly dramatic, or realistic. He had promised her that he would never take that way out, but that was a long time ago. They stood there in silence, not knowing what to do now. Billowing clouds had gathered on the horizon with patches of misty rain coming in their direction, and Baz suggested that they get back to shelter before the rain came.

By the time they arrived back at the cabin, it had begun to pour. The rain on the tin roof was deafening. The water became rushing streams running into the forest, and a mist descended as though they had been lifted into the clouds.

Vladimir was bleating with distress, and Baz brought the goat under the shelter of the deck. Eric, on the other hand, was thoroughly enjoying himself, making happy little squawks as he ruffled his feathers. 'Baz baz!' he called cheerfully. 'Nightmare!'

It was cold now and Elizabeth went inside. She thought how depressing it must have been for Ray here when he was forced indoors by the weather. It seemed impossible that he could have lived here for so long with so little. There was a single overhead light that ran off a solar panel, and a couple of camping lamps. The only heating was the pot-belly stove but, in Ray's usual organised way, there was plenty of firewood stacked behind it.

Elizabeth showed Zach how to light the fire and found one of Ray's jumpers for him. She washed out his hoodie and hung it over a chair near the fire to dry.

Zach wandered around listlessly, chose a book from the bookshelf and lay down on the bed to read it. A few minutes later he was fast asleep.

Elizabeth couldn't relax. They had been here all day and were no further ahead. She had no idea what to do next. Was he actually missing or simply somewhere else? Should they report it to the authorities? She went out and sat on the deck with Baz.

'She's a widow, you know . . .' he said.

'You've lost me,' said Elizabeth.

'Susie. Next door. Her hubby died a couple of years ago.'

'Are you looking for a wife, Baz?'

'Well, I'm half-blind, domestically inept and lonely as hell . . . so that would be a yes. We had a bit of a thing going back then, you know. Bit of a *thing*,' he repeated with a wobble of his head. 'Before she was married, obviously. She was very cute. How did she look to you?'

'Honestly, Baz . . . you need to get those eyes fixed. Anyway, let's talk about —'

'Baz baz baz!' cried Eric. 'Ba-az!'

Baz laughed his wheezy laugh. 'Eric sounds like my old mum – Baa-z!'

Elizabeth could see the track was streaming water, and she wondered aloud how they would get out of there. 'It'll ease off,' Baz reassured her. 'But the road will be smashed. Your little run-about won't get out, that's for sure.'

'What are we going to do about Ray?' asked Elizabeth.

'We're stuck here the night, so he could come back. If he doesn't, we'll think of something else in the morning,' said Baz unhelpfully.

'We can go into Wissam, ask around. He'd know people there.'

'First thing in the morning, we can go back to Susie's. I know what you're thinking, Liz, but she knows everyone around here.'

Late in the afternoon, the rain eased off a little but the sky was heavy with another deluge to come. It made sense to stay, in case Ray came back, and because they had nowhere else to go.

Zach helped Elizabeth bring a few things up from the car and gather some vegetables from the garden. She made a soup and they ate off their laps by the warmth of the fire. Baz brought his swag up from the car. He would sleep on the deck with Vladimir. Zach would take the sofa and Elizabeth the bed, with Eric in his cage on the bedside table.

Elizabeth lay awake listening to the sounds of the night and going over what she knew of Ray's habits. He collected his mail down in Wissam where he bought whatever supplies he needed. She knew he went into Mullumbimby once a month to sell vegetables and bush food on market day. She'd never had the impression that he stayed overnight, but it was possible. Perhaps she was overthinking the whole thing; after all, he'd managed here for all these years without her keeping track of him. He would probably turn up in the morning and wonder what the fuss was about. But somehow she didn't think that would happen.

She was startled by the crash of a possum landing on the tin roof. It thundered across the metal and then all was quiet, apart from the thrum of insects and murmur of night animals. Despite the hardness of the bed, she was grateful for it after the previous night in the car, but still she couldn't sleep. They'd let the fire go out but the cabin was still stuffy and too warm. She got up and opened the door, took a deep breath of cool night air and stood in the doorway listening to the clicking frogs.

Baz sat on the deck chair smoking a joint. The goat lay beside the chair, his legs neatly tucked under his torso. The cloying sweetness of marijuana almost masked the rank smell of the damp goat.

'Brings back a few memories, being here,' said Baz, as she sat down beside him. 'Woke up one morning after a week of rain like this and drove away. Just drove away. Couldn't stand another minute. Not one fucking minute.' He paused. 'Maybe that's what Ray's done.'

He offered her the joint but she shook her head. 'It's possible,' she said. 'But after all these years I think it's unlikely. Something's not right. I just know it. We need to keep going until we find him.'

'Ray's been through a lot, Liz. And I mean, a lot. He's not going to do something stupid at this stage of the game, if that's what you're thinking. Like jump off the escarpment, for example. No, that's not him. Don't even think about it. Not that.'

'I always imagined this place as some sort of utopia where the sun always shone,' said Elizabeth. 'I saw him living here at peace with nature. That was the impression I got from his letters. But I can see it is also . . . isolated and depressing.'

'You need to be pretty strong-minded. Self-sufficient.'

'What if he's had an accident, Baz? Somewhere out in the bush. A snake. Or a fall.'

'There's worse ways to go,' said Baz. 'Say, for example, trapped in a lift.'

'You're not going to be trapped in a lift for three or four days,' said Elizabeth. 'That's how long it would take without water.'

'You could be in an abandoned building. What about that?'

'Well, why would you be in the lift if the building was abandoned?'

'My point is, at least here you're surrounded by nature, birds and buzzing things. Pleasant things. Not having muzak drilled into your head . . . Barry Manilow or Neil Sedaka. That sort of nonsense.'

'It's obviously a long time since you've been in a lift, Baz. And why is the lift in the abandoned building playing muzak?' Elizabeth deeply regretted becoming involved in this pointless squabble and changed the subject. 'Tell me, if you had to pick a song that represented you and your life – your anthem – what would it be? Don't overthink it.'

'Hmm . . . okay, interesting . . . "Riders on the Storm", ol' Jimmy Morrison.'

'Is that inspired by the weather?'

'No, no . . . I've always related to that song about being thrown into the world. Tossed about. That's me. Tumbling around, tryna find something to hang on to. It's not like I've given up so much as forgotten what I was looking for in the first place. Long forgotten what I'm supposed to be doing here.'

They fell silent for a while. 'I wanted to believe Ray was doing well,' said Elizabeth. 'I just wanted to believe it.'

'You were busy with kids for years, Liz. You had your work cut out getting food on the table. Now you've got your sons, and your grandkids. Your little blue bird. You've got it all.'

Elizabeth wanted to tell him that she had also lost her place in the world and was tumbling around just like him. But she had so much more by comparison, it would seem ungrateful, and he wouldn't believe her anyway.

28

one big happy family

1979 Lizzy lies flat on the floor to reach under Danny's bed. His new black leather shoes have been pushed into the far corner as part of his quiet rebellion against starting school in the new year. Tom was the opposite, begging to go for months before he was old enough. Despite Danny's trepidation, she knows he will make friends once he gets there. He always does.

'Come on, Danny! Here they are. Put them on please,' she calls, walking down the hall to the kitchen. 'We've got to go now. Quick sticks!'

'Where were they?' Danny asks, the picture of innocence.

Lizzy laughs. 'They hid themselves under the bed.'

He sits at the dining table carefully colouring in, with the bright textas from his Christmas stocking scattered over the table. 'Why do I have to wear them today? You said they're school shoes.'

'Danny, you know Christmas Day is special and we have to dress nicely when we go to Grandma and Grandad's.'

Lizzy twists his chair slightly so she can kneel down and put his shoes on. He could easily do it himself but, in this mood, would take forever. She hears the tight bounce of Tom's new soccer ball off the walls in the front hall. 'Tom, no kicking the ball inside. Go and get in the car please.'

She watches Danny tighten his grip on the texta. 'I can't go 'til I finish this,' he says. He flinches as if in pain. 'That sock hurts. It's got crunchy bits!'

The front door rattles on its hinges as the ball hits it hard.

Lizzy counts backwards from ten under her breath. She bends down and pulls Danny's shoes and socks off, turns the socks inside out and slips them back on. He hunches over his colouring-in book with renewed determination. 'Don't want to go to Grandma and Grandad's. Why can't we stay here? I only like staying home.'

'Bring your textas and everything with you, darling. Uncle Andy will be there. You can show him your colouring in. Come on, let's go.'

Danny ignores her. She hears something smash in the hall-way, does a quick mental audit and suspects it's the vase Gwen gave them as a wedding present. 'TOM! Do as you are told! Go and get in the car!' Shouting doesn't relieve her frustration, it makes her angrier as though a barrier has been broken and all patience evaporated. 'Danny! Get up now!'

Danny's head slumps onto his arms as he weeps softly. Normally she's endlessly patient with him but right now his behaviour is more frustrating than tragic.

She collects her handbag and the gifts: a scarf for Cynthia, a book for Ray's dad and socks for Andy, and walks briskly away from Danny into the entry hall where Tom is pushing the broken vase into the corner with his foot. Without a word, she opens the front door and ushers him out to the car.

In the driveway, Ray laboriously wipes the car down with a chamois, apparently unaware that they're going to be late and his father will be annoyed. Lizzy straps Tom into the back seat. 'Could you get Danny please, darling?' she asks Ray.

He steps back to examine the car, touches up several spots and goes inside. Five minutes later, he emerges carrying Danny, the boy's head resting on his father's shoulder. With an expression of deep suffering, Danny is strapped into the back seat and, at last, they set off.

These days, Ray and Lizzy and their boys live in Roseville, in a house they purchased the year before Tom was born. The previous owners converted the garage into a workshop, which is now a study for Ray and allows him to write in relative peace, or at least retreat from the chaos of family life when he needs to.

In the month after Lizzy brought Ray home, he managed to secure a cadetship at the *Sydney Morning Herald*. The first year was difficult for him, the pace of the work exhausting, and there were many days when he struggled to get up in the morning. The second year was easier and he was offered a full-time position but, within months, he'd quit after an argument with the editor. Lizzy convinced him to return and apologise, but a few months later he was sacked. For a while it became a pattern, and she began to worry that he might run out of publications. In a small industry, he had gained a reputation for himself as talented but temperamental.

In those early years there was a simmering anger and a sense of frustration at his lack of control, and when he drank it became so much worse. He couldn't deal with criticism or any sort of conflict, and would simply walk away. It was only when they bought the house in Roseville and Tom was born that Ray began to settle down. He took fatherhood seriously, and his love for the children seemed to change his focus.

The trip to Marrickville takes over an hour. Ray drives and Lizzy makes an effort to entertain the boys with I-spy, alphabet songs and spotting different-coloured cars. Visiting Ray's family has become easier now that attention is more on the children, and the boys adore their Uncle Andy, now at university. But Ray is still on edge when they visit, and sensitive to his father's criticism.

Lizzy glances over at him. She rests her hand on his thigh and he gives her a smile.

Cynthia waits at the front door and rushes out to the car, waving her arms excitedly as they park. She opens the car door and pulls each of the boys into a hug. 'Jingle bells, Jingle bells . . . Merry Christmas! Come on in – there's pressies and Uncle Andy's here . . .' Her enthusiasm makes the boys shy, but they allow themselves to be shepherded inside. 'Come on, Mummy and Daddy,' she urges. 'Lunch is ready.'

Ray sits at the wheel; he takes a deep breath. Lizzy gives his neck a gentle rub. 'It's only an hour or two, darling, and we'll be on our way home.' He leans over and gives her a quick kiss.

Andy gets everyone drinks while Lizzy helps Cynthia bring dishes to the table: roast pork and potatoes, beans and pumpkin, and green peas. The routine is always the same. There's no time for convivialities; Cynthia wants to make sure everyone gets fed before something goes wrong.

As usual, Ray's father watches from the comfort of his arm-chair until everything is ready, then takes his place at the head of the table. The boys sit at the card table, seated on plastic chairs with cushions that bolster them up and make them wobbly at the same time. They kick each other quietly under the table while Ray's father says grace.

Lizzy takes a gulp of wine and feels the tension headache that's been building all morning begin to ease slightly. Occasionally wine has the opposite effect, but not today.

For a while, all goes well. Cynthia has a gift for keeping things light, and over the years Lizzy has learned to work with her. Andy and Ray have the same sense of humour and enjoy sparring with each other. But sooner or later, Ray's dad will ask, 'So how's the job going, Ray?' Despite his neutral tone, everyone at the table knows this is a loaded question, and his father doesn't know the half of it.

'Job is fine, thanks, Dad.' Ray glances across at Lizzy. She winks back at him.

'Still with the same paper?' his father persists.

'I'm with AAP now. Australian Associated Press. We're a news agency. Like Reuters.'

'Am I supposed to know who Reuters are?' asks his father.

'Come on, Dad,' says Andy in a teasing tone. 'You know who Reuters are.'

Cynthia changes the subject: 'Andy's been getting high distinctions for his essays.'

'Just scraped through on some subjects,' admits Andy.

'What about you, Liz?' asks Cynthia. 'What are you going to do with yourself when your two big boys are both at school next year?'

'Actually, I'm starting at Sydney Uni doing a degree part-time.'

'Oh, how exciting!' says Cynthia. 'And what will you study?'

'An Arts degree initially. I'm not sure after that. I might do teaching like Ginny – that would fit in with the boys. I'd like to do something useful, I think.'

Ray's father looks annoyed. 'I don't see the point.' He makes a helpless gesture towards Tom and Danny. 'These ones turn into latchkey kids so you can be a "career woman" – why not get a shop job and work school hours? What do you think of all this, Ray?'

Ray shrugs. 'Dad, you don't have to have such a definite opinion. Lizzy's been home with the kids the last few years, she's smart and she deserves to —'

'Better to have you both working and that house of yours paid off then. You owe money – that's your first priority.' Ray's father helps himself to extra potatoes while he waits for the explanation he believes he deserves.

'Everyone has mortgages now, Dad,' says Ray. 'There's no rush to pay it off.'

'This generation, drowning in debt. I don't know why you didn't stay in the army. You might have been able to stretch yourself a bit higher than lance corporal. Good secure job. All this flitting from one thing to another —'

'Let's not forget I was forced into the army, Dad. It wasn't a career choice.'

Andy speaks up. 'Dad, just leave it. Lizzy and Ray know what they're doing.'

'There are other things to talk about than my legion of disappointments,' adds Ray bitterly.

'If I don't ask, next thing you'll say I don't take an interest.'

Ray drops his cutlery on the plate with a clang. 'I've never in my life said that. And it's not "interest" that I object to – it's the criticism. Inferred or otherwise. I don't want to hear your opinions on everything, Dad. Let alone on what Lizzy does. It's really none of your business.'

Lizzy glances across at Tom and Danny, who have gone very still and watchful. She knows they're wary of Ray's outbursts and it's not the first time they've seen conflict at this table.

'Let's talk about something else,' says Cynthia, but she can't seem to think of anything. 'Come on, someone, anyone – all suggestions considered.'

Ray stares at his father. 'And for once, I'd like to hear that you approve of something we do. You have a knack for finding something negative in everything. Maybe that's why Mum left the way she did? Maybe if she'd had more support, she might still be here.' He glances at Cynthia. 'Sorry, Cynthia . . . I didn't mean . . .'

Lizzy can hardly breathe. Never in all the disputes with his father over the years has Ray brought up the subject of his mother. There is an unspoken but ironclad rule that Kathleen is never mentioned in this house.

'You don't know what you're talking about,' says his father savagely.

'Dad, Ray, let's drop this subject . . .' says Andy urgently.

'In these last years, since I've become a father, I've realised Mum didn't leave "us". She left you,' says Ray. 'And I've been asking myself why? Why didn't she take me? Why has she never written to me? I don't believe that she would leave and never contact me again. Did you destroy her letters? Or do you still have them?'

Cynthia puts her face in her hands and even Andy falls silent.

Lizzy and Ray have puzzled over these questions for years but he's never before had the courage to bring them up with his father.

Ray's father stares at him for a long moment. 'There's no letters. She left because she didn't give a shit – about me or you.

Get that through your head. She was neurotic . . . and selfish.'
He leans towards Ray and taps the side of his own head. 'You're
going the same way. Can't have a discussion without going off
your nut. Seen it all before.'

Cynthia knows there's no hope of changing the subject now.
She casts an agonised look at the two children, as if wondering
when she'll ever see them again.

Ray says nothing and, for a terrible moment, Lizzy doesn't
know what he's going to do next. Then, dignity intact, he gets
to his feet, thanks Cynthia and walks out the door. Christmas
lunch is over and possibly for the last time.

Lizzy gathers the boys and hurries them out to the car.
Cynthia follows, pressing gifts into their little hands, apologising
to everyone all at once. Andy comes outside and takes Ray aside;
they talk quietly for a moment and exchange hugs. Without a
word, Ray gets in the passenger seat of the car. He looks pale, his
hands restless and trembling.

As Lizzy drives past the nearby park, she notices a toilet block.
'Want me to stop?' He nods, and she pulls over and watches him
walk into the Men's, his sensitive gut another unhappy legacy of
his time away.

While they wait in the car, Tom decides he doesn't care for
his jigsaw puzzle and he grabs Danny's Etch A Sketch and begins
to scribble on it. Danny screams for its return and Lizzy leans
over to confiscate both gifts. Now they will compete to see who
can be silent for the longest with ice-cream in a cone for all con-
testants when they get home, and a double serve for the winner.
Danny soon goes to sleep and becomes the winner by default
and they enjoy a quiet drive home.

When the boys are in bed, Lizzy opens a bottle of wine and

puts *Kind of Blue* on the stereo, still Ray's favourite after all these years. They sit down on the sofa and wish each other a happy Christmas, but he's clearly still upset by the conversation with his father.

'I don't believe him,' he says. 'Mum wasn't neurotic. She was sad sometimes, I do remember that. Perhaps she was depressed. I was too young to know. Dad wasn't even around that much. He was either at work or the pub.'

'She must have been lonely,' says Lizzy. 'With no family here.'

Ray nods. 'When I was in that boys' home, I used to fantasise all the time about Mum coming back to get me. As if she'd forgotten me by accident or something. Or I'd imagine Dad died and I'd somehow get the money out of his bank account and buy a ticket and go back to Ireland.' He smiles. 'I used to plan it all when I was going to sleep. I remember that, later on, I felt guilty about Cynthia so I revised the story to me and Cynthia going to Ireland together to find Mum.'

'One big happy family.' Lizzy smiles. 'We'll go one day, Ray. Our family.'

'We will,' he agrees. 'We'll get to the bottom of it one day.'

'Let's go away for Christmas next year, darling,' says Lizzy. 'Take the boys camping. Let's not put ourselves through this again.'

'We could spend Christmas with your family,' suggests Ray. They both laugh at that idea; her parents are still in the shop in Nullaburra and becoming more eccentric every year.

Ray looks at her with the tender smile that still brings a flutter to her heart. He pats his thigh. She gets up and sits down on his lap, her arm around his shoulders. He lifts her hand to his lips and kisses each knuckle. 'Te amo, my sweet Lizzy. Happy Christmas.'

'Te amo too, darling,' she says. She lays her head on his shoulder. Even when Ray is difficult and stubborn, even when he walks away while she's talking to him. Even when he shuts down and goes deep inside himself so that nothing can touch him. Even when he drinks until he falls asleep on the sofa. There is never a time when she doubts that she is loved. He's simply doing what he has to in order to survive.

29

caged animals

1982 Lizzy hurries towards the entrance of Taronga Zoo, holding Danny and Tom's hands. She can see Ginny waiting with Polly, and Adam in his pushchair.

Polly looks pretty in a floral skirt and a straw hat with a yellow daisy on the crown. 'Hi, Danny! Hi, Tom!' she calls, skipping towards them.

Danny responds with a shy wave but Tom, almost nine, is too cool to get excited by a six-year-old girl. 'Can we see the elephants first, Mum?' asks Tom quietly.

'We'll see,' says Lizzy. 'As long as everyone else wants to —'

'Mum,' he says. 'Polly only ever wants to see the koalas. That's all she wants to do. They're boring. Mum? Please, Mum. Can you tell them?'

'I said we will see . . . Just wait.' Lizzy and Ginny exchange hugs and embrace each other's children. After some discussion, they decide to put the picnic bag in the pushchair while it's heavy and later swap it for Adam when he gets tired.

As predicted, Polly wants to see the koalas first but Ginny

insists they take a democratic vote. Thanks to some quiet lob-bying by Tom, the elephants win out. As they walk down to the elephant house, Polly sulks and slides her feet along the path like a robot low on power. When they get close, the boys run ahead and she gives in and chases after them.

'That's got rid of that lot,' says Ginny. 'Let's find a bar. My shout.'

Lizzy laughs. 'They'd track us down and we'd get done for parental neglect.'

'They're not neglected enough, if you ask me. They live a sweet life.'

'Not mine,' says Lizzy. 'The boys have to look after them-selves at the moment. I'm up to my neck in assignments, and now that Ray's on crimes and court reports, he's late home prac-tically every day.'

'Crime and courts sounds depressing to me,' says Ginny. 'Seeing the worst of people every day. How's he doing at the moment?'

From the outside, the O'Reillys look like a model family and Lizzy works hard to maintain that image. In reality, Ray's drink-ing is worse than ever because it's become part of his job and he regularly socialises with other journos, off-duty cops and crimi-nals. He almost never comes home completely sober. Work has become the centre of his life and it seems that drinking is central to his work. Ginny is the only person Lizzy can confide in.

'He's okay,' she says. 'I just wish he'd cut down on the booze.'

Ginny gives her arm a squeeze. 'Have you talked to him about it again?'

'It's such a touchy subject. He's such a different person when he drinks.'

'He knows it's a problem,' says Ginny. 'He's a smart guy. He'll get it under control.'

They've had this conversation a dozen times in the past few years and nothing has changed. But Ginny is always sympathetic towards Ray. Never once has she criticised him or blamed him for the way he is; she understands, and Lizzy values this more than she can say.

They arrive at the elephant house to find the children in a state of high excitement. Ranee the elephant has a new toy, a huge truck tyre on a chain. Supervised by the keeper, the children can roll the tyre towards her and she rolls it back to them. The elephant is only a few feet away with no barrier between her and the children. Lizzy quickly picks up Adam and sits him on her hip, while Ginny takes Danny's hand and tells the children to stand well back.

Tom's face is alight with excitement and he pushes the tyre as hard as he can towards the elephant. Ranee sits back on her hind legs and uses her front foot to roll the tyre back. Even Polly is entranced. She's afraid to touch the tyre herself but urges Tom to do it again, giggling delightedly when he does. Lizzy helps the two younger boys each have a turn until everyone is satisfied, then it's on to the koalas, followed by the monkeys, where Polly's hat somehow ends up inside the enclosure. A large male chimp tests it for edibility, and finding it not to his taste, walks off wearing it comically perched on his head. The Charlie Chaplin gait adds to the effect and makes the spectators laugh and Polly cry.

They find a spot on the grass and set out the picnic. Polly's still tearful at the memory of her lost hat but is eventually consoled by the promise of a new one. The boys can't stop talking about the elephant and how dangerous it all was.

Lizzy and Ginny sit in the sun chatting while the children practise handstands and cartwheels on the grass, and Lizzy has a sudden feeling that these days may be the best days of her life. It's only later, years later, she realises the truth of that.

30

the search goes on

Elizabeth was woken by an odd sensation that turned out to be Vladimir nibbling at her hair. She batted the goat away and rolled over to the other side of the bed. A moment later, feeling a presence hovering over her, she opened her eyes to find this time it was Zach, wanting to know when they were leaving. She asked him to take Vladimir outside and hauled herself out of bed. She washed her face at the sink and made a cup of tea, chopped up the beans and celery from the fridge for Eric and took his cage outside to the deck.

In the morning sun, the rainforest was luminescent, the trees sequinned with raindrops, and Elizabeth could practically see them growing. The dawn chorus was in full voice and she remembered reading somewhere that birds called to let each other know that they had made it through the night. What a different world it would be if humans could adopt this practice and sing to each other when they woke in the morning.

Hidden inside his swag, Baz snored like an old bellows, occasionally speaking in tongues. There was hardly any milk left, so Zach, looking very disgruntled, spread several dry Weet-Bix from the packet Elizabeth had brought along with peanut butter. Vladimir was easily pleased, happy breakfasting on a piece of rope he'd discovered hanging from the roof.

Elizabeth drank her tea while she waited for Baz to come to consciousness so they could get going. She tried to imagine what it was like to wake up every day here quite alone. Since her retirement, for the first time in her life, she had developed a fear of boredom that sent her scurrying out to the shops or the library, where she collected pamphlets and considered joining something – but never did. All her life she had been busy, driven by a sense of urgency. Now there was so much time that she had to recalibrate and do things slowly, but it didn't come naturally. She wondered if Ray had truly found the peace he was seeking and had mastered the slow life, or if he'd simply found a place to be lost beyond the gaze of the world. Eager to get going, she gathered some tomatoes, beans, spinach, corn and coriander, chopped them all up and tossed them with a couple of eggs in a pan on the gas ring.

Baz rolled out of his swag and staggered to his feet. He pounded his chest and let out a Tarzan yell, followed by a nasty bout of coughing. The performance cheered Zach up and even Vladimir paused mid-chew to watch the spectacle.

'That air!' Baz shouted. 'How fresh is it? It's a tonic! A tonic for the soul!'

'Baz!' cried Eric. 'Baaaaaz!' He seemed to have abandoned his entire vocabulary in favour of repeating Baz's name like a faulty car alarm.

'Do you reckon there are guns here?' asked Zach. 'Or a bunker?'

'Ray?' said Baz. 'Not on your life. No fan of guns. He's a pacifist.'

'Is that like a religion?' asked Zach.

'More a belief that all problems can be resolved by non-violent means,' explained Elizabeth, as she handed Baz a plate of food.

'Oh, hippie thing,' said Zach, dismissively. 'Probs why he doesn't have the internet.'

'I'm not sure the two are related,' Elizabeth said. She sat in a patch of sun on the steps with her breakfast. 'Okay, so we're all agreed we'll go to Susie's first? If she doesn't know anything she might be able to point us in the right direction.'

'Maybe Ray doesn't want to be found,' said Baz. 'Maybe he wants to stay in the shadows.'

Elizabeth had considered this possibility, but there was no evidence that Ray was actually hiding. 'We'll keep looking until we find him,' she said firmly.

Baz gave her a snappy salute. 'You're in charge, Liz. You're the ringmaster. We're just the clowns doing what we're told – eh, Zach?'

Zach, evidently not impressed at being called a clown, ignored him.

'I think I'd prefer to be ringleader,' said Elizabeth. 'Sounds a bit more gangsta.'

'Gotcha. I can see the movie,' said Baz, gesturing towards an invisible screen or billboard. 'A gang of misfits road-tripping across the country. Sleeping rough. Eating off the land. A woman, a man, a boy, a goat and a budgie. Searching for a man called Ray.'

'I wouldn't bother,' said Zach grumpily. 'Sounds boring.'

'And I don't see myself as a misfit, thank you,' added Elizabeth, slightly offended.

Susie opened her front door looking like an elderly fairy princess in an emerald-green dressing gown, her red hair cascading over her shoulders. 'I'm sure he hasn't gone far. He'll be around somewhere,' she said, making Ray sound like a lost pet. 'He goes into Mullum quite often to take stuff to the market, perhaps his car broke down . . . Come inside, let me make a couple of calls.'

Elizabeth followed Baz into the house, beckoning to Zach to come in as well. He wore a mutinous expression and it seemed that he was going to stay in the car, but a few minutes later he appeared with Eric's cage, which Elizabeth found strangely touching.

The house had one large main room dominated by a series of tables pushed end to end. These were covered in paints, paper and canvases, jars of brushes and a surprising number of stuffed wild animals mounted on blocks or branches: snakes, rabbits, a fox, a goanna and a large tawny frogmouth owl. There were branches of eucalyptus and bamboo, palm fronds and other greenery in buckets. Bones and animal skulls were littered about like leftovers from a medieval feast. On another table, pushed against the wall, there was a small stuffed crocodile and a wombat. Some of the creatures looked relatively at peace, while others had frightening grimaces, and the fox wore a disturbing leer.

An easel held a huge canvas with a painting in progress of a brown snake unfurling from the background foliage, poised to

strike. It was rendered in a fantastical way and even more terrifying than the snake it was modelled on, which was rigid and
lifeless, fixed on a timber base.

Susie poked around, searching for her phone. She picked up
things and looked under them in a haphazard way that made
Elizabeth itch to take charge. Zach stood holding Eric's cage and
looking around the room.

'What's all this, Susie?' asked Baz. 'It's like a zoo but everything's dead.'

'You know I love to paint the natural world, but it's so difficult to get it to keep still.' Susie laughed at her own well-worn
joke. 'Someone showed me how to taxidermy a few years ago
and I just loved it. I feel like I'm giving the animals a second
life, honouring their beauty and wildness. When they make their
spirit journey into the great beyond, their earthly body stays here
with me.'

'What do you kill them with?' asked Zach, suddenly coming to life. He bent down and eyeballed the crocodile. 'Do you
like . . . stun them and inject them. Or snipe them?' Elizabeth
wondered if he was thinking of volunteering his services.

Susie gave a melodic laugh. 'No, no. They're roadkill or
died a natural death. The croc was from a farm up north, not
round here. People bring them to me now. I don't have to go
out looking.' She glanced around helplessly. 'Now, where is
that phone?'

Elizabeth was getting frustrated; there seemed to be one
distraction after another and no one had any sense of urgency
but her.

Zach eventually located the phone but the battery was dead.
Susie explained that she never talked on her phone while it was

charging, in case it exploded, and while Elizabeth thought this highly unlikely, she had no choice but to accept another ten-minute delay. She reassured herself that they were getting closer, just in painfully tiny increments.

While they waited, Susie showed Zach inside the large chest freezer where she kept dead animals waiting for their taxidermy treatment.

'Nano, when Eric dies, you could have him stuffed,' suggested Zach. 'What do you reckon, Eric?' he said, looking into the cage. 'Maybe I could do it?'

'Baz!' cried Eric. 'Baz!'

'I don't think he'd be very good company stuffed,' said Elizabeth.

'It's a fascinating hobby,' said Susie with conviction. 'Addictive. You need to not be squeamish, of course.'

'Meaning?' asked Zach.

'You need to be okay with a bit of gore,' Elizabeth told him.

'Cool. Do you use a really sharp knife?' Zach watched over Susie's shoulder as she unzipped a leather tool case to reveal an array of sharp items: scissors, scalpels, knives and various other instruments – the sorts of items that were banned in carry-on luggage. The whole conversation was making Elizabeth queasy. She asked to use the bathroom, hoping it was reasonably civilised, although it could hardly be worse than the one at the cabin.

'Oh, of course,' said Susie. 'You should have a bath! Get your things and I'll run it for you. By the time you come out, I'm sure I'll have some answers.' Without waiting for a reply, she disappeared off into the back of the house and, after a moment of resistance, Elizabeth had to admit that the idea of a bath and a clean change of clothes was very appealing.

Exceeding all expectations, the bathroom was like an atrium, timber framed with a glass ceiling and walls, and looked out into the rainforest. The floor was made of multicoloured ceramic tiles in greens and blues. Steam rose invitingly as water poured into the bath from two brass taps. Susie fussed around showing her where to hang her clothes and gave her several towels, soap and shampoo, and left her to it. Elizabeth stripped off the clothes she'd been wearing for two days, lowered herself into the warm water and slid under the surface. Her anxiety about finding Ray had become all consuming. She had to keep reminding herself that there was most likely a simple explanation, and for a few minutes she allowed herself to luxuriate in the joys of soap and water.

Refreshed and clean, wearing one of her new dresses and a touch of 'Sugar Plum' on her lips, Elizabeth rejoined the others in the living room. Baz was following Susie around, gazing at her adoringly and lavishing compliments on her paintings, her dead creatures – basically anything in range.

Elizabeth wondered what Susie thought of him. He was hardly an ideal suitor with his rocky teeth and dodgy eyesight, and Susie didn't know about his haemorrhoids (a topic he mentioned regularly despite Elizabeth's obvious lack of interest). On the other hand, when Baz explained that Vladimir was a reincarnated member of the Romanov family, Susie embraced this idea with enthusiasm – so perhaps they were better suited than it first appeared.

'Would you like me to defrost something for you to practise on, Zach? I've got a couple of rats in the freezer you might like to try,' suggested Susie.

'Not right now,' said Elizabeth, interrupting Zach's inspection of the fleshing tools and Baz's flirtation. 'We don't have time for that. How's the phone charge going?'

'Of course,' said Susie as she hurried over to her phone. 'Now, let me think who might be able to help.'

'He must have some friends around here,' said Elizabeth.

'Oh yes, of course,' said Susie. 'Actually, I have a friend along the road a bit – Sian knows absolutely everyone. I'll call her.' She spent a few moments navigating her phone and finally said, 'Hello, darling, it's me. There's some friends here looking for Ray . . . Oh . . . When was that? But not in the last week? No . . .' She caught Elizabeth's eye and shook her head. 'All right. Can you call around and get back to me? These people have come from *Sydney*. Yes. Okay.'

'She's ringing around now,' Susie informed them. 'Let's have coffee while we wait.' She floated off to the kitchen in her long gown and came back with coffee, and banana cake. Zach took a mug of coffee without comment and a large slice of cake. He got out his phone and took some selfies with various animals, revealing himself to be quite the comedian as he pulled expressions of shock and terror. Susie laughed at his antics and Baz wheezed along with her. Vladimir appeared in the midst of it all, having escaped and found a door open, and Susie laughed some more and gave the goat some banana cake too.

Just as the joviality was getting out of hand and Elizabeth was about to explode with built-up tension, Susie's phone rang. She picked it up, listened and nodded solemnly. 'Oh . . . Oh dear . . . When was this? Sorry to hear that. Do we know if it's serious? Okay . . . Thanks, I'll let them know.'

She terminated the call and turned to Elizabeth. 'Not good news, I'm afraid. It seems he collapsed down in Mullum a few days ago and was taken to Gold Coast Hospital. She didn't know any more, I'm sorry. It's only an hour away but perhaps you could call? You might find out . . .'

For a moment Elizabeth was paralysed by indecision but Zach picked up Eric's cage. 'Come on, Nano – let's just go.'

31

going for gold

'Why is Baz driving so slowly? I don't know why on earth we have to follow him – it's not that difficult!' said Elizabeth. She was frantic to get to the hospital and now they were forced to follow Baz, who had insisted on guiding them to the hospital.

'Nano. Chill, can you? You just said Ray might've had a fall or something —'

'Or something! I just want Baz to get out of the way. Next chance, I'm passing him.'

'Baz!' chirped Eric. 'Baz!'

'Zach, *please* teach that bird something new! He's driving me crazy!'

Zach ignored her request and continued to read aloud from a beginner's guide to taxidermy and remark on the sharpness of the instruments Susie had given him. Leaving Susie's in the flurry of goodbyes and good wishes, they had somehow ended up with a frozen rat, now packed in Baz's esky in the back of the car. And, despite being dead, Elizabeth sensed the rat would give them trouble at some point.

But, right now, all her thoughts were with Ray and what might have happened to him. He loathed hospitals, having spent months in Concord after his breakdown but, if he'd fallen or collapsed, he would have been admitted whether he liked it or not. Best case, it could be low blood pressure or a virus. Perhaps she should have called the hospital to find out more, but it would only delay them. She tried to calm her thoughts and concentrate on the road, watching for an opportunity to overtake Baz.

'Snakes are pretty easy,' Zach explained. 'Frogs are tricky. Very tricky.' As usual he barely glanced out the window and perhaps he imagined they were crossing the Serengeti, since he turned his attentions to the intricacies of stuffing lions and elephants, and wildebeests.

Elizabeth listened patiently while he explained how to clean out a skull. When he noticed a dead wallaby on the side of the road, he wanted to check to see if it was viable but she sped on. They were on a mission and the last thing she needed was another animal on board. Dead or alive. As soon as a passing lane appeared, she put her foot down and took the lead.

Elizabeth pulled into the hospital carpark and instructed Zach to wait in the car while she went inside to find out what was going on.

'Can I get something to eat?' he asked.

'It's relentless,' said Elizabeth, handing him a twenty. 'Buy something for Baz too. And come straight back. Keep the windows open – Eric doesn't like the heat.'

'Baz!' said Eric. 'Baz! Baz!'

As she got out of the car, Baz cruised past looking for a parking space. She indicated to him that she was going inside and he gave her a nod.

At the reception desk, she was given the number of Ray's room on the third floor. She waited for the lift to slowly move between floors, her face reflected in the bright metal door pale and worried. As she walked along the polished linoleum hallway, every footstep felt significant. Her heart pounded, her hands were trembling and she paused for a moment to gather herself and take a deep breath. Whatever the situation with Ray, the last thing she wanted to do was burst into tears.

There were four beds in the room. One had the curtains pulled around it, another was empty. Two beds were inhabited by dozing men, neither of whom were Ray. She tweaked the curtain to reveal an elderly man who was sitting up in bed working on a laptop. He glanced up and gave her a nod, but he was not Ray. She looked again at the inhabited beds. Moving closer to the one nearest the door, she saw the name O'Reilly on the card above the bed. But the sleeping man was nothing like Ray. He had stubbly grey hair, his face weatherbeaten and gaunt, the skin stretched over his cheekbones tissue thin.

As she turned to leave, a voice said, 'Lizzy?'

She spun back in surprise to find the man staring at her. His warm brown eyes were just as she remembered and, in a moment, this stranger was as familiar as her own reflection.

'Lizzy . . . Lizzy . . .' Ray struggled up into a sitting position. She helped with his pillows. Afraid to speak, she bit her lip hard to stop herself from crying out. This was not how she hoped to find him.

He gazed at her in wonderment. 'I wake to find an angel at

my side,' he said, with a smile. 'I can't believe you're real. What are you doing here?'

'I knew something was wrong. I knew it . . . I should have come sooner.' She sat down heavily in the chair beside the bed. 'Oh Ray, why didn't you tell me? This must have been going on for a long time.' Each word came out as a sigh. 'I could have . . . done something.'

Ray smiled. 'Your sixth sense. I might have known.'

Grief had Elizabeth by the throat and it was a struggle to get the words out. 'What are they doing for you here, Ray? Are they treating you?'

He shook his head. 'I'm waiting for a place in palliative care. The cancer's all through my body now. As you know, this is not a place I wanted to end up but I'm glad to see you one last time, Lizzy.'

'I'm surprised you even recognised me.'

'You're just as I remember. Beautiful. Although . . .' He paused and searched her features. '. . . I'm not sure I've seen that lipstick on you.'

Despite herself, Elizabeth laughed. There were so many things she had planned to say to him but none of them seemed to matter now. All she could think of was how long he had, how many weeks or days? One thing she knew for certain was that she would not leave his side again.

'Ray, come home and let me take care of you,' she said thickly.

'I thought of it a hundred times, Lizzy. I've never wanted to impose on anyone, let alone you, and not in this state. I've been living day to day, not making any plans, just letting the day take its course. I suppose I thought I'd fade away gracefully, but it didn't happen quite like that.' His face softened. 'It's *so* good to see you.'

A trolley came rattling along the hallway and he closed his eyes tight for a moment until the squeak of the wheels receded. The man in the next bed sat upright with a start; he swung his legs over the side of the bed and carefully lowered his feet to the floor. He wasn't as old as Elizabeth had first thought, perhaps in his fifties, but ravaged looking. He wore baggy pyjama pants and an AC/DC t-shirt that revealed arms covered in the sort of amateur black ink tattoos she associated with prison inmates.

Ray glanced over at the man, 'You okay, mate?'

'Yeah, I'm good thanks, Ray. Nature calls,' said the man, pain evident in his face as he put the weight on his feet. 'All okay once I get moving.'

'This is my wife, Lizzy. Or Mrs O'Reilly to you.' Ray grinned.

'Aww . . . look at you two lovebirds,' said the man, pausing in his efforts. 'Good to meet you, Mrs O'Reilly. You can call me Moon Dog.'

'Nice to meet you, Mister Dog,' said Elizabeth.

The man laughed, hitched his pants up and shuffled off towards the bathroom.

'He's had an interesting life,' said Ray, and Elizabeth could see the old spark of enthusiasm for people and their stories was still in him.

'Don't tell me . . . international diplomat? Rock star?' she mused.

'Close. Sergeant-at-arms for the Comancheros. And this guy opposite me, Laurie,' said Ray, lowering his voice. 'Ex-cop. Been some interesting discussions. People always have more in common than you think – illness is the great equaliser. We have a pyjama republic in here.'

Elizabeth smiled, her emotions reined in so tightly that the strain of making pleasant conversation was becoming unbearable. She wondered if she could leave the room and let loose for a few minutes – but could she pull herself together again?

'How much time have we got, Lizzy?' asked Ray. 'When do you have to leave?'

'I didn't come on my own. I've brought Zach with me.'

Ray's face lit up. 'Zach! Where is he? Bring him in. Or do you think it's too much?'

'Well, actually . . . there's a whole entourage. Baz is here – with his goat – and I brought Eric, my budgie.' Elizabeth decided to leave Zach's rat out of it for the moment.

Ray leaned back on his pillows, shuddering with laughter. 'Bring them all in. I'd like to see you smuggle a goat in here – that'd be something to remember.'

Elizabeth wasn't in the mood for levity. 'Ray, please let me take you home. Let's do this together.'

He closed his eyes and was silent for a long minute. 'It's too late now. Too late.' His voice was scratchy and breathless. 'I should have come home years ago. I was afraid that nothing had changed and I'd make a mess of it again. I'm sorry.'

'That doesn't matter now. Let me take care of you.'

'Come back when I'm gone if you want to,' he said quietly. 'Scatter my ashes off the escarpment. It won't really matter to me, but it would be nice to think I'll settle there as part of the earth. Come on, don't cry, Lizzy, let's celebrate being here together. Bring the boy up – I'd like to see him. And Baz. Definitely the goat . . . and Eric, was it?'

He took in her miserable expression and beckoned her closer. She got up and sat on the side of the bed. He offered his open arms and, although it felt strange after all these years apart, she accepted and rested her head on his chest while he stroked her hair tenderly. 'I don't get why you're all here – and why now?' he said.

Elizabeth sat up and mopped her eyes. 'Ginny died.'

'Oh, Lizzy. I'm so sorry to hear that.'

'She left me a note saying I needed to find you. And on top of that, I didn't quite believe that excuse about you being "under the weather" – I knew there was more to it.'

'So you gathered up friends and family and pets . . .'

Elizabeth smiled. 'Not quite how I planned it, to be honest.'

Moon Dog came back from the bathroom. 'You guys want the curtain pulled?'

'We're good, thanks, mate. Lizzy's bringing my grandson up here to meet me.'

Moon Dog walked over and pulled the curtains open around Laurie's bed. 'Forget your memoir, mate. You're missing real-life action out here.'

Elizabeth grabbed a tissue from the bedside table. 'I'll be back in a minute, Ray.'

By the time she walked out of the hospital doors, the tissue was a wet ball. She paused in the driveway and, after a moment, walked back inside and found the bathrooms. She splashed her face with water and stared at herself in the mirror. Dashing away tears with the back of her hand, she patted her face dry with a paper towel. She didn't want Zach seeing her like this.

Halfway across the carpark, Vladimir passed her trotting off in the other direction and she made no attempt to stop the silly creature. Baz and Zach sat on the bonnet of the Land Cruiser engrossed in something she suspected was the book on taxidermy. 'Baz! Baz! Get your goat!' she shouted.

Baz slid down off the bonnet and looked around in confusion as Elizabeth jabbed a finger in the direction of the goat. She got into her car and leaned her head on the steering wheel. Her chest hurt as though her heart was aching.

Zach slipped into the passenger's seat. 'Nano? Are you okay?' He put his hand on her shoulder. It felt strong and full of life.

She lifted her head and they sat in silence for a moment watching Baz zigzag across the carpark after the goat. He gave that up, put two fingers in his mouth and delivered a piercing whistle that brought Vladimir skipping back towards him.

Zach turned to Elizabeth. 'So, not good?' he asked.

As she explained the situation, he nodded and looked so serious she wanted to hug him and offer some reassurances. But she had to be honest with him.

Having secured Vladimir, Baz came over and Elizabeth got out. They talked everything through and agreed that he would go up and spend a few minutes with Ray, then go on his way.

Zach and Elizabeth sat in the car waiting for him to return. 'I want to take Ray home,' she said. 'But he doesn't want to come.'

'Isn't he better in a hospital?' asked Zach.

'Not necessarily. He needs painkillers and all that, but he could be cared for at home. Anyway, he won't do it. He thinks it's too much.'

'It's pretty heavy if he's really sick,' agreed Zach.

'I want to take care of him.' She pushed the balled-up tissue into her eyes.

'We could stay here and, like . . . visit him.'

'I have to get you home, Zach. I'm going to put you on a flight. We'll call Mum after you've seen Ray, and get it organised.'

'I don't want to go home.'

'Zach, please . . .' Elizabeth's voice cracked and he turned away from her to stare out the window.

When Baz returned, the three of them stood together in the carpark and said their goodbyes. Baz shook his head sadly, his eyes red-rimmed. 'I'm sorry, Liz. I thought this story would have a happy ending.' He turned to Zach, brightening up a little. 'Zach, my man. Come up to the farm, anytime. Bring your mates. Your mates' mates. We'll get a lamb on the spit and roll some fat spli—'

'Perhaps when he's a bit older,' interrupted Elizabeth. 'Baz, could you take the esky and the rat home with you?'

'Wouldn't dream of it! My gift to you, Zach. Happy stuffing.' He got in his Cruiser and drove away, Vladimir gazing sorrowfully out the window.

Zach was nervous going up in the lift to the ward. Elizabeth touched his shoulder and gave him a reassuring smile, but he pulled away irritably. She noticed that he never seemed able to accept comfort when it was offered, as though he had to find it in himself.

He followed her into the room and stood halfway between Ray's bed and the door. He'd wrapped Eric's cage in his hoodie to hide it and now didn't know what to do with it.

'Hello, Zach.' Ray smiled and reached out to shake his hand. 'I'm Ray.'

Zach put the cage on the floor, stepped forward and shook Ray's hand solemnly.

Laurie and Moon Dog watched the meeting with interest.

Ray introduced Zach and he walked over to Moon Dog's bedside and shook his hand too.

'Good to meet you, brother,' said Moon Dog.

Zach shook hands with Laurie. He picked up the cage and removed the hoodie. 'This is Uncle Eric,' he said.

'What the hell what the hell?' Eric strutted around his cage indignantly. 'Baz!'

Ray laughed and shook his head. 'It's one surprise after another today. Am I dreaming or is this really happening?'

'He's pretty clever,' Zach said, a note of pride in his voice. He placed the cage on Ray's bedside table and began to coach Eric to say hello to Ray. Eric refused to cooperate. He looked at Ray and then at Zach and after a moment said, 'Wassup stickybeak.'

'What did he say?' asked Ray, leaning over to hear him better.

'Aw, nothing,' said Zach. 'Don't worry about it.'

Elizabeth stood at the end of the bed. 'Ray, would you at least consider the idea of coming home?'

'I wanted to come home in health, Lizzy. Not in sickness.'

'Until death do us part,' she said, attempting a light tone. 'That was the deal.'

Zach looked from one to the other and said nothing.

A nurse came in and checked Moon Dog's blood pressure. As she was leaving, Elizabeth said, 'Excuse me, Sister. I'm Mrs O'Reilly. Is it possible to speak to my husband's doctor?'

The nurse studied the clipboard on the end of Ray's bed. 'He's due to go across to the hospice in the next day or so. Is there something you need, Mr O'Reilly?'

Ray shook his head. 'No, I'm fine.'

'I'd still like to speak to a doctor,' insisted Elizabeth.

'There's a locum on. You can speak to her. She's doing the rounds now.'

Elizabeth thanked the nurse and turned back to find Zach giving her one of his dubious looks. 'What?' she asked.

'Why are you calling her "sister"? She's not your sister.'

'That's her title, Zach. She's a nursing sister.'

'Oh, okay. I thought you were like "yo sista!" – not cool.'

Ray caught her eye and winked. She left them together and went in search of the doctor. She checked each of the rooms until she spotted a young woman who looked barely older than Zach but wore a white coat and stethoscope. When the doctor came out into the hallway, Elizabeth introduced herself. The woman listened patiently as Elizabeth explained that she'd like to take Ray home.

'Mrs O'Reilly, there's nothing to stop your husband leaving here if the appropriate home care is available. But he may not want to. Sometimes people prefer to be in a hospital environment. It's really up to him. He can discharge himself if he wishes to.'

Elizabeth thanked her and walked back to Ray's room. She stopped on the way to get Zach a snack and stood at the vending machine lost in thought. Was this the right thing for Ray or something she wanted for herself? She remembered how he'd flinched at the rattle of the trolley and the distant slam of a door, and wondered how he could possibly cope with this place after the tranquility of his forest home.

When she got back to Ray's room, Zach was entertaining everyone with the story of Baz and his gun and a highly dramatised version of Nano fighting off the goat, which had Moon Dog roaring with laughter.

Elizabeth sat down on the side of Ray's bed. 'The doctor said there is nothing stopping you coming home with us, Ray.'

Ray smiled and took her hand. 'It's a kind thought, Lizzy. I do appreciate it.'

'How come you don't want to?' asked Zach.

'It's not that I don't want to, Zach. It's not that. Taking care of someone in my situation . . . it's too much to ask.'

'Go on, Ray,' said Laurie. 'That's an offer you can't refuse.'

'You can take me home anytime, Mrs O'Reilly,' offered Moon Dog.

Ray closed his eyes for a moment and Elizabeth could see this conversation was tiring him. 'We'll go now,' she said, patting his hand. 'I'll find somewhere to stay but I need to get Zach on a flight home.'

'Debatable,' said Zach with a scowl.

'De-bate-able,' agreed Eric. 'De-bate-able debatable.'

'I might get you both on a flight, actually.'

'Thanks, Lizzy,' said Ray. 'You don't need to stay, you know . . . but thank you. Good to meet you, Zach. You're a fine young man. I wish . . . I wish I'd known you better.'

Elizabeth kissed Ray on the cheek. He held her close, their faces pressed together for a moment. 'See you soon,' she whispered.

Zach shook Ray's hand, and Moon Dog and Laurie said their goodbyes.

By the time Elizabeth and Zach reached the lifts, the petulant teenager was back in business. 'Why do I have to go home? If he's, you know . . . why leave him? It's not fair,' he argued.

'It could be days, but what if it's weeks or a month? There's no telling how long the body can hold out. Besides, Angela still has to report on you every two weeks, and that's not negotiable. Plus you have to go back to school.'

'We could take Ray back to the forest . . . to the cabin, and look after him.'

Elizabeth shook her head. 'It's too isolated. He needs medical support.'

Zach was still arguing when they got back to the car, and she sent him off for food so she could call Claire and explain the situation without his input. She watched him lope away, head down. She was touched that he wanted to stay and care for Ray but wished he could see it was more helpful to fit in with her and not be so difficult.

Claire answered the phone immediately. 'Oh Liz, what's happened? Zach messaged to say Ray was in hospital. How is he?'

'He's very sick, Claire. Not long to go, I would think,' said Elizabeth.

'I'm so sorry. But good you saw him?'

Elizabeth agreed and explained that she planned to stay and send Zach and Eric back. As they chatted, she realised the other problem was the rat now defrosting in the back. She'd have to find somewhere to dispose of the thing.

'Leave everything to me, Liz,' said Claire. 'I'll check out flights for Zach and let you know. I've moved back home and left your place sparkling clean for when you get back.'

Zach returned and dropped into the passenger's seat with a bag of food. He fished out two chicken rolls and gave one to Elizabeth. She'd forgotten all about eating and was grateful both for the food and his consideration.

'Nano, I've been thinking.' He paused to ensure he had her full attention. 'This is kinda like a hostage situation.'

'In what way?' asked Elizabeth with a sigh.

He took a bite of his roll. 'Ray wants to get out. You want him out.'

Elizabeth hoped he might have something useful to offer but now expected it would involve high-velocity assault weapons. 'Not sure where you're going with this, Zach. No one is holding him against his will.'

He gave her a despairing look. 'You both want the same thing.'

'Got that. But I can't make him come home. What else can I do?'

'Don't give up so easily,' he said.

'I don't know what else to do,' said Elizabeth.

'*Dhurr,* have to do everything myself.' He dumped his roll on the dashboard, opened the door and walked off back towards the hospital.

Elizabeth got out to call him back but something made her hesitate, and she got back in the car to wait.

32

the day of the parade

1987 Patrick O'Reilly's wake is being held in the Molly Malone Bar of the Mercantile Hotel. With everything she knows of him, Lizzy is surprised to discover how well-liked her father-in-law was, judging by the number of people who attended his Mass and have gathered in this bar to celebrate his life.

Danny and Tom are now twelve and fourteen, handsome young men wearing three-piece suits that Ray had insisted on buying them for the funeral. Lizzy knows they'll grow out of them before the year is over but it was important to Ray that the boys look smart at his father's funeral.

Cynthia wanders around, her smile more strained as the evening wears on. Bringing a bottle of whiskey and two glasses, she joins Lizzy at a quiet table in the corner and sits down with a groan, 'These shoes, honestly. What was I thinking?' She pours two generous glasses and raises a toast. 'To Pat.'

Lizzy smiles and murmurs her agreement as they tip glasses. Not a whiskey drinker herself, she takes a pretend sip and places the glass back on the table. 'What will you do now,

Cynthia? I suppose you haven't even had time to think about it.'

'No, my head's still spinning. I'm sixty-three next week – is that young to be a widow, do you think? Probably not.' She gazes at Lizzy sadly. 'He wasn't a bad man, you know. Yes, he had a temper that got the better of him sometimes – you know that all too well – but he had many fine points, and he was always good to me.'

'I'm sure he was, Cynthia,' says Lizzy, although she finds that hard to believe.

'Liz, can I tell you something? Just between you and me. The truth is, I was very grateful to meet Patrick and find a man who wanted to marry me. I was high on the shelf when we met. I'd given up on love and having children. Patrick needed a mum for Ray and that's why he married me. He never got over Kathleen, and I knew that from the start. So we each had our own reasons, but we came to love one another. And we brought up two lovely lads. I don't want you and Ray, or the boys, to think badly of him. Truly, I don't. Look at all these people who loved him. They saw the other side of him.'

Lizzy nods. She understands that for some reason they never saw the best of Patrick's nature. He had mellowed in later years, but his relationship with Ray was always tenuous. She watches Ray and Andy in conversation with two men in checked sports-jackets. Ray has a fixed smile on his face and she will need to rescue him soon and get him home.

Cynthia touches her arm. 'I have some photos you might like . . . Kathleen and Ray in the early days. Back in Ireland when he was just a little boy, and with Caitlin as well. I hid them away all these years to give to Ray one day. He's the spitting image of his mother. She was what they call "black Irish" – not gypsies or anything like that, just dark looking. She was a beauty, no doubt about that. A real beauty —' Cynthia stops abruptly and gives a sob. 'I just can't believe he's gone.'

Lizzy takes her hand and holds it for a moment. 'Cynthia, I want you to know you'll always be welcome in our home, even for the long term if you don't want to live alone.'

'That's very kind but I'm not sure Ray would —'

'It was Ray's idea – we've already discussed it. We would be happy to have you.'

'There's something I need to talk to you about.' Cynthia's mouth pulls down at the corners, her chin trembling. 'Not here. Not today. Today is Patrick's day. He wasn't a saint, I know that, but let's face it, who is? He tried to do the right thing. But we never know, do we? We never know what's the right thing at the time.'

In the week after his father's funeral, Ray is in a strange mood. Restless and irritable, he refuses to discuss whatever's bothering him. They have a longstanding agreement that Lizzy won't ask him how he *feels* about things. He's explained that it's difficult enough for him to monitor his emotions without having to lay them bare for her. Mostly it works, but now there's something complicated to do with his father's death that is troubling him, and all she can do is wait until he's ready to discuss it.

Ray agrees to take a few days off work and go up to Baz's farm with the boys. It's September; the farm is quieter than usual and Baz has a bedroom free for her and Ray. The boys always camp outside anyway. Lizzy cleans the bedroom and makes up the beds with their own linen while Ray helps the boys pitch the pup tents.

Baz is always pleased to see them and he adores the boys. The first time Lizzy came to Lennox all those years ago to bring Ray home, he had only recently taken over the farm, and in these past few years he's turned it into an alternative community. His enthusiasm and generosity, and his penchant for late-night philosophising over home-brew, are a magnet for young people and troubled women.

Wendy, his current girlfriend, served as an army nurse in Vietnam. She has a hard, angular face and smokes continuously to keep her restless hands occupied. Lizzy's heard it said that people age ten years for each year they served in that war, and this is true of Wendy. In the late afternoon, everyone sits around the fire pit while the boys build up the fire and the adults sample Baz's latest batch of honey-fermented cider. They are joined by a young German couple who live in a caravan behind the house and play didgeridoos. As darkness closes in, the air around them rumbles with the sound of the ancient instruments. Tom and Danny are mesmerised, their faces glowing in the firelight. Lizzy glances over at Ray. He looks relaxed and happy, and it's not just the moonshine weaving its magic.

The days here are quiet and predictable and suit Ray very well. Tonight they'll eat sausages with Wendy's homemade bread and vegetables from the garden. In the morning they'll prepare a lamb for the spit, and tomorrow night they'll feast. The boys will take themselves to bed without argument, exhausted from running over the paddocks and swimming in the dam despite the chilly water. For Lizzy there's the sense of being cocooned, away from the world's pressures and expectations. Darkness around them, a bright moon above and fire at their feet, this is a time she will always remember with nostalgia.

Late in the evening, Wendy and Baz discuss veterans they know in common. Over the years, this has become an increasingly dispiriting conversation: some mates ill, mentally or physically, others dead through accident or suicide.

Wendy asks Ray if he's going to the Welcome Home Parade in Sydney next month. 'I reckon we should all go,' she says. 'Just get out there and show ourselves. Get out from under our rocks.'

'Fifteen years too late,' says Ray. 'What's the point now?'

'The point,' says Wendy, 'is that we get on board. It's not saying we approve of the war. Or think we're heroes. Nothing like that. We're not being hypocrites about it. We're just saying we exist.'

'Solidarity,' agrees Baz. 'Being there with the rest of our mates, fucked as we may be. We need a decent showing. Not just decent . . . huge! And not just for us but for the poor bastards who didn't make it back – Macca, Freddo . . . and the others.'

'It's supposed to be a kind of apology, Ray,' says Wendy. 'Or at least recognition that we did our bit when we were asked to. It's the best we're going to get. I'm sick of being ashamed that I was a part of that whole shitty mess. And I was there saving people, not killing them. Not that I mean . . . sorry – that was poorly put.'

'Too late,' says Baz. 'You've put your foot in the swamp now. Doesn't matter where you start, you just get sucked into it. Sucked down into the vortex —'

'Yeah, okay, Bazza,' says Wendy, rolling a cigarette on her knee with a practised hand. 'Hold the poetry and keep the cider coming.'

Ray is reluctant to commit to the parade but, after further debate, he agrees to go along and march with the others. At the end of the evening, Lizzy and Ray walk out into the front paddock before they go to bed. From the top of the rise, they can see a cluster of lights along the coast. The moon is bright and high, casting light and shadow around them, the only sound the rhythmic click of insects.

Ray gives a deep sigh. 'So quiet.'

'That's only because Baz has shot everything for miles around,' says Lizzy. Somewhere in the distance, a cow bellows as if to agree and stops just as suddenly, and she and Ray laugh quietly together. 'We could move up here, Ray. Do something different, live a more simple life,' she suggests, not for the first time.

'What sort of work would we get up here? I don't think we're farming types – we're not really cut out for that.'

'Maybe when the boys leave home. We could think about it then.'

'That's a very long time away . . . Maybe. I don't know,' he says.

'Ray, you don't have to go to the parade, you know. Not if you don't want to.'

'I know. It could be a good thing though. Close that chapter for a lot of us. I feel obliged to some extent. On the other hand, it could just bring up shit I really don't want to think about again.'

'You're not under any obligation. Just decide on the day.'

He pulls her to him and hugs her tightly. 'Thank you.'

'For what?'

'Everything you do for me. And the boys. Everything you put up with. Everything you manage. Without complaint. Without putting me under pressure. Don't think I don't see you, Lizzy – I do.' He crushes her against his chest and she squeezes her eyes tight so as not to ruin the moment with tears.

When they return to Sydney, Ray falls back into a despondent mood. He agrees to visit Cynthia for the first time since the funeral, on the proviso that the boys don't come along. Lizzy wonders if there are legalities to discuss but Ray won't be drawn on the subject.

Cynthia bakes scones and sets the table with the good china, and the three of them sit down together to exchange pleasantries. Lizzy notices that Ray, who has been tense all morning, is now sweating, as he often does under duress. He brings the light conversation to an abrupt halt and says, 'Cynthia, now Dad's gone, I want to hear the truth.'

Cynthia nods as if she's been expecting this moment.

'I know Mum's dead,' says Ray. 'People at the wake referred to her in the past tense. Not one of them asked after her, so it seems to me that they know more than I do.'

Cynthia gets up and goes over to the sideboard, opens a drawer and gets out a shoebox. She places it on the table and sits down. 'Firstly, Ray, I want to say that no one meant to deceive you. Your father was . . .' She sighs and lifts the lid off the box. 'You have to understand that what happened was all before my time. Lies had been told, and I understand why that happened, but it wasn't thought about properly. Your father wasn't in his right mind. He should have told you. I begged him to talk about it – I was worried you'd go back to Ireland and try to find her and —'

'Cynthia, please,' says Ray gently. 'I don't know what you're talking about.'

She takes two pieces of paper out of the box and passes them across the table. One is a small newspaper story from 10 September 1959, concerning the death of a 27-year-old woman who stepped off the platform in front of the 8.45 am train at Marrickville Station, causing a two-hour delay at rush hour. The second is a death certificate for the same date: *Kathleen Mary O'Reilly. Cause of Death: Misadventure.*

'I'm so sorry,' says Cynthia tearfully. 'So very sorry.'

On the day of the Welcome Home Parade, Lizzy and the boys leave early to get a good position up at the front of the crowd. Ray has gone on ahead to meet his battalion at the assembly point for the march. Lizzy's been worried about him for the past couple of weeks. The revelations about his mother have been devastating, and although he's talked about it almost every day since, he has still not shed a single tear. He discusses it like a journalist, going over and over that day when his mother walked him to school and then to the station to end her life. He's put a timeline together, gathered facts and dredged memories. He's been to the cemetery to visit her grave several times. And what worries Lizzy the most is the way he talks about this as if it happened to someone else, to some other child's mother.

Tom and Danny know so little about Ray's military service, they don't understand the purpose of the parade, but the Prime Minister, Mr Hawke, will be present, so it must be important. On the train going into the city, Lizzy explains the difference between regular army soldiers and conscripts, and how the system of the birthdates and the lottery worked. Tom takes a real interest – he's doing history at high school – but Danny fidgets, interrupting to ask how long it will take and if they'll be home in time for his favourite television show, *Hey Hey It's Saturday*.

They find a good position in Martin Place, and she buys a couple of flags to wave as the crowds gather. After a long wait, the brass band strikes up and motorcycle police lead the parade, followed by two long lines of army Land Rovers. The atmosphere is one of celebration, with thousands of people on the sidelines cheering as those marching wave to onlookers.

Lizzy spots Ray walking with his battalion. He looks handsome in his dark blue suit and carries one of the five hundred flags representing the men who died.

Tom and Danny wave and cheer, pointlessly shouting, 'Dad!' to get his attention.

When five army helicopters hover overhead, a hush falls on the parade and Lizzy recognises the expressions of trepidation on the faces of these men. She has seen this look on Ray's face many times.

As Ray passes them, he turns towards her briefly and she realises that something terrible is happening to him. He looks like a man facing his own death, terrified and desperate. She wants to rush into the parade and get him out. She looks around wildly. Someone has to help him. The boys seem unaware, waving their flags and cheering, then Danny says in a stricken voice, 'Mum, Dad's crying.'

33

the morning light

Elizabeth focused on the road ahead. It was almost midnight, the heavy traffic of the Gold Coast was behind them and now there were long stretches of empty highway. Zach sat beside her with Eric's cage on his lap. Ray was asleep on the back seat under a blanket.

She stopped conscientiously every two hours and walked around the car or got a cup of tea if she could find one at a road-side service centre. And then she drove on, hour after hour, until they arrived back home in the early dawn.

Ray was stiff from the discomfort of the back seat, and Elizabeth and Zach helped him up the front steps and into the wheelchair Claire had delivered. Zach took command of it and wheeled Ray to the bathroom, waiting outside the door for him.

Elizabeth brought Eric inside and saw that Claire had thoughtfully dropped over his large cage and Elizabeth's suit-case. She had stocked the fridge, and the kitchen smelled of fresh bread. There was fruit in the bowl on the bench.

Elizabeth gave Eric a piece of cuttlefish and some of his

favourite seeds. 'We're home! We're home!' she told him. 'We're home!'

'Baz! Baz! Baz!' he said, wandering around his cage.

'I'll put you in the post if you don't stop that,' threatened Elizabeth.

She opened the patio doors to let fresh air in, made tea and toast and they sat down to eat. Silent with fatigue, they watched the morning sun creep into the garden. She tried to imagine how Ray must feel being back here after all this time, but when a magpie began its chortling song in the big elm, he smiled. 'Tree's grown,' he said.

After breakfast, Zach went off to Tom's room to sleep.

When they were alone, Ray said, 'Lizzy, let's make the best of this time together but I don't want to pretend that things are other than they are.' He reached for her hand across the table. 'I'd like to see the boys, if they are willing.'

'Of course,' she said. 'Anything you want.'

'And I'd like to talk about old times with you, but when I'm gone, I want you to put all this behind you for good.'

Elizabeth agreed, although as far as she could see, the past was a more pleasant place to dwell than the future. She wheeled him down the hall to her room, helped him onto the bed and laid a rug over him. 'Sleep as long as you like,' she said, as she tucked it around him.

'Not sure what you mean by that,' he joked as he closed his eyes.

While he slept, she took the opportunity to call Danny and break the news.

'What do you mean "Dad's home"?' he asked in a shocked voice. 'He just turned up?'

'Not exactly. Zach and I brought him home,' said Elizabeth, already wishing she'd started with a less dramatic opening statement.

'This is getting more confusing. You and Zach went and found Dad?'

'It's a little more complicated than that, but in essence, yes. He'd like to see you . . . but make it soon – he doesn't have long.'

'When's he leaving?' Danny asked, dismayed.

Elizabeth was furious with herself for making such a mess of this conversation. She was exhausted, and should have waited until she'd had some rest. Now she struggled to set things right. 'Danny, I'm sorry. He's not leaving, he's very ill . . .' The silence on the other end was so long, she added, 'I'm sorry.'

'Okay. I just need to get my head around it. I really wasn't expecting this.' Danny liked to consider all aspects of a situation, weighing up the pros and cons, sometimes until it was too late and he missed out.

'Think about it, Dan. But don't leave it too long.'

'Yeah, okay. I'll come this evening after work.'

Elizabeth rang the correctional centre and put in a request for Tom to call her. Then there was nothing more she could do. She lay down on the bed in Danny's room and went straight to sleep.

When she woke, the day was sunny and warm. She helped Ray out onto the patio and made him comfortable. Zach wandered outside and sat down. He and Ray chatted while Elizabeth organised food and put several loads of washing on.

Late in the afternoon, Claire arrived with flowers.

'You didn't need to, Claire,' said Elizabeth as she stood in the kitchen. 'You've already done so much.'

'I want to help you,' said Claire with a sympathetic smile. 'This is going to be tough.'

Elizabeth put the flowers on the bench and knelt down to search the cupboard under the sink for a vase. On her knees, and not being able to find one, she suddenly began to sob.

'Liz?' said Claire. 'Oh Liz, take my hand. Let me help you.'

Elizabeth allowed herself to be helped up and accepted a hug. 'I don't want Ray to see me. I don't want to be sad and make him miserable.'

'Liz, you think you need to be invincible, and you don't. How could you not be sad? I'm sure Ray would understand.'

'I pressured him to come home. I want it to be a happy time for him.' They stood together at the kitchen window and watched Ray and Zach playing cards out on the patio. 'Poker,' said Elizabeth. 'Ray's teaching him poker.'

'Good to have further education,' said Claire. 'How's our boy been?'

'We had our moments, but overall it's been good for both of us. Although he has a new hobby you're probably not going to like. Which reminds me, I've got something in the freezer for you when you go.'

Claire turned to her. 'I can't thank you enough for what you've done, Liz.'

'I'm not saying he's reformed, but if we can just get through these next few months without incident —'

'I mean for taking him to give me a break. I was a mess, flipping out over everything.'

'You're looking well,' said Elizabeth. 'The break has done you good.'

'I'm so relieved that op's behind me – I'd been dreading

it. I think we deserve a G and T, don't we?' said Claire with a laugh.

'We do,' agreed Elizabeth. She reached up and took down a couple of tumblers from the cupboard. 'Claire, I haven't actually told Ray about Tom yet. I didn't want to discuss it in front of Zach.'

Claire frowned. 'But I thought you wrote to Ray regularly.'

'I do. I did . . . but I only tell him the good things.'

'So, we've all got a clean slate,' said Claire brightly. 'Suits me. I'm a bit nervous. I really want him to like me.'

'He will, Claire.' Elizabeth smiled. 'I wouldn't worry about that.'

Out on the patio, Claire introduced herself and Ray offered his hand. 'Sorry I can't get up,' he said.

'No one gets up these days – you're in good company.' Claire gave a nervous laugh. Zach got to his feet and gave her a hug. 'You've grown, Zachy!' she said.

He pulled away with a frown. 'Can you not?'

'Sorry, sorry, Zach.' Claire grimaced and Elizabeth wondered why she struggled to behave naturally around him, always trying too hard.

They sat down at the table and Ray pointed out a pile of leaves that represented Zach's winnings. 'He's a fast learner. Raking it in.'

Zach grinned with a flash of metal. Ray laid down his cards.

'Ohhh . . . owned!' Zach dropped his cards on the table in defeat. 'Ray's teaching me Five-card draw and Texas hold 'em. Can you play cards, Mum?'

'We used to play gin rummy years ago,' said Claire. 'It's the only one I know.'

Zach shuffled the cards with great concentration and they played a hand, which Claire won. Zach won the next two games, pronounced gin rummy boring and went back to poker. 'Do I have to go home?' he asked. 'Can't I stay here?'

'Back to school on Monday,' said Claire.

'They might try and suspend me again,' Zach said, dealing cards to himself and Ray.

'Why did they want to suspend you?' asked Ray, assessing his cards.

'Chucking stuff into the ceiling fan.'

Ray picked up his cards and put them in order. 'Doesn't seem that serious.'

'He'd already had several warnings,' added Claire.

'What did you throw into the fan?' Ray sounded genuinely curious, as if it was something he might be interested in trying.

'The best thing *ever* was one of those freezy gel packs.' Zach fought the urge to smile at the memory. 'It like . . . exploded and rained blue gel over everyone.'

'Sounds quite spectacular,' agreed Ray.

Zach nodded enthusiastically. 'Sandwiches are cool. Or a piece of fruit, like an orange. Once, I threw a whole box of tissues. That was *epic* . . . like it was snowing. One tissue sort of floated down really slowly and landed on the maths teacher's head. He was messing around on the whiteboard and didn't even know.'

'The class must have thought that was funny,' said Ray.

'One girl wet herself. Kids still talk about it. But what I got in trouble for was throwing this guy's phone into the fan,' he admitted. 'It wasn't for fun. It was revenge.'

Claire and Elizabeth exchanged glances. It was the first time

Elizabeth had heard the motive behind this crime, and by Claire's expression, a first for her as well.

'Must take some skill,' suggested Ray.

'Timing,' Zach confirmed with a modest nod. 'All about the timing.'

'What did he do to deserve that?' asked Ray.

Zach studied his cards. 'Said stuff . . .' He laid down a royal flush. 'About Dad.'

34

Danny Boy

When Claire and Zach had gone, Elizabeth helped Ray inside and onto the bed so he could rest before Danny's visit. He lay down with a groan of relief. 'I'm not used to such a frantic social life. I'm worn out,' he said.

She made him comfortable and settled herself on the other side of the bed. 'About Tom . . .' she began.

'It's okay, Zach told me. I noticed you'd been avoiding the topic of Tom. I thought it might be something else.'

'Like what?' asked Elizabeth.

'That he didn't want to see me, which would be understandable. I'd like to hear the whole story, when you're ready.'

'Later – there's no rush,' said Elizabeth. 'Get some rest.'

'Lizzy, I never wanted you to have to do this.'

'Most couples end up this way,' she said. 'Someone's always going to go first.'

'Who will look after you? You should have . . .'

'There won't be anyone else, Ray. It's only ever been you. Nothing's changed.'

'I hope that I've changed, but it's hard to tell. I still get shaken up easily but the anger has burned itself out. I'm sorry I couldn't be more help to you over the years . . . with the boys.'

'I know you are, Ray.' Elizabeth stroked his rough stubble of hair, leaned down and kissed him lightly. The touch of his lips was just as she remembered. They kissed again, and smiled at each other. She lay down and curled up beside him, her face tucked into the crook of his neck, and dozed until they were woken by the doorbell.

'That will be Danny,' Elizabeth said. 'You stay here, you don't need to get up.'

As she opened the front door, she realised how nervous she was about this meeting and how important it was that it go well. Danny gave her a peck on the cheek and glanced past her. 'Where is he?' he asked.

'He's in the bedroom. He gets very tired. Do you want a beer? Have you eaten?'

'I'm fine, Mum. So, in your room?' he asked, already walking that way.

She nodded and was about to follow him, then reconsidered, realising that she wasn't needed. Instead, she went into the kitchen, opened the fridge and stared blindly into it, wondering what they would say to each other. She closed the patio doors and laid out some apple slices and seeds on the windowsill, and let Eric out of his cage. 'Hello, buddy. How's things?' she asked him. 'Hello, buddy.'

He wasn't in a chatty mood and strutted along the windowsill, pecking at the seeds.

'You're cute,' she encouraged him. 'You're cute.'

He seemed to not hear her but finally conceded, 'You're cute too.'

Elizabeth rubbed his little throat and he hopped onto her finger. She held a piece of apple for him to peck at, relieved by his good spirits. She pottered about in the kitchen until Danny came in half an hour later. 'How did you go?' she asked.

'Mum, you hadn't told Dad about Tom before now? Stop trying to manage everyone. That's half the problem.'

Elizabeth was taken aback by his annoyance. 'I haven't had a chance to explain the circumstances. I was getting to it . . . What do you mean "half the problem"?'

Danny walked around the dining room restlessly, stopped at the patio doors and stared out into the twilight. 'Mum, Tom assaulted someone – not just anyone, his friend and business partner. But even though he's admitted to it and been convicted, you still seem to have the idea that he was some helpless victim of circumstance.'

Elizabeth crossed the room and closed the door to the hallway.

'Dad's asleep,' said Danny. 'Besides, everything doesn't need to be a secret in this family. We can just deal with the facts, instead of this fake "poor Tom" bullshit.'

'I don't think he's a victim . . . He was going through a difficult patch —'

'Of his own making,' interrupted Danny. 'He had a good practice. Nathan cut him a lot of slack. He didn't need to get involved in all this restaurant shit. He could have spent some time with his family, for example. He just wanted to be the big man.'

'That's a bit harsh, Dan. And Claire —'

Danny threw his head back in frustration. '*Arghh*, Mum, you don't have a clue. Claire is a fucking *saint*! Okay, she had a thing going with Nathan, but she put up with Tom messing around for *years*. She was the one trying to hold things together. You only see what you want to see, Mum. You have your own warped reality. Before Tom got done, you were forever going on about what a genius he was and how wonderful Claire was, blah blah blah. I'm not a genius, but I've been in my job ten years. I have a fantastic wife and kids. I spend my weekends at playgrounds with them. I never hear you ranting to people about that.' He stared at her with a bewildered expression. 'And waiting around for thirty years for Dad to come home is just *ridiculous*.'

'Maybe so. But here he is,' she said triumphantly. She was bluffing and they both knew it. She sat down at the dining table. It had seemed right at the time to defend Tom and show her loyalty to him. But now she could see that, from Danny's and Claire's perspectives, it could be seen as excessive and irrational. 'Is that why Melissa doesn't like me?' she asked in a small voice.

'Who said she doesn't like you? Listen, her mum is tougher than you but she's equally tough on all the sisters. She doesn't favour one of them over the others. And anyway, you're the one who acts weirdly around her family when all they're trying to do is be hospitable. You've just got this one-eyed approach . . .'

'It's not that I think Tom is better than you, Danny.' Elizabeth was shocked at the idea.

'I should hope not. The only thing Tom is a victim of is his own stupidity. Claire and Zach are the ones who suffered through all this.' He paused. 'And, another thing, Dad said Zach told him that he's under a Juvenile Justice order. Been up in front of the courts. How come I didn't know anything about this?'

'He hasn't been in front of the courts, exactly.' Elizabeth realised this was a minor detail to someone not familiar with the justice system and not a loophole she should take. 'Yes, he's been in some trouble. That's why I was living at Claire's – to give her a break and keep an eye on him.'

'So the kitchen's not being renovated anytime soon?'

Elizabeth shook her head. 'I'm not much of a liar, am I?'

Danny gave a dry laugh. 'It's not your strength, no.' He had been standing on the other side of the dining table and, much as she was not enjoying this conversation, she worried that he would walk out, as he often did when family discussions got heated. But instead he said, 'Can I have that beer now?'

Elizabeth nodded. She got two beers out of the fridge and flipped the caps off. Danny took one and put his arm around her shoulders. 'Let's sit outside for a bit, Mum. I need to calm down before I go home.'

Elizabeth nodded. It would be cool outside now but she didn't feel she could refuse. She slid open the door to the patio and Danny followed her outside. 'Shut the door behind you,' she told him.

He sat down and took a long draught of beer. 'My memories of Dad are really confused. The strongest ones are what a short fuse he had, how he would be so sweet sometimes, kind and patient, and then sort of erupt over nothing. I remember once a rescue helicopter was hovering overhead and he went into meltdown. It was really frightening for us, that unpredictability.' He paused and took a quick swig of his beer. 'What I realised tonight is . . . he's a really lovely man. And even though you can be a massive pain in the neck sometimes, Mum, you did a good thing bringing him home. You don't even know how much it means to me.'

Elizabeth looked up into the sky, watching it turn from mauve to grey in the dusk. She thought again of Ginny's letter, and while she'd never thought it would be an easy task to bring the family back together, neither had she anticipated it would be so painful for everyone. Trying to think of something wise and consoling to say, she turned to Danny and, in the spill of the out-door light, saw a flutter of blue and realised the patio door had been left slightly open. 'Oh no . . .' she murmured. 'Oh no . . .'

She stood up to give chase but Danny pressed on and she sat down again.

'And Mum, while we're having this heart-to-heart, I know you're not, but . . . you come across as a bit racist with Melissa's family. It's like you think their cultural practices are, like, I don't know . . . like a game? Something unnecessary and pretend —'

'I don't think that,' Elizabeth protested, forcing herself to focus. 'It's just unfamiliar.' But there was a grain of truth in the accusation, some deep-rooted idea – perhaps inherited from her parents – that these were ways from the old country and it was unnecessary to perpetuate them. Now it had been brought to her attention, she felt ashamed to think that she might have become the sort of person who believed everyone should become homog-enised, as if being Australian was one single thing.

'I'm just saying, that's how it seems. You don't know what Melissa and her family have to put up with from ignorant peo-ple all the time. It's made them very sensitive and more insular, I guess. You want to see more of the girls but on your own terms and preferably in your territory. Can you see that's kind of . . . insulting?'

Elizabeth nodded. A moment earlier she had been basking in Danny's gratitude, now all she could do was apologise and promise to do better. It was no good trying to explain her intentions, it was her actions she had to improve on.

'Have you actually spoken to Tom?' he asked.

'I've requested a call. Maybe tonight or in the morning. It's up to him to apply for a leave permit. I don't know how long the process of approval takes and there has to be an officer available to accompany him.'

'And he might not want to come,' said Danny.

Elizabeth nodded. 'I don't know about that. Do you think Melissa and the girls . . .?'

'I'll talk to Mel,' he said. 'I better go.'

She followed him through the house to the front door. As they said goodbye, to her surprise, he pulled her into a tight hug.

'You're a lovely man too, Danny.'

He laughed lightheartedly. 'Thanks, Mum. I do my best.'

She waved him off and hurried out into the back garden. It was dark now and there was no chance of being able to spot a tiny blue bird. She stood under the elm tree and called his name. She wandered around the periphery of the garden and poked around the larger shrubs. She tried to recall some of his favourite phrases and, circling the garden, called, 'Baz! Baz! What the hell?' She crouched down and called into the shrubby undergrowth, 'You're cute too! Good girl!' She realised the hopelessness of the situation and for a moment lost her mind, and stood in the middle of the lawn shouting, 'Head shot! Head shot!'

Next door's outside light flicked on. Geoffrey and his wife came outside to stare fearfully in her direction and she was tempted to finish the performance with 'Wassup stickybeak?' but instead scurried inside, bursting into tears at the sight of his empty cage. Eric was out in the big wild world now and she didn't hold out much hope for his return, or his survival.

She checked on Ray and was pleased to see him sleeping peacefully. She left a fresh glass of water for him and went down to sleep in Danny's room. She'd never spent the night in this room before, but it was a place of fond memories of reading Danny bedtime stories and settling him in for sleep with a cuddle. She recalled times when Tom had considered himself too old for story time, but would come in and lie on the end of the bed to listen to her read aloud. If only it were so simple to bring her sons together now.

Waiting for sleep, she turned over Danny's criticisms and attempted to defend herself against them. But she knew this was exactly what Ginny had tried to tell her. Instead of digging her heels in, she had to keep an open mind and listen to other points of view.

She thought about Tom, and back to the first time she had realised something was seriously wrong. Tom, Claire and Zach had come over for dinner. Elizabeth hadn't seen them for weeks, which wasn't unusual, but from the moment they arrived, there was tension in the air. Zach had just turned twelve. Normally cheerful, he looked sulky, and Elizabeth wondered if there had been an argument in the car. Tom could be grumpy, especially when he was tired or hungry, but Claire was always calm and never seemed to take things personally.

After dinner, Zach watched *Home Alone* on television and the adults moved outside onto the patio. Elizabeth and Claire had moved from wine to peppermint tea, but Tom opened a second bottle of wine.

'Looks like Claire will be driving home,' Elizabeth said, trying for a lightness of tone to mask her concern about his drinking.

'Thanks, Mum. I'm an adult now. I can figure those things out for myself.'

'I'm not trying to —' she began.

'Stress at work. Stress at home. I don't need stress here, thanks, Mum.' He poured a full glass and took a gulp.

'What's all this stress then?' asked Elizabeth. But Tom wouldn't meet her eye.

'There's been problems with the restaurant —' said Claire.

'What the fuck, Claire? Did I ask you to explain things to my mother? Je-sus!' Tom had always had a quick temper but Elizabeth had *never* heard him speak to Claire like that. She was stunned by his response.

'Sorry, Liz. He'll explain when —' began Claire.

Elizabeth was startled by the sound of glass breaking and turned to see red wine splattered like blood on the cream bricks of the house. Before she could say anything, Tom got up and stalked inside, and she could hear his raised voice telling Zach to turn off the television, they were leaving.

'It's only just started . . .' protested Zach.

'You've seen it a hundred times! Get in the car.'

Elizabeth and Claire hurried inside to see Tom levering Zach off the sofa by his armpit, forcing him to his feet. 'Tom, stop it! What are you doing?' said Elizabeth.

Zach was angry and tearful as Tom guided him from behind and frogmarched him to the front door. Elizabeth turned to Claire. 'What on earth is going on?'

Claire was looking around frantically for her bag. 'I'll speak to you later, Liz.'

When they had gone, Elizabeth stood in the middle of the living room, stunned by what she'd witnessed – and ashamed.

It was the first time she had ever felt truly ashamed of either of her sons and it was deeply uncomfortable. She'd barely slept that night and called Tom several times over the next few days, but he didn't return her calls. She tried Claire but was fobbed off. Finally, perhaps feeling sorry about her being shut out, Claire agreed to meet for coffee.

The day had been a late summer scorcher followed by a cloudburst and, as Elizabeth walked to the cafe, the dense humidity and the anxiety made her breathless. She sat at a table outside under the awning and waited for Claire to arrive, every possible scenario running through her head. Bankruptcy. Illness. Divorce.

Claire arrived looking pale and tense, and Elizabeth felt like a bully. Once their order had been taken, Claire said, 'I agree with Tom. It's really up to him to tell you what's going on. He just . . . he can't talk about it at the moment.'

'Claire, I'm worried sick.'

'Okay, but don't tell Tom we had this conversation, please. It will make things so much worse.' Elizabeth nodded her agreement and Claire continued. 'He discovered that the kitchen staff at the bistro were stealing from him and he shut the place down. The rent is four thousand a week and he's locked into a lease.' Claire paused. 'I know you're thinking that was a stupid move, Liz, and I completely agree, but it gets worse. Much worse. He needed money to pay everyone out. The staff have filed a joint action against him for unfair dismissal. He was desperate to get the place going again and . . . he borrowed money from a trust fund. A client's trust fund.'

Elizabeth put her face in her hands. She wanted to weep with disappointment and the fear of what would happen next. But she braced herself and asked Claire to go on.

'He was counting on the fact that, once he got the restaurant back up and running, the bank would extend his line of credit and he'd return the money before it was noticed. But Nathan found out. If it got out, Tom would be struck off.' Claire was silent for a moment. 'I didn't hear the full story from Tom, by the way. Nathan told me.'

'Nathan told you?' Elizabeth asked.

Claire blushed. 'Nathan's a good friend, Liz. He's saved the situation . . . put his own money into the trust to cover for Tom. Things have been horrible at home, Liz. I didn't know what was going on. I had to ask someone. Anyway, I shouldn't be telling you. It feels terrible talking about Tom behind his back. He felt under pressure the other night. He doesn't want to let you down.'

Elizabeth asked what would happen now, but Claire said she had no idea – it was out of her hands. As they parted, Elizabeth wondered what else she didn't know. This was the first time she had ever been shut out of Tom's life; even in his teen years they'd had frank conversations. But not any more, it seemed.

The next time she heard from Tom, he'd been arrested and charged with assault.

35

casserole night

1989 Lizzy has spent the afternoon making a casserole to take up to Ray's place for dinner this evening. It's Saturday night, both boys are home and pizzas have been ordered. She knocks on the door of Tom's bedroom, where he's entertaining his new girl-friend, Sophie, in the dark.

'Tom, I'm going up to Dad's but I'd like this door left open, please.' A muffled reply from within. 'Tom?' She waits a moment. 'I'm still here.'

The door cracks open and Tom's face appears. He's suffering from what used to be called a 'pash rash' in her teenage years. 'Mum, it's 1989. Not the fifties.'

'Thanks for the history lesson. I still have a responsibility to Sophie's parents, so door open, thanks. Why don't you watch a video with Danny?'

'Because he's watching *The Princess Bride* again?'

'I love *The Princess Bride*,' declares Sophie in the back-ground.

Tom grimaces at his mother. He pushes one of the many

socks fermenting on the floor into the gap between the door and jamb. 'Okay?'

'As you wish. I shall take my leave and bid you a fond adieu,' says Lizzy.

'Okay, see yah.' Tom squints at her through the crack in the door.

Danny lies on the sofa eating potato chips and watching his video. Lizzy pauses for a moment. 'You okay, Dan? Sure you don't want to get another video?'

'Nah, I like this one. It's funny,' he says, eyes fixed on the screen.

'I'm going to Dad's. I'll only be a couple of hours. Listen out for the pizza guy.'

'Okay. Say hi to Dad for me.'

Lizzy stands behind the sofa holding the casserole between two oven mitts. She watches the scene where Westley is unmasked and he and Buttercup embrace passionately. Danny pauses, a potato chip poised halfway to his mouth; he wears the smile of a thirteen-year-old dreaming of romance.

It's a mild autumn evening and only a few minutes' walk to Ray's flat. She often wanders up here before she goes to bed, just to reassure herself that he's okay. On Fridays, Ray always comes home for dinner and the boys rent whatever video they want to watch. Their taste runs to *Die Hard* and *Rambo*, probably the last thing Ray would choose for entertainment, but he loves these evenings together. Other times, she drops into his place and they chat or watch television, usually current affairs programs on the ABC. After his breakdown eighteen months ago, Ray spent almost six months in the psychiatric ward of Concord Hospital. Since his release, he lives a smaller life. He stays close to home and lives alone at his own insistence. These days, the man who once planned to travel the world and speak its languages barely has the confidence to leave the house. The hospital psychiatrist explained to Lizzy that many of the problems Ray was dealing with would normally occur in the first months after returning from a war zone, but he had managed to bury his trauma for almost two decades. Now it had caught up with him and consumed him. There was a new term, post-traumatic stress disorder, being applied to his condition but while it had been recognised, the psychiatrist explained, there was a long way to go before it was fully understood.

Lizzy knocks at Ray's front door and lets herself in with her key. He gets up and gives her a kiss, flicking off the television. 'Mmm, that smells good,' he says.

'Beef casserole,' she says, taking it through to the kitchen.

The flat is like an extension of their home: the furniture, crockery and cutlery all comfortingly familiar. Ray doesn't care much for aesthetics; it was Lizzy who bought the framed prints and the pottery bowls to make the place look more like a home than a halfway house. He lays placemats, plates and cutlery on the table, opens a bottle of red wine and pours them each a glass. He hands her one and leans against the bench while she serves up the casserole.

'How are the boys? Danny get his essay back?' he asks as they sit down.

'Not yet. I'm sure it will be fine though.'

'Lizzy, you've surpassed yourself,' he says, after the first mouthful. 'You've come a long way since you asked me how to cook a carrot.'

'I don't know why I asked you, it's not as if you knew how to cook anyway.'

'True, but we muddled through together somehow, didn't we?'

'Very happily,' she says with a smile.

'What are the boys up to tonight?'

'Tom's romancing Sophie behind closed doors and Danny's watching *The Princess Bride* again.'

Ray smiles fondly. 'He's a creature of habit.' After a moment he says, 'I had a letter back from the agent today. They're not renewing the lease. The owner wants the flat for his mother, apparently.'

'Oh no. That's a shame. It's such a good spot,' says Lizzy. 'Ray, it's only another few years and the boys will both be at uni. We can look at selling the house —'

'I don't want the boys to feel they're being pushed out of home.'

'You don't need to martyr yourself. Once the boys are independent . . .' Lizzy sighs – they've had this conversation so many times. He doesn't like to plan ahead, fearful of change or causing problems. It frustrates her, given the limited life he has these days. 'Anyway, we'll find something nearby for you. Even if we have to pay a bit more. I'll sort something out.'

'Lizzy, I can do it,' says Ray. 'I'll speak to the agent tomorrow.'

After dinner they sit on the sofa and watch the news. Ray has been following the Fitzgerald Inquiry into police corruption in Queensland and is familiar with many of the identities from his Associated Press days. Lizzy suggests he could write a freelance piece on it. He doesn't immediately dismiss the idea, but she knows from experience nothing will come of it. He tinkers with writing and is occasionally motivated to start pieces, but then she never hears about them again.

When the Minister for Corrective Services, Michael Yabsley, makes an appearance to discuss the implementation of the government's 'tough on crime' policy, Lizzy gives an exasperated sigh. 'They're going about this the wrong way,' she says. 'It's going to be disastrous for young offenders and push more of them into the prison system. We should be doing everything in our power to keep them out of it. We already know locking up kids isn't a deterrent – it just turns them into better criminals.'

'Conservative government and a director-general who's an ex-cop, not surprising the justice system's gone in that direction,' says Ray.

'I think most of us working in probation feel it would be better to intervene early, before these kids come under supervision, and get them into something more like a rehabilitation program. That's where the money should be spent. Building them up. Not locking them up.'

'You're there on the front line, Lizzy. Your department should be making recommendations and putting forward a proposal to the minister. You could be the one to drive it.'

'I don't know about that – there's plenty of people more senior than me in the department and a few old guard up the ranks who would resist anything progressive,' says Lizzy.

'But it's something you really care about. And you've got the energy for it.'

'I do . . . I could, I suppose.' Lizzy's not as sure of herself but she trusts Ray's judgement.

'Of course you could,' says Ray.

'I need to think about it more, figure out how it might work,' says Lizzy thoughtfully.

Ray puts his arm around her shoulders and gives her a kiss on the cheek. 'I like your hair like that. It suits you.'

'Going grey and overdue for a cut?'

He laughs under his breath. 'Let's face it, you make anything look good.'

'I'm glad you think so, darling.' She gives him a peck on the cheek.

After a moment, he says quietly, 'Lizzy, we need to get a divorce.'

'Let's see if there's a movie starting.' She picks up the remote and flicks through the channels. Back and forth. Bright faces. People laughing and crying. People killing each other.

'I'm serious. We need to go our separate ways. You're not even forty and that grey hair is because of me. I don't want that. There's plenty of time for you to start again.'

'I'm not interested, Ray. I've told you that. You're my one and only.'

'That's very romantic and sweet, but I don't actually want you giving up your life for me. You just need to open your mind to the idea. If you were free, it would make a difference to your thinking . . .'

'One day you will be well again. And when that happens, we'll get out that bloody map and stick those pins back in it, and we'll go – we'll go to Ireland and . . .'

'That's a beautiful dream, darling. I'd love to think that could happen. I'm tired of living like an old man, zonked out on these drugs. But I don't want you pinning your hopes on that.' He gives her a squeeze and kisses the top of her head absent-mindedly. It's rare to hear him complain and always brings on a creeping dread in her. Her thoughts inevitably turn to Kathleen, wondering for the thousandth time whether the decision to end her life was premeditated or a wild impulse. Had her judgement been clouded by an argument or incident, or did she feel trapped and desperately homesick? What was the tipping point that made her choose something so final?

'If I told you that I didn't love you, would you consider a divorce?' Ray asks.

'Hardly. I know that's not true.'

He laughs out loud, his head thrown back. 'It must be nice to feel so secure in my affections.'

'It is. I've never doubted it. So that's going to work against you now.'

He leans down and kisses her tenderly. 'As you wish. So did you find a movie to watch?'

Lizzy and Ray have promised Danny a family night out at a local Sizzler for his fourteenth birthday but, from the moment they step into the restaurant, Lizzy knows this is the wrong choice. It's packed on a Saturday night and more like a cafeteria, with people going back and forth to the buffet to refill their plates.

Noise and crowds are two things that Ray does not handle well. He pretends to enjoy himself and makes an effort at conversation but, to Lizzy, he sounds like a bad actor reading lines from a script. The first bottle of wine disappears quickly and another takes its place. The boys, distracted by food and friends from school, don't seem to notice the tension at the table. But on the drive home, Tom teases Danny about a girl who said hello to him. A fight breaks out in the back seat and the evening takes a definite turn for the worse.

Ray had planned to come home with them for an hour or two, but now says he'd prefer to be dropped at his place. He's moved to a block of flats on the Pacific Highway where he has neighbours who come home at all hours and play loud music. He's already had an argument with the neighbour above him. When they drop him off, he seems dopey and disoriented. He wishes Danny a happy birthday and wanders off without saying goodbye.

'Dad's so pissed,' says Tom as they drive away.

'He's probably taken a Valium,' Lizzy says. 'Not good to mix with alcohol.'

'Why does he do it then?' asks Danny.

'Valium helps him stay calm and . . . I don't know, the drinking's a habit, I suppose.'

'He's a pisshead,' says Tom. 'You're just making excuses for him. As usual.'

Lizzy pulls into their driveway and switches off the engine. 'Don't talk about him like that, please, Tom. Dad's got a lot to cope with. He's doing his best.'

'Yeah, right,' says Tom. 'Freaking out over a war from twenty years ago. I don't get why it's suddenly a big deal. He was better *before* he went into hospital.'

'Not really,' says Danny. 'Remember when he punched his fist through the kitchen window? And then that other time on cracker night you let off the rocket . . .'

Tom opens the car door. 'Yeah, how could I forget? Never heard the end of it from Mum. At least we don't have to hear him screaming in the middle of the night like a crazy vampire.'

Lizzy knows all of these incidents happened when Ray had been drinking, but that's hardly an excuse she can offer.

'Vampires are really quiet,' says Danny as they follow Tom inside. 'They sneak up on people. It's more like a werewolf howling, and what about —'

'Yes, okay, thank you,' says Lizzy. 'We don't need to relive these incidents. At least he takes it out on things, not on us.'

Tom turns on her angrily. 'Are you kidding? Are we supposed to be happy that he doesn't bash us up?'

'No, of course not. I didn't mean that . . . I just meant —'

'I feel sorry for Dad,' interrupts Danny. 'He can't help getting upset.'

'He needs to get over it,' says Tom furiously. 'He was embarrassing tonight. He looked like he was actually in the middle of a battle. People were staring at him.'

'What did he do?' asks Danny. 'He was just sitting there.'

'Like a retard!' Tom walks off down to his room and she waits for the inevitable slam of the door. There it is. The house trembles slightly and stills.

'Dad should come and live at home again,' says Danny. 'I don't mind him doing those things and he doesn't like that place he's living anyway.'

Lizzy puts her hands on his shoulders and looks into his dear face with its childlike innocence. 'Happy birthday, Danny.'

'Thanks, Mum. You too.' They laugh and hug each other and say goodnight.

Lizzy's mind drifts to the other side of the highway. Her best hope is that Ray can wind down now and watch something on television. Sometimes he's too agitated to settle for long and paces around drinking, then falls asleep in front of the television.

She calls him before she goes to bed. He takes so long to

answer, she begins to glance around for her car keys. When he picks up the phone, he says nothing for a moment, only the hum of the line between them. 'Night, Lizzy,' he says, his voice full of sadness. 'Sleep well.'

36

the days ahead

On Monday morning, Elizabeth called their family doctor and explained the situation with Ray. She was put in touch with hospice care and made an appointment for a palliative care nurse to come and see him. She ordered a walking frame, a shower chair and a stick to be delivered so he had every option for mobility.

Elizabeth's phone, normally so silent, buzzed all morning with messages and calls from Baz, Danny and Claire – even one from Zach, asking if he could come on Friday afternoon and stay the weekend. Finally there was a call from Tom. This time, Elizabeth made sure she explained properly how they had found Ray and brought him home. 'That was Zach's doing,' she added. 'He made it happen.'

Tom was silent for a moment. 'So how long has Dad got?'

'I don't know, Tom. I'm sorry . . . but not long.' She noticed there was less than two minutes left on the call. 'You need to put in an application for compassionate leave straight away. I know those things can take time.'

Tom seemed reluctant. 'Yeah. I can try . . . Sorry, Mum.'

'Sorry for what, Tom?'

'For being in here. Not being able to help. I always thought you wanted Dad to come back so he could see what a good job you'd done with everything.'

'I just wanted him to know —' She wasn't sure what she wanted Ray to know, she had simply been doing her best to compensate for his absence over the years.

'It wasn't an insult. I meant —' began Tom. But before he could finish, his time was up and the call disconnected.

Afterwards, Elizabeth felt unsettled. There was something in Tom's tone that made her less certain that he would make the effort to see Ray, and she realised she'd neglected to ask if he actually wanted to see his father.

She went out into the garden and called for Eric, wondering how long he could survive around those aggressive Indian mynas. She chopped up some strawberries and put them on the outdoor table, then added some blueberries and almonds: a feast that attracted plenty of birds but none of them her little blue buddy.

When Ray woke in the early afternoon, she helped him shower and made him comfortable on the sofa with a few snacks on the side table. He had no appetite and only ate to please her. She made tea for them and entertained him with the story of Ginny's funeral, how she had worn her dress back to front and ended up locked in the funeral home. The part about her stuffing her mouth full of blinis had Ray laughing so hard that he had to ask her to stop several times so he could catch his breath. When he'd recovered, she continued with the tale of her Olympian efforts to conquer the blowfly, and mimicked the shocked reaction of Zach's friends.

'Poor Zach,' said Ray, wiping away tears of laughter. 'You've got to hand it to him for quick thinking, disowning you like that. Oh, I wish I could have seen that . . .'

Elizabeth laughed. 'You haven't heard about the night he had me running up and down the beach and hiding from the police in my pyjamas yet.'

'It's good that he gets you out and about,' said Ray.

'I suppose so.' Elizabeth turned to look out the patio doors, hoping for a flash of blue. There was a sprinkle of rain and the garden was quiet. She hoped Eric was enjoying it wherever he was and felt a pang of missing the little fellow.

'I'm sorry about Eric, Lizzy. He may turn up, you know. Budgies can be surprising.'

Elizabeth wasn't holding out much hope. The day turned gloomy as the rain set in. She got up and turned on a couple of lamps and made more tea. When she sat down, Ray smiled across at her. Despite the circumstances, there was contentment in these moments.

'Lizzy . . . you didn't need to hide Tom's troubles from me.'

'It wasn't so much hiding as censoring, which I suppose is the same thing. And what could you do anyway?'

'I feel guilty for thinking everything was running smoothly and the boys were fine. That must have been terrible for you.'

'All of us really,' agreed Elizabeth. 'I think he just snapped under the strain. They were in the carpark when the argument started. Tom threw a punch, Nathan barely defended himself. Someone called the police and the whole thing was caught on security cameras.'

'I understand that urge, wanting to lash out at someone just to get some relief from the tension.'

'I know you do,' she said. 'But you managed to restrain yourself.' She got up and went to the dresser, and got out Ginny's letter. She handed it to him; he put his glasses on and read it slowly several times.

'I am very honoured to be your one love, Lizzy, but waiting all these years . . .' Ray shook his head as he read the letter again. 'What does she mean about withdrawing?'

'I seem to have developed a gift for alienating people, one way or another.'

'You're not being too hard on yourself? I didn't get that impression from Danny. And Zach obviously thinks the world of you.'

Elizabeth laughed out loud. 'Now you're exaggerating. You know, I never really worried about Danny. I always thought he would be fine. It was Tom with his moods and frustrations . . . anyway, seems I might have overcompensated.'

'Danny and I had such a good talk,' said Ray fondly. 'I was exhausted at the end but I just wanted to keep on talking with him.'

'I blame myself that Tom didn't feel he could confide in me.'

'You're being hard on yourself again, Lizzy.' He held up the letter and turned it over. 'Was there more? Looks like the bottom of this letter has been torn off.'

'Ah, yes. There was a bit about making friends with Judith. I chucked that away. I don't have to do everything Ginny says.'

Ray laughed and handed the letter back to her. 'And Judith was a bridge too far.'

Over the next few days, apart from a visit from the palliative care nurse, they were mostly left to themselves and fell into an easy routine. Each morning, Elizabeth brought Ray a cup of tea in bed and they sat together talking, mainly about the past. They pieced together forgotten anecdotes and remembered the names of forgotten friends, as they went through the photo albums that Elizabeth had painstakingly assembled over the years, almost as if she had been preparing for this time.

When he was able, she helped him up and into the shower. Remembering how strong he'd once been, it tore at her heart that he was now so frail that he needed her support. In the afternoons, she ran errands quickly while he rested, not wanting to be away from his side. In the evenings they watched old movies they had loved: *12 Angry Men*, *Rear Window*, *La Dolce Vita* – they called it the O'Reilly Film Festival. Ray had little exposure to the online world and was both bewildered and entranced by instantaneous streaming.

At Ray's request she contacted Andy, who had lived in London for many years where he worked as a lawyer. Elizabeth hadn't seen him since Cynthia's funeral but now he and Ray had a long conversation and said their goodbyes. She called Paul and explained the situation, and he also had a chat to Ray. Baz rang every few days and Susie had sent a kind message. Tom had arranged to visit the next weekend.

On Friday the sun came out and the sky cleared to a vivid blue. With the help of the stick and Elizabeth's arm, Ray was able to sit outside on the bench seat under the shade of the elm. 'What was it really like, up there in the cabin?' she asked him. 'You made it sound idyllic.'

'Well, it wasn't one thing, obviously. From what I remember of my first weeks there, I felt relief to be left to my own devices. After a couple of months, I realised that I had to give up drinking or I would drink myself to death. It wasn't as hard as I thought, but it made the days seem longer.'

'It must have been lonely though,' suggested Elizabeth.

'Of course, but you get used to that over time and you become better company to yourself. You're forced to stop complaining or feeling sorry for yourself, and try to be a more cheerful friend.'

'That's why I got Eric, so I didn't have to talk to myself,' said Elizabeth. 'It was when I started to call myself "Missy", like my mother used to. I knew it was all downhill from there.'

'The first year was the hardest,' admitted Ray. 'By then I had a routine, kept myself busy, allowed myself to rest if I hadn't slept. I did feel the pressure was off and I'd felt under pressure for so long. I don't know where the years have gone – just disappeared one day at a time.'

'Neither do I,' said Elizabeth. It seemed to her that this time together now was expanding and connecting those decades spent apart.

When Ray's back began to hurt, she helped him to his feet. As he shifted his weight to the stick, it slipped out from under him. Before she could grab him, he lost his balance and fell hard on his hip, his face rigid from the pain of the impact. Once she'd established that nothing was broken, Elizabeth tried to lift him but he was too heavy.

'Just wait, Lizzy. Don't hurt your back. Give me a moment to recover.'

Elizabeth sat down on the damp grass beside him and made his head comfortable on her lap. 'Now we're both down here,' said Ray. 'Will we ever get up again?'

'I don't mind it down here, actually. It smells kind of earthy.'

She stroked his head, running her fingers over the soft bristles. 'It's quite lovely.'

She knew the end was coming a little closer every day, and when she let that thought intrude, a sick dread washed over her. So she pushed it away, determined not to make a misery of this time together. She would remember the touch of his hand and every smile exchanged when there was no hand to hold, no gaze to meet. Her love for Ray, dormant all these years, glowed warm inside her now.

'I think I'm going to have to call an ambulance, darling. We can't stay here all day.'

'No. We can do it,' insisted Ray. 'I don't want to end up back in hospital after all that.'

Elizabeth eased his head off her lap and got to her feet. 'Let's try and get you sitting up, at least.' She knelt down and helped him into a sitting position, but there was no way she could get him to his feet – he was just too weak. She stood up and looked around for something he could hold on to and noticed the next-door neighbour, the one with the dreadlocks, standing on his back step talking on his phone. Without hesitation, she waved in his direction. 'Help! Can you help us?'

He turned her way with a look of surprise and a moment later vaulted over the fence.

'Where did you come from?' asked Ray, startled.

'I just dropped out of this tree,' said the man. 'I'm Brendan, your neighbour. Anything broken?'

Ray shook his head. 'Just don't have the manpower to get up.'

Brendan squatted down and, seemingly without effort, scooped Ray up and onto his feet. With Ray's arm across his shoulders, the two of them walked slowly towards the house.

Elizabeth rushed ahead and led the way to the bedroom, where Brendan gently helped Ray onto the bed. 'Thanks,' said Ray, lying back on the pillows. 'Thank you, neighbour.'

''S'okay, mate. Anytime. I'll leave my number. Take care.'

In the kitchen, the young man wrote his number down and Elizabeth thanked him again.

'I'm sorry about the bin thing,' he said. She wasn't sure if he was reminding her what a nark she had been or putting the incident behind them. She apologised too. It was less painful than she anticipated. 'Take care, Mrs O'Reilly,' he said again.

To Elizabeth, this phrase usually sounded like a veiled threat from a gangster movie, but coming from Brendan it was comforting. He had a nice smile and well-tended teeth. He seemed kind and friendly. He'd remembered her name from the crabby notes she had left him. 'Elizabeth,' she said. 'Please call me Elizabeth.'

37

stories and songs

Zach arrived after school on Friday. He slung his backpack on the floor in the living room and made himself at home. He sat on the kitchen bench, the way he used to when he was little, so that she could keep an eye on him.

'Where's Ray?' he asked as he watched her make a sandwich for him.

'He's having a nap. He'll be up soon. He knows you're coming over. How did you go with Angela this week?' she asked him.

'All good,' he said. 'Winning.'

'Well, you need to keep on winning, Zach. You've still got three more months before the hearing – don't blow it now.'

He made no comment. She knew it annoyed him when she brought the subject up but she wasn't going to let that stop her reminding him to stay on track.

'Do you think Ray could get a bit better?' he asked. 'Like, not cured, but, you know . . .'

'Have a longer life?' asked Elizabeth. 'I don't want to give you false hope, Zach. He's very sick and with more than one type of cancer. When he was in Vietnam in the war, he was exposed to a very nasty herbicide called Agent Orange – it causes lots of different cancers. He's not the only one suffering from this.'

'Rough,' he muttered under his breath. He slid down off the bench and took the sandwich from her. 'Dad called me yesterday. He said he's coming on Sunday.'

Elizabeth nodded. 'Provided there's an officer to escort him. It's just for a few hours but it'll be nice for us all to be together.'

Zach stood at the patio doors looking into the garden while he ate his sandwich. 'I thought you said Uncle Eric wasn't allowed outside,' he said after a moment.

It took Elizabeth a second to grasp what he meant. She leaned over to look out the window. Eric was on the outdoor table pecking at the berries she had continued putting out every day since he'd gone missing, even though she'd lost all hope.

'I don't believe it! Get the small cage from the hall cupboard, Zach.' She walked outside making kissing sounds. 'Hello, Eric, sweet thing . . . *tsk* . . . *tsk* . . .' She leaned over slowly and offered her knuckle. He glanced away, wilfully ignoring her. She slid her finger under his chest and, after a moment's consideration, he daintily stepped onto her knuckle and was transported to the safety of his waiting cage.

'That was very careless, Nano. He could've gone anywhere,' said Zach. 'Where you been, li'l buddy? Where you been?'

'Well spotted, Zach,' said Elizabeth. 'I honestly thought —'

'Whatever,' Zach interrupted. 'Can I go and see Ray now?'

Elizabeth nodded. 'Just pop your head in and see if he's awake.'

When he'd gone, she transferred Eric to his large cage. 'Clever boy,' she told him. 'Clever boy. Welcome home.'

'Happy days,' Eric agreed. He went over to his tiny mirror to welcome his reflection home. 'Happy days.'

Elizabeth went down to the bedroom to find Ray settled comfortably on his pillows while Zach sat cross-legged on the end of the bed, entertaining him with stories from school. 'Mrs Jennings, the geography teacher, she's like a real bogan. Thinks she's gangsta. Shouts things like, "If youse lot don't shuddup o'm sending the lot of yis to the proncapol's office." Honestly,' Zach said sniffily, 'her English is *appalling* and she throws stuff at us all the time. Markers and things, throws like a ninja . . .' He demonstrated her loose wrist technique accompanied by a maniacal expression.

Ray was laughing. 'How's her aim?' he asked.

'Hmm . . . not bad. She gets a lot of practice.'

'And what do you do when she throws things?' asked Elizabeth, her sympathies leaning towards Mrs Jennings despite her poor diction and old-style methods of discipline.

'We throw them at each other . . . I mean, why give people ammunition?'

'I can see your logic, Zach,' said Elizabeth. 'But you're not compelled to throw things.'

'Debatable. It is basically a war zone.'

'Used to be blackboard dusters and chalk when we were at school,' said Ray. 'Remember the science teacher, Lizzy? Mr Kennedy used to do this overarm bowl with a duster. He'd played for Australia, never missed.'

'Chalk was the lesser evil,' agreed Elizabeth. 'I can actually remember the thunk of the duster bouncing off certain students' heads.'

'Empty vessels,' said Ray with a smile.

Zach frowned. 'What's an empty vessel?'

Ray explained the expression to him and Zach continued to regale them with tales from school. Elizabeth was struck by his powers of observation for the various tics and idiosyncrasies of his teachers and fellow students. Telling these stories, it was hard to believe this was the taciturn, monosyllabic boy of recent times, but Elizabeth had no doubt he could revert without notice.

On Saturday afternoon, Danny arrived with Melissa and the girls. Elizabeth baked a cake, and the adults sat outside and watched Zach chase the girls around the garden. Melissa was quiet but Elizabeth made a concerted effort to be natural, rather than tripping over herself to make her daughter-in-law feel comfortable, which would likely have the opposite effect.

When Danny realised Ray was getting tired, he said they would go and be back the next day when both Tom and Claire would be there. When they'd gone, Zach sprawled on the sofa to watch something dark and violent on Netflix while Elizabeth ordered takeaway and tidied the house ready for the next day.

Ray slept through the evening. Every day he was a little weaker, and Elizabeth hoped he would be able to get out of bed for Tom's visit and be with the whole family.

When Zach had gone to bed, she sat with Ray and watched him sleep. Every day she wished for one more day, one more night and then another day. As if he sensed her presence, he opened his eyes and turned his head towards her. 'What have I missed?' he asked, his voice a hoarse whisper.

'Nothing at all.' She leaned over and gave him a sip of water from a bottle on the bedside table.

He patted the bed beside him. 'Stay with me, Lizzy.'

She nodded, took off her dressing gown and slipped into bed. All these years she'd slept alone in this bed, yet it felt like the most natural thing in the world to settle in beside Ray once more.

'Do you ever think about how different our lives might have been?' he asked. 'It's been on my mind the last few days.'

'Mine too. I wonder what we'd be doing now if things had gone to plan. A lot of people seem to go on cruises at our time of life,' said Elizabeth.

Ray gave a shudder of laughter. 'That really is a stretch. I'm not sure we're cruise people, are we?'

'You can cruise down the Rhine in a slow boat that stops at every city – say, start in Amsterdam, then Cologne and Strasbourg. I don't remember the order of the cities. Or maybe a canal trip through France would be better. Just the two of us.'

'Sounds more our style,' agreed Ray.

'They have bikes and you can cycle into the villages on the way.'

'I can see us picnicking under an olive tree with a bottle of wine, fromage and a baguette . . .'

'Are you wearing a beret and playing the accordion?'

'Absolutely, and you are too. We could hire a car and drive to Spain or Italy.'

'Or both,' said Elizabeth. 'We're not in any hurry.'

With some effort, Ray inched over onto his side to face her. He touched her cheek tenderly. 'Do you ever regret climbing out that window, Lizzy?'

'Never,' said Elizabeth. 'That was the most exciting night of my life.'

'I'm glad,' said Ray. 'I thought you must have had second thoughts by now.'

They lay quietly for a moment. Ray stroked her hair and took her hand.

'Ray, if I had a song that represented me, what do you think it would be?'

'I'm not sure what you mean.'

'At Ginny's funeral they played "You Raise Me Up" and I thought it captured her so perfectly. I've been wondering what my song might be.'

Ray rolled onto his back and gave a breathless laugh. 'What about "Don't Bring Me Down"?'

'Very funny. I'm being serious.'

'There was that one about being as sweet as a honey bee. I remember us dancing to that tune.'

Elizabeth laughed. 'I'm not sure that describes me, sad to say.'

'Okay, I've got it – "Heaven Must Be Missing an Angel".' He hummed the opening bars under his breath.

'Ray, seriously? If they play that at my funeral people will think they're in the wrong chapel.'

Ray sighed. 'Perhaps your song hasn't been written yet, Lizzy. It's being written now and you have to stay on this earth until your song is complete.'

'What about you, darling? What's your song?' she asked.

'You're my song, Lizzy.'

Elizabeth laughed. 'Good try, you ol' charmer. I'm more like an annoying tune you can't get out of your head.'

'Not everyone has a great love, Lizzy. We're lucky to have experienced that.' He was silent for a while, his breathing shallow as if he was running out of breath. Finally he whispered,

'Te amo, Lizzy, my love.' And, without hesitation, she replied, 'Te amo.'

With slow careful movements, he turned and curled on his side away from her. She fitted herself into his body, her arms around him, feeling bones where there was once flesh but his heartbeat still strong beneath her hand. She nestled her face between his shoulder blades and fell asleep.

When Elizabeth woke at dawn, Ray lay on his back, breathing quietly. She went into the kitchen and watched the sun creep into the garden as she made the tea. She thought about the day ahead with the family all here and ran through the menu in her head, calculating what time she needed to put the meat in the oven.

She was only away a few minutes, but when she walked back into the bedroom it was full of silence. And she knew he'd gone. She stood over him, not wanting it to be true, hoping he would gasp and take a breath, but he was quite still, his expression peaceful. She lay down beside him and put her head on his chest. All she wanted was another day, another hour, but it was not to be, and even though she had endured many lonely days and nights in her life, nothing had prepared her for the loneliness that overtook her now. The emptiness of a world without Ray.

38

letter under the door

1 November 1989

My darling Lizzy, I know how much this will hurt you and I'm so sorry, but I see no other way. Every time I come out of hospital, we talk about a new era and a fresh start. But we both know this has become a cycle, and it's difficult to see how that cycle will ever be broken.

Ward 29 is full of broken men, like me. Each time we leave and venture out into the real world, we believe things will be different. And perhaps for a while they are – then something goes wrong and we're back where we started. Not coping, falling apart and dragging people we love down with us. Each time someone goes back there, they have a little less in their lives. Some are filled with loathing for themselves, others with self-pity and resentment. I don't want to be one of them, and I don't want to wear out the patience of the people I love.

I see more clearly now the toll this has taken on the boys.

You can see it in their eyes. Last night at Danny's birthday dinner, I saw the resentment in Tom and a growing contempt. He sees right through my attempts to be upbeat, and that must be painful for him. Danny is torn between disappointment and anxiety, but is still optimistic and encouraging – he is his mother's son.

The time has come to stop fooling ourselves, my darling. We must face the situation as it is, not as we wish it could be. I have to gather all my strength and break the cycle to release you from the burden I have become. It's not fair on you, and it's not fair on the boys.

I promised myself many years ago that however much I was drawn to ending my life – as I have been many times – I would resist. Even when the suffering feels unbearable, I have to grit my teeth and bear it. Even when I'm convinced beyond all doubt that the world would be better off without me, that I am nothing but a dead-weight on society and on you, I have to keep going and remind myself that Mum had these same thoughts of despair and hopelessness. She must have felt there was no other way out. If only she could have waited another day, another week, until her thinking was clearer. But she acted and the pain of that act will be with me until the end of my days.

There has never been a time when I questioned your love, my beautiful Lizzy. You have done too much at your own cost and I fear it will damage your relationship with the boys in the future. Now that they are young men, convinced of their own immortality, as I once was, they are losing respect for me. Perhaps Tom has already lost it. They see me, through the harsh eyes of the young, as a hopeless broken man. They judge my actions as weak. And who can blame them?

I need to go away, Lizzy. Far away from here and from everything I know, to a place where I know nothing and no one. I need to be alone. I must find a way to sublimate the storm raging inside me and find some peace. All these years I have expended so much energy trying to be the person I once was. The person I know others want me to be. Yet that man continues to elude me, and searching for him exhausts me every day.

The happiest days of my life have been spent with you. Last week, sitting on the sofa, holding your hand and watching *Funniest Home Videos* with the boys, laughing together, as if our lives are a series of small mishaps we look back on and see the funny side of. But, as always, when the evening draws to a close I feel myself go cold knowing that soon my only companions will be fear and agitation.

I know you believe that one day I will recover, but the truth is that, despite the passing of time, the things I experienced are just as vivid in my dreams, perhaps more so. They have mutated and in the dead of night they come to me like a horror film that I'm doomed to watch over and over. There are times when I do sleep but, even now, the slightest sound and I'm out of bed, drenched in sweat, searching for my weapon in the dark. It was a brief period in my life and a long time ago but I'm beginning to doubt I can ever outrun it. I left things too long.

When Baz came to see me in hospital, he offered me his place up in the mountains near Wissam. I need to try it as a way to break this cycle.

You've done everything for me. Cared for me, cleaned up after me, talked me down off clifftops. But this can't continue to be your life. Don't fight it. Let me go, Lizzy. Heal your heart, knowing I am safe in a quiet place among trees and birds, under the wide blue sky with the mountains at my back. Living the simple life.

I know you'll be angry that I slipped away without saying goodbye. Right now my resolve is threadbare. Saying goodbye to you would be impossible. If you were to put your arms around me, I would abandon all plans and stay. And stay. And stay. And nothing would ever change. Life will be easier for you if you let me go. I will write to you. Not love letters, simply letters from a distant relative. Someone you once knew.

The one thing I ask of you is not to try and find me. Don't come and rescue me. It's time I rescued myself. Write to me care of the Post Office at Wissam with your news, and news of the boys, but please don't ask me to come home. Because if you do, I will feel I must.

If only we can forget these past few years and remember the happy days we had together and the early years with our little boys. The sweetest of times.

I wish more sweet times for you, Lizzy, my darling. Think of me now and then and know I love you, but think of me as a past love, a lost love. One day your heart will mend and find new love with my blessing.

Yours, Ray.

39

slippery noodles

Elizabeth watched Lily and Grace as they ran squealing through the water fountains that spurted up from the pavement. Like many other children tonight, the girls were both dressed in red with pretty lace tops, full satin skirts, and red ribbons in their hair. Grace zigzagged across the square, dodging the jets, and Lily followed her, as did other children, all watched by smiling parents and grandparents. The girls' shoes would be soaked but Melissa didn't seem to mind; she and her mother, Doris, were laughing at their antics.

The whole of Chinatown had been given over to the Lunar New Year celebrations. Families roamed the streets and watched the lion dancers who wore fantastical costumes in yellow and red, writhing and dancing to beating drums. Some streets were blocked off with stages and performances by musicians and dancers from Asian countries. Women of all ages, many older than Elizabeth, wore spectacular costumes: towering headdresses of flowers and brightly patterned robes. They danced and sang in high voices, and banged drums with bright smiles on their faces.

Doris came over and stood next to Elizabeth. 'You look pretty in red blouse. You should wear more often, Liz. Nice bright colour.'

Elizabeth glanced down at her shirt. 'I've never thought of red as one of my colours. But if it brings me luck, why not?'

'We already lucky,' said Doris, gesturing widely, and Elizabeth had to agree.

'Okay, ladies,' said Danny, coming over to them. 'We're going to eat now before the restaurants get too crowded. Follow me.'

Doris called to Lily and Grace, then she and Elizabeth took the girls' hands and followed Melissa and Danny through the crowded streets. Everywhere Elizabeth looked there was colour: paper lanterns in red, pink, orange and purple; sideshows with enormous stuffed toys in bright greens, blue and pink. Swirls of colour all around them and, despite the crowds, Elizabeth felt safe and comfortable. The atmosphere was one of quiet celebration, nothing like drunken yobbos that roamed the streets on New Year's Eve.

Danny pushed open the door to a noodle restaurant and ushered the family in. 'You okay with this, Mum? The girls love noodles.'

'Of course,' said Elizabeth, although she lacked much experience with noodles.

The family jammed around a table and, menus in hand, the adults began an earnest discussion in Cantonese. Elizabeth knew that Danny had made an effort to learn the language over the years but was amazed that he could clearly hold his own in this discussion. It was odd to hear these foreign sounds coming from her son, that gentle boy who found the world such a mysterious place. She was reminded of Ray and his efforts to learn Spanish all those years ago; Danny had inherited his dedication.

From time to time, Doris asked: 'You like Lanzhou noodle, Liz?' 'Sichuan noodle?' Elizabeth agreed to each proposal without any idea what they were.

Doris beckoned the waiter over and, although Elizabeth couldn't understand a word, she was impressed by Doris's confidence, asking questions, consulting with Melissa and Danny and returning to the waiter with specific instructions. Doris watched him note down the order and asked him to read it back. She clarified several points and finally gave her approval.

'All okay, Mum?' asked Danny.

'Lovely,' said Elizabeth. 'I'm having a lovely time.' She reached across the table and patted his hand. 'You don't need to worry about me, Danny.'

He blinked and smiled. Melissa turned to Lily and Grace. 'Pretty good having two nanas here for New Year, isn't it, girls?'

'Yay,' said Lily.

'Yay, yay,' repeated Grace.

Lily, always the excitable one, shouted 'Yay! Yay!' Melissa held her hand up to halt the escalation of celebrations and Lily reduced her voice to a whisper. 'Yay.'

Whatever the volume, Elizabeth was pleased they were happy. Melissa was still reserved around her, and the idea that her daughter-in-law may have misinterpreted her awkwardness as disapproval still made Elizabeth feel dreadful. She wasn't entirely at home or relaxed in this environment, but she could see a place for herself in Danny's family and she would earn it.

Two waiters arrived at the table, bearing large bowls of

steaming noodles, smelling of ginger and garlic and a dozen delicious fragrances that Elizabeth couldn't identify. Using a serving spoon, she helped herself to the nearest one.

Seeing her fumble with the chopsticks, Danny said, 'I'll get you some cutlery, Mum.'

'Not necessary,' said Doris. 'Let me show you, Liz.' She held up her chopsticks and demonstrated. She helped Elizabeth grasp them correctly and use the tweezer action to pick up the noodles, neglecting her own meal to watch and correct until Elizabeth understood the technique.

Elizabeth thanked her. 'My husband, Ray – Danny's father . . . and Tom's father too, of course. And Lily and Grace's grandfather . . .' Elizabeth had no idea why she was making such a long introduction, as if he was about to be presented with an award, when everyone at the table knew perfectly well who he was. It was just fortunate she didn't have a trumpet on her. 'Well, what I'm getting to is that Asian food gave him migraines, so we never —'

'MSG,' interrupted Doris.

'No, it wasn't that,' Elizabeth said. 'It was to do with his war service. Perhaps Danny told you about Ray . . .' She looked at Danny and saw that he hadn't. All these years he had kept that secret close. She gave him an apologetic smile. 'Ray was traumatised in Vietnam. He had nothing against the people there, it wasn't that. He felt great compassion for them. But the smell of Asian food triggered these migraines. He couldn't help it. Even later, I never got into the habit of eating —'

'Next week, you come to yum cha with us. Sunday morning,' said Doris.

'Yay,' whispered Lily, adding a silent handclap.

Elizabeth agreed and everyone turned their attentions to their meals. She struggled determinedly with the chopsticks slipping and sliding over each other. Eventually she managed to grasp a fat wad of noodles. Lifting it to her mouth, she splattered sauce down her chin and all down her red shirt, but it was the most delicious thing she had ever tasted.

40

packing boxes

'Mum, are they Dad's clothes in Danny's wardrobe? Or are you dating a man with a taste for eighties clothes?' asked Tom. 'Mum? Where are you?'

'Mum!' cried Eric, sitting on the top perch of his cage. 'Mum!'

'I'm here,' said Elizabeth, coming out of the kitchen.

'The problem is that you've never moved before,' said Tom when they met in the living room. 'You need to get rid of way more stuff. These clothes can go. I'll do a run down to the Red Cross bin, get that out of the way.'

Elizabeth followed him to Danny's old room and together they packed up half-a-dozen bags with shirts, jackets, trousers and pairs of shoes. Tom was right, they were all hopelessly out of fashion. It had been foolish to keep them for so long.

Once Tom drove off with that load, there were a few less things to worry about. The packing had started off in an organised way, but then Tom got involved and had his own strategies. Now every room had become chaotic and Elizabeth found herself moving boxes from one room to another without a clear plan. Tom was right: she lacked experience. This was her first move in more than forty years. She thought about people who moved every few years and wondered how they could bear the disruption, but at least they regularly culled their belongings. Now she had to deal with toys and books from the boys' childhood, framed prints sitting in the backs of wardrobes, a dozen different corkscrews – none of which were foolproof. She had found things she'd lost, and things she'd forgotten about.

When Tom got back from his errand, he went outside and stood on the lawn as he had done often since his release. He gazed up at a flock of birds flying across the pale afternoon sky until they had disappeared, then he turned away and came back into the house. Elizabeth had been worried he would be depressed when he was released and had to face the world. But he'd quickly found a job making pizzas and had rented a small flat near Claire's place. She had yet to hear him complain about his lot.

Elizabeth baked a couple of pieces of salmon for dinner with rice and a salad. She opened a bottle of white wine and poured two glasses. Tom sat down at the table and inhaled the smell of his meal. 'Looks delicious, Mum. Thanks.' After a moment he said, 'Looking through those clothes of Dad's really brought back some memories for me. I was putting them in the clothing bin and, I don't know . . . I felt really emotional.'

'What sort of memories?' asked Elizabeth.

'All sorts. Things I'd forgotten about, I suppose. Over the years, I've always painted Dad in a bad light. Most of what I remember are the crazy incidents, like when Danny and I might have a bit of a squabble, or kicked each other under the table, and Dad would just charge out the door and not come back for hours. I thought it was a sort of manipulation.'

'Really?' asked Elizabeth.

'I know, Mum. I get it. You don't have to go on defending him. I met veterans inside and the sons of vets. I understand PTSD more now. I get that's why he walked out and also why he drank and went off about things.' Tom paused, took a deep breath and gathered himself. 'Seeing his clothes, like that Eagles t-shirt he used to wear around the house, I started to remember more ordinary things, like playing cricket in the backyard, him making us slingshots and taking us camping in the national park.' Tom put his knife and fork down and rubbed his face in an agonised way. 'I regret not seeing him. If I'd put in the request straight away . . . but I put it off and —'

'I'm sure you had your reasons,' said Elizabeth gently.

'It wasn't that I didn't want to see him. I was ashamed of *my* behaviour. I made him out to be a shit parent, and then I turned into one myself.'

'Tom, you're being too hard on yourself —'

He cut her off with a shake of his head. 'When I saw Claire's jacket in Nathan's car that day, and I knew they'd been together . . . I went into blind rage. It was like being possessed. I don't actually remember hitting him. When I listened to those witnesses in court, it was like they were talking about someone else. Some violent, messed-up nut-job I didn't recognise. But it was *me*.'

Elizabeth could have wept to see him in such pain. But now was the time for him to reassess the man he'd become and find the man he wanted to be. Tears and sympathy from her would not help, and she resisted the urge to excuse him or to make things right.

After dinner, they began to pack up the bookshelves in the living room. Elizabeth was still reluctant to part with the books that had been so important to Ray all those years ago and tried to convince Tom to take them. He refused to be saddled with *Spanish Verb Conjugations*, *History of the Spanish Civil War* and collections of Truman Capote stories, but agreed to take a couple about Scott of the Antarctic and several Raymond Carvers. Tucked in between the books, Elizabeth found the world map that had once been taped to the wall of their Paddington flat. She spread it out on the dining table. 'I wondered where this had got to – I wanted to show Ray. Look, you can see all the pinholes. All the places he planned to visit.' She smiled. 'The optimism of youth.'

Tom stood beside her and looked over the map. 'Very ambitious. Ecuador, Argentina, Europe . . . Antarctica . . . England. Ireland, obviously.'

'Tom, why don't you take it? You could go to some of these places.'

He put his arm across her shoulders. 'So could you, Mum.'

Elizabeth sighed. 'Maybe. Not sure I have the courage now.'

'Well, I won't be travelling anytime soon, but sure . . . if it's a family heirloom. I kept the Eagles t-shirt, by the way.'

Later when he'd gone home, Elizabeth noticed he'd left the map behind. Perhaps it was meant to be hers. She tucked it away safely in a box; it could go up on the wall somewhere in her new flat. And perhaps she could put a pin somewhere on that map and see how that felt.

On her way to bed, she wandered around the house to assess the readiness of each room for the move. Her new flat was half the size of this house, but it was still spacious and light. It was close enough to the beach to smell the salt in the air and within walking distance of Claire's and Tom's places. It had a sheltered garden courtyard where she could put Eric's cage in the mornings for fresh air. She'd recently been offered a female budgie called Violet and had decided to take her. Eric would enjoy the company.

Now she walked through the house she had lived in for all these years. Every room held a thousand tiny memories of family life. She switched off the lights as she went and it seemed to her like the end of a play, when darkness falls on the stage, the story complete. She said goodnight to Eric and was about to put the cover on his cage when it occurred to her that once the lights go down, the cast must take a bow. She thought of all the things she had to be proud of in her life; the people she had helped through her work, her two sons and grand-children, the long and loving friendship with Ginny, her devoted love for Ray undimmed through all those years and their last days together. She took a bow, modest at first, but then took several more and added a flourish or two.

Eric was her only audience so there was no expectation of applause. His head followed her as she bobbed up and down and he said, 'What the hell?'

41

the final determination

Elizabeth, Tom, Claire and Zach sat in a silent row outside the conference room waiting for the convenor. Elizabeth had already briefed Zach on the importance of body language and not to fold his arms, slump or lounge in his chair. He'd been dismissive at the time, but had obviously taken it on board because he was sitting up straight, hands folded in his lap, although his right knee jiggled nervously, his heel tapping the floor.

Elizabeth was worried about today – they all were. Mrs Giles was an experienced and fair convenor, but she wasn't one to brush things aside and hope for the best. Zach had completed the main requirements of his Outcome Plan but there was no supporting report from his school. The final warning of a suspension for destruction of property and disruptive behaviour was still hanging over him and, if there was any risk that Zach would reoffend, the convenor would be obliged to refer him into the corrections system.

Mrs Giles arrived and they all filed into the conference room. It was a different room to last time but with identical decor, the same brown carpet tiles and circle of vinyl-covered chairs. They sat down and Mrs Giles went through the opening formalities, explaining that the purpose of the conference was to make the final determination on Zach's case. In the last conference she had seemed almost sympathetic. Today she was cooler, and more business-like. It may have been related to Zach or just the lingering effect of an earlier conference, but Elizabeth sensed a definite chill in the room.

As Mrs Giles spoke, Tom and Claire hung on her every word. Tom glanced at Zach from time to time, as if he were a ticking bomb that might explode.

'Zach,' said Mrs Giles. 'I can see from the caseworker notes that there have been some further problems. Can you explain what's been happening for you?'

Zach looked at his parents and then at Elizabeth as if hoping one of them would speak for him but, when no one volunteered, he began in the offhand tone that always rankled with Elizabeth and would not do him any favours with Mrs Giles. 'I didn't really . . . like . . . care that much . . .' He paused and stared out the window. There was nothing to see but blue sky, but it held his interest for a long moment.

'Zach, Mrs Giles wants to hear that —' began Elizabeth in a desperate attempt to get his attention and keep him on task.

'I'd like to hear from Zach's perspective if you don't mind,' interrupted Mrs Giles. 'What didn't you care about, Zach?'

'I didn't care about what I did or if it . . . like . . . bothered other people . . . I just kinda did whatever I wanted.' Zach paused and shrugged.

Tom gave Elizabeth an agonised look. She knew he was thinking about his own conviction, which, handled better, would have resulted in a suspended sentence instead of a prison term. Now they were witnessing Zach sabotage this opportunity to escape the system.

Mrs Giles waited for him to continue. 'Yes, okay. Anything else?' she asked patiently.

'I didn't care about having to do the community stuff for the surf club or writing the apology letter or anything. I thought it was a bit . . . stupid.' He glanced around to gauge the effect of that statement. His gaze rested for a moment on Claire, who was fighting back tears of frustration. She mouthed something at him but he frowned and turned away. His leg began to jiggle again, the heel of his shoe vibrating softly on the carpet.

Mrs Giles glanced down at her file and made several notes. 'Is that it?' she asked, looking up. 'Anything you'd like to add?'

Elizabeth caught Zach's eye. She gave him a nod to urge him on.

'But what happened is that me and Nano – my nana, I mean.' Zach tipped his head towards Elizabeth. 'And Uncle Eric . . . well, he's just a bird really but he's pretty smart. We went on this road trip and . . . I dunno . . . We met crazy people and there was this goat . . . and also I got a rat and I stuffed it and it was really cool. It's not as difficult as you think.' He took a deep breath and for a horrible moment Elizabeth thought he was going to offer Mrs Giles an insight into taxidermy methods.

'But, anyway, we found my granddad, Ray, and the hardest thing was that he was really sick. And Nano really loved him . . . but it was too late.' Zach's voice cracked and he paused to wipe his nose on the sleeve of his jacket, his eyes drawn again to the sky outside.

'Is there anything else you'd like to say about that, Zach?' asked Mrs Giles.

'He was a cool guy. Also I found out a lot of really bad things happened to him that weren't his fault, and it made me think . . . he didn't have the chance to do what he wanted with his life. It wasn't fair.'

Tom's chin dropped to his chest and his shoulders began to shake. Claire edged her chair closer and rested her hand on Tom's arm.

Elizabeth watched Mrs Giles, who seemed interested but not entirely convinced. Over the years, she'd probably encountered too many young men with swagger and stories who didn't deliver on their promises.

'Well, it sounds like that experience had quite an impact on you, Zach,' said Mrs Giles. 'And this all took place since the incident at school?'

Zach nodded. He gripped his knees to stop himself fidgeting and gave Elizabeth a fearful look, as if he had only now grasped that his actions had consequences, ones he may not be able to talk his way out of.

'We don't always have a face-to-face meeting for the final determination,' Mrs Giles continued. 'If the Outcome Plan is complete, then that's the end of it. It's not necessary to meet again. But when we met six months ago, it seemed that you were possibly saying what we wanted to hear and didn't properly understand the gravity of your situation —'

'That was before,' interrupted Zach. 'It's different now. I *do* understand.'

'I can see that, Zach. But what do you think you can do differently in the future so you make better decisions?'

He thought about this for a while. His foot tapped a rhythm on the floor and then stilled and the room was silent. He nodded, coming to some agreement with himself. 'I'll think about what Ray would do. Yeah, I can do that.'

Silent tears slipped down Claire's face and Tom intertwined his hand with hers. Barely holding on to her emotions, Elizabeth racked her brain for anything she could add to convince Mrs Giles of Zach's sincerity. But she understood that he was on his own and he'd given it all he had.

Mrs Giles gave him a long look. She consulted her file, made a note and glanced around at each member of the family. 'I take it we all approve of Zach's proposal,' she said with a smile. 'So all that remains for us to do is run through the formalities and this matter will be closed. You will be free to go, Zach. Okay?'

Zach nodded his agreement and closed his eyes with sweet relief.

42

the escarpment

'Can we *not* stay in Coffs Harbour this time?' asked Zach as they headed up the freeway. This trip, he was behind the wheel of Elizabeth's car. He'd recently turned sixteen and was learning to drive, so she had suggested he come along to clock up some hours.

'There's nothing wrong with Coffs, Zach. That incident with the dump bin could have happened anywhere. Operator error. Anyway, I don't mind . . . let's see how we go.' Elizabeth gripped the seat. 'Zach! Watch the road. Stay in your lane!'

'Stay in yo laaaa-ne . . . stay in yooo lane,' Zach rapped. 'Okay, Nano, listen up. Don't snap at me. Makes me nervous. Let's use our inside voices and quit holding on to the seat.'

Elizabeth released her grip and tried to relax. She had taught both Tom and Danny to drive but had forgotten how nerve-racking it was to be hurtling along the freeway with an overconfident teen behind the wheel.

As the hours passed, they swapped places, squabbled over the choice of music and whether singing along was allowed (it wasn't, but quiet humming was permissible). Sharing the driving over the day, they made it as far as Byron Bay by nightfall.

They checked into a motel and walked down to the foreshore, where they bought fish and chips and sat on a bench in the park, which was lively with young people sitting in groups on the grass. There was a young man demonstrating his firestick twirling, a group of backpackers singing along as someone strummed a guitar. There were shaved heads, dreadlocks and tie-dye: hippie regalia that Elizabeth hadn't seen in years. It was as if these young people were a nomadic tribe searching for that lost world of the previous generation.

Zach watched them without comment. Elizabeth remembered the experience she'd had with her mother in Hyde Park all those years ago. It wouldn't be long before Zach stepped away to become one of these independent young people travelling the world.

They watched a couple set up a line made of webbing, like a safety belt, between two trees. It didn't seem tight enough to walk on but Zach explained it was a 'slackline'.

When it was secure, the woman stepped up onto the line with one foot. She waited a moment for the line to absorb her weight, and lifted her other foot in a practised, fluid movement. Her partner, a handsome young man in a blue beanie, chatted to people nearby, encouraging them to try it for a small fee.

'That seems like the worst of both worlds,' remarked Elizabeth to Zach. 'A tightrope that's not tight.'

'Wouldn't be that hard,' said Zach, with his usual bravado.

'Have you tried it?' asked Elizabeth.

He shook his head and gave a dismissive sniff. 'Don't think it would be that difficult, is all.'

'Most things don't *look* difficult, Zach.'

'Like being a nano, for example,' he suggested with a grin.

'Nanoing is up there with extreme sports, buddy, like running with the bulls. Why don't you give it a go then? The line, I mean. Not the bulls.'

'Nah.'

'Why not?' she asked. 'You said it was easy.'

'When?'

'When what?' asked Elizabeth, confused.

He gave her a sly look. 'I will if you will.'

'No, I'm too old for that, Zach.'

'Oh, bad attitude!'

'I'll tell you what,' said Elizabeth, against her better judgement. 'If you can do it then I'll give it a try.'

Zach shrugged. They got up and walked over. The young woman turned a brilliant smile on Zach, which made him stare at his feet. 'Have you done this before?' she asked. He shook his head. 'Okay, think of it as baby steps. When you stand up, the world will start wobbling. You need to find your frequency and balance your energy. Slowly.'

Zach nodded. He listened carefully while she explained the mechanics and technique. He placed one foot firmly on the line. Staring straight ahead, he was still for a moment while the line bounced under his weight. Suddenly, it began to wobble violently from side to side and he jumped off. He tried again and again. After a dozen tries, he waited patiently until the line stilled, lifted his body and placed the other foot on the line. He managed to resist windmilling his arms and balanced himself, arms bent, fingers pointed to the sky. He put one foot in front of the other, waited, then took another step. He walked three or four steps along the line and jumped down with a broad grin on his face. The woman congratulated him and, although he shrugged it off, Elizabeth could see he was really pleased with his performance. 'It's not that easy, Nano,' he admitted.

'I said I'd give it a try,' Elizabeth said, half hoping the young woman would refuse her. But she didn't. She simply suggested Elizabeth take her shoes off to get a better feel for the vibrations. It sounded a little mystical for Elizabeth's taste but she obeyed.

The man in the blue beanie came over and suggested that he and Zach could hold Elizabeth's hands and help her balance. 'I'll give you one tip,' said Beanie. 'Focus your mind on forward movement. You can't stay where you are, you have to move.'

Elizabeth nodded and placed her foot on the line. Even that was a stretch and she still had one foot on the ground. She stood there feeling foolish. Zach held one hand and Beanie the other, and she pushed down firmly as instructed and lifted herself onto the line. It swung wildly from side to side and she gave a little shriek, but her two helpers steadied her. She had a vision of herself being catapulted across the park cartoon-style, all flapping arms and legs. But the realisation that Zach would be telling that story for years focused her mind.

She put one foot in front of the other and trusted in her helpers, gripping their hands in a hot sweaty hold. She loosened her fingers using their hands for balance and took two more steps. Then, distracted by her success, she slipped and was caught in Beanie's muscular arms, which, frankly, was the highlight of the whole experience.

She and Zach thanked the couple and wandered over to the foreshore to take a look at the surf. Down on the beach, a group of people danced to the beat of a drum by the light of flares. One of them was a tall balding man with a stringy ponytail. He wore orange and grey mechanic's overalls.

'Do you reckon they're the lefties, hippies, nihilists or whatever he was going on about?' asked Zach.

'Hard to tell from this distance,' Elizabeth replied. As they turned away to walk back to the motel, she asked, 'Aren't you going to ask me what a nihilist is?'

'I *know* what a nihilist is,' he said irritably, which had Elizabeth chuckling all the way back to the motel.

They left Byron Bay early the next morning. Zach was driving but, as they headed up into the mountains, gentle rain began to fall and Elizabeth took control. The dirt road up to the cabin was slippery and slow going, with the wheels losing traction occasionally, which Zach found so thrilling that he began a campaign to drive down the mountain.

By the time they reached the cabin, the rain had stopped and sun had broken through the clouds. It was almost six months since they had last been here and the forest had begun its work reclaiming the man-made structures. Vines grew thickly over the wire fence surrounding the vegetable garden and twisted around the railings of the deck, as if the cabin was being slowly devoured by the forest.

Elizabeth had a good look inside the place to see if there was anything worth recovering. She found the package of old photos that Cynthia had given Ray after his father died, and a penknife that Zach might like to keep as a memento. There was a box packed full of her letters to Ray. She leafed through them, debating whether to take them home, but in the end she put them in the stove and lit a match.

Beyond that, it seemed fitting that the place be left as it was. One day it would disappear altogether, or perhaps some other lost soul would inhabit it and find a little peace here. They left the cabin and continued along the path that wound up the mountain. The track was overgrown in places without Ray making his regular trips into the bush. After the rain, the frogs were singing their odd cry, *okay, okay, okay*, and birds called from high in the trees.

Elizabeth followed Zach, who carried the urn, up to the escarpment, and they stood together on the flat rocks and gazed over the valley to the green mountains rising in the distance and the brightening sky.

'Do you want to say something? Or like . . . what do we do?' asked Zach.

'I haven't actually done this before. I guess we can make it up as we go along.' Elizabeth put her finger in her mouth and held it up to test the wind direction.

'What are you doing?' asked Zach, trying not to laugh. 'The ocean's that direction, right? It's blowing an easterly.'

'Okay. Just hand me the top of the urn. Give it a shake so the ashes go up into the air – and obviously away from us. You might have to do it a couple of times.'

Elizabeth had thought Zach might find this difficult but he was more concerned with doing the job well. He gave the urn a shake and a cloud of ash lifted into the air and swept away over the valley.

She'd worried she would be saying goodbye all over again, but she had already said her goodbyes and now she blew a kiss into the air. 'Do you want to say something, Zach?'

'Bye, Ray. Kinda wish we had more time but . . . bye.' Zach

glanced over at her. 'If this was, like, a movie . . . you'd probably expect a hug in this scene.'

'Would that be too much to ask?'

'Maybe later,' he said, but allowed her a gentle fist bump. He turned his attention back to the urn, lifting it up to shake the rest of the ashes out.

'Wait!' said Elizabeth. 'Wait. I'll keep the rest. I've got another destination in mind.'

Zach turned to her. 'Like?'

'Somewhere Ray always wanted to go,' said Elizabeth.

Zach bestowed his princely nod of approval on the plan and fixed the lid back on the urn. As they walked back down the track, he led the way, his head nodding to some internal rhythm, his gaze lifted to the treetops. There was a sound that may have been a distant bird but Elizabeth was almost sure it was Zach, singing.

acknowledgements

My heartfelt gratitude to friends who took the time to read and critique various drafts: Helen Thurloe, Danica Beaudoin, Linda Beltrame, Joseph Furolo, Catherine Hersom, Heather Mackie and Tula Wynyard.

Special thanks to Joanna Nell for taking the time to read my manuscript and provide such a generous and fulsome endorsement.

Thank you to those who shared experiences, contributed expert information or provided contacts: Helen Bain, Giles Hohnen, Stephen Hutcheon, Tasman Trinder, Richard Woolveridge and Milan Wynyard.

Many thanks, as always, to the wonderful and supportive team at Penguin Random House: Ali Watts, Amanda Martin, Sonja Heijn, Louise Ryan and Nerrilee Weir. Adam Laszczuk for the fabulous cover design, Maddie Garratt for publicity, Emily Hindle for marketing, as well as the many dedicated people behind the scenes who each play an essential role in delivering a book into the world.

My appreciation to the authors of these books, which were invaluable to my research: *Vietnam: A Reporter's War*, Hugh Lunn;

ACKNOWLEDGEMENTS

The Way Home, Mark Boyle; *Minefields and Miniskirts*, Siobhán McHugh; *Well Done Those Men*, Barry Heard; *Ashes of Vietnam*, Stuart Rintoul; *Out of the Forest*, Gregory P Smith; *Budgerigar*, Sarah Harris and Don Baker.

book club notes

1. What did you make of the main character, Elizabeth, and how did your impression of her change over the course of the book?
2. Do you think Elizabeth did the right thing standing by Ray? What could she have done differently?
3. Elizabeth states that 'grief catches up with you at some point'. Discuss the ways in which we see this play out in the novel.
4. Elizabeth tells her daughter-in-law Louise: 'You'll bounce back. Women always do. We have no choice.' What do you think she means by this?
5. Elizabeth believes she is the only person who can appreciate Ray in all his dimensions, because she knew him as his young self, full of ambitions. Do you agree?
6. Do you understand Ray's decision to leave his family and go to live in isolation? Do you think it was right?
7. What were the main themes of the book, and how were they brought to life?
8. Which character or moment in the novel prompted the strongest emotional reaction for you?

9. What were the most important things Elizabeth and Zach taught each other?

10. Elizabeth loves to imagine the songs that sum up people's lives, yet struggles to identify a song for herself. What do you think your theme song could be?

11. What do you imagine Elizabeth will do next with her life?

12. Have you read any other books by Amanda Hampson, and if so, what recurring themes did you find?